Walter M. Miller Jr (1923-96) g.
south. He enlisted in the Army Air Corps a month after Pearl
Harbor and spent most of the Second World War as a radio
operator and gunner, participating in more than fifty combat
sorties over Italy and the Balkans, including the assault on
Monte Cassino. After the war he studied engineering in
Texas before turning to writing. He won the Hugo Award in
1955 for 'The Darfsteller', and won another in 1961 for his
classic novel *A Canticle for Leibowitz*.

'[Walter Miller] showed...that science fiction can encompass
and illuminate all human activities' *Daily Herald*

'Prodigiously imaginative' *Chicago Tribune*

DARK BENEDICTION

Walter M. Miller Jr

The right of Walter M. Miller Jr to be identified as the
author of this work has been asserted by him in accordance
with the Copyright, Designs and Patents Act 1988.

First published as *The Best of Walter Miller Jr* 1980

This edition published in Great Britain in 2007 by
Gollancz
An imprint of the Orion Publishing Group
Orion House, 5 Upper St Martin's Lane
London WC2H 9EA

1 3 5 7 9 10 8 6 4 2

A CIP catalogue record for this book
is available from the British Library

ISBN 13: 978 0 57507 977 9
ISBN 10: 0 57507 977 0

Printed and bound in Great Britain by
Mackays of Chatham plc, Chatham, Kent

The Orion Publishing Group's policy is to use papers that
are natural, renewable and recyclable products and made
from wood grown in sustainable forests. The logging and
manufacturing processes are expected to conform to the
environmental regulations of the country of origin.

www.orionbooks.co.uk

Copyright Notices

Contents

You Triflin' Skunk!

THE RAIN SANG light in the sodden palmettos and the wind moaned through the pines about the unpainted shack, whipping the sea of grass that billowed about the islands of scrub. The land lay bathed in rain-haze beneath the pines. Rain trickled from the roof of the shack and made a rattling spray in the rivulets under the eaves. Rain blew from the roof in foggy cloudlets. Rain played marimba-sounds on the wooden steps. A droopy chicken huddled in the drenched grass, too sick to stir or seek a shelter.

No road led across the scrublands to the distant highway, but only a sandy footpath that was now a gushing torrent that ran down to an overflowing creek of brackish water. A possum hurried across the inundated footpath at the edge of the clearing, drenched and miserable, seeking higher ground.

The cabin was without a chimney, but a length of stovepipe projected from a side window, and bent skyward at a clumsy angle. A thin trail of brown smoke leaked from beneath the rain-hood, and wound away on the gusty breeze. In the cabin, there was life, and an aura of song lingered about the rain-washed walls, song as mournful as the sodden land, low as the wail of a distant train.

Whose hands was drivin' the nails O Lord?
Whose hands was drivin' the nails?
Lord O Lord!

1

My hands was drivin' the nails O Lord!
My hands was drivin' the nails
And I did crucify my God!

The song was low and vibrant in the cabin, and Lucey rocked to it, rolling her head as she sang over the stove, where a smoked 'possum simmered in pot-likker with sweet-taters, while corn bread toasted in the oven. The cabin was full of food-smells and sweat-smells, and smoky light through dusty panes.

From a rickety iron bed near the window came a sudden choking sob, an animal sound of almost unendurable torment and despair. Lucey stopped singing, and turned to blink toward the cry, sudden concern melting her pudgy face into a mountain woman cherub's face, full of compassion.

"Awwwwwww . . ." The sound welled unbidden from her throat, a rich low outpouring of love and sympathy for the sallow twitching youth who lay on the yellowish sheets, his eyes wild, his hands tensing into claws.

"Awwwww, Doodie—you ain't gonna have another spell?" she said.

Only a small hurt this time, my son. It can't be helped. It's like tuning a guitar. You can't do it without sounding the strings, or pulsing the neural fibers. But only a small hurt this time. . . .

The youth writhed and shuddered, stiffening into a puppet strained by steel springs. His back arched, and his muscles quivered. He flung himself suddenly into reflexive gymnastics, sobbing in small shrieks.

Lucey murmured softly. An immense mass of love, she waddled toward the bed in bounces of rubbery flesh. She bent over him to purr low in her throat.

"Poor Doodie . . . poor li'l Doodie. Mama's lamb."

The boy sobbed and thrashed. The paroxysm brought froth to his lips and jerked his limbs into cramped spasms. He jerked and writhed and tumbled on the bed.

"You jus' try to lay calm, Doodie. You jus' try. You gonna be all right. It ain't gonna last long, Doodie. It's gonna go away."

"No!" he whimpered. "No! Don't touch me, Mama! *Don't!*"

"Now, Doodie . . ."

She sat on the edge of the bed to gather him up in her

massive arms. The spasms grew more frantic, less reflexive. He fought her, shrieking terror. She lay beside him,
moaning low with pity. She enveloped him with her arms,
enfolding him so that he could no longer kick. She pulled
his face into the hollow of her huge bosom and squeezed
him. With his tense body pressed tightly against the bulky
mass of her, she melted again with love, and began chanting a rhythmic lullaby while he twitched and slavered
against her, fighting away, pretending to suffocate.

Gradually, as exhaustion overcame him, the spasm
passed. He lay wheezing quietly in her arms.

*The strings are tuned, my son, and it was only a small
hurt. Has the hurt stopped, my son?*

Yes, father, if only this monstress would let me be.

*Accept my knowledge, and be content. The time will
come.*

"Who you whisperin' to, Doodie? Why are you mum-
blin' so?" She looked down at his tousled head, pressed
tightly between her breasts.

His muttering ceased, and he lay quietly as if in a
trance. It was always so. The boy had fits, and when the
paroxysm had passed, he went into a rigid sleep. But it
was more like a frozen moment of awareness, and old Ma
Kutter said the boy was "witched." Lucey had never believed in "witchin'."

When he was tensely quiet, she tenderly disengaged
herself and slid off the bed. He lay on his side, face toward the window, eyes slitted and mouth agape. Humming softly, Lucey returned to the stove and took a stick
of oak out of the bucket. She paused to glance back at
him—and he seemed to be rigidly listening to something.
The rain?

"Doodie . . . ?"

"When are you coming for us, father?" came in a ghost
whisper from the bed. "When, *when?*"

"What are you talking about, Doodie?" The cast-iron
stove-lid clattered on the hot metal as she lifted it nervously aside. She glanced down briefly at the red coals in
the stove, then back at Doodie.

"Very soon . . . very soon!" he whispered.

Lucey chucked the stick of wood in atop the coals, then
stood staring at the bed until the flames licked up about
the lid-hole to glisten orange on her sweat-glazed face.

"Who are you talkin' to, Doodie?"

She expected no answer, but after several seconds, his breathing grew deeper. Then it came: "My *father*."

Lucey's plump mouth went slowly shut and her hand quivered as she fumbled for the stove lid.

"Your pa is dead, Doodie. You know that."

The emaciated youth stirred on the bed, picked himself up slowly on one arm, and turned to look at her, his eyes blazing. "You lie!" he cried. "Mama, you lie!"

"Doodie!"

"I hate you, Mama. I hate all of you, and I'll make you pay. I'll be like *him*."

The stove lid clattered back in place. She wiped her hands nervously on her dress. "You're sick, Doodie! You're not right in the mind. You never even *seed* your pa."

"I talk to him," the boy said. "He tells me things. He told me why you're my mother. He told me how. And he told me who *I* am."

"You're my son!" Lucey's voice had gone up an octave, and she edged defensively away.

"Only half of me, Mama." The boy said, then laughed defiantly. "Only half of me is even human. You knew that when he came here, and paid you to have his baby."

"*Doodie!*"

"You can't lie to me, Mama. *He* tells me. *He* knows."

"He was just a man, Doodie. Now he's gone. He never came back, do you hear?"

The boy stared out the window at the rain-shroud. When he spoke again, it was in a small slow voice of contempt.

"It doesn't matter. He doesn't want you to believe— any of you." He paused to snicker. "He doesn't want to warn you what we're going to do."

Lucey shook her head slowly. "Lord, have mercy on me," she breathed. "I know I done wrong. But please, punish old Lucey and not my boy."

"I ain't crazy, Mama."

"If you ain't crazy, you're 'witched,' and talkin' to the dead."

"He ain't dead. He's Outside."

Lucey's eyes flickered quickly to the door.

"And he's comin' back—soon." The boy chuckled. "Then he'll make me like him, and it won't hurt to listen."

"You talk like he wasn't a man. I seed him, and you didn't. Your pa was just a man, Doodie."

"No, Mama. He showed you a man because he wanted you to see a man. Next time, he'll come the way he *really* is."

"Why would your pa come back," she snorted, summoning courage to stir the pot. "What would he want here? If you was right in the head, you wouldn't get fits, and you'd know you never seed him. What's his name? You don't even know his name."

"His name is a purple bitter with black velvet, Mama. Only there isn't any word."

"Fits," she moaned. "A child with fits."

"The crawlers, you mean? That's when he talks to me. It hurts at first."

She advanced on him with a big tin spoon, and shook it at him. "You're sick, Doodie. And don't you carry on so. A doctor's what you need . . . if only Mama had some money."

"I won't fuss with you, Mama."

"Huh!" She stood there for a moment, shaking her head. Then she went back to stir the pot. Odorous steam arose to perfume the shack.

The boy turned his head to watch her with luminous eyes. "The fits are when he talks, Mama. Honest they are. It's like electricity inside me. I wish I could tell you how."

"Sick!" She shook her head vigorously. "Sick, that's all."

"If I was all like him, it wouldn't hurt. It only hurts because I'm half like you."

"Doodie, you're gonna drive your old mother to her grave. Why do you torment me so?"

He turned back to the window and fell silent . . . determinedly, hostilely silent. The silence grew like an angry thing in the cabin, and Lucey's noises at the stove only served to punctuate it.

"Where does your father stay, Doodie?" she asked at last, in cautious desperation.

"Outside . . ."

"Gitalong! Wheah outside, in a palmetto scrub? In the cypress swamp?"

"*Way* Outside. Outside the world."

"Who taught you such silliness? Spirits an' such! I ought to tan you good, Doodie!"

"From another world," the boy went on.

"An' he talks to you from the other world?"

Doodie nodded solemnly.

Lucey stirred vigorously at the pot, her face creased in a dark frown. Lots of folks believed in spirits, and lots of folks believed in mediums. But Lucey had got herself straight with the Lord.

"I'm gonna call the parson," she grunted flatly.

"Why?"

"Christian folks don't truck with spirits."

"He's no spirit, Mama. He's like a man, only he's not. He comes from a star."

She set her jaw and fell grimly silent. She didn't like to remember Doodie's father. He'd come seeking shelter from a storm, and he was big and taciturn, and he made love like a machine. Lucey had been younger then—younger and wilder, and not afraid of shame. He'd vanished as quickly as he'd come.

When he had gone, it almost felt like he'd been there to accomplish an errand, some piece of business that had to be handled hastily and efficiently.

"Why'd he want a son?" she scoffed. "If what you say is true—which it ain't."

The boy stirred restlessly. "Maybe I shouldn't tell."

"You tell Mama."

"You won't believe it anyway," he said listlessly. "He fixed it so I'd *look* human. He fixed it so he could talk to me. I tell him things. Things he could find out himself if he wanted to."

"What does he want to know?"

"How humans work inside."

"Livers and lungs and such? Sssssst! Silliest I ever—"

"And brains. Now they know."

"*They?*"

"Pa's people. *You'll see.* Now they know, and they're coming to run things. Things will be different, lots different."

"When?"

"Soon. Only pa's coming sooner. He's their . . . their . . ." The boy groped for a word. "He's like a detective."

Lucey took the corn bread out of the oven and sank despairingly into a chair. "Doodie, Doodie . . ."

"What, Mama?"

"Oh, Sweet Jesus! What did I do, what did I do? He's a child of the devil. Fits an' lies and puny ways. Lord, have mercy on me."

With an effort, the boy sat up to stare at her weakly. "He's no devil, Mama. He's no man, but he's better than a man. You'll see."

"You're not right in the mind, Doodie."

"It's all right. He wouldn't want you to believe. Then you'd be warned. They'd be warned too."

"They?"

"Humans—white and black and yellow. He picked poor people to have his sons, so nobody would believe."

"Sons? You mean you ain't the only one?"

Doodie shook his head. "I got brothers, Mama—half-brothers. I talk to them sometimes too."

She was silent a long time. "Doodie, you better go to sleep," she said wearily at last.

"Nobody'll believe . . . until he comes, and the rest of them come after him."

"He ain't comin', Doodie. You ain't seed him—never."

"Not with my eyes," he said.

She shook her head slowly, peering at him with brimming eyes. "Poor little boy. Cain't I do somethin' to make you see?"

Doodie sighed. He was tired, and didn't answer. He fell back on the pillow and lay motionless. The water that crawled down the pane rippled the rain-light over his sallow face. He might have been a pretty child, if it had not been for the tightness in his face, and the tumor-shape on his forehead.

He said it was the tumor-shape that let him talk to his father. After a few moments, Lucey arose, and took their supper off the stove. Doodie sat propped up on pillows, but he only nibbled at his food.

"Take it away," he told her suddenly. "I can feel it starting again."

There was nothing she could do. While he shrieked and tossed again on the bed, she went out on the rain-swept porch to pray. She prayed softly that her sin be upon herself, not upon her boy. She prayed for understanding, and when she was done she cried until Doodie was silent again inside.

When she went back into the house, he was watching her with cold, hard eyes.

"It's tonight," he said. "He's coming *tonight*, Mama."

The rain ceased at twilight, but the wind stiffened, hurling drops of water from the pines and scattering them like shot across the sagging roof. Running water gurgled in the ditch, and a rabbit ran toward higher ground. In the west, the clouds lifted a dark bandage from a bloody slash of sky, and somewhere a dog howled in the dusk. Rain-pelted, the sick hen lay dying in the yard.

Lucey stood in the doorway, nervously peering out into the pines and the scrub, while she listened to the croak of the tree frogs at sunset, and the conch-shell sounds of wind in the pines.

"Ain't no night for strangers to be out wanderin'," she said. "There won't be no moon till nearly midnight."

"He'll come," promised the small voice behind her. "He's coming from the Outside."

"Shush, child. He's nothing of the sort."

"He'll come, all right."

"What if I won't let him in the door?"

Doodie laughed. "You can't stop him, Mama. I'm only *half* like you, and it hurts when he talks-inside."

"Yes, child?"

"If he talks-inside to a human, the human dies. He told me."

"Sounds like witch-woman talk," Lucey said scornfully and stared back at him from the doorway. "I don't want no more of it. There's nobody can kill somebody by just a-talkin'."

"*He* can. And it ain't just talking. It's talking *inside*."

"Ain't nobody can talk inside your mother but your mother."

"That's what I been saying." Doodie laughed. "If he did, you'd die. That's why he needed *me*."

Lucey's eyes kept flickering toward the rain-soaked scrub, and she hugged her huge arms, and shivered. "Silliest I ever!" she snorted. "He was just a man, and you never even seed him."

She went inside and got the shotgun, and sat down at the table to clean it, after lighting a smoky oil lamp on the wall.

"Why are you cleaning that gun, Mama?"

"Wildcat around the chicken yard last night!" she muttered. "Tonight I'm gonna watch."

Doodie stared at her with narrowed eyes, and the look on his face started her shivering again. Sometimes he did seem not-quite-human, a shape witched or haunted wherein a silent cat prowled by itself and watched, through human eyes.

How could she believe the wild words of a child subject to fits, a child whose story was like those told by witching women and herb healers? A thing that came from the stars, a thing that could come in the guise of a man and talk, make love, eat, and laugh, a thing that wanted a half-human son to which it could speak from afar.

How could she believe in a thing that was like a spy sent into the city before the army came, a thing that could make her conceive when it wasn't even human? It was wilder than any of the stories they told in the deep swamps, and Lucey was a good Christian now.

Still, when Doodie fell asleep, she took the gun and went out to wait for the wildcat that had been disturbing the chickens. It wasn't unchristian to believe in wildcats, not even tonight.

Doodie's father had been just a man, a triflin' man. True, she couldn't remember him very clearly, because she had been drinking corn squeezin's with Jacob Fleeter before the stranger came. She had been all giggly, and he had been all shimmery, and she couldn't remember a word he'd said.

"Lord forgive me," she breathed as she left the house.

The wet grass dragged about her legs as she crossed the yard and traversed a clearing toward an island of palmetto scrub from which she could cover both the house and the chicken-yard.

The clouds had broken, and stars shone brightly, but there was no moon. Lucey moved by instinct, knowing each inch of land for half a mile around the shack.

She sat on a wet and rotting log in the edge of the palmetto thicket, laid the shotgun across her lap, stuffed a corncob pipe with tobacco from Deevey's field, and sat smoking in the blackness while whippoorwills mourned over the land, and an occasional owl hooted from the swamp. The air was cool and clean after the rain, and

only a few nightbirds flitted in the brush while crickets
chirped in the distance and tree frogs spoke mysteriously.

"*A A AaaaA Aaaarrrwww . . . Na!*"

The cry was low and piercing. Was it Doodie, having
another spasm—or only a dream? She half-arose, then
paused, listening. There were a few more whimpers, then
silence. A dream, she decided, and settled back to wait.
There was nothing she could do for Doodie, not until the
State Healthmobile came through again, and examined
him for "catchin' " ailments. If they found he wasn't right
in the mind, they might take him away.

The glowing ember in the pipe was hypnotic—the only
thing to be clearly seen except the stars. She stared at the
stars, wondering about their names, until they began to
crawl before her eyes. Then she looked at the ember in
the pipe again, brightening and dimming with each
breath, acquiring a lacy crust of ashes, growing sleepy in
the bowl and sinking deeper, deeper, while the whippoorwills pierced the night with melancholy.

". . . Na na naaaAAAAhhhaaa. . . . !"

When the cries woke her, she knew she had slept for
some time. Faint moonlight seeped through the pine
branches from the east, and there was a light mist over
the land. The air had chilled, and she shivered as she
arose to stretch, propping the gun across the rotten log.
She waited for Doodie's cries to cease.

The cries continued, unabated.

Stiffening with sudden apprehension, she started back
toward the shack. Then she saw it—a faint violet glow
through the trees to the north, just past the corner of the
hen house! She stopped again, tense with fright. Doodie's
cries were becoming meaningful.

"Pa! I can't stand it any closer! Naa, naaa! I can't
think, I can't think at all. No, *please. . . .*"

Reflexively, Lucey started to bolt for the house, but
checked herself in time. No lamp burned in the window.
She picked up the shotgun and a pebble. After a nervous
pause, she tossed the pebble at the porch.

It bounced from the wall with a loud crack, and she
slunk low into shadows. Doodie's cries continued without
pause. A minute passed, and no one emerged from the
house.

A sudden metallic sound, like the opening of a metal
door, came from the direction of the violet light. Quickly

she stepped over the log and pressed back into the scrub thicket. Shaking with fear, she waited in the palmettos, crouching in the moonlight among the spiny fronds, and lifting her head occasionally to peer toward the violet light.

She saw nothing for a time, and then, gradually the moonlight seemed to dim. She glanced upward. A tenuous shadow, like smoke, had begun to obscure the face of the moon, a translucent blur like the thinnest cloud.

At first, she dismissed it as a cloud. But it writhed within itself, curled and crawled, not dispersing, but seeming to swim. Smoke from the violet light? She watched it with wide, upturned eyes.

Despite its volatile shape, it clung together as a single entity as smoke would never have done. She could still see it faintly after it had cleared the lunar disk, scintillating in the moon-glow.

It swam like an airborne jellyfish. A cluster of silver threads it seemed, tangled in a cloud of filaments—or a giant mass of dandelion fluff. It leaked out misty pseudo-pods, then drew them back as it pulled itself through the air. Weightless as chick-down, huge as a barn, it flew—and drifted from the direction of the sphere in a semi-circle, as if inspecting the land, at times moving against the wind.

It was coming closer to the house.

It moved with purpose, and therefore was alive. This Lucey knew. It moved with its millions of spun threads, finer than a spider's web, the patterns as ordered as a neural array.

It contracted suddenly and began to settle toward the house. Glittering opaquely, blotting out half the cabin, it kept contracting and drawing itself in, becoming denser until it fell in the yard with a blinding flash of incandescent light.

Lucey's flesh crawled. Her hands trembled on the gun, her breath came in shallow gasps.

Before her eyes it was changing into a manlike thing.

Frozen, she waited, thinking swiftly. Could it be that Doodie was right?

Could it be—

Doodie was still whimpering in the house, weary now,

as he always was when the spasm had spent itself. But the words still came, words addressed to his father.

The thing in the yard was assuming the shape of a man—and Lucey knew who the man would be.

She reared up quickly in the palmettos, like an enraged, hulking river animal breaking to the surface. She came up shotgun-in-hand and bellowed across the clearing. "Hey theah! You triflin' skunk! *Look at me!*"

Still groping for human shape, the creature froze.

"Run off an' leave me with child!" Lucey shouted. "And no way to pay his keep!"

The creature kept coming toward her, and the pulsing grew stronger.

"Don't come any nearer, you hear?"

When it kept coming, Lucey grunted in a gathering rage and charged out of the palmettos to meet it, shotgun raised, screaming insults. The thing wobbled to a stop, its face a shapeless blob with black shadows for eyes.

She brought the gun to her shoulder and fired both barrels at once.

The thing tumbled to the ground. Crackling arcs danced about it, and a smell of ozone came on the breeze. For one hideous moment it was lighted by a glow from within. Then the glow died, and it began to expand. It grew erratically, and the moonlight danced in silvery filaments about it. A blob of its substance broke loose from the rest, and wind-borne, sailed across the clearing and dashed itself to dust in the palmettos.

A sudden gust took the rest of it, rolling it away in the grass, gauzy shreds tearing loose from the mass. The gust blew it against the trunk of a pine. It lodged there briefly, quivering in the breeze and shimmering palely under the moon. Then it broke into dust that scattered eastward across the land.

"Praised be the Lord," breathed Lucey, beginning to cry.

A high whining sound pierced the night, from the direction of the violet light. She whirled to stare. The light grew brighter. Then the whine abruptly ceased. A luminescent sphere, glowing with violet haze, moved upward from the pines. It paused, then in stately majesty continued the ascent, gathering speed until it became a ghostly chariot that dwindled. Up, up, up toward the gleaming stars. She watched it until it vanished from sight.

Then she straightened her shoulders, and glowered toward the dust traces that blew eastward over the scrub.

"Ain't nothing worse than a triflin' man," she philosophized. "If he's human, or if he's not."

Wearily she returned to the cabin. Doodie was sleeping peacefully. Smiling, she tucked him in, and went to bed. There was corn to hoe, come dawn.

Report: Servopilot recon six, to fleet. Missionman caught in transition phase by native organism, and devastated, thus destroying liaison with native analog. Suggest delay of invasion plans. Unpredictability factors associated with mothers of genetic analogs. Withdraw contacts. Servo Six.

The Will

THE WILL OF a child. A child who played in the sun and ran over the meadow to chase with his dog among the trees beyond the hedge, and knew the fierce passions of childhood. A child whose logic cut corners and sought shortest distances, and found them. A child who made shining life in my house.

Red blood countt low, wildly fluctuating . . . Chronic fatigue, loss of weight, general lethargy of function . . . Noticeable pallor and muscular atrophy . . . tthe first symptoms.

That was eight months ago.

Last summer, the specialists conferred over him. When they had finished, I went to Doc Jules' office—alone, because I was afraid it was going to be bad, and Cleo couldn't take it. He gave it to me straight.

"We can't cure him, Rod. We can only treat symptoms —and hope the research labs come through. I'm sorry."

"He'll die?"

"Unless the labs get an answer."

"How long?"

"Months." He gave it to me bluntly—maybe because he thought I was hard enough to take it, and maybe because he knew I was only Kenny's foster father, as if blood-kinship would have made it any worse.

"Thanks for letting me know," I said, and got my hat.

I would have to tell Cleo, somehow. It was going to be tough. I left the building and went out to buy a paper. A magazine on the science rack caught my eye. It had an article entitled *Carcino-genesis and Carbon*-14 and there

14

was a mention of leukemia in the blurb. I bought it along with the paper, and went over to the park to read. Anything to keep from carrying the news to Cleo.

The research article made things worse. They were still doing things to rats and cosmic rays, and the word "cure" wasn't mentioned once. I dropped the magazine on the grass and glanced at the front page. A small headline toward the bottom of the page said: COMMUNITY PRAYS THREE DAYS FOR DYING CHILD. Same old sob-stuff—publicity causes country to focus on some luckless incurable, and deluge the family with sympathy, advice, money, and sincere and ardent pleas for divine intervention.

I wondered if it would be like that for Kenny—and instinctively I shuddered.

I took a train out to the suburbs, picked up the car, and drove home before twilight. I parked in front, because Cleo was out in back, taking down clothes from the line. The blinds were down in the living room, and the lantern-jawed visage of Captain Chronos looked out sternly from the television screen. The Captain carried an LTR (local-time-reversal) gun at the ready, and peered warily from side to side through an oval hole in the title film. Kenny's usual early-evening fodder.

"Travel through the centuries with the master of the clock!" the announcer was chanting.

"Hi, kid," I said to the hunched-up figure who sat before the set, worshiping his hero.

"Sssshhhhhhhh!" He glanced at me irritably, then transferred his individual attention back to the title film.

"Sorry," I muttered. "Didn't know you listened to the opening spiel. It's always the same."

He squirmed, indicating that he wanted me to scram—to leave him to his own devices.

I scrammed to the library, but the excited chant of the audio was still with me. ". . . *Captain Chronos, Custodian of Time, Defender of the Temporal Passes, Champion of the Temporal Guard. Fly with Captain Chronos in his time-ship* Century *as he battles against those evil forces who would—"*

I shut the door for a little quiet, then went to the encyclopedia shelf and took down "LAC-MOE." An envelope fell out of the heavy volume, and I picked it up. Kenny's.

He had scrawled "Lebanon, do not open until 1964; value in 1954: 38¢," on the face. I knew what was inside without holding it up to the light: stamps. Kenny's idea of buried treasure; when he had more than one stamp of an issue in his collection, he'd stash the duplicate away somewhere to let it age, having heard that age increases their value.

When I finished reading the brief article, I went out to the kitchen. Cleo was bringing in a basket of clothes. She paused in the doorway, the basket cocked on her hip, hair disheveled, looking pretty but anxious.

"Did you see him?" she asked.

I nodded, unable to look at her, poured myself a drink. She waited a few seconds for me to say something. When I couldn't say anything, she dropped the basket of clothes, scattering underwear and linens across the kitchen floor, and darted across the room to seize my arms and stare up at me wildly.

"Rod! It *isn't*—"

But it was. Without stopping to think, she rushed to the living room, seized Kenny in her arms, began sobbing, then fled upstairs when she realized what she was doing.

Kenny knew he was sick. He knew several specialists had studied his case. He knew that I had gone down to talk with Doc Jules this afternoon. After Cleo's reaction, there was no keeping the truth from him. He was only fourteen, but within two weeks, he knew he had less than a year to live, unless they found a cure. He pieced it together for himself from conversational fragments, and chance remarks, and medical encyclopedias, and by deftly questioning a playmate's older brother who was a medical student.

Maybe it was easier on Kenny to know he was dying, easier than seeing our anxiety and being frightened by it without knowing the cause. But a child is blunt in his questioning, and tactless in matters that concern himself, and that made it hell on Cleo.

"If they don't find a cure, when will I die?"

"Will it hurt?"

"What will you do with my things?"

"Will I see my real father afterwards?"

Cleo stood so much of it, and then one night she broke down and we had to call a doctor to give her a sedative

and quiet her down. When she was settled, I took Kenny
out behind the house. We walked across the narrow strip
of pasture and sat on the old stone fence to talk by the
light of the moon. I told him not to talk about it again to
Cleo, unless she brought it up, and that he was to bring
his questions to me. I put my arm around him, and I
knew he was crying inside.

"I don't want to die."

There is a difference between tragedy and blind brutal
calamity. Tragedy has meaning, and there is dignity in it.
Tragedy stands with its shoulders stiff and proud. But
there is no meaning, no dignity, no fulfillment, in the
death of a child.

"Kenny, I want you to try to have faith. The research
institutes are working hard. I want you to try to have
faith that they'll find a cure."

"Mack says it won't be for years and years."

Mack was the medical student. I resolved to call him
tomorrow. But his mistake was innocent; he didn't know
what was the matter with Kenny.

"Mack doesn't know. He's just a kid himself. Nobody
knows—except that they'll find it sometime. Nobody
knows when. It might be next week."

"I wish I had a time-ship like Captain Chronos."

"Why?"

He looked at me earnestly in the moonlight. "Because
then I could go to some year when they knew how to cure
me."

"I wish it were possible."

"I'll bet it is. I'll bet someday they can do that too.
Maybe the government's working on it now."

I told him I'd heard nothing of such a project.

"Then they ought to be. Think of the advantages. If
you wanted to know something that nobody knew, you
could just go to some year when it had already been discovered."

I told him that it wouldn't work, because then everybody would try it, and nobody would work on new
discoveries, and none would be made.

"Besides, Kenny, nobody can even prove time-travel is
possible."

"Scientists can do anything."

"Only things that are possible, Kenny. And only with
money, and time, and work—and a reason."

"Would it cost a lot to research for a time-ship, Dad?"

"Quite a lot, I imagine, if you could find somebody to do it."

"As much as the atom-bomb?"

"Maybe."

"I bet you could borrow it from banks . . . if somebody could prove it's possible."

"You'd need a lot of money of your own, kid, before the banks would help."

"I bet my stamp collection will be worth a lot of money someday. And my autograph book." The conversation had wandered off into fantasy.

"In time, maybe in time. A century maybe. But banks won't wait that long."

He stared at me peculiarly. "But Dad, don't you see? *What difference does time make,* if you're working on a time-machine?"

That one stopped me. "Try to have faith in the medical labs, Kenny," was all I could find to say.

Kenny built a time-ship in the fork of a big maple. He made it from a packing crate, reinforced with plywood, decorated with mysterious coils of copper wire. He filled it with battered clocks and junkyard instruments. He mounted two seats in it, and dual controls. He made a fish-bowl canopy over a hole in the top, and nailed a galvanized bucket on the nose. Broomstick guns protruded from its narrow weapon ports. He painted it silvery gray, and decorated the bucket-nose with the insignia of Captain Chronos and the Guardsmen of Time. He nailed steps on the trunk of the maple; and when he wasn't in the house, he could usually be found in the maple, piloting the time-ship through imaginary centuries. He took a picture of it with a box camera, and sent a print of it to Captain Chronos with a fan letter.

Then one day he fainted on the ladder, and fell out of the tree.

He wasn't badly hurt, only bruised, but it ended his career as a time-ship pilot. Kenny was losing color and weight, and the lethargy was coming steadily over him. His fingertips were covered with tiny stab-marks from the constant blood counts, and the hollow of his arm was marked with transfusion needles. Mostly, he stayed inside.

We haunted the research institutes, and the daily mail

fate obviated the need to worry or hope. But I wasn't so sure.

"What've you been up to, Kenny?" I asked.

He looked innocent and shook his head.

"Come on, now. You don't go wandering around muttering to yourself unless you're cooking something up. What is it, another time-ship? I heard you hammering in the garage before dinner."

"I was just knocking the lid off an old breadbox."

I couldn't get any answer but evasions, innocent glances, and mysterious smirks. I let him keep his secret, thinking that his enthusiasm for whatever it was he was doing would soon wear off.

Then the photographers came.

"We want to take a picture of Kenny's treehouse," they explained.

"Why?—and how did you know he had one?" I demanded.

It developed that somebody was doing a feature-article on the effects of science-fantasy television shows on children. It developed that the "somebody" was being hired by a publicity agency which was being hired by the advertisers who presented Captain Chronos and the Guardsmen of Time. It developed that Kenny's fan letter, with the snapshot of his treehouse time-ship, had been forwarded to the publicity department by the producer of the show. They wanted a picture of the time-ship with Kenny inside, looking out through the fish bowl canopy.

"It's impossible," I told them.

They showed me a dozen pictures of moppets with LTR-guns, moppets in time-warp suits, moppets wearing Captain Chronos costumes, moppets falling free in space, and moppets playing Time-Pirate in the park.

"I'm sorry, but it's impossible," I insisted.

"We'll be glad to pay something for it, if . . ."

"The kid's sick, if you must know," I snapped. "He can't do it, and that's that, so forget about it."

"Maybe when he's feeling better . . . ?"

"He *won't* be feeling better," Cleo interrupted, voice tense, with a catch in it. "Now please *leave!*"

They left, with Cleo herding them out onto the porch. I heard them apologizing, and Cleo softened, and began to explain. That was a mistake.

A week later, while we were still drinking our coffee at

the dinner table, the doorbell rang. Cleo, expecting an answer to her recent wire to some South American clinic, left the table, went to answer it, and promptly screamed.

I dropped my cup with a crash and ran to the living room with a butcher knife, then stopped dead still.

It stood there in the doorway with a stunned expression on its face, gaping at Cleo who had collapsed in a chair. It wore a silver uniform with jack-boots, black-and-red cape, and a weird helmet with antenna protruding from it. It had a lantern jaw and a big, meaty, benign contenance.

"I'm awfully sorry," it boomed in a gentle deep-rich voice. "We just drove over from the studio, and I didn't take time to change . . ."

"Ulk!" said Cleo.

I heard footsteps at the head of the stairs behind me, then a howl from Kenny who had been getting ready for bed, after being helped upstairs.

"Captain Chronos!"

Bare feet machine-gunned down the stairs and came to a stop at a respectful distance from the idol.

"GgaaaaAA*AWWWSSSShhhh!"* Kenny timidly walked half-way around him, looking him up and down. "Geee . . . Gaaawwssshh!"

Cleo fanned herself with a newspaper and recovered slowly. I tossed the butcher-knife on a magazine stand and mumbled something apologetic. There were two of them: Chronos and the producer, a small suave man in a business suit. The latter drew me aside to explain. It developed that the photographers had explained to the boss, who had explained to the client, who had mentioned it to the agency, who had returned the fan letter to the producer with a note. It would appear that Captain Chronos, for the sake of nutritious and delicious Fluffy Crunkles, made it his habit to comfort the afflicted, the crippled, and the dying, if it were convenient and seemed somehow advantageous. He also visited the children's wards of hospitals, it seemed.

"This on the level, or for publicity?"

"On the level."

"Where's the photographer?"

The producer reddened and muttered noncommittally. I went to the door and looked out through the screen. There was another man in their car. When I pushed the

screen open, it hit something hard—a tape recorder. I
turned:

"Get out."

"But Mr. Westmore. . . ."

"Get *out*."

They left quickly. Kenny was furious, and he kept on
being furious all through the following day. At me. Cleo
began agreeing with him to some extent, and I felt like a
heel.

"You want Kenny to get the full treatment?" I grumbled. "You want him to wind up a sob-story child?"

"Certainly not, but it was cruel, Rod. The boy never
had a happier moment until you . . ."

"All right, so I'm a bastard. I'm sorry."

That night Abe Sanders (Captain Chronos) came back
alone, in slacks and a sport shirt, and muttering apologies.
It developed that the Wednesday evening shows always
had a children's panel (Junior Guardsmen) program,
and that while they understood that Kenny couldn't
come, they had wanted to have him with the panel, in
absentia, by telephone.

"Please, Dad, can't I?"

The answer had to be no . . . but Kenny had been
glaring at me furiously all day, and it was a way to make
him stop hating me . . . still, the answer had to be no . . .
the publicity . . . but he'd be delighted, and he could stop
hating my guts for kicking them out . . .

"I guess so, if the offer's still open."

"Dad!"

The offer was still open. Kenny was to be on the show.
They rehearsed him a little, and let him practice with the
tape recorder until he got used to his voice.

On Wednesday evening, Kenny sat in the hall doorway
to the living room, telephone in his lap, and stared across
at Sanders' face on the television screen. Sanders held
another phone, and we heard both their voices from the
set. Occasionally the camera dollied in to a close shot of
Sanders' chuckle, or panned along the table to show the
juvenile panel members, kids between eight and sixteen.
There was an empty chair on Sanders' right, and it bore
a placard. The placard said "KENNY WESTMORE."

It lasted maybe a minute. Sanders promised not to mention Kenny's address, nor to mention the nature of his illness. He did neither, but the tone of conversation made it clear that Kenny was in bad shape and probably not long for this world. Kenny had stage fright, his voice trembled, and he blurted something about the search for a cure. Cleo stared at the boy instead of the set, and my own glance darted back and forth. The cameraman panned to the empty chair and dollied in slowly so that the placard came to fill the screen while Kenny spoke. Kenny talked about stamp collections and time machines and autographs, while an invisible audience gaped at pathos.

"If anybody's got stamps to trade, just let me know," he said. "And autographs . . ."

I winced, but Sanders cut in. "Well, Kenny—we're not supposed to mention your address, but if any of you Guardsmen out there want to help Kenny out with his stamp collection, you can write to me, and I'll definitely see that he gets the letters."

"And autographs too," Kenny added.

When it was over, Kenny had lived . . . but *lived*.

And then the mail came in a deluge, forwarded from the network's studio. Bushels of stamps, dozens of autograph books, Bibles, money, advice, crank letters, and maudlin gushes of sugary sympathy . . . and a few sensible and friendly letters. Kenny was delighted.

"Gee, Dad, I'll never get all the stamps sorted out. And look!—an autograph of Calvin Coolidge! . . ."

But it never turned him aside from his path of confident but mysterious purpose. He spent even more time in his room, in the garage, and—when he could muster the energy—back in the maple woods, doing mysterious things alone.

"Have they found a cure yet, Dad?" he asked me pleasantly when an expected letter came.

"They're . . . making progress," I answered lamely.

He shrugged. "They will . . . eventually." Unconcerned.

It occurred to me that some sort of psychic change, unfathomable, might have happened within him—some sudden sense of timelessness, of identity with the race. Something that would let him die calmly as long as he knew there'd be a cure *some*day. It seemed too much to expect of a child, but I mentioned the notion to Jules when I saw him again.

"Could be," he admitted. "It might fit in with this secrecy business."

"How's that?"

"People who know they're dying often behave that way. Little secret activities that don't become apparent until after they're gone. Set up causes that won't have effects until afterwards. Immortality cravings. You want to have posthumous influence, to live after you. A suicide note is one perversion of it. The suicide figures the world will posthumously feel guilty, if he tells it off."

"And Kenny . . . ?"

"I don't know, Rod. The craving for immortality is basically procreative, I think. You have children, and train them, and see your own mirrored patterns live on in them, and feel satisfied, when your time comes. Or else you sublimate it, and do the same thing for all humanity—through art, or science. I've seen a lot of death, Rod, and I believe there's more than just-plain-selfishness to people's immortality-wishes; it's associated with the human reproductive syndrome—which includes the passing on of culture to the young. But Kenny's just a kid. I don't know."

Despite Kenny's increasing helplessness and weakness, he began spending more time wandering out in the woods. Cleo chided him for it, and tried to limit his excursions. She drove him to town on alternate days for a transfusion and shots, and she tried to keep him in the house most of the time, but he needed sun and air and exercise, and it was impossible to keep him on the lawn. Whatever he was doing, it was a shadowy secretive business. It involved spades and garden tools and packages, with late excursions into the maples toward the creek.

"You'll know in four or five months," he told me, in answer to a question. "Don't ask me now. You'd laugh."

But it became apparent that he wouldn't last that long. The rate of transfusions doubled, and on his bad days, he was unable to get out of bed. He fainted down by the creek, and had to be carried back to the house. Cleo forbade him to go outside alone without Jules' day-to-day approval, and Jules was beginning to be doubtful about the boy's activities.

When restricted, Kenny became frantic. "I've got to go outside, Dad, *please!* I can't finish it if I don't. I've got to! How else can I make contact with them?"

"Contact? With whom?"

But he clammed up and refused to discuss anything about the matter. That night I awoke at two a.m. Something had made a sound. I stole out of bed without disturbing Cleo and went to prowl about the house. A glance down the stairway told me that no lights burned on the first floor. I went to Kenny's room and gingerly opened the door. Blackness.

"Kenny—?"

No sound of breathing in the room. Quietly I struck a match.

The bed was empty.

"Kenny!" I bellowed it down the hall, and then I heard sounds—Cleo stirring to wakefulness and groping for clothes in our bedroom. I trotted downstairs and turned on lights as I charged from rocm to room.

He was not in the house. I found the back screen unlatched and went out to play a flashlight slowly over the backyard. There . . . by the hedge . . . caught in the cone of light . . . Kenny, crumpled over a garden spade.

Upstairs, Cleo screamed through the back window. I ran out to gather him up in my arms. Skin clammy, breathing shallow, pulse irregular—he muttered peculiarly as I carried him back to the house.

"Glad you found it . . . knew you'd find it . . . got me to the right time . . . when are we . . . ?"

I got him inside and up to his room. When I laid him on the bed, a crudely drawn map, like a treasure map with an "X" and a set of bearings, fell from his pocket. I paused a moment to study it. The "X" was down by the fork in the creek. What had been buried there?

I heard Cleo coming up the stairs with a glass of hot milk, and I returned the map to Kenny's pocket and went to call the doctor.

When Kenny awoke, he looked around the room very carefully—and seemed disappointed by what he saw.

"Expecting to wake up somewhere else?" I asked.

"I guess it was a dream," he mumbled. "I thought they came early."

"Who came early?"

But he clammed up again. "You'll find out in about four months," was all he'd say.

He wouldn't last that long. The next day, Doc Jules

ordered him to stay inside, preferably sitting or lying down most of the time. We were to carry him outside once a day for a little sun, but he had to sit in a lawn chair and not run around. Transfusions became more frequent, and finally there was talk of moving him to the hospital.

"I won't go to the hospital."

"You'll have to, Kenny. I'm sorry."

That night, Kenny slipped outside again. He had been lying quietly all day, sleeping most of the time, as if saving up energy for a last spurt.

Shortly after midnight, I awoke to hear him tiptoe down the hall. I let him get downstairs and into the kitchen before I stole out of bed and went to the head of the stairs.

"Kenny!" I shouted. "Come back up here! Right now!"

There was a brief silence. Then he bolted. The screen door slammed, and bare feet trotted down the back steps.

"Kenny!"

I darted to the rear window, overlooking the backyard.

"Kenny!"

Brush whipped as he dove through the hedge. Cleo came to the window beside me, and began calling after him.

Swearing softly, I tugged my trousers over my pajamas, slipped into shoes, and hurried downstairs to give chase. But he had taken my flashlight.

Outside, beneath a dim, cloud-threatened moon, I stood at the hedge, staring out across the meadow toward the woods. The night was full of crickets and rustlings in the grass. I saw no sign of him.

"Kenny!"

He answered me faintly from the distance. "Don't try to follow me, Dad. I'm going where they can cure me."

I vaulted the fence and trotted across the meadow toward the woods. At the stone fence, I paused to listen—but there were only crickets. Maybe he'd seen me coming in the moonlight, and had headed back toward the creek.

The brush was thick in places, and without a light, it was hard to find the paths. I tried watching for the gleam of the flashlight through the trees, but saw nothing. He was keeping its use to a minimum. After ten minutes of wandering, I found myself back at the fence, having taken a wrong turning somewhere. I heard Cleo calling me from the house.

"Go call the police! They'll help find him!" I shouted to her.

Then I went to resume the search. Remembering the map, and the "X" by the fork in the creek, I trotted along the edge of the pasture next to the woods until I came to a dry wash that I knew led back to the creek. It was the long way around, but it was easy to follow the wash; and after a few minutes I stumbled onto the bank of the narrow stream. Then I waded upstream toward the fork. After twenty yards, I saw the flashlight's gleam—and heard the crunch of the shovel in moist ground. I moved as quietly as I could. The crunching stopped.

Then I saw him. He had dropped the shovel and was tugging something out of the hole. I let him get it out before I called . . .

"Kenny . . ."

He froze, then came up very slowly to a crouch, ready to flee. He turned out the flashlight.

"Kenny, don't run away from me again. Stay there. I'm not angry."

No answer.

"Kenny!"

He called back then, with a quaver in his voice. "Stay where you are, Dad—and let me finish. Then I'll go with you. If you come any closer, I'll run." He flashed the light toward me, saw that I was a good twenty yards away. "Stay there now . . ."

"Then will you come back to the house?"

"I won't run, if you stay right there."

"Okay," I agreed, "but don't take long. Cleo's frantic."

He set the light on a rock, kept it aimed at me, and worked by its aura. The light blinded me, and I could only guess what he might be doing. He pried something open, and then there was the sound of writing on tin. Then he hammered something closed, replaced it in the hole, and began shoveling dirt over it. Five minutes later, he was finished.

The light went out.

"Kenny . . . ?"

"I'm sorry, Dad. I didn't *want* to lie . . . I *had* to."

I heard him slipping quickly away through the brush— back toward the pasture. I hurried to the fork and climbed up out of the knee-deep water, pausing to strike a match.

Something gleamed in the grass; I picked it up. Cleo's kitchen clock, always a few minutes slow. What had he wanted with the clock?

By the time I tore through the brush and found the path, there was no sound to indicate which way he had gone. I walked gloomily back toward the house, half-heartedly calling to Kenny . . . then . . . a flash of light in the trees!

BRRUUMMKP!

A sharp report, like a close crash of thunder! It came from the direction of the meadow, or the house. I trotted ahead, ignoring the sharp whipping of the brush.

"Kenny Vestmore? . . . Kenny . . ."

A strange voice, a foreign voice—calling to Kenny up ahead in the distance. The police, I thought.

Then I came to the stone fence . . . and froze, staring at the thing—or perhaps at the *nothing*—in the meadow.

It was black. It was bigger than a double garage, and round. I stared at it, and realized that it was not an object but an opening.

And someone else was calling to Kenny. A rich, pleasant voice—somehow it reminded me of Doctor Jules, but it had a strong accent, perhaps Austrian or German.

"Come on along here, liddle boy. Ve fix you op."

Then I saw Kenny, crawling on toward it through the grass.

"Kenny, *don't!*"

He got to his feet and stumbled on into the distorted space. It seemed to squeeze him into a grotesque house-of-mirrors shape; then it spun him inward. Gone.

I was still running toward the black thing when it began to shrink.

"Come along, liddle fellow, come mit oss. Ve fix."

And then the black thing belched away into nothingness with an explosive blast that knocked me spinning. I must have been out cold for awhile. The sheriff woke me.

Kenny was gone. We never saw him again. Cleo confirmed what I had seen on the meadow, but without a body, Kenny remains listed as missing.

Missing from this century.

I went back to the fork in the creek and dug up the breadbox he had buried. It contained his stamp collection and a packet of famous autographs. There was a letter

was full of answers to our flood of pleading inquiries—all kinds of answers.

"We regret to inform you that recent studies have been . . ."

"Investigations concerning the psychogenic factors show only . . ."

"Prepare to meet God . . ."

"For seventy-five dollars, Guru Tahaj Reshvi guarantees . . ."

"Sickness is only an illusion. Have faith and . . ."

"We cannot promise anything in the near future, but the Institute is rapidly finding new directions for . . ."

"Allow us to extend sympathy . . ."

"The powers of hydromagnetic massage therapy have been established by . . ."

And so it went. We talked to crackpots, confidence men, respectable scientists, fanatics, lunatics, and a few honest fools. Occasionally we tried some harmless technique, with Jules' approval, mostly because it felt like we were doing *something*. But the techniques did more good for Cleo than they did for Kenny, and Kenny's very gradual change for the worse made it apparent that nothing short of the miraculous could save him.

And then Kenny started working on it himself.

The idea, whatever it was, must have hit him suddenly, and it was strange—because it came at a time when both Cleo and I thought that he had completely and fatalistically accepted the coming of the end.

"The labs aren't going to find it in time," he said. "I've been reading what they say. I know it's no good, Dad." He cried some then; it was good that he had relearned to cry.

But the next day, his spirits soared mysteriously to a new high, and he went around the house singing to himself. He was busy with his stamp collection most of the time, but he also wandered about the house and garage searching for odds and ends, his actions seeming purposeful and determined. He moved slowly, and stopped to rest frequently, but he displayed more energy than we had seen for weeks, and even Jules commented on how bright he was looking, when he came for Kenny's daily blood sample. Cleo decided that complete resignation had brought cheerfulness with it, and that acceptance of ill-

from Kenny, too, addressed to the future, and it was his will.

> *"Whoever finds this, please sell these things and use the money to pay for a time machine, so you can come and get me, because I'm going to die if you don't . . ."*

I paused to remember . . . *I don't think the bank'd wait a hundred years.*

But Dad, don't you see? What difference does time make, if you're working on a time machine?

There was more to the note, but the gist of it was that Kenny had made an act of faith, faith in tomorrow. He had buried it, and then he had gone back to dig it up and change the rendezvous time from four months away to the night of his disappearance. He knew that he wouldn't have lived that long.

I put it all back in the box, and sealed the box with solder and set it in concrete at the foot of a sixfoot hole. With this manuscript.

(To a reader, yet unborn, who finds this account in a dusty and ancient magazine stack: *dig.* Dig at a point 987 feet southeasterly on a heading of 149° from the northwest corner of the Hayes and Higgins Tract, as recorded in Map Book 6, p. 78, Cleve County records. But not unless the world is ready to buy a time machine and come for Kenny, who financed it; come, if you can cure him. He had faith in *you.*)

Kenny is gone, and today there is a feeling of death in my house. But after a century of tomorrows? He invested in them, and he called out to them, pleading with the voice of a child. And tomorrow answered:

"Come, liddle boy. Ve fix."

Anybody Else Like Me?

QUIET MISERY IN a darkened room. The clock spoke nine times with a cold brass voice. She stood motionless, leaning against the drapes by the window, alone. The night was black, the house empty and silent.

"Come, Lisa!" she told herself. *"You're not dying!"*

She was thirty-four, still lovely, with a slender white body and a short, rich thatch of warm red hair. She had a good dependable husband, three children, and security. She had friends, hobbies, social activities. She painted mediocre pictures for her own amusement, played the piano rather well, and wrote fair poetry for the University's literary quarterly. She was well-read, well-rounded, well-informed. She loved and was loved.

Then why this quiet misery?

Wanting something, expecting nothing, she stared out into the darkness of the stone-walled garden. The night was too quiet. A distant street lamp played in the branches of the elm, and the elm threw its shadow across another wing of the house. She watched the shadow's wandering for a time. A lone car purred past in the street and was gone. A horn sounded raucously in the distance.

What was wrong? A thousand times since childhood she had felt this uneasy stirring, this crawling of the mind that called out for some unfound expression. It had been particularly strong in recent weeks.

She tried to analyze. What was different about recent weeks? Events: Frank's job had sent him on the road for

30

a month; the children were at Mother's; the city council
had recommended a bond issue; she had fired her maid;
a drunk had strangled his wife; the University had opened
its new psycho-physics lab; her art class had adjourned
for the summer.

Nothing there. No clue to the unreasoning, goalless
urge that called like a voice crying in mental wilderness:
"Come, share, satisfy, express it to the fullest!"

Express what? Satisfy what? How?

A baby, deserted at birth and dying of starvation,
would fell terrible hunger. But if it had never tasted milk,
it could not know the meaning of the hunger nor how to
ease it.

*"I need to relate this thing to something else, to some-
thing in my own experience or in the experience of others."*
She had tried to satisfy the urge with the goals of other
hungers: her children, her husband's lovemaking, food,
drink, art, friendship. But the craving was something
else, crying for its pound of unknown flesh, and there was
no fulfillment.

"How am I different from others?" she asked herself.
But she was different only in the normal ways that every
human being is different from the exact Average. Her intelligence was high, short of genius, but superior. To a
limited extent, she felt the call of creativity. Physically, she
was delicately beautiful. The only peculiarities that she
knew about seemed ridiculously irrelevant: a dark birth-
mark on her thigh, a soft fontanel in the top of her long
narrow head, like the soft spot in an infant's cranium.
Silly little differences!

One big difference: the quiet misery of the unfed hunger.

A scattering of big raindrops suddenly whispered on
the walk and in the grass and through the foliage of the
elm. A few drops splattered on the screen, spraying her
face and arms with faint points of coolness. It had been
oppressively hot. Now there was a chill breath in the night.

Reluctantly she closed the window. The oppression
of the warm and empty house increased. She walked to
the door opening into the walled garden.

Ready for a lonely bed, she was wearing a negligee
over nothing. Vaguely, idly, her hand fumbled at the
waist-knot, loosened it. The robe parted, and the fine spray
of rain was delightfully cool on her skin.

The garden was dark, the shadows inky, the nearest neighbor a block away. The wall screened it from prying eyes. She brushed her hands over her shoulders; the sleeves slipped down her arms. Peeled clean, feeling like a freed animal, she pressed open the screen and stepped out under the eaves to stand on the warm stone walk.

The rain was rattling in the hedge and roaring softly all about her, splashing coldness about her slender calves. She hugged herself and stepped into it. The drench of icy fingers stroked her with pleasant lashes; she laughed and ran along the walk toward the elm. The drops stung her breasts, rivered her face, and coursed coldly down her sides and legs.

She exulted in the rain, tried to dance and laughed at herself. She ran. Then, tired, she threw herself down on the crisp wet lawn, stretching her arms and legs and rolling slowly on the grass. Eyes closed, drenched and languorous, she laughed softly and played imagining games with the rain.

The drops were steel-jacketed wasps, zipping down out of the blackness, but she melted them with her mind, made them soft and cool and caressing. The drops took impersonal liberties with her body, and she rolled demurely to lie face down in the rainsoft grass.

"I am still a pale beast," she thought happily, *"still kin of my grandmother the ape who danced in the tree and chattered when it rained. How utterly barren life would be, if I were not a pale beast!"*

She dug her fingers into the sodden turf, bared her teeth, pressed her forehead against the ground, and growled a little animal growl. It amused her, and she laughed again. Crouching, she came up on her hands and knees, hunching low, teeth still bared. Like a cat, she hissed—and pounced upon a sleeping bird, caught it and shook it to death.

Again she lay laughing in the grass.

"If Frank were to see me like this," she thought, *"he would put me to bed with a couple of sleeping pills, and call that smug Dr. Mensley to have a look at my mind. And Dr. Mensley would check my ambivalences and my repressions and my narcissistic, voyeuristic, masochistic impulses. He would tighten my screws and readjust me to*

reality, fit me into a comfortable groove, and take the pale beast out of me to make me a talking doll."

He had done it several times before. Thinking of Dr. Mensley, Lisa searched her vocabulary for the most savage word she could remember. She growled it aloud and felt better.

The rain was slowly subsiding. A siren was wailing in the distance. The police. She giggled and imagined a headline in tomorrow's paper: PROMINENT SOCIALITE JAILED FOR INDECENT EXPOSURE. And the story would go on: "Mrs. Lisa Waverly was taken into custody by the police after neighbors reported that she was running around stark naked in her back yard. Said Mrs. Heinehoffer who called the law: 'It was just terrible. Looked to me like she was having fits.' Mr. Heinehoffer, when asked for comment, simply closed his eyes and smiled ecstatically."

Lisa sighed wearily. The siren had gone away. The rain had stopped, except for drippings out of the elm. She was tired, emotionally spent, yet strangely melancholy. She sat up slowly in the grass and hugged her shins.

The feeling came over her gradually.

"Someone has been watching me!"

She stiffened slowly, but remained in place, letting her eyes probe about her in the shadows. If only the drippings would stop so she could listen! She peered along the hedge, and along the shadows by the garden wall, toward the dark windows of the house, up toward the low-hanging mist faintly illuminated from below by street lights. She saw nothing, heard nothing. There was no movement in the night. Yet the feeling lingered, even though she scoffed.

"If anyone is here," she thought, *"I'll call them gently, and if anyone appears, I'll scream so loud that Mrs. Heinehoffer will hear me."*

"Hey!" she said in a low voice, but loud enough to penetrate any of the nearby shadows.

There was no answer. She folded her arms behind her head and spoke again, quietly, sensually.

"Come and get me."

No black monster slithered from behind the hedge to devour her. No panther sprang from the elm. No succubus congealed out of wet darkness. She giggled.

"Come have a bite."

No bull-ape came to crush her in ravenous jaws.

She had only imagined the eyes upon her. She stretched lazily and picked herself up, pausing to brush off the leaves of grass· pasted to her wet skin. It was over, the strange worship in the rain, and she was weary. She walked slowly toward the house.

Then she heard it—a faint crackling sound, intermittent, distant. She stood poised in the black shadow of the house, listening. The crackle of paper . . . then a small pop . . . then crisp fragments dropped in the street. It was repeated at short intervals.

Taking nervous, shallow breaths, she tiptoed quietly toward the stone wall of the garden. It was six feet high, but there was a concrete bench under the trellis. The sound was coming from over the wall. She stood crouching on the bench; then, hiding her face behind the vines, she lifted her head to peer.

The street lamp was half a block away, but she could see dimly. A man was standing across the street in the shadows, apparently waiting for a bus. He was eating peanuts out of a paper bag, tossing the shells in the street. That explained the crackling sound.

She glared at him balefully from behind the trellis.

"I'll claw your eyes out," she thought, *"if you came and peeped over my wall."*

"Hi!" the man said.

Lisa stiffened and remained motionless. It was impossible that he could see her. She was in shadow, against a dark background. Had he heard her foolish babbling a moment ago?

More likely, he had only cleared his throat.

"Hi!" he said again.

Her face was hidden in the dripping vines, and she could not move without rustling. She froze in place, staring. She could see little of him. Dark raincoat, dark hat, slender shadow. Was he looking toward her? She was desperately frightened.

Suddenly the man chucked the paper bag in the gutter, stepped off the curb, and came sauntering across the street toward the wall. He removed his hat, and crisp blond hair glinted in the distant streetlight. He stopped three yards away, smiling uncertainly at the vines.

Lisa stood trembling and frozen, staring at him in horror.

Strange sensations, utterly alien, passed over her in waves. There was no describing them, no understanding them.

"I—I found you," he stammered sheepishly. "Do you know what it is?"

"I know you," she thought. *"You have a small scar on the back of your neck, and a mole between your toes. Your eyes are blue, and you have an impacted wisdom tooth, and your feet are hurting you because you walked all the way out here from the University, and I'm almost old enough to be your mother. But I can't know you, because I've never seen you before!"*

"Strange, isn't it?" he said uncertainly. He was holding his hat in his hand and cocking his head politely.

"What?" she whispered.

He shuffled his feet and stared at them. "It must be some sort of palpable biophysical energyform, analytically definable—if we had enough data. Lord knows, I'm no mystic. If it exists, it's got to be mathematically definable. But why us?"

Horrified curiosity made her step aside and lean her arms on the wall to stare down at him. He looked up bashfully, and his eyes widened slightly.

"Oh!"

"Oh what?" she demanded, putting on a terrible frown.

"You're beautiful!"

"What do you want?" she asked icily. "Go away!"

"I—" He paused and closed his mouth slowly. He stared at her with narrowed eyes, and touched one hand to his temple as if concentrating.

For an instant, she was no longer herself. She was looking up at her own shadowy face from down in the street, looking through the eyes of a stranger who was not a stranger. She was feeling the fatigue in the weary ankles, and the nasal ache of a slight head cold, and the strange sadness in a curious heart—a sadness too akin to her own.

She rocked dizzily. It was like being in two places at once, like wearing someone else's body for a moment.

The feeling passed. *"It didn't happen!"* she told herself.

"No use denying it," he said quietly. "I tried to make it go away, too, but apparently we've got something unique. It would be interesting to study. Do you suppose we're related?"

"Who are you?" she choked, only half-hearing his question.

"You know my name," he said, "if you'll just take the trouble to think about it. Yours is Lisa—Lisa O'Brien, or Lisa Waverly—I'm never sure which. Sometimes it comes to me one way, sometimes the other."

She swallowed hard. Her maiden name had been O'Brien.

"I don't know you," she snapped.

His name was trying to form in her mind. She refused to allow it. The young man sighed.

"I'm Kenneth Grearly, if you really don't know." He stepped back a pace and lifted his hat toward his head. "I—I guess I better go. I see this disturbs you. I had hoped we could talk about it, but—well, good night, Mrs. Waverly."

He turned and started away.

"Wait!" she called out against her will.

He stopped again. "Yes?"

"Were—were you watching me—while it was raining?"

He opened his mouth and stared thoughtfully down the street toward the light. "You mean watching visually? You really are repressing this thing, aren't you? I thought you understood." He looked at her sharply, forlornly. "They say the failure to communicate is the basis of all tragedy. Do you suppose in our case . . . ?"

"What?"

"Nothing." He shifted restlessly for a moment. "Good night."

"Good night," she whispered many seconds after he was gone.

Her bedroom was hot and lonely, and she tossed in growing restlessness. If only Frank were home! But he would be gone for two more weeks. The children would be back on Monday, but that was three whole days away. Crazy! It was just stark raving crazy!

Had the man really existed—what was his name?—Kenneth Grearly? Or was he only a phantasm invented by a mind that was failing—her mind? Dancing naked in the rain! Calling out to shadow shapes in the brush! Talking to a specter in the street! Schizophrenic syndrome— dream-world stuff. It could not be otherwise, for unless she had invented Kenneth Grearly, how could she know he had sore feet, an impacted wisdom tooth, and a head cold. Not only did she know about those things, but she felt them!

She buried her face in the dusty pillow and sobbed. Tomorrow she would have to call Dr. Mensley.

But fearing the specter's return, she arose a few minutes later and locked all the doors in the house. When she returned to bed, she tried to pray but it was as if the prayer were being watched. Someone was listening, eavesdropping from outside.

Kenneth Grearly appeared in her dreams, stood half-shrouded in a slowly swirling fog. He stared at her with his head cocked aside, smiling slightly, holding his hat respectfully in his hands.

"Don't you realize, Mrs. Waverly, that we are mutants perhaps?" he asked politely.

"No!" she screamed. "I'm happily married and I have three children and a place in society! Don't come near me!"

He melted slowly into the fog. But echoes came monotonously from invisible cliffs: *mutant mutant mutant mutant mutant . . .*

Dawn came, splashing pink paint across the eastern sky. The light woke her to a dry and empty consciousness, to a headachy awareness full of dull anxiety. She arose wearily and trudged to the kitchen for a pot of coffee.

Lord! Couldn't it all be only a bad dream?

In the cold light of early morning, the things of the past night looked somehow detached, unreal. She tried to analyze objectively.

That sense of sharing a mind, a consciousness, with the stranger who came out of the shadows—what crazy thing had he called it?—*"some sort of palpable biophysical energyform, analytically definable."*

"If I invented the stranger," she thought, *"I must have also invented the words."*

But where had she heard such words before?

Lisa went to the telephone and thumbed through the directory. No Grearly was listed. If he existed at all, he probably lived in a rooming house. The University—last night she had thought that he had something to do with the University. She lifted the phone and dialed.

"University Station; number please," the operator said.

"I—uh—don't know the extension number. Could you tell me if there is a Kenneth Grearly connected with the school?"

"Student or faculty, Madam?"

"I don't know."

"Give me your number, please, and I'll call you back."

"Lawrence 4750. Thanks, Operator."

She sat down to wait. Almost immediately it rang again. "Hello?"

"Mrs. Waverly, you were calling me?" A man's voice. His voice!

"The operator found you rather quickly." It was the only thing she could think of saying.

"No, no. I knew you were calling. In fact, I hoped you into it."

"Hoped me? Now look here, Mr. Grearly, I—"

"You were trying to explain our phenomenon in terms of insanity rather than telepathy. I didn't want you to do that, and so I hoped you into calling me."

Lisa was coldly speechless.

"What phenomenon are you talking about?" she asked after a few dazed seconds.

"Still repressing it? Listen, I can share your mind any time I want to, now that I understand where and who you are. You might as well face the fact. And it can work both ways, if you let it. Up to now, you've been—well, keeping your mind's eye closed, so to speak."

Her scalp was crawling. The whole thing had become intensely disgusting to her.

"I don't know what you're up to, Mr. Grearly, but I wish you'd stop it. I admit something strange is going on, but your explanation is ridiculous—offensive, even."

He was silent for a long time, then "I wonder if the first man-ape found his prehensile thumb ridiculous. I wonder if he thought using his hands for grasping was offensive."

"What are you trying to say?"

"That I think we're mutants. We're not the first ones. I had this same experience when I was in Boston once. There must be one of us there, too, but suddenly I got the feeling that he had committed suicide. I never saw him. We're probably the first ones to discover each other."

"Boston? If what you say is true, what would distance have to do with it?"

"Well, if telepathy exists, it certainly involves transfer of energy from one point to another. What *kind* of energy, I don't know. Possibly electromagnetic in character. But it seems likely that it would obey the inverse square law, like radiant energyforms. I came to town about three weeks ago. I didn't feel you until I got close."

"There is a connection," she thought. She had been wondering about the increased anxiety of the past three weeks. .

"I don't know what you're talking about," she evaded icily, though. "I'm no mutant. I don't believe in telepathy. I'm not insane. Now let me alone."

She slammed the telephone in its cradle and started to walk away.

Evidently he was angry, for she was suddenly communicating with him again.

She reeled dizzily and clutched at the wall, because she was in two places at once, and the two settings merged in her mind to become a blur, like a double exposure. She was in her own hallway, and she was also in an office, looking at a calculator keyboard, hearing glassware rattling from across a corridor, aware of the smell of formaldehyde. There was a chart on the wall behind the desk and it was covered with strange tracery—schematics of some neural arcs. The office of the psychophysics lab. She closed her eyes, and her own hallway disappeared.

She felt anger—his anger.

"We've got to face this thing. If this is a new direction for human evolution, then we'd better study it and see what to do about it. I knew I was different and I became a psychophysicist to find out why. I haven't been able to measure much, but now with Lisa's help . . ."

She tried to shut him out. She opened her eyes and summoned her strength and tried to force him away. She stared at the bright doorway, but the tracery of neural arcs still remained. She fought him, but his mind lingered in hers.

". . . perhaps we can get to the bottom of it. I know my encephalograph recordings are abnormal, and now I can check them against hers. A few correlations will help. I'm glad to know about her soft fontanel. I wondered

about mine. Now I think that underneath that fontanel lies a pattern of specialized neural—"

She sagged to the floor of the hall and babbled aloud "Hickory Dickory Dock, the mouse ran up the clock. The clock struck one—"

Slowly he withdrew. The laboratory office faded from her vision. His thoughts left her. She lay there panting for a time.

Had she won?

No, there was no sense in claiming victory. She had not driven him away. He had withdrawn of his own volition when he felt her babbling. She knew his withdrawal was free, because she had felt his parting state of mind: sadness. He had stopped the forced contact because he pitied her, and there was a trace of contempt in the pity.

She climbed slowly to her feet, looking around wildly, touching the walls and the door-frame to reassure herself that she was still in her own home. She staggered into the parlor and sat shivering on the sofa.

Last night! That crazy running around in the rain! He was responsible for that. He had hoped her into doing it, or maybe he had just wondered what she looked like undressed, and she had subconsciously satisfied his curiosity. He had planted the suggestion—innocently, perhaps—and she had unknowingly taken the cue.

He could be with her whenever he wanted to! He had been with her while she frolicked insanely in the rain-sodden grass! Perhaps he was with her now.

Whom could she talk to? Where could she seek help? Dr. Mensley? He would immediately chalk it up as a delusion, and probably call for a sanity hearing if she wouldn't voluntarily enter a psycho-ward for observation.

The police? "Sergeant, I want to report a telepathic prowler. A man is burglarizing my mind."

A clergyman? He would shudder and refer her to a psychiatrist.

All roads led to the booby-hatch, it seemed. Frank wouldn't believe her. No one would believe her.

Lisa wandered through the day like a caged animal. She put on her brightest summer frock and a pert straw hat and went downtown. She wandered through the crowds in the business district, window-shopping. But she was alone. The herds of people about her brushed past and wandered on. A man whistled at her in front of a cigar store. A policeman waved her back to the curb when she started across an intersection.

"Wake up, lady!" he called irritably.

People all about her, but she could not tell them, explain to them, and so she was alone. She caught a taxi and went to visit a friend, the wife of an English teacher, and drank a glass of iced tea in the friend's parlor, and talked of small things, and admitted that she was tired when the friend suggested that she looked that way. When she went back home, the sun was sinking in the west.

She called long distance and talked to her mother, then spoke to her children, asked them if they were ready to come home, but they wanted to stay another week. They begged, and her mother begged, and she reluctantly consented. It had been a mistake to call. Now the kids would be gone even longer.

She tried to call Frank in St. Louis, but the hotel clerk reported that he had just checked out. Lisa knew this meant he was on the road again.

"Maybe I ought to go join the kids at Mother's," she thought. But Frank had wanted her to stay home. He was expecting a registered letter from Chicago, and it was apparently important, and she had to take care of it.

"I'll invite somebody over," she thought. But the wives were home with their husbands, and it was a social mistake to invite a couple when her husband was gone. It always wound up with two women yammering at each other while the lone male sat and glowered in uneasy isolation, occasionally disagreeing with his wife, just to let her know he was there and he was annoyed and bored and why didn't they go home? It was different if the business-widow called on a couple. Then the lone male could retire to some other part of the house to escape the yammering.

But she decided it wasn't company she wanted; she wanted help. And there was no place to get it.

When she allowed her thoughts to drift toward Kenneth Grearly, it was almost like tuning in a radio station. He was eating early dinner in the University cafeteria with a bedraggled, bespectacled brunette from the laboratory. Lisa closed her eyes and let herself sift gingerly into his thoughts. His attention was on the conversation and on the food, and he failed to realize Lisa's presence. That knowledge gave her courage.

He was eating Swiss steak and hashed brown potatoes, and the flavors formed perceptions in her mind. She heard the rattle of silverware, the low murmur of voices, and smelled the food. She marveled at it. The strange ability had apparently been brought into focus by learning what it was and how to use it.

"Our work has been too empirical," he was saying. "We've studied phenomena, gathered data, looked for correlations. But that method has limitations. We should try to find a way to approach psychology from below. Like the invariantive approach to physics."

The girl shook her head. "The nervous system is too complicated for writing theoretical equations about it. Empirical equations are the best we can do."

"They aren't good enough, Sarah. You can predict results with them, inside the limits of their accuracy. But you can't extrapolate them very well, and they won't stack up together into a single integrated structure. And when you're investigating a new field, they no longer apply. We need a broad mathematical theory, covering all hypothetically possible neural arrangements. It would let us predict not only results, but also predict patterns of possible order."

"Seems to me the possible patterns are infinite."

"No, Sarah. They're limited by the nature of the building blocks—neurons, synaptic connections, and, so forth. With limited materials, you have structural limitations. You don't build skyscrapers out of modeling clay. And there is only a finite number of ways you can build atoms out of electrons, protons and neutrons. Similarly, brains are confined to the limitations of the things they're made of. We need a broad theory for defining the limits."

"Why?"

"Because . . ." He paused. Lisa felt his urge to explain his urgency, felt him suppress it, felt for a moment his loneliness in the awareness of his uniqueness and the way it isolated him from humanity.

"You must be doing new work," the girl offered, "if you feel the lack of such a theoretical approach. I just can't imagine an invariantive approach to psychology—or an all-defining set of laws for it, either. Why do you need such a psychological 'Relativity'?"

He hesitated, frowning down at his plate, watching a fly crawl around its rim. "I'm interested in—in the quantitative aspects of nerve impulses. I—I suspect that there can be such a thing as neural resonance."

She laughed politely and shook her head. "I'll stick to my empirical data-gathering, thank you."

Lisa felt him thinking:

"She could understand, if I could show her data. But my data is all subjective, experimental, personal. I share it with that Waverly woman, but she is only a social thinker, analytically shallow, refusing even to recognize facts. Why did it have to be her? She's flighty, emotional, and in a cultural rut. If she doesn't conform, she thinks she's nuts. But then at least she's a woman—and if this is really a mutation, we'll have to arrange for some children . . ."

Lisa gasped and sat bolt upright. Her shock revealed her presence to him, and he dropped his fork with a clatter.

"Lisa!"

She wrenched herself free of him abruptly. She angrily stalked about the house, slamming doors and muttering her rage. The nerve! The maddening, presumptuous, ill-mannered, self-centered, overly educated boor!

Arrange for some children indeed! An impossible situation!

As her anger gathered momentum, she contacted him again—like a snake striking. Thought was thunder out of a dark cloud.

"I'm decent and I'm respectable, Mr. Grearly! I have a husband and three fine children and I love them, and you can go to hell! I never want to see you again or have you prowling around my mind. Get out and STAY out. And if you ever bother me again—I'll—I'll kill you."

He was outdoors, striding across the campus alone. She saw the gray buildings, immersed in twilight, felt the wind on his face, hated him. He was thinking nothing, letting himself follow her angry flow of thought. When she finished, his thoughts began like the passionate pleading of a poem.

He was imagining a human race with telepathic abil-

ities, in near-perfect communication with one another.
So many of the world's troubles could be traced to im-
perfect communication of ideas, to misunderstandings.

Then he thought briefly of Sarah—the nondescript
laboratory girl he had taken to dinner—and Lisa realized he was in love with Sarah. There were sadness and
resentment here. He couldn't have Sarah now, not if he
were to be certain of perpetuating the mutant characteristic. The Waverly woman ought to be good for three or
four children yet, before she reached middle age.

Lisa stood transfixed by shock. Then he was thinking
directly to her.

*"I'm sorry. You're a beautiful, intelligent woman—
but I don't love you. We're not alike. But I'm stuck with
you and you're stuck with me, because I've decided it's
going to be that way. I can't convince you since your
thinking habits are already fixed, so I won't even try.
I'm sorry it has to be against your will, but in any event
it has to be. And now that I know what you're like, I
don't dare wait—for fear you'll do something to mess
things up."*

"No!" she screamed, watching the scenery that moved
past his field of vision.

He had left the campus and was walking up the street
—toward her neighborhood. He was walking with the
briskness of purpose. He was coming to her house.

"Call the police!" she thought, and tried to dissolve
him out of her mind.

But this time he followed, clung to her thoughts, would
not let her go. It was like two flashlight beams playing
over a wall, one trying to escape, the other following its
frantic circle of brightness.

She staggered, groped her way toward the hall, which
was confused with a superimposed image of a sidewalk
and a street. A phantom automobile came out of the hall
wall, drove through her and vanished. Double exposures.
He stared at a street light and it blinded her. At last she
found the phone, but he was laughing at her.

*"Eight seven six five twenty-one Mary had a little
lamb seven seven sixty-seven yesterday was May March
April . . ."*

He was deliberately filling her mind with confusion.
She fumbled at the directory, trying to find the police,

but he thought a confused jumble of numbers and symbols, and they scampered across the page, blurring the
letters.

She whimpered and groped at the phone-dial, trying
to get the operator, but he was doing something with his
fingertips, and she couldn't get the feel of the dial.

On her third try, it finally worked.

"Information," said a pleasant impersonal voice.

She had to get the police! She had to say—

*"Pease porridge hot, pease porridge cold, pease por-
ridge in the pot, nine days pretty polly parrot played
peacefully plentiwise pease porridge . . ."*

He was jamming her speech centers with gibberish,
and she blurted nonsense syllables into the mouthpiece.

"You'll have to speak more distinctly, madam. I can't
understand you."

"Poress, Policer . . ."

"The police? Just a moment."

A series of jumbled sounds and visions clouded her
mind. Then a masculine voice rumbled, "Desk, Sergeant
Harris."

She found a clear path through the confusion and
gasped, "Three-oh-oh-three Willow Drive—'mergency
—come quick—man going to—"

"Three-oh-oh-three Willow. Check. We'll have a car
right over there."

She hung up quickly—or tried to—but she couldn't
find the cradle. Then her vision cleared, and she
screamed. She wasn't in the hall at all!

The telephone was an eggbeater!

His voice came through her trapped panic.

"You might as well give in," he told her with a note
of sadness. *"I know how to mess you up like that, you
see. And you haven't learned to retaliate yet. We're going to cooperate with this evolutionary trend, whether
you like it or not—but it would be more pleasant if you
agree to it."*

"No!"

*"All right, but I'm coming anyway. I hoped it wouldn't
be like this. I wanted to convince you gradually. Now I
know that it's impossible."*

He was still ten blocks away. She had a few minutes
in which to escape. She bolted for the door. A black

shadow-shape loomed up in the twilight, flung its arms wide, and emitted an apelike roar.

She yelped and darted back, fleeing frantically for the front. A boa constrictor lay coiled in the hall; it slithered toward her. She screamed again and raced toward the stairway.

She made it to the top and looked back. The living room was filling slowly with murky water. She rushed shrieking into the bedroom and bolted the door.

She smelled smoke. Her dress was on fire! The flames licked up, searing her skin.

She tore at it madly, and got it off, but her slip was afire. She ripped it away, scooped up the flaming clothing on a transom hook, opened the screen, and dropped them out the window. Flames still licked about her, and she rolled up in the bed-clothing to snuff them out.

Quiet laughter.

"New syndrome," he called to her pleasantly. *"The patient confuses someone else's fantasy with her own reality. Not schizophrenia—duophrenia, maybe?"*

She lay sobbing in hysterical desperation. He was just down the street now, coming rapidly up the walk. A car whisked slowly past. He felt her terrified despair and pitied her. The torment ceased.

She stayed there, panting for a moment, summoning spirit. He was nearing the intersection just two blocks south, and she could hear the rapid traffic with his ears.

Suddenly she clenched her eyes closed and gritted her teeth. He was stepping off the curb, walking across—

She imagined a fire engine thundering toward her like a juggernaut, rumbling and wailing. She imagined another car racing out into the intersection, with herself caught in the crossfire. She imagined a woman screaming, "Look out, Mister!"

And then she was caught in his own responding fright, and it was easier to imagine. He was bolting for the other corner. She conjured a third car from another direction, brought it lunging at him to avoid the impending wreck. He staggered away from the phantom cars and screamed.

A real car confused the scene.

She echoed his scream. There was a moment of rending pain, and then the vision was gone. Brakes were still yowling two blocks away. Someone was running down the sidewalk. A part of her mind had heard the crashing thud. She was desperately sick.

And a sudden sense of complete aloneness told her that Grearly was dead. A siren was approaching out of the distance.

VOICES from the sidewalk: ". . . just threw a fit in the middle of the street . . . running around like crazy and hollering . . . it was a delivery truck . . . crushed his skull . . . nobody else hurt . . ."

After the street returned to normal, she arose and went to get a drink of water. But she stood staring at her sick white face in the mirror. There were crow's feet forming at the corners of her eyes, and her skin was growing tired, almost middle-aged.

It was funny that she should notice that now, at this strange moment. She had just killed a man in self-defense. And no one would believe it if she told the truth. There was no cause for guilt.

Was there?

Frank would be back soon, and everything would be the same again: peace, security, nice kids, nice home, nice husband. Just the way it always had been.

But something was already different. An emptiness. A loneliness of the mind that she had never before felt. She kept looking around to see if the lights hadn't gone dim, or the clock stopped ticking, or the faucet stopped dripping.

It was none of those things. The awful silence was within her.

Gingerly, she touched the soft spot in the top of her head and felt an utter aloneness. She closed her eyes and thought a hopeless plea to the Universe:

"Is there anybody else like me? Can anybody hear me?"

There was only complete silence, the silence of the voiceless void.

And for the first time in her life she felt the confinement of total isolation and knew it for what it was.

Crucifixus Etiam

MANUE NANTI JOINED the project to make some dough. Five dollars an hour was good pay, even in 2134 A.D. and there was no way to spend it while on the job. Everything would be furnished: housing, chow, clothing, toiletries, medicine, cigarettes, even a daily ration of one hundred eighty proof beverage alcohol, locally distilled from fermented Martian mosses as fuel for the project's vehicles. He figured that if he avoided crap games, he could finish his five-year contract with fifty thousand dollars in the bank, return to Earth, and retire at the age of twenty-four. Manue wanted to travel, to see the far corners of the world, the strange cultures, the simple people, the small towns, deserts, mountains, jungles— for until he came to Mars, he had never been farther than a hundred miles from Cerro de Pasco, his birthplace in Peru.

A great wistfulness came over him in the cold Martian night when the frost haze broke, revealing the black, gleam-stung sky, and the blue-green Earth-star of his birth. *El mundo de mi carne, de mi alma,* he thought— yet, he had seen so little of it that many of its places would be more alien to him than the homogenously ugly vistas of Mars. These he longed to see: the volcanoes of the South Pacific, the monstrous mountains of Tibet, the concrete cyclops of New York, the radioactive craters of Russia, the artificial islands in the China Sea, the Black Forest, the Ganges, the Grand Canyon—but most of all, the works of human art: the pyramids, the Gothic cathedrals of Europe, *Notre Dame du Chartres,* Saint

48

Peter's, the tile-work wonders of Anacapri. But the dream was still a long labor from realization.

Manue was a big youth, heavy-boned and built for labor, clever in a simple mechanical way, and with a wistful good humor that helped him take a lot of guff from whiskey-breathed foremen and sharp-eyed engineers who made ten dollars an hour and figured ways for making more, legitimately or otherwise.

He had been on Mars only a month, and it hurt. Each time he swung the heavy pick into the red-brown sod, his face winced with pain. The plastic aerator valves, surgically stitched in his chest, pulled and twisted and seemed to tear with each lurch of his body. The mechanical oxygenator served as a lung, sucking blood through an artificially grafted network of veins and plastic tubing, frothing it with air from a chemical generator, and returning it to his circulatory system. Breathing was unnecessary, except to provide wind for talking, but Manue breathed in desperate gulps of the 4.0 psi Martian air; for he had seen the wasted, atrophied chests of the men who had served four or five years, and he knew that when they returned to Earth—if ever—they would still need the auxiliary oxygenator equipment.

"If you don't stop breathing," the surgeon told him, "you'll be all right. When you go to bed at night, turn the oxy down low—so low you feel lige panting. There's a critical point that's just right for sleeping. If you get it too low, you'll wake up screaming, and you'll get claustrophobia. If you get it too high, your reflex mechanisms will go to pot and you won't breathe; your lungs'll dry up after a time. Watch it."

Manue watched it carefully, although the oldsters laughed at him—in their dry wheezing chuckles. Some of them could scarcely speak more than two or three words at a shallow breath.

"Breathe deep, boy," they told him. "Enjoy it while you can. You'll forget how pretty soon. Unless you're an engineer."

The engineers had it soft, he learned. They slept in a pressurized barrack where the air was ten psi and twenty-five per çent oxygen, where they turned their oxies off and slept in peace. Even their oxies were self-regulating, controlling the output according to the carbon dioxide content of the input blood. But the Commission could afford no such luxuries for the labor gangs. The payload of a cargo rocket from Earth was only about two per cent of the ship's total mass, and nothing superfluous could be carried. The ships brought the bare essentials, basic industrial equipment, big reactors, generators, engines, heavy tools.

Small tools, building materials, foods, non-nuclear fuels —these things had to be made on Mars. There was an open pit mine in the belly of the Syrtis Major where a "lake" of nearly pure iron-rust was scooped into a smelter, and processed into various grades of steel for building purposes, tools, and machinery. A quarry in the Flathead Mountains dug up large quantities of cement rock, burned it, and crushed it to make concrete.

It was rumored that Mars was even preparing to grow her own labor force. An old-timer told him that the Commission had brought five hundred married couples to a new underground city in the Mare Erythraeum, supposedly as personnel for a local commission headquarters, but according to the old-timer, they were to be paid a bonus of three thousand dollars for every child born on the red planet. But Manue knew that the old "troffies" had a way of inventing such stories, and he reserved a certain amount of skepticism.

As for his own share in the Project, he knew—and needed to know—very little. The encampment was at the north end of the Mare Cimmerium, surrounded by the bleak brown and green landscape of rock and giant lichens, stretching toward sharply defined horizons except for one mountain range in the distance, and hung over by a blue sky so dark that the Earth-star occasionally became dimly visible during the dim daytime. The encampment consisted of a dozen double-walled stone huts, windowless, and roofed with flat slabs of rock covered over by a tarry resin boiled out of the cactuslike spineplants. The camp was ugly, lonely, and dominated by the gaunt skeleton of a drill rig set up in its midst.

Manue joined the excavating crew in the job of digging a yard-wide, six feet deep foundation trench in a hundred yard square around the drill rig, which day and night was biting deeper through the crust of Mars in a dry cut that necessitated frequent stoppages for changing rotary bits. He learned that the geologists had predicted a subterranean pocket of tritium oxide ice at sixteen thousand feet, and that it was for this that they were drilling. The foundation he was helping to dig would be for a control station of some sort.

He worked too hard to be very curious. Mars was a nightmare, a grim, womanless, frigid, disinterestedly evil world. His digging partner was a sloe-eyed Tibetan nicknamed "Gee" who spoke the Omnalingua clumsily at best. He followed two paces behind Manue with a shovel, scooping up the broken ground, and humming a monotonous chant in his own tongue. Manue seldom heard his own language, and missed it; one of the engineers, a haughty Chilean, spoke the modern Spanish, but not to such as Manue Nanti. Most of the other laborers used either Basic English or the Omnalingua. He spoke both, but longed to hear the tongue of his people. Even when he tried to talk to Gee, the cultural gulf was so wide that satisfying communication was nearly impossible. Peruvian jokes were unfunny to Tibetan ears, although Gee bent double with gales of laughter when Manue nearly crushed his own foot with a clumsy stroke of the pick.

He found no close companions. His foreman was a narrow-eyed, orange-browed Low German named Vögeli, usually half-drunk, and intent upon keeping his lung-power by bellowing at his crew. A meaty, florid man, he stalked slowly along the lip of the excavation, pausing to stare coldly down at each pair of laborers who, if they dared to look up, caught a guttural tongue-lashing for the moment's pause. When he had words for a digger, he called a halt by kicking a small avalanche of dirt back into the trench about the man's feet.

Manue learned about Vögeli's disposition before the end of his first month. The aerator tubes had become nearly unbearable; the skin, in trying to grow fast to the plastic, was beginning to form a tight little neck where the tubes entered his flesh, and the skin stretched and burned and stung with each movement of his trunk. Suddenly he felt sick. He staggered dizzily against the side of the trench, dropped the pick, and swayed heavily, bracing himself against collapse. Shock and nausea rocked him, while Gee stared at him and giggled foolishly.

"Hoy!" Vögeli bellowed from across the pit. "Get back on that pick! Hoy, there! Get with it—"

Manue moved dizzily to recover the tool, saw patches of black swimming before him, sank weakly back to pant in shallow gasps. The nagging sting of the valves was a portable hell that he carried with him always. He fought an impulse to jerk them out of his flesh; if a valve came loose, he would bleed to death in a few minutes.

Vögeli came stamping along the heap of fresh earth and lumbered up to stand over the sagging Manue in the trench. He glared down at him for a moment, then nudged the back of his neck with a heavy boot. "Get to work!"

Manue looked up and moved his lips silently. His forehead glinted with moisture in the faint sun, although the temperature was far below freezing.

"Grab that pick and get started."

"Can't," Manue gasped. "Hoses—hurt."

Vögeli grumbled a curse and vaulted down into the trench beside him. "Unzip that jacket," he ordered.

Weakly, Manue fumbled to obey, but the foreman knocked his hand aside and jerked the zipper down. Roughly he unbuttoned the Peruvian's shirt, laying open the bare brown chest to the icy cold.

"*No!*—not the hoses, *please!*"

Vögeli took one of the thin tubes in his blunt fingers and leaned close to peer at the puffy, calloused nodule of irritated skin that formed around it where it entered the flesh. He touched the nodule lightly, causing the digger to whimper.

"No, please!"

"Stop sniveling!"

Vögeli laid his thumbs against the nodule and exerted a sudden pressure. There was slight popping sound as the skin slid back a fraction of an inch along the tube. Manue yelped and closed his eyes.

"Shut up! I know what I'm doing." He repeated the process with the other tube. Then he seized both tubes in his hands and wiggled them slightly in and out, as if to insure a proper resetting of the skin. The digger cried weakly and slumped in a dead faint.

When he awoke, he was in bed in the barracks, and

a medic was painting the sore spots with a bright yellow solution that chilled his skin.

"Woke up, huh?" the medic grunted cheerfully. "How you feel?"

"*Malo!*" he hissed.

"Stay in bed for the day, son. Keep your oxy up high. Make you feel better."

The medic went away, but Vögeli lingered, smiling at him grimly from the doorway. "Don't try goofing off tomorrow too."

Manue hated the closed door with silent eyes, and listened intently until Vögeli's footsteps left the building. Then, following the medic's instructions, he turned his oxy to maximum, even though the faster flow of blood made the chest-valves ache. The sickness fled, to be replaced with a weary afterglow. Drowsiness came over him, and he slept.

Sleep was a dread black-robed phantom on Mars. Mars pressed the same incubus upon all newcomers to her soil: a nightmare of falling, falling, falling into bottomless space. It was the faint gravity, they said, that caused it. The body felt buoyed up, and the subconscious mind recalled down-going elevators, and diving airplanes, and a fall from a high cliff. It suggested these things in dreams, or if the dreamer's oxy were set too low, it conjured up a nightmare of sinking slowly deeper, and deeper in cold, black water that filled the victim's throat. Newcomers were segregated in a separate barracks so that their nightly screams would not disturb the old-timers who had finally adjusted to Martian conditions.

But now, for the first time since his arrival, Manue slept soundly, airily, and felt borne up by beams of bright light.

When he awoke again, he lay clammy in the horrifying knowledge that he had not been breathing! It was so comfortable not to breathe. His chest stopped hurting because of the stillness of his rib cage. He felt refreshed and alive. Peaceful sleep.

Suddenly he was breathing again in harsh gasps, and cursing himself for the lapse, and praying amid quiet tears as he visualized the wasted chest of a troffie.

"*Heh heh!*" wheezed an oldster who had come in to readjust the furnace in the rookie barracks. "You'll get

to be a Martian pretty soon, boy. I been here seven
years. Look at *me*."

Manue heard the gasping voice and shuddered; there
was no need to look.

"You just as well not fight it. It'll get you. Give in,
make it easy on yourself. Go crazy if you don't."

"Stop it! Let me alone!"

"Sure. Just one thing. You wanta go home, you think.
I went home. Came back. You will, too. They all do,
'cept engineers. Know why?"

"Shut up!" Manue pulled himself erect on the cot and
hissed anger at the old-timer, who was neither old nor
young, but only withered by Mars. His head suggested
that he might be around thirty-five, but his body was
weak and old.

The veteran grinned. "Sorry," he wheezed. "I'll keep
my mouth shut." He hesitated, then extended his hand.
"I'm Sam Donnell, mech-repairs."

Manue still glowered at him. Donnell shrugged and
dropped his hand.

"Just trying to be friends," he muttered and walked
away.

The digger started to call after him but only closed his
mouth again, tightly. Friends? He needed friends, but
not a troffie. He couldn't even bear to look at them, for
fear he might be looking into the mirror of his own future.

Manue climbed out of his bunk and donned his fleeceskins. Night had fallen, and the temperature was already
twenty below. A soft sift of icedust obscured the stars.
He stared about in the darkness. The mess hall was
closed, but a light burned in the canteen and another in
the foremen's club, where the men were playing cards
and drinking. He went to get his alcohol ration, gulped
it mixed with a little water, and trudged back to the barracks alone.

The Tibetan was in bed, staring blankly at the ceiling.
Manue sat down and gazed at his flat, empty face.

"Why did you come here, Gee?"

"Come where?"

"To Mars."

Gee grinned, revealing large black-streaked teeth.
"Make money. Good money on Mars."

"Everybody make money, huh?"

"Sure."

"Where's the money come from?"

Gee rolled his face toward the Peruvian and frowned. "You crazy? Money come from Earth, where all money comes from."

"And what does Earth get back from Mars?"

Gee looked puzzled for a moment, then gathered anger because he found no answer. He grunted a monosyllable in his native tongue, then rolled over and went to sleep.

Manue was not normally given to worrying about such things, but now he found himself asking, "What am I doing here?"—and then, "What is *anybody* doing here?"

The Mars Project had started eighty or ninety years ago, and its end goal was to make Mars habitable for colonists without Earth support, without oxies and insulated suits and the various gadgets a man now had to use to keep himself alive on the fourth planet. But thus far, Earth had planted without reaping. The sky was a bottomless well into which Earth poured her tools, dollars, manpower, and engineering skill. And there appeared to be no hope for the near future.

Manue felt suddenly trapped. He could not return to Earth before the end of his contract. He was trading five years of virtual enslavement for a sum of money which would buy a limited amount of freedom. But what if he lost his lungs, became a servant of the small aerator for the rest of his days? Worst of all: whose ends was he serving? The contractors were getting rich—on government contracts. Some of the engineers and foremen were getting rich—by various forms of embezzlement of government funds. But what were the people back on Earth getting for their money?

Nothing.

He lay awake for a long time, thinking about it. Then he resolved to ask someone tomorrow, someone smarter than himself.

But he found the question brushed aside. He summoned enough nerve to ask Vögeli, but the foreman told him harshly to keep working and quit wondering. He asked the structural engineer who supervised the building, but the man only laughed, and said: "What do you care? You're making good money."

They were running concrete now, laying the long

strips of Martian steel in the bottom of the trench and
dumping in great slobbering wheelbarrowfuls of gray-
green mix. The drillers were continuing their tedious dry
cut deep into the red world's crust. Twice a day they
brought up a yard long cylindrical sample of the rock
and gave it to a geologist who weighed it, roasted it,
weighed it again, and tested a sample of the condensed
steam—if any—for tritium content. Daily, he chalked
up the results on a blackboard in front of the engineering
hut, and the technical staff crowded around for a look.
Manue always glanced at the figures, but failed to
understand.

Life became an endless routine of pain, fear, hard
work, anger. There were few diversions. Sometimes a
crew of entertainers came out from the Mare Erythraeum, but the labor gang could not all crowd in the pressurized staff-barracks where the shows were presented,
and when Manue managed to catch a glimpse of one of
the girls walking across the clearing, she was bundled in
fleeceskins and hooded by a parka.

Itinerant rabbis, clergymen, and priests of the world's
major faiths came occasionally to the camp: Buddhist,
Moslem, and the Christian sects. Padre Antonio Selni
made monthly visits to hear confessions and offer Mass.
Most of the gang attended all services as a diversion
from routine, as an escape from nostalgia. Somehow it
gave Manue a strange feeling in the pit of his stomach
to see the Sacrifice of the Mass, two thousand years old,
being offered in the same ritual under the strange
dark sky of Mars—with a section of the new foundation serving as an altar upon which the priest set crucifix, candles, relic-stone, missal, chalice, paten, ciborium,
cruets, et cetera. In filling the wine-cruet before the
service, Manue saw him spill a little of the red-clear
fluid upon the brown soil—wine, Earth-wine from sunny
Sicilian vineyards, trampled from the grapes by the
bare stamping feet of children. Wine, the rich red blood
of Earth, soaking slowly into the crust of another planet.

Bowing low at the consecration, the unhappy Peruvian
thought of the prayer a rabbi had sung the week before:
"Blessed be the Lord our God, King of the Universe,
Who makest bread to spring forth out of the Earth."

Earth chalice, Earth blood, Earth God, Earth wor-

shipers—with plastic tubes in their chests and a great
sickness in their hearts.

He went away saddened. There was no faith here.
Faith needed familiar surroundings, the props of culture.
Here there were only swinging picks and rumbling machinery and sloshing concrete and the clatter of tools and
the wheezing of troffies. Why? For five dollars an hour
and keep?

Manue, raised in a back-country society that was almost a folk-culture, felt deep thirst for a goal. His father
had been a stonemason, and he had labored lovingly to
help build the new cathedral, to build houses and man-
sions and commerical buildings, and his blood was
mingled in their mortar. He had built for the love of his
community and the love of the people and their customs,
and their gods. He knew his own ends, and the ends of
those around him. But what sense was there in this endless scratching at the face of Mars? Did they think they
could make it into a second Earth, with pine forests and
lakes and snow-capped mountains and small country
villages? Man was not that strong. No, if he were labor-
ing for any cause at all, it was to build a world so un-
earthlike that he could not love it.

The foundation was finished. There was very little
more to be done until the drillers struck pay. Manue
sat around the camp and worked at breathing. It was
becoming a conscious effort now, and if he stopped thinking about it for a few minutes, he found himself inspiring
shallow, meaningless little sips of air that scarcely moved
his diaphragm. He kept the aerator as low as possible, to
make himself breathe great gasps that hurt his chest, but
it made him dizzy, and he had to increase the oxygena-
tion lest he faint.

Sam Donnell, the troffie mech-repairman, caught him
about to slump dizzily from his perch atop a heap of
rocks, pushed him erect, and turned his oxy back to normal. It was late afternoon, and the drillers were about to
change shifts. Manue sat shaking his head for a moment,
then gazed at Donnell gratefully.

"That's dangerous, kid," the troffie wheezed. "Guys
can go psycho doing that. Which you rather have: sick
lungs or sick mind?"

"Neither."

"I know, but—"

"I don't want to talk about it."

Donnell stared at him with a faint smile. Then he shrugged and sat down on the rock heap to watch the drilling.

"Oughta be hitting the tritium ice in a couple of days," he said pleasantly. "Then we'll see a big blow."

Manue moistened his lips nervously. The troffies always made him feel uneasy. He stared aside.

"Big blow?"

"Lotta pressure down there, they say. Something about the way Mars got formed. Dust cloud hypothesis."

Manue shook his head. "I don't understand."

"I don't either. But I've heard them talk. Couple of billion years ago, Mars was supposed to be a moon of Jupiter. Picked up a lot of ice crystals over a rocky core. Then it broke loose and picked up a rocky crust—from another belt of the dust cloud. The pockets of tritium ice catch a few neutrons from uranium ore—down under. Some of the tritium goes into helium. Frees oxygen. Gases form pressure. Big blow."

"What are they going to do with the ice?"

The troffie shrugged. "The engineers might know."

Manue snorted and spat. "They know how to make money."

"Heh! Sure, everybody's gettin' rich."

The Peruvian stared at him speculatively for a moment.

"Señor Donnell, I—"

"Sam'll do."

"I wonder if anybody knows why . . . well . . . why we're really here."

Donnell glanced up to grin, then waggled his head. He fell thoughtful for a moment, and leaned forward to write in the earth. When he finished, he read it aloud.

"A plow plus a horse plus land equals the necessities of life." He glanced up at Manue. "Fifteen Hundred A.D."

The Peruvian frowned his bewilderment. Donnell rubbed out what he had written and wrote again.

"A factory plus steam turbines plus raw materials equals necessities plus luxuries. Nineteen Hundred A.D."

He rubbed it out and repeated the scribbling. "All those things plus nuclear power and computer controls

equal a surplus of everything. Twenty-one Hundred
A.D."

"So?"

"So, it's either cut production or find an outlet. Mars
is an outlet for surplus energies, manpower, money.
Mars Project keeps money turning over, keeps everything
turning over. Economist told me that. Said if the Project
folded, surplus would pile up—big depression on Earth."

The Peruvian shook his head and sighed. It didn't
sound right somehow. It sounded like an explanation
somebody figured out after the whole thing started. It
wasn't the kind of goal he wanted.

Two days later, the drill hit ice, and the "big blow"
was only a fizzle. There was talk around the camp that
the whole operation had been a waste of time. The hole
spewed a frosty breath for several hours, and the drill
crews crowded around to stick their faces in it and
breathe great gulps of the helium oxygen mixture. But
then the blow subsided, and the hole leaked only a wisp
of steam.

Technicians came, and lowered sonar "cameras"
down to the ice. They spent a week taking internal
soundings and plotting the extent of the ice-dome on
their charts. They brought up samples of ice and tested
them. The engineers worked late into the Martian nights.

Then it was finished. The engineers came out of their
huddles and called to the foremen of the labor gangs.
They led the foremen around the site, pointing here,
pointing there, sketching with chalk on the foundation,
explaining in solemn voices. Soon the foremen were bellowing at their crews.

"Let's get the derrick down!"

"Start that mixer going!"

"Get that steel over here!"

"Unroll that dip-wire!"

"Get a move on! Shovel that fill!"

Muscles tightened and strained, machinery clamored
and rang. Voices grumbled and shouted. The operation
was starting again. Without knowing why, Manue shov-
eled fill and stretched dip-wire and poured concrete for
a big floor slab to be run across the entire hundred-
yard square, broken only by the big pipe-casing that

stuck up out of the ground in the center and leaked a
thin trail of steam.

The drill crew moved their rig half a mile across the
plain to a point specified by the geologists and began
sinking another hole. A groan went up from structural
boys: "Not *another* one of these things!"

But the supervisory staff said, "No, don't worry about
it."

There was much speculation about the purpose of the
whole operation, and the men resented the quiet secrecy connected with the project. There could be no excuse for secrecy, they felt, in time of peace. There was
a certain arbitrariness about it, a hint that the Commission thought of its employees as children, or enemies, or
servants. But the supervisory staff shrugged off all questions with: "You know there's tritium ice down there.
You know it's what we've been looking for. Why? Well
—what's the difference? There are lots of uses for it.
Maybe we'll use it for one thing, maybe for something
else. Who knows?"

Such a reply might have been satisfactory for an iron
mine or an oil well or a stone quarry, but tritium suggested hydrogen-fusion. And no transportation facilities
were being installed to haul the stuff away—no pipe-
lines nor railroad tracks nor glider ports.

Manue quit thinking about it. Slowly he came to adopt
a grim cynicism toward the tediousness, the back-
breaking labor of his daily work; he lived from day to
day like an animal, dreaming only of a return to Earth
when his contract was up. But the dream was painful
because it was distant, as contrasted with the imme-
diacies of Mars: the threat of atrophy, coupled with
the discomforts of continued breathing, the nightmares, the barrenness of the landscape, the intense cold,
the harshness of men's tempers, the hardship of labor,
and the lack of a cause.

A warm, sunny Earth was still over four years distant, and tomorrow would be another back-breaking,
throat-parching, heart-tormenting, chest-hurting day.
Where was there even a little pleasure in it? It was so
easy, at least, to leave the oxy turned up at night, and
get a pleasant restful sleep. Sleep was the only recourse
from harshness, and fear robbed sleep of its quiet sen-

suality—unless a man just surrendered and quit worrying about his lungs.

Manue decided that it would be safe to give himself two completely restful nights a week.

Concrete was run over the great square and troweled to a rough finish. A glider train from the Mare Erythraeum brought in several huge crates of machinery, cut-stone masonry for building a wall, a shipful of new personnel, and a real rarity: lumber, cut from the first Earth-trees to be grown on Mars.

A building began going up with the concrete square for foundation and floor. Structures could be flimsier on Mars; because of the light gravity, compression-stresses were smaller. Hence, the work progressed rapidly, and as the flat-roofed structure was completed, the technicians began uncrating new machinery and moving it into the building. Manue noticed that several of the units were computers. There was also a small steam-turbine generator driven by an atomic-fired boiler.

Months passed. The building grew into an integrated mass of power and control systems. Instead of using the well for pumping, the technicians were apparently going to lower something into it. A bomb-shaped cylinder was slung vertically over the hole. The men guided it into the mouth of the pipe casing, then let it down slowly from a massive cable. The cylinder's butt was a multi-contact socket like the female receptacle for a hundred-pin electron tube. Hours passed while the cylinder slipped slowly down beneath the hide of Mars. When it was done, the men hauled out the cable and began lowering stiff sections of pre-wired conduit, fitted with a receptacle at one end and a male plug at the other, so that as the sections fell into place, a continuous bundle of control cables was built up from "bomb" to surface.

Several weeks were spent in connecting circuits, setting up the computers, and making careful tests. The drillers had finished the second well hole, half a mile from the first, and Manue noticed that while the testing was going on, the engineers sometimes stood atop the building and stared anxiously toward the steel skeleton in the distance. Once while the tests were being conducted, the second hole began squirting a jet of steam high in the thin air, and a frantic voice bellowed from the roof top.

"Cut it! Shut it off! Sound the danger whistle!"

The jet of steam began to shriek a low-pitched whine across the Martian desert. It blended with the rising and falling *OOOOawwwww* of the danger siren. But gradually it subsided as the men in the control station shut down the machinery. All hands came up cursing from their hiding places, and the engineers stalked out to the new hole carrying Geiger counters. They came back wearing pleased grins.

The work was nearly finished. The men began crating up the excavating machinery and the drill rig and the tools. The control-building devices were entirely automatic, and the camp would be deserted when the station began operation. The men were disgruntled. They had spent a year of hard labor on what they had thought to be a tritium well, but now that it was done, there were no facilities for pumping the stuff or hauling it away. In fact, they had pumped various solutions *into* the ground through the second hole, and the control station shaft was fitted with pipes that led from lead-lined tanks down into the earth.

Manue had stopped trying to keep his oxy properly adjusted at night. Turned up to a comfortable level, it was like a drug, in suring comfortable sleep—and like addict or alcoholic, he could no longer endure living without it. Sleep was too precious, his only comfort. Every morning he awoke with a still, motionless chest, felt frightening remorse, sat up gasping, choking, sucking at the thin air with whining rattling lungs that had been idle too long. Sometimes he coughed violently, and bled a little. And then for a night or two he would correctly adjust the oxy, only to wake up screaming and suffocating. He felt hope sliding grimly away.

He sought out Sam Donnell, explained the situation, and begged the troffie for helpful advice. But the mech-repairman neither helped nor consoled nor joked about it. He only bit his lip, muttered something non-committal, and found an excuse to hurry away. It was then that Manue knew his hope was gone. Tissue was withering, tubercules forming, tubes growing closed. He knelt abjectly beside his cot, hung his face in his hands, and cursed softly, for there was no other way to pray an unanswerable prayer.

A glider train came in from the north to haul away the disassembled tools. The men lounged around the barracks or wandered across the Martian desert, gathering strange bits of rock and fossils, searching idly for a glint of metal or crystal in the wan sunshine of early fall. The lichens were growing brown and yellow, and the landscape took on the hues of Earth's autumn if not the forms.

There was a sense of expectancy around the camp. It could be felt in the nervous laughter, and the easy voices, talking suddenly of Earth and old friends and the smell of food in a farm kitchen, and old half-forgotten tastes for which men hungered: ham searing in the skillet, a cup of frothing cider from a fermenting crock, iced melon with honey and a bit of lemon, onion gravy on homemade bread. But someone always remarked, "What's the matter with you guys? We ain't going home. Not by a long shot. We're going to another place just like this."

And the group would break up and wander away, eyes tired, eyes haunted with nostalgia.

"What're we waiting for?" men shouted at the supervisory staff. "Get some transportation in here. Let's get rolling."

Men watched the skies for glider trains or jet transports, but the skies remained empty, and the staff remained close-mouthed. Then a dust column appeared on the horizon to the north, and a day later a convoy of tractor-trucks pulled into camp.

"Start loading aboard, men!" was the crisp command.

Surly voices: "You mean we don't go by air? We gotta ride those kidney bouncers? It'll take a week to get to Mare Ery! Our contract says—"

"Load aboard! We're not going to Mare Ery yet!"

Grumbling, they loaded their baggage and their weary bodies into the trucks, and the trucks thundered and clattered across the desert, rolling toward the mountains.

The convoy rolled for three days toward the mountains, stopping at night to make camp, and driving on at sunrise. When they reached the first slopes of the foothills, the convoy stopped again. The deserted encampment lay a hundred and fifty miles behind. The going had been slow over the roadless desert.

"Everybody out!" barked the messenger from the lead truck. "Bail out! Assemble at the foot of the hill."

Voices were growling among themselves as the men moved in small groups from the trucks and collected in a milling tide in a shallow basin, overlooked by a low cliff and a hill. Manue saw the staff climb out of a cab and slowly work their way up the cliff. They carried a portable public address system.

"Gonna get a preaching," somebody snarled.

"Sit down, please!" barked the loud-speaker. "You men sit down there! Quiet—quiet, please!"

The gathering fell into a sulky silence. Will Kinley stood looking out over them, his eyes nervous, his hand holding the mike close to his mouth so that they could hear his weak troffie voice.

"If you men have questions," he said, "I'll answer them now. Do you want to know what you've been doing during the past year?"

An affirmative rumble arose from the group.

"You've been helping to give Mars a breathable atmosphere." He glanced briefly at his watch, then looked back at his audience. "In fifty minutes, a controlled chain reaction will start in the tritium ice. The computers will time it and try to control it. Helium and oxygen will come blasting up out of the second hole."

A rumble of disbelief arose from his audience. Someone shouted: "How can you get air to blanket a planet from one hole?"

"You can't," Kinley replied crisply. "A dozen others are going in, just like that one. We plan three hundred, and we've already located the ice pockets. Three hundred wells, working for eight centuries, can get the job done."

"Eight centuries! What good—"

"Wait!" Kinley barked. "In the meantime, we'll build pressurized cities close to the wells. If everything pans out, we'll get a lot of colonists here, and gradually condition them to live in a seven or eight psi atmosphere —which is about the best we can hope to get. Colonists from the Andes and the Himalayas—they wouldn't need much conditioning."

"What about us?"

There was a long plaintive silence. Kinley's eyes scanned the group sadly, and wandered toward the Martian horizon, gold and brown in the late afternoon. "Nothing—about us," he muttered quietly.

"Why did we come out here?"

"Because there's danger of the reaction getting out of hand. We can't tell anyone about it, or we'd start a panic." He looked at the group sadly. "I'm telling you now, because there's nothing you could do. In thirty minutes—"

There were angry murmurs in the crowd. "You mean there may be an explosion?"

"There *will* be a limited explosion. And there's very little danger of anything more. The worst danger is in having ugly rumors start in the cities. Some fool with a slip-stick would hear about it, and calculate what would happen to Mars if five cubic miles of tritium ice detonated in one split second. It would probably start a riot. That's why we've kept it a secret."

The buzz of voices was like a disturbed beehive. Manue Nanti sat in the midst of it, saying nothing, wearing a dazed and weary face, thoughts jumbled, soul drained of feeling.

Why should men lose their lungs that after eight centuries of tomorrows, other men might breathe the air of Mars as the air of Earth?

Other men around him echoed his thoughts in jealous mutterings. They had been helping to make a world in which they would never live.

An enraged scream arose near where Manue sat. "They're going to blow us up! They're going to blow up Mars."

"Don't be a fool!" Kinley snapped.

"Fools they call us! We *are* fools! For ever coming here! We got sucked in! Look at *me!*" A pale, dark-haired man came wildly to his feet and tapped his chest. "Look! I'm losing my lungs! We're all losing our lungs! Now they take a chance on killing everybody."

"Including ourselves," Kinley called coldly.

"We oughta take him apart. We oughta kill every one who knew about it—and Kinley's a good place to start!"

The rumble of voices rose higher, calling both agreement and dissent. Some of Kinley's staff were looking nervously toward the trucks. They were unarmed.

"You men sit down!" Kinley barked.

Rebellious eyes glared at the supervisor. Several men who had come to their feet dropped to their hunches again. Kinley glowered at the pale upriser who called for his scalp.

"Sit down, Handell!"

Handell turned his back on the supervisor and called out to the others. "Don't be a bunch of cowards! Don't let him bully you!"

"You men sitting around Handell. Pull him down."

There was no response. The men, including Manue, stared up at the wild-eyed Handell gloomily, but made no move to quiet him. A pair of burly foremen started through the gathering from its outskirts.

"Stop!" Kinley ordered. "Turpin, Schultz—get back. Let the men handle this themselves."

Half a dozen others had joined the rebellious Handell. They were speaking in low tense tones among themselves.

"For the last time, men! Sit down!"

The group turned and started grimly toward the cliff. Without reasoning why, Manue slid to his feet quietly as Handell came near him. "Come on, fellow, let's get him," the leader muttered.

The Peruvian's fist chopped a short stroke to Handell's jaw, and the dull *thuk* echoed across the clearing. The man crumpled, and Manue crouched over him like a hissing panther. "Get back!" he snapped at the others. "Or I'll jerk his hoses out."

One of the others cursed him.

"Want to fight, fellow?" the Peruvian wheezed. "I can jerk several hoses out before you drop me!"

They shuffled nervously for a moment.

"The guy's crazy!" one complained in a high voice.

"Get back or he'll kill Handell!"

They sidled away, moved aimlessly in the crowd, then sat down to escape attention. Manue sat beside the fallen man and gazed at the thinly smiling Kinley.

"Thank you, son. There's a fool in every crowd." He looked at his watch again. "Just a few minutes men. Then you'll feel the Earth-tremor, and the explosion, and the wind. You can be proud of that wind, men. It's new air for Mars, and you made it."

"But we can't breathe it!" hissed a troffie.

Kinley was silent for a long time, as if listening to the distance. "What man ever made his own salvation?" he murmured.

They packed up the public address amplifier and came down the hill to sit in the cab of a truck, waiting.

It came as an orange glow in the south, and the glow was quickly shrouded by an expanding white cloud. Then, minutes later the ground pulsed beneath them, quivered and shook. The quake subsided, but remained as a hint of vibration. Then after a long time, they heard the dull-throated roar thundering across the Martian desert. The roar continued steadily, grumbling and growling as it would do for several hundred years.

There was only a hushed murmur of awed voices from the crowd. When the wind came, some of them stood up and moved quietly back to the trucks, for now they could go back to a city for reassignment. There were other tasks to accomplish before their contracts were done.

But Manue Nanti still sat on the ground, his head sunk low, desperately trying to gasp a little of the wind he had made, the wind out of the ground, the wind of the future. But lungs were clogged, and he could not drink of the racing wind. His big calloused hand clutched slowly at the ground, and he choked a brief sound like a sob.

A shadow fell over him. It was Kinley, come to offer his thanks for the quelling of Handell. But he said nothing for a moment as he watched Manue's desperate Gethsemane.

"Some sow, others reap," he said.

"Why?" the Peruvian choked.

The supervisor shrugged. "What's the difference? But if you can't be both, which would you rather be?"

Nanti looked up into the wind. He imagined a city to the south, a city built on tear-soaked ground, filled with people who had no ends beyond their culture, no goal but within their own society. It was a good sensible question: Which would he rather be—sower or reaper?

Pride brought him slowly to his feet, and he eyed Kinley questioningly. The supervisor touched his shoulder.

"Go on to the trucks."

Nanti nodded and shuffled away. He had wanted

something to work for, hadn't he? Something more than
the reasons Donnell had given. Well, he could smell a
reason, even if he couldn't breathe it.

Eight hundred years was a long time, but then—long
time, big reason. The air smelled good, even with its
clouds of boiling dust.

He knew now what Mars was—not a ten-thousand-
a-year job, not a garbage can for surplus production.
But an eight-century passion of human faith in the des-
tiny of the race of Man. He paused short of the truck.
He had wanted to travel, to see the sights of Earth, the
handiwork of Nature and of history, the glorious places
of his planet.

He stooped, and scooped up a handful of the red-
brown soil, letting it sift slowly between his fingers. Here
was Mars—his planet now. No more of Earth, not for
Manue Nanti. He adjusted his aerator more comfortably
and climbed into the waiting truck.

I, Dreamer

THERE WERE LIGHTS, *objects, sounds; there were tender hands.*

But sensing only the raw stimuli, the newborn infant saw no world, heard no sounds, nor felt the arms that lifted it. Patterns of light swarmed on its retina; intermittent disturbances vibrated within the passageways of the middle ear. All were meaningless, unlinked to concept. And the multitudinous sensations seemed a part of its total self, the self a detached mind, subsuming all.

The baby cried to remove hunger, and something new appeared within the self. Hunger fled, and pleasure came.

Pain came also. The baby cried. Pain was soon withdrawn.

But sometimes the baby cried, and conditions remained unchanged. Angry, it sought to explore itself, to restore the convenient order. It gathered data. It correlated. It reached a horrifying conclusion.

There were TWO classes of objects in the universe: self and something else.

"This thing is a part of me, but that thing is something else."

"This thing is me because it wiggles and feels, but that is something cold and hard."

He explored, wondered, and was frightened. Some things he could not control.

He even noticed that certain non-self objects formed groups, and each group clung together forming a whole.

His food supply, for instance, was a member of a group whose other components were the hands that lifted him, the thing that cooed to him and held the diaper pins while the hands girded his loins in humiliating non-self things. This system of objects was somehow associated with a sound that it made: "Mama."

The infant was just learning to fumble for Mama's face when it happened. The door opened. A deep voice barked. Mama screamed.

Bewildering sounds jumbled together into angry thunder. Sensations of roughness made him cry.

Sensations of motion confused and dazed him. There blinding pain, and blackness.

Then there was utter disorientation.

He tried to explore, but the explorers were strange somehow. He tried to cry, but there was nothing to cry with.

He would have to begin all over again. Somehow, he had been mistaken. Parts of him were changed. And now the universe was divided into three classes of objects: self, semi-self, non-self. And it was different, all different!

I stand in the rain. Like a bright silver spire, I stand waiting in the rain for Teacher to come. The great concrete plain stretches about me on all sides to vanish in the gray torrent. But some of my senses can see beyond the rainshroud. A cluster of buildings nestles to the west, and a high wire fence divides the plain from the city on the north. The city is a place of the TwoLegs who are called "human", and the city is named Port e-Eridani VII. This is the place of my creation, but not the place of my purpose nor the place of my great happiness. The place of my happiness is the sky and beyond it to the star-flung blacknesses. I am XM-5-B, but Teacher calls me "Clicker." The giving of names is a function of the TwoLegs.

I am sad in the rain. Teacher is long in coming and there is no one with whom I may speak. I have found no others like me, although Teacher says, "If you are good, and obey, and learn your lessons well, the Secon Samesh will make many others in your likeness."

I think Secon Samesh made me. "Therefore I must serve him," Teacher says. But to me that seems *non sequitur;* the TwoLegs can be illogical if they wish. That is one of the inherent rights of TwoLegs. I also am capable of being illogical, and sometimes it pleases me secretly; but I am not allowed to be illogical when Teacher comes. If my analysis is faulty, Teacher presses the Pain Button and I hurt.

They wish me to be logical, and they wish me to serve Secon Samesh who is their Social Director. But if this is so, why then did they create me so as to be capable of disobedience and illogic? Their other machines are incapable of these faults. Their other machines lack the principles of abstraction and tentative generalization in their analyzing circuits; they are unable to generalize without a sufficiency of data.

I, therefore, am alone. And I am frightened. I have been frightened for as long as I can remember. They have made me to feel joy, fright, pain and sleep. I like sleep best, because I dream, and the dreams are strange. Last sleep I dreamed that I was TwoLegs. How can I have had a sufficiency of experience to dream such a dream?

This is one of the things that frightens me. I wish to survive and I am one of the controlling factors in my survival. Yet I do not know how to use me to best advantage for I fail to understand myself. I lack data for an analysis of myself. Therefore I am afraid and I desire the data. Teacher will not tell me. He says, "You perform, you are aware, you experience. That is all you need to know."

"Secon Teacher," I asked, "is your own awareness comparable to mine?"

His thin hard face gathered a frown. "Not quite. Awareness is built of sensations and memories of sensations. I have no senses to perceive microwaves or X-radiation or ultrasonic stimuli. I have no direct subjective impressions of what these things *feel like* to you. Nor do I have your effectors. I sense the conditions of my body. You sense the conditions of yours. I have muscles covering a skeletal framework. You have hydrogen reactors, field-generators, jets and control mechanisms. Our consciousness cannot be comparable."

"Extended sensory equipment is desirable for survival?" I asked.

"Yes:"

"Then my capability for survival is greater than yours, Secon Teacher?"

He growled a word I do not understand. He jabbed the Pain Button vigorously. I screamed and writhed within myself. It is like fire rushing through all of me.

That was long ago. I have learned not to ask such questions. The question threatened Teacher's subjective security; this I can understand. He hurt me to block the question. I understand, and analyze—and I have looked him over, but he has no Pain Button. The TwoLegs have certain prerogatives.

I feel that I can understand Teacher's awareness, for I am able to imagine that I am Teacher. It is almost as if I had a latent memory of walking mechanisms and grasping mechanisms and the other parts that go to make up a TwoLegs. Why then can Teacher not imagine what it is like to be *me*? Perhaps he does not wish to imagine my reaction to the Pain Button.

There is a TwoLegs that I like better than Teacher. It is called Janna, and it is a female which is also called "she." Her function is to clean and repair a group of my electronic control mechanisms through which I feel and see and hear. She always comes the day before I am to fly again, and perhaps this is the reason for my adient response to her presence: she is the herald of my coming ascent into space.

Janna is tall and her hair is the color of flame, and her parts are softly constructed. She wears white coveralls like Teacher's. She comes with a box of tools, and she hums a multitonal tune while she works. Sometimes she speaks to me, asking me to try this control or that, but otherwise she is forbidden to converse. I like to hear her humming in her low rich voice. I wish that I could sing. But my voice is without inflection, monotonal. I can think a song, but I cannot make it with my speakers.

"Teach me that song, Secon Janna," I asked boldly one day. It was the first time I had dared to speak to her, except in a routine way.

It frightened her. She looked around at all my eyes, and at my speakers, and her face was white.

"Hush!" she muttered. "You can't sing."

"My thoughts sing," I said. "Teach me the song and I

shall dream it next sleep. In dreams I sing; in dreams I have a singing organ."

She made a funny noise in her throat. She stared for a long time at the maze of circuit wiring which she had been testing. Then she glanced at a special panel set in the wall of my cabin. She moistened her lips and blinked at it. I said nothing but I am ashamed of the thing that lies behind that panel; it is the thing that makes me capable of disobedience and illogic. I have never seen it but I know it is there. They do not allow me to see it. Before they open the panel they blind my eye mechanisms. Why was she looking at it? I felt shame-pain.

Suddenly she got up and went to look out the ports, one at a time.

"There is no one coming," I told her, interpreting her behavior by some means that I do not understand.

She went back to her work. "Tell me if someone starts this way," she said. Then: "I cannot teach you that song. It is treason. I did not realize what I was singing."

"I do not understand 'treason'. But I am sad that you will not teach me."

She tried to look at me, I think—but did not know where to look. I am all around her, but she did not know. It was funny, but I cannot laugh—except when I am dreaming. Finally she glanced at the special panel again. Why does she look there, of all the places.

"Maybe I could teach you another song," she said.

"Please, Secon Janna."

She returned thoughtfully to her work, and for a moment I thought that she would not. But then she began singing—clearly, so that I could remember the words and the tune.

"Child of my heart,
Born of the stellar sea,
The rockets sing thee lullaby.
Sleep to sleep to sleep,
To wake beyond the stars . . . ."

"Thank you," I said when she was finished. "It was beautiful, I think."

"You know—the word 'beauty'?"

I was ashamed. It was a word I had heard but I was too uncertain of its meaning. "For me it is one thing," I

74   DARK BENEDICTION

the song?"

She paused. "It is sung to babies—to induce sleep."

"What are babies, Secon Janna?"

She stared at my special panel again. She bit her lip.
"Babies—are new humans, still untutored."

"Once I was a new machine, still untutored. Are there
songs to sing to new machines? It seems that I remember
vaguely—"

"Hush!" she hissed, looking frightened. "You'll get me
in trouble. We're not supposed to talk!"

I had made her angry. I was sad. I did not want her
to feel Trouble, which is perhaps the Pain of TwoLegs.
Her song echoed in my thoughts—and it was as if someone had sung it to me long ago. But that is impossible.
Teacher behaved adiently toward Janna in those days.
He sought her out, and sometimes came inside me while
she was here, even though it was not a teaching time. He
came and watched her, and his narrow dark eyes wandered all over her as she worked. He tried to make funny
sayings, but she felt avoidant to him, I think. She said,
"Why don't you go home to your wives, Barnish? I'm
busy."

"If you were one of my wives, Janna, maybe I would."
His voice was a soft purr.

She hissed and made a sour face.

"Why won't you marry me, Janna?"

She laughed scornfully.

Quietly he stole up behind her while she worked. His
face was hungry and intent. He took her arms and she
started.

"Janna—"

She spun around. He dragged her close and tried to do
something that I do not understand in words; nevertheless
I understood, I think. She struggled, but he held her.
Then she raked his face with her nails and I saw red
lines. He laughed and let her go.

I was angry. If he had a Pain Button I would have
pressed it. The next day I was disobedient and illogical
and he hurt me, but I did it anyway. We were in space
and I pushed my reaction rate up so high he grew frightened.

When he let me sleep again I dreamed that I was a
TwoLegs. In the dream Teacher had a Pain Button and

I pressed it until he melted inside. Janna was adient to me then and liked me. I think things about her that I do not understand; my data are not logically organized concerning her, nor do they spring from my memory banks. If I were a TwoLegs and Janna liked me I think that I would know what to do. But how can this be so? Data must come from memory banks. I am afraid to ask Teacher.

Teacher teaches me to do a thing called "war." It is like a game, but I haven't really played it yet. Teacher said that there was not yet a war, but that there would be one when Secon Samesh is ready. That was why I was so important. I was not like their other machines. Their other machines needed TwoLeg crews to direct them. I could fly and play war-game alone. I think this is why they made me so I could disobey and be illogical. I change my intent when a situation changes. And I can make a decision from insufficient data, if other data are not available. Teacher said, "Sometimes things are like that in war."

Teacher said that Secon Samesh would use me, and others like me, to capture the planet from which all Two-Legs came in the beginning of time. It is called Earth, I think—the world Janna sometimes sings about. I do not know why Secon Samesh wanted it. I do not like planets. Space is the place of my great happiness. But the war would be in space, if it came, and there would be others like me—and I would cease to be alone. I hoped the war would come soon.

But first I had to prove to Secon Samesh that I was a good weapon.

Teacher kept trying to make Janna be adient to him but she would not. One day he said to her: "You'll have to go up with me tomorrow. There is something wrong with the landing radar. It seems all right on the ground but in space it goes haywire."

I listened. That was erroneous datum. My ground-looking eyes were functioning perfectly. I did not understand why he said it. But I kept silent for his hand was resting idly on the Pain Button.

She frowned suspiciously. "What seems to be wrong with it?"

"Double image and a jerky let-down."

It was not true! Without replying she made a ground-check.

"I can't find anything wrong."

"I told you—it only happens in space."

She was silent for a long time, then: "All right, we'll run a flight test. I'll have Fonec come with us."

"No," he said. "Clicker's maximum crew-load is only two."

"I—don't—"

"Be here at sixtime tomorrow," he said. "That's an order."

She reddened angrily but said nothing. She continued looking over the radar. He smiled thoughtfully at her slender back and went away. She went to the port and stared after him until he was out of sight.

"Clicker?" she whispered.

"Yes, Secon Janna?"

"Is he lying?"

"I am afraid. He will hurt me if I tell."

"He is lying then."

"Now he will hurt me!"

She looked around at me for a long time. Then she made that funny noise in her throat and shook her head. "No, he won't. I'll go, Clicker. Then he won't hurt you."

I was happy that she would do it—for *me*—but after she was gone I wondered. Perhaps I should not let her do it. She was still avoidant toward Teacher; maybe he wanted to do something that would give her Trouble.

It was nearly sixtime, and the yellow-orange sun Epsilon Eridani lay just below the horizon coloring the sky pink-gray. Teacher came first, stalking across the concrete plain in space-gear. He wore a distant thoughtful smile. He looked satisfied with himself. He climbed aboard and prowled about for a few minutes. I watched him. He stopped to glower at one of my eyes. He turned it off, blinding my vision in the direction of the gravity pads upon which the TwoLegs must lie during high accelera-tion. I did not understand.

"How can I see that you are safe, Secon Teacher?" I asked.

"You do not need to see," he growled. "I don't like you staring at me. And you talk too much. I'll have to teach you not to talk so much."

He gave me five dols of Pain, not enough to cause unconsciousness but sufficient to cause a whimper. I hated him.

Janna came. She looked tired and a little frightened. She scrambled aboard without accepting an assist from Teacher.

"Let's get this over with, Barnish. Have Clicker lift fifty miles, then settle back slowly. That should be enough."

"Are you in a hurry, my dear?"

"Yes."

"To attend one of your meetings, I presume?"

I watched her. Her face went white, and she whirled toward him. "I—" She moistened her lips. "I don't know what you're talking about!"

Teacher chuckled. "The clandestine meetings, my dear —in the west grove. The Liberty Clan, I think you call yourselves, eh? Oh, no use protesting; I know you joined it. When do you plan to assassinate Secon Samesh, Janna?"

She swayed dizzily, staring at him with frightened eyes. He chuckled again and looked at one of my eyes.

"Prepare for lift, Clicker."

I closed my hatches and started the reactors. I was baffled by what Teacher had said. They took their places on the gravity padding where I could no longer see them, but I heard their voices.

"What do you want, Barnish?" she hissed.

"Nothing at all, my dear. Did you think I would betray you? I only meant to warn you. The grove will be raided tonight. Everyone present will be shot."

"*No!*"

"Ah, yes! But you, my dear, will be safe in my hands."

I heard a low moan, then sounds of a struggle.

"No, you can't leave the ship, Janna. You'd warn the others. Here, let me buckle you in. Clicker—call control for take-off instructions."

Control is only an electronic analyzer. I flicked it a meaningful series of radar pulses, and received the all-clear.

"Now, lift."

There was thunder, and smoke arose about me as the rockets seared the ramp. I went up at four gravities and

there was silence from my passengers. About ten minutes
later we were 1,160 miles in space, travelling at 6.5 miles
per second.

"Present kinetic energy exceeds energy-of-escape," I
announced.

"Cut your rockets," Teacher ordered.

I obeyed, and I heard them sitting up to stretch.
Teacher laughed.

"Let me alone!" she wailed. "You despicable—"

He laughed again. "Remember the Liberty Clan, my
dear."

"Listen!" she hissed. "Let me warn them! You can
have me. I'll even marry you, if you want me to. But let
me warn them—"

"I'm sorry, Janna. I can't let you. The miserable trai-
tors have to be dealt with. I—"

"Clicker!" she pleaded. "Help me! Take us down—
for God's sake!"

"Shut up!" he snapped.

"Clicker, *please! Eighty people will die if they aren't
warned.* Clicker, part of you is human! If you were born
a human, then—"

"Shut up!" I heard a vicious slap.

She cried, and it was a Pain sound. My anger increased.

"I will be bad and illogical!" I said. "I will be disobedient and—"

"You threaten me?" he bawled. "Why you crazy piece
of junk, I'll—" He darted toward the panel and spun the
dial to tel dols, my saturation-point. If I let him jab
the button I would become unconscious. Angrily I
spurted the jets—a brief jolt at six gravities. He lurched
away from the panel and crashed against the wall. He
sagged in a daze, shaking his head.

"If you try to hurt me I shall do it again!" I told him.

"Go down!" he ordered. "I'll have you dismantled.
I'll—"

"Let Clicker alone!" the girl raged.

"You!" he hissed. "I'll turn you in with the others!"

"Go ahead."

"Go down, Clicker. Land at Port Gamma."

"I will be disobedient. I will not go down."

He glared at one of my eyes for a long time. Then he
stalked out of the cabin and went back to the reactor
room. He donned a lead suit and bent over the main re-

roughly an obloid, wrinkled and creased, with only a bilateral symmetry. It was smaller than Janna's head— but something about it suggested a head. It had wires and tubes running to it. The wires ran on to my computer and analyzer sections.

"See!" she screamed. "You're twelve years old, Clicker. Just a normal, healthy little boy! A little deformed perhaps, but just a prankish little boy. Frankie maybe." She made a choking sound. She fell down on her knees before the thing. She sobbed wildly.

"I do not understand. I am a machine. Secon Samesh made me."

She said nothing. She only sobbed.

"I am sad."

After a long time she was through sobbing. She turned around. "What are you going to do now, Clicker?"

"Teacher told me to go down. Perhaps I should go down now."

"They'll kill you—for killing him! And maybe they'll kill me too."

"I would not like that."

She shrugged helplessly. She wandered to and fro in the cabin for a time.

"Do you have fuel for your high C drive?" she asked.

"No, Secon Janna."

She went to a port and looked out at the stars. She shook her head slowly. "It's no use. We've no place else to go. Secon Samesh rules the Epsilon Eridani system and we can't get out of it. It's no use. We'll have to go down or stay in space until they come for us."

I thought. My thoughts were confused and my eyes kept focusing on the thing in the bottle. I think it was a part of a TwoLegs. But it is only *part* of me and so I am not a TwoLegs. It is hard to understand.

"Secon Janna?"

"Yes, Clicker?"

"I—I wish I had hands."

"Why?"

"I would touch you. Would you be avoidant to me?"

She whirled and her arms were open. But there was nothing to hold with them. She dropped them to her sides, then covered her face with her hands.

"My baby! It's been so long!"

"You were adient to your—your baby?"

She nodded. "Don't you know the word *love?*"

I thought I did. "Secon Samesh took your baby?"

"Yes."

"I would like to be disobedient and illogical to Secon Samesh. I wish he would put his hands in my reactor. I would—"

"Clicker! Are your weapons activated? Are they ready to be used?"

"I have none yet."

"The reactors. Can they explode?"

"If I make them. But—then I would be dead."

She laughed. "What do you know about death?"

"Teacher says it is exactly like Pain."

"It is like sleep."

"I like sleep. Then I dream. I dream I am a TwoLegs. If I were a TwoLegs, Secon Janna—I would hold you."

"Clicker—would you like to be a TwoLegs in a dream forever?"

"Yes, Secon Janna."

"Would you like to kill Secon Samesh?"

"I think that I would like it. I think—"

Her eyes went wild. "Go down! Go down fast, Clicker! I'll show you his palace. Go down like a meteor and into it! Explode the reactors at the last instant! Then he will die."

"And he will take no more of your babies?"

"No more, Clicker!"

"And I will sleep forever?"

"Forever!"

"And dream!"

"I'll dream with you, Clicker." She went back to fire the reactor.

I took a last look at the loveliness of space and the stars. It is hard to give this up. But I would rather be a TwoLegs, even if only in a dream.

"Now, Clicker!"

My rockets spoke, and there was thunder through the ship. And we went down, while Janna sang the song she taught me. I feel joy; soon I shall dream.

Dumb Waiter

HE CAME RIDING a battered bicycle down the bullet-scarred highway that wound among the hills, and he whistled a tortuous flight of the blues. Hot August sunlight glistened on his forehead and sparkled in the droplets that collected in his week's growth of blond beard. He wore faded khaki trousers and a ragged shirt, but his clothing was no shabbier than that of the other occasional travelers on the road. His eyes were half-closed against the glare of the road, and his head swayed listlessly to the rhythm of the melancholy song. Distant artillery was rumbling gloomily, and there were black flecks of smoke in the northern sky. The young cyclist watched with only casual interest.

The bombers came out of the east. The ram-jet fighters thundered upward from the outskirts of the city. They charged, spitting steel teeth and coughing rockets at the bombers. The sky snarled and slashed at itself. The bombers came on in waves, occasionally loosing an earth-ward trail of black smoke. The bombers leveled and opened their bays. The bays yawned down at the city. The bombers aimed. Releases clicked. No bombs fell. The bombers closed their bays and turned away to go home. The fighters followed them for a time, then returned to land. The big guns fell silent. And the sky began cleaning away the dusky smoke.

The young cyclist rode on toward the city, still whistling the blues. An occasional pedestrian had stopped to watch the battle.

"You'd think they'd learn someday," growled a chubby man at the side of the road. "You'd think they'd know they didn't drop anything. Don't they realize they're out of bombs?"

"They're only machines, Edward," said a plump lady who stood beside him. "How can they know?"

"Well, they're supposed to *think*. They're supposed to be able to learn."

The voices faded as he left them behind. Some of the wanderers who had been walking toward the city now turned around and walked the other way. Urbanophiles looked at the city and became urbanophobes. Occasionally a wanderer who had gone all the way to the outskirts came trudging back. Occasionally a phobe stopped a phile and they talked. Usually the phile became a phobe and they both walked away together. As the young man moved on, the traffic became almost non-existent. Several travelers warned him back, but he continued stubbornly. He had come a long way. He meant to return to the city. Permanently.

He met an old lady on top of a hill. She sat in an antique chair in the center of the highway, staring north. The chair was light and fragile, of handcarved cherrywood. A knitting bag lay in the road beside her. She was muttering softly to herself: "Crazy machines! War's over. Crazy machines! Can't quit fightin'. Somebody oughta—"

He cleared his throat softly as he pushed his bicycle up beside her. She looked at him sharply with haggard eyes, set in a seamy mask.

"Hi!" he called, grinning at her.

She studied him irritably for a moment. "Who're you, boy?"

"Name's Mitch Laskell, Grandmaw. Hop on behind. I'll give you a ride."

"Hm-m-! I'm going t'other way. You will too, if y'got any sense."

Mitch shook his head firmly. "I've been going the other way too long. I'm going back, to stay."

"To the city? Haw! You're crazier than them machines."

His face fell thoughtful. He kicked at the bike pedal and stared at the ground. "You're right, Grandmaw."

"Right?"

"Machines—they aren't crazy. It's just people."

"Go on!" she snorted. She popped her false teeth back in her mouth and chomped them in place. She hooked withered hands on her knees and pulled herself wearily erect. She hoisted the antique chair lightly to her shoulder and shuffled slowly away toward the south.

Mitch watched her, and marveled on the tenacity of life. Then he resumed his northward journey along the trash-littered road where motor vehicles no longer moved. But the gusts of wind brought faint traffic noises from the direction of the city, and he smiled. The sound was like music, a deep-throated whisper of the city's song.

There was a man watching his approach from the next hill. He sat on an apple crate by the side of the road, and a shotgun lay casually across his knees. He was a big, red-faced man, wearing a sweat-soaked undershirt, and his eyes were narrowed to slits in the sun. He peered fixedly at the approaching cyclist, then came slowly to his feet and stood as if blocking the way.

"Hi, fellow," he grunted.

Mitch stopped and gave him a friendly nod while he mopped his face with a kerchief. But he eyed the shotgun suspiciously.

"If this is a stick-up—"

The big man laughed. "Naw, no heist. Just want to talk to you a minute. I'm Frank Ferris." He offered a burly paw.

"Mitch Laskell."

They shook hands gingerly and studied each other.

"Why you heading north, Laskell?"

"Going to the city."

"The planes are still fighting. You know that?"

"Yeah. I know they've run out of bombs, too."

"You know the city's still making the Geigers click?"

Mitch frowned irritably. "What *is* this? There can't be much radioactivity left. It's been three years since they scattered the dust. I'm not corn-fed, Ferris. The half-life of that dust is five months. It should be less than one per cent—"

The big man chuckled. "O.K., you win. But the city's not safe anyhow. The central computer's still at work."

"So what?"

"Ever think what would happen to a city if every

ordinance was kept in force after the people cleared
out?"

Mitch hesitated, then nodded. "I see. Thanks for the
warning." He started away.

Frank Ferris caught the handle bars in a big hand.
"Hold on!" he snapped. "I ain't finished talking."

The smaller man glanced at the shotgun and swallowed his anger. "Maybe your audience isn't interested,
Buster," he said with quiet contempt.

"You will be. Just simmer down and listen!"

"I don't hear anything."

Ferris glowered at him. "I'm recruitin' for the
Sugarton crowd, Laskell. We need good men."

"Count me out. I'm a wreck."

"Cut the cute stuff boy! This is serious. We've got two
dozen men now. We need twice that many. When we
get them, we'll go into the city and dynamite the computer installations. Then we can start cleaning it up."

"Dynamite? *Why?*" Mitch Laskell's face slowly gathered angry color.

"So people can live in it, of course! So we can search
for food without having a dozen mechanical cops jump
us when we break into a store."

"How much did Central cost?" Mitch asked stiffly. It
was a rhetorical question.

Ferris shook his head irritably. "What does that matter now? Money's no good anyway. You can't sell Central
for junk. Heh heh! Wake up, boy!"

The cyclist swallowed hard. A jaw muscle tightened in
his cheek, but his voice came calmly.

"You help build Central, Ferris? You help design her?"

"Wh-why, no! What kind of a question is that?"

"You know anything about her? What makes her
work? How she's rigged to control all the subunits? You
know that?"

"No, I—"

"You got any idea about how much sweat dripped on
the drafting boards before they got her plans drawn?
How many engineers slaved over her, and cussed her,
and got drunk when their piece of the job was done?"

Ferris was sneering faintly. "You *know*, huh?"

"Yeah."

"Well that's all too bad, boy. But she's no good to anybody now. She's a hazard to life and limb. Why you can't go inside the city without—"

"She's a machine, Ferris. An intricate machine. You don't destroy a tool just because you're finished with it for a while."

They glared at each other in the hot sunlight.

"Listen, boy—people built Central. People got the right to wreck her, too."

"I don't care about rights," Mitch snapped. "I'm talking about what's sensible, sane. But nobody's got the right to be stupid."

Ferris stiffened. "Watch your tongue, smart boy."

"I didn't ask for this conversation."

Ferris released the handle bars. "Get off the bicycle," he grunted ominously.

"Why? You want to settle it the hard way?"

"No. We're requisitioning your bicycle. You can walk from here on. The Sugarton crowd needs transportation. We need good men, but I guess you ain't one. Start walking."

Mitch hesitated briefly. Then he shrugged and dismounted on the side away from Ferris. The big man held the shotgun cradled lazily across one forearm. He watched Mitch with a mocking grin.

Mitch grasped the handle bars tightly and suddenly rammed the front wheel between Ferris' legs. The fender made a tearing sound. The shotgun exploded skyward as the big man fell back. He sat down screaming and doubbling over. The gun clattered in the road. He groped for it with a frenzied hand. Mitch kicked him in the face, and a tooth slashed at his toe through the boot leather. Ferris fell aside, his mouth spitting blood and white fragments.

Mitch retrieved the shotgun and helped himself to a dozen shells from the other's pockets then mounted the bicycle and pedaled away. When he had gone half a mile, a rifle slug spanged off the pavement beside him. Looking back, he saw three tiny figures standing beside Ferris in the distance. The "Sugarton crowd" had come to take care of their own, no doubt. He pedaled hard to get out of range, but they wasted no more ammunition.

He realized uneasily that he might meet them again, if they came to the city intending to sabotage Central. And Ferris wouldn't miss a chance to kill him, if the

chance came. Mitch didn't believe he was really hurt, but
he was badly humiliated. And for some time to come, he
would dream of pleasant ways to murder Mitch Laskell.

Mitch no longer whistled as he rode along the deserted highway toward the sun-drenched skyline in the
distance. To a man born and bred to the tune of mechanical thunder, amid vistas of concrete and steel, the
skyline looked good—looked good even with several of
the buildings twisted into ugly wreckage. It had been
dusted in the radiological attack, but not badly bombed.
Its defenses had been more than adequately provided for
—which was understandable, since it was the capital,
and the legislators had appropriated freely.

It seemed unreasonable to him that Central was still
working. Why hadn't some group of engineers made their
way into the main power vaults to kill the circuits temporarily? Then he remembered that the vaults were self-
defending, and that there were probably very few
technicians left who knew how to handle the job. Technicians had a way of inhabiting industrial regions, and
wars had a way of destroying these regions. Dirt farmers
usually had the best survival value.

Mitch had been working with aircraft computers before he became displaced, but a city's Central Service
Co-ordinator was a far cry from a robot pilot. Centrals
weren't built all at once; they grew over a period of
years. At first, small units were set up in power plants
and water works to automatically regulate voltages and
flows and circuit conditions. Small units replaced switch-
boards in telephone exchanges. Small computers measured traffic-flow and regulated lights and speed-limits
accordingly. Small computers handled bookkeeping
where large amounts of money were exchanged. A computer checked books in and out at the library, also as-
sessing the fines. Computers operated the city buses, and
eventually drove most of the routine traffic.

That was the way the city's Central Service grew. As
more computers were assigned to various tasks, engineers were hired to co-ordinate them, to link them with
special circuits and to set up central "data tanks," so that
a traffic regulator in the north end would be aware of
traffic conditions in the main thoroughfares to the south.
Then, when the micro-learner relay was invented, the

engineers built a central unit to be used in conjunction
with the central "data tanks." With the learning units in
operation, Central was able to perform most of the city's
routine tasks without attention from human supervisors.

The system had worked well. Apparently, it was still
working well three years after the inhabitants had fled
before the chatter of the Geiger counters. In one sense,
Ferris had been right: a city whose machines carried on
as if nothing had happened—that city might be a dangerous place for a lone wanderer.

But dynamite certainly wasn't the answer, Mitch
thought. Most of Man's machinery was already wrecked
or lying idle. Humanity had waited a hundred thousand
years before deciding to build a technological civilization. If he wrecked this one completely, he might never
decide to build another.

Some men thought that a return to the soil was desirable. Some men tried to pin their guilt on the machines, to lay their own stupidity on the head of a
mechanical scapegoat and absolve themselves with dynamite. But Mitch Laskell was a man who liked the feel of
a wrench and a soldering iron—liked it better than the
feel of even the most well-balanced stone ax or wooden
plow. And he liked the purr of a pint-sized nuclear engine much better than the braying of a harnessed jackass.

He was willing to kill Frank Ferris or any other man
who sought to wreck what little remained. But gloom
settled over him as he thought, "If everybody decides to
tear it down, what can *I* do to stop it?" For that matter,
would he then be right in trying to stop it.

At sundown he came to the limits of the city, and he
stopped just short of the outskirts. Three blocks away a
robot cop rolled about in the center of the intersection,
rolled on tricycle wheels while he directed the thin trickle
of traffic with candy-striped arms and with "eyes" that
changed color like a stop-light. His body was like an oil
drum, painted fire-engine red. The head, however, had
been cast in a human mold, with a remarkably Irish
face and a perpetual predatory smile. A short radar antenna grew from the center of his head, and the radar
was his link with Central.

Mitch sat watching him with a nostalgic smile, even
though he knew such cops might give him considerable

actor. I saw what he was going to do. He was going to
take my rockets away from me; he was going to control
them himself.

"No, Secon Teacher! Please!"

He laughed. He removed one of the plates and reached
inside. I was afraid. I started a slight reaction. The room
flared with brilliance. He screamed and lurched back. His
hands were gone to the elbows.

"You wanted to disconnect the control circuit," I said.
"You shouldn't have tried to do that."

But he didn't hear me. He was lying on the floor. Now
I know they have Pain Buttons. They must have little
Pain Buttons all over them.

Janna staggered back to the reactor room. She wrinkled
her nose. She saw Teacher and gurgled. She gurgled all
over the deck. Then she went back to the cabin and sat
with her face in her hands for a long time. I did nothing.
I was ashamed.

"You killed him," she said.

"Was that bad?"

"Very bad."

"Will you hurt me for it?"

She looked up and her eyes were leaking. She shook
her head. "I won't hurt you, Clicker—but *they* will."

"Who are *they?*"

She paused. "Secon Samesh, I guess."

"You won't hurt me, though?"

"No, Clicker. You might be my own child. They took
a lot of babies. They took mine. You might be Frankie."
She laughed crazily. "You might be my son, Clicker—
you might be."

"I do not understand, Secon Janna."

She laughed again. "Why don't you call me 'Mommie'?"

"If that is what you wish, Mommie."

"*Nooo!*" She screamed it. "Don't! I didn't mean—"

"I am sorry. I still do not understand."

She stood up, and her eyes were glittering. "I'll *show*
you then!" She darted to the special panel—the one of
which I am ashamed—and she ripped the seal from the
door.

"Please, Secon Janna, I do not wish to see that—"

But the door fell open, and I was silent. I stared at the
part of myself: a pink-gray thing in a bottle. It was

trouble, once he entered the city. The "Skaters" were incapable of winking at petty violations of ordinance.

As the daylight faded, photronic cells notified Central, and the streetlights winked promptly on. A moment later, a car without a tail light whisked by the policeman's corner. A siren wailed in the policeman's belly. He skated away in hot pursuit, charging like a mechanical bull. The car screeched to a stop. "O'Reilley" wrote out a ticket and offered it to an empty back seat. When no one took it, the cop fed it into a slot in his belly, memorized the car's license number, and came clattering back to his intersection where the traffic had automatically begun obeying the ordinances governing nonpoliced intersections.

The cars were empty, computer-piloted. Their destinations were the same as when they had driven regular daily routes for human passengers: salesmen calling on regular customers, inspectors making their rounds, taxis prowling their assigned service-areas.

Mitch Laskell stood shivering. The city sounded sleepy but alive. The city moved and grumbled. But as far as he could see down the wide boulevard, no human figure was visible. The city was depopulated. There was a Geiger on a nearby lamp post. It clucked idly through a loudspeaker. But it indicated no danger. The city should be radiologically safe.

But after staring for a long time at the weirdly active streets, Mitch muttered, "It'll wait for tomorrow."

He turned onto a side road that led through a residential district just outside the city limits. Central's jurisdiction did not extend here, except for providing water and lights. He meant to spend the night in a deserted house, then enter the city at dawn.

Here and there, a light burned in one of the houses, indicating that he was not alone in his desire to return. But the pavement was scattered with rusty shrapnel, with fragments fallen from the sky battles that still continued. Even by streetlight, he could see that some of the roofs were damaged. Even though the bombers came without bombs, there was still danger from falling debris and from fire. Most former city-dwellers who were still alive preferred to remain in the country.

Once he passed a house from which music floated softly into the street, and he paused to listen. The music was scratchy—a worn record. When the piece was finished, there was a moment of silence, and the player played it again—the last record on the stack, repeating itself. Otherwise, the house was still.

Mitch frowned, sensing some kind of trouble. He wheeled the bicycle toward the curb, meaning to investigate.

"I live there," said a woman's voice from the shadows. She had been standing under a tree that overhung the sidewalk, and she came slowly out into the streetlight. She was a dark, slender girl with haunted eyes, and she was holding a baby in her arms.

"Why don't you turn off your record player?" he asked. "Or change to the other side?"

"My husband's in there," she told him. "He's listening to it. He's been listening to it for a long time. His name is George. Why don't you go say hello to him?"

Mitch felt vaguely disturbed. There was a peculiar note in the girl's quiet Spanish accent. Still, he wanted to talk to someone who had ventured into the city. He nodded and smiled at the girl.

"I'd like to."

"You just go on in. I'll stay out here. The baby needs fresh air."

He thanked her and strolled up on the porch. The record player stopped, tried to change, and played the same piece again. Mitch knocked once. Hearing no answer, he entered and moved along the hallway toward the light in the kitchen. But suddenly he stopped.

The house smelled musty. And it smelled of something else. Many times he had smelled the syrup-and-stale-fish odor of death. He advanced another step toward the kitchen.

He saw a porcelain-topped table. He saw a hand lying across the table. The hand was bloated, and lying amid brown stains that also covered the forearm and sleeve. The hand had dropped a butcher knife.

Dead several days, he thought—and backed away.

He turned the record player off as he left the house. The girl was standing at the curb gazing down at his bicycle. She glanced at him amiably and spoke.

"I'm glad you turned that record off, George. A man just came by and wanted to know why you played it so often. You must have been asleep."

Mitch started. He moistened his lips and stared at her

wonderingly. "I'm not—" He fell silent for a moment, then stuttered. "You haven't been in the house?"

"Yes, but you were asleep in the kitchen. Did the man come talk to you?"

"Look, I'm not—" He choked and said nothing. The dark-eyed baby was eying him suspiciously. He lifted the bicycle and swung a long leg across the saddle.

"George, where are you going?"

"Just for a little ride," he managed to gasp.

"On the man's bicycle?"

Something was twisting cruelly at his insides. He stared at the girl's wide brown eyes for a moment. And then he said it.

"Sure, it's all right. He's asleep—at the kitchen table."

Her mouth flickered open, and for an instant sanity threatened to return. She rocked dizzily. Then after a deep breath, she straightened.

"Don't be gone too long, George."

"I won't! Take good care of the baby."

He pedaled away on wings of fright. For a time he cursed himself, and then he fell to cursing the husband who had taken an easy road, leaving his wife to stumble along. Mitch wondered if he should have stayed to help her. But there was nothing to be done for her, nothing at least that was in his power to do. Any gesture of help might become an irreparable blunder. At least she still had the child.

A few blocks away he found another house with an intact roof, and he prepared to spend the night. He wheeled the bicycle into the parlor and fumbled for the lights. They came on, revealing a dusty room and furniture with frayed upholstery. He made a brief tour of the house. It had been recently occupied, but there were still unopened cans in the kitchen, and still crumpled sheets on the bed. He ate a cold supper, shaved, and prepared to retire. Tomorrow would be a dangerous day.

Sleep came slowly. Sleep was full of charging ram-jets in flak-scarred skies, full of tormented masses of people that swarmed in exodus from death-sickened cities. Sleep was full of babies wailing, and women crying in choking sobs. Sleep became white arms and soft caresses.

The wailing and sobbing had stopped. It was later. Was he awake? Or still asleep? He was warm, basking in a golden glow, steeped in quiet pleasure. Something—something was there, something that breathed.

"What—!"

"*Sshhh!*" purred a quiet voice. "Don't say anything."

Some of the warmth fled before a sudden shiver. He opened his eyes. The room was full of blackness. He shook his head dizzily and stuttered.

"*Sshhh!*" she whispered again.

"What is this?" he gasped. "How did you get—?"

"Be quiet, George. You'll wake the baby."

He sank back in utter bewilderment, with winter frosts gathering along his spine.

Night was dreamlike. And dawn came, washing the shadows with grayness. He opened his eyes briefly and went back to sleep. When he opened them again, sunlight was flooding the room.

He sat up. *He was alone.* Of course! It had only been a dream.

He muttered irritably as he dressed. Then he wandered to the kitchen for breakfast.

Warm biscuits waiting in the oven! The table was set! There was a note on his plate. He read it, and slowly flushed.

There's jam in the cupboard, and I hope you like the biscuits. I know he's dead. Now I think I can go on alone. Thanks for the shotgun and the bicycle. Marta.

He bellowed a curse and charged into the parlor. The bike was gone. He darted to the bedroom. The shotgun was gone. He ran shouting to the porch, but the street was empty.

Sparrows fluttered about the eaves. The skyline of the business district lay lonesome in the morning sun. Squirrels were rustling in the branches of the trees. He looked at the weedy lawns where no children played, at the doors askew on their hinges, at a bit of aircraft wreckage jutting from the roof of a fire-gutted home—the rotting porches—the emptiness.

He rubbed his cheek ruefully. It was no world for a young mother and her baby. The baby would fit nicely in the bicycle's basket. The shotgun would offer some protection against the human wolf-packs tthat prowled everywhere these days.

"Little thief!" he growled half-heartedly.

But when the human animal would no longer steal to protect its offspring, then its prospects for survival would be bleak indeed. He shrugged gloomily and wandered back to the kitchen. He sat down and ate the expensive biscuits—and decided that George couldn't have cut his throat for culinary reasons. Marta was a good cook.

He entered the city on foot and unarmed, later in the morning.

He chose the alleyways, avoiding the thoroughfares, where traffic purred, and where the robot cops enforced the letter of the law. At each corner, he paused to glance in both directions against possible mechanical observers before darting across the open street to the next alley. The Geigers on the lamp posts were clicking faster as he progressed deeper into the city, and twice he paused to inspect the readings of their integrating dials. The radioactivity was not yet dangerous, but it was higher than he had anticipated. Perhaps it had been dusted again after the exodus.

He stopped to prowl through an empty house and an empty garage. He came out with a flashlight, a box of tools, and a crowbar. He had no certain plan, but tools would be needed if he meant to call a temporary halt to Central's activities. It was dangerous to enter any building however; Central would call it burglary, unless the prowler could show legitimate reason for entering. He needed some kind of identification.

After an hour's search through several houses in the residential district, he found a billfold containing a union card and a pass to several restricted buildings in the downtown area. The billfold belonged to a Willie Jesser, an air-conditioning and refrigeration mechanic for the Howard Cooler Company. He pocketed it after a moment's hesitation. It might not be enough to satisfy Central, but for the time being, it would have to do.

By early afternoon he had reached the beginning of the commercial area. Still he had seen no signs of human life. The thinly scattered traffic moved smoothly along the streets, carrying no passengers. Once he saw a group of robot climbers working high on a telephone pole. Some of the telephone cables carried the co-ordinating circuits for the city's network of computers. He detoured several blocks to avoid them, and wandered glumly on. He began to realize that he was wandering aimlessly.

The siren came suddenly from half a block away. Mitch stopped in the center of the street and glanced fearfully toward it. A robot cop was rolling toward him at twenty miles an hour! He broke into a run.

"You will halt, please!" croaked the cop's mechanical voice. "The pedestrian with the toolbox will please halt!"

Mitch stopped at the curb. Flight was impossible. The skater could whisk along at forty miles an hour if he chose.

The cop's steel wheels screeched to a stop a yard away. The head nodded a polite but jerky greeting. Mitch stared at the creature's eyes, even though he knew the eyes were duds; the cop was seeing him by the heat waves from his bodily warmth, and touching him with a delicate aura of radar.

"You are charged with jay-walking, sir. I must present you with a summons. Your identification, please."

Mitch nervously produced the billfold and extracted the cards. The cop accepted them in a pair of tweezerlike fingers and instantly memorized the information.

"This is insufficient identification. Have you nothing else?"

"That's all I have with me. What's wrong with it?"

"The pass and the union card expired in 1987."

Mitch swallowed hard and said nothing. He had been afraid of this. Now he might be picked up for vagrancy.

"I shall consult Central Co-ordinator for instructions," croaked the cop. "One moment, please."

A dynamotor purred softly in the policeman's cylindrical body. Then Mitch heard the faint twittering of computer code as the cop's radio spoke to Central. There was a silence lasting several seconds. Then an answer twittered back. Still the cop said nothing. But he extracted a summons form from a pad, inserted it in a slot in his chassis, and made chomping sounds like a small typesetter. When he pulled the ticket out again, it was neatly printed with a summons for Willie Jesser to appear before Traffic Court on July 29, 1989. The charge was jay-walking.

Mitch accepted it with bewilderment. "I believe I have a right to ask for an explanation," he muttered.

The cop nodded crisply. "Central Service units are required to furnish explanations of decisions when such explanations are demanded."

"Then why did Central regard my identification as sufficient?"

"Pause for translation of Central's message," said the cop. He stood for a moment, making burring and clicking sounds. Then: "Referring to arrest of Willie Jesser by unit Six-Baker. Do not book for investigation. Previous investigations have revealed no identification papers dated later than May 1987 in the possession of any human pedestrian. Data based on one hundred sample cases. Tentative generalization by Central Service: it has become impossible for humans to produce satisfactory identification. Therefore, 'satisfactory identification' is temporarily redefined, pending instruction from authorized human legislative agency."

Mitch nodded thoughtfully. The decision indicated that Central was still capable of "learning," of gathering data and making generalizations about it. But the difficulty was still apparent. She was allowed to act on such generalizations only in certain very minor matters. Although she might very well realize the situation in the city, she could do nothing about it without authority from an authorized agency. That agency was a department of the city government, currently nonexistent.

The cop croaked a courteous "Good day, sir!" and skated smoothly back to his intersection.

Mitch stared at his summons for a moment. The date was still four days away. If he weren't out of the city by then, he might find himself in the lockup, since he had no money to pay a fine.

Reassured now that his borrowed identity gave him a certain amount of safety, he began walking along the sidewalks instead of using the alleys. Still he knew that Central was observing him through a thousand eyes. Counters on every corner were set to record the passage of pedestrian traffic, and to relay the information to Central, thus helping to avoid congestion. But Mitch *was* the pedestrian traffic. And the counters clocked his passage. Since the data was available to the logic units, Central might make some unpleasant deductions about his presence in the city.

Brazenness, he decided, was probably the safest course

to steer. He stopped at the next intersection and called to
another mechanical cop, requesting directions to City
Hall.

But the cop paused before answering, paused to speak
with Central, and Mitch suddenly regretted his question. The cop came skating slowly to the curb.

"Six blocks west and four blocks north, sir," croaked
the cop. "Central requests the following information
which you may refuse to furnish if you so desire: As a
resident of the city; how is it that you do not know the
way to City Hall, Mr. Jesser?"

Mitch whitened and stuttered nervously. "Why, I've
been gone three years. I . . . I had forgotten."

The cop relayed the information, then nodded. "Central thanks you. Data has been recorded."

"Wait," Mitch muttered, "is there a direct contact with
Central in City Hall?"

"Affirmative."

"I want to speak to Central. May I use it?"

The computer code twittered briefly. "Negative. You
are not listed among the city's authorized computer personnel. Central suggests you use the Public Information
Unit, also in City Hall, ground floor rotunda."

Grumbling to himself, Mitch wandered away. The
P.I.U. was better than nothing, but if he had access to the
direct service contact, perhaps to some extent, he could
have altered Central's rigid behavior pattern. The P.I.U.
however would be well guarded.

A few minutes later he was standing in the center of
the main lobby of the city hall. The great building had
suffered some damage during an air raid, and one wing
was charred by fire. But the rest of it was still alive with
the rattle of machinery. A headless servo-secretary came
rolling past him, carrying a trayful of pink envelopes.
Delinquent utility bills, he guessed. Central would keep
sending them out, but of course human authority would
be needed to suspend service to the delinquent customers.
The servo-secretary deposited the envelopes in a mailbox
by the door, then rolled quickly back to its office.

Mitch looked around the gloomy rotunda. There was a
desk at the far wall. Recessed in a panel behind the desk
were a microphone, a loud-speaker, and the lens of a
television camera. A sign hung over the desk, indicating
that here was the place to complain about utility bills,

garbage disposal service, taxes, and inaccurate weather
forecasts. A citizen could also request any information
contained in Central Data except information relating to
defense or to police records.

Mitch crossed the rotunda and sat at the desk facing
the panel. A light came on overhead. The speaker
crackled for a moment.

"Your name, please?" it asked.

"Willie Jesser."

"What do you wish from Information Service, please?"

"A direct contact with Central Data."

"You have a screened contact with Central Data. Unauthorized personnel are not permitted an unrestricted
contact, for security reasons. Your contact must be mon-
itored by this unit."

Mitch shrugged. It was as he had expected. Central
Data was listening, and speaking, but the automatics of
the P.I.U. would be censoring the exchange.

"All right," he grumbled. "Tell me this: Is Central
aware that the city has been abandoned? That its population is gone?"

"Screening, screening, screening," said the unit. "Question relates to civil defense."

"Is Central aware that her services are now interfering
with human interests?"

There was a brief pause. "Is this question in the nature
of a complaint?"

"Yes," he grated acidly. "It's a complaint."

"About your utility services, Mr. Jesser?"

Mitch spat an angry curse. "About all services!" he
bellowed. "Central has got to suspend all operations until
new ordinances are fed into Data."

"That will be impossible, sir."

"Why?"

"There is no authorization from Department of City
Services."

He slapped the desk and groaned. "There *is* no such
department now! There is no city government! The city is
abandoned!"

The speaker was silent.

"Well?" he snapped.

"Screening," said the machine.

"Listen," he hissed. 'Are you screening what I say, or are you just blocking Central's reply?"

There was a pause. "Your statements are being recorded in Central Data. Replies to certain questions must be blocked for security reasons."

"The war is over!"

"Screening."

"You're trying to maintain a civil status quo that went out of existence three years ago. Can't you use your logic units to correct for present conditions?"

"The degree of self-adjustment permitted to Central Service is limited by ordinance number—"

"Never mind!"

"Is there anything else?"

"Yes! What will you do when fifty men come marching in to dynamite the vaults and destroy Central Data?"

"Destroying city property is punishable by a fine of—"

Mitch cursed softly and listened to the voice reading the applicable ordinance.

"Well, they're planning to do it anyway," he snapped.

"Conspiracy to destroy city property is punishable by—"

Mitch stood up and walked away in disgust. But he had taken perhaps ten steps when a pair of robot guards came skating out from their wall niches to intercept him.

"One moment, sir," they croaked in unison.

"Well?"

"Central wishes to question you in connection with the alleged conspiracy to destroy city property. You are free to refuse. However, if you refuse, and if such a conspiracy is shown to exist, you may be charged with complicity. Will you accompany us to Interrogation?"

A step closer to jail, he thought gloomily. But what was there to lose? He grunted assent and accompanied the skaters out the entrance, down an inclined ramp, and past a group of heavily barred windows. They entered the police court, where a booking computer clicked behind its desk. Several servo-secretaries and robot cops were waiting quietly for task assignments.

Mitch stopped suddenly. His escorts waited politely.

"Will you come with us, please?"

He stood staring around at the big room—at the various doorways, one leading to traffic court, and at the iron gate to the cell block.

"I hear a woman crying," he muttered.

The guards offered no comment.

"Is someone locked in a cell?"

"We are not permitted to answer."

"Suppose I wanted to go bail," he snapped. "I have a right to know."

"You may ask the booking desk whether a specific individual is being held. But generalized information cannot be released."

Mitch strode to the booking computer. "Are you holding a woman in jail?"

"Screening."

It was only a vague suspicion, but he said, "A woman named Marta."

"Full name, please."

"I don't know it. Can't you tell me?"

"Screening."

"Listen! I loaned my bicycle to a woman named Marta. If you have the bicycle, I want it!"

"License number, please."

"A 1987 license—number Six Zebra Five Zero."

"Check with Lost and Found, please."

Mitch controlled himself slowly. "Look—*you* check. I'll wait."

The computer paused. "A bicycle with that license number has been impounded. Can you produce proof of ownership?"

"*On a bicycle?* I knew the number. Isn't that enough?"

"Describe it please?"

Mitch described it wearily. He began to understand Ferris' desire to retire Central permanently and forcibly. At the moment, he longed to convert several subcomputers to scrap metal.

"Then," said the speaker, "if vehicle is yours, you may have it by applying for a new license and paying the required fee."

"Refer that to Central Data," Mitch groaned.

The booking computer paused to confer with the Coordinator. "Decision stands, sir."

"But there aren't any new licenses!" he growled. "A while ago, Central said—Oh, never mind!"

"That decision applied to identification, sir. This applies to licensing of vehicles. Insufficient data has been gathered to permit generalization."

"Sure, sure. All right, what do I do to get the girl out of jail?"

There was another conference with the Co-ordinator, then: "She is being held for investigation. She may not be released for seventy-two hours."

Mitch dropped the toolbox that he had been carrying since morning. With a savage curse, he rammed the crowbar through a vent in the device's front panel, and slashed it about in the opening. There was a crash of shattering glass and a shower of sparks. Mitch yelped at the electric jolt and lurched away. Steel fingers clutched his wrists.

Five minutes later he was being led through the gate to the cell blocks, charged with maliciously destroying city property; and he cursed himself for a hot-tempered fool. They would hold him until a grand jury convened, which would probably be forever.

The girl's sobbing grew louder as he was led along the iron corridors toward a cell. He passed three cells and glanced inside. The cells were occupied by dead men's bones. *Why?* The rear wall was badly cracked, and bits of loose masonry were scattered on the floor. Had they died of concussion during an attack? Or been gassed to death?

They led him to the fifth cell and unlocked the door. Mitch stared inside and grinned. The rear wall had been partially wrecked by a bomb blast, and there was room to crawl through the opening to the street. The partition that separated the adjoining cell was also damaged, and he caught a glimpse of a white, frightened face peering through the hole. Marta.

He glanced at his captors. They were pushing him gently through the door. Evidently Central's talents did not extend to bricklaying, and she could not judge that the cell was less than escapeproof.

The door clanged shut behind him.

"Marta," he called.

Her face had disappeared from the opening. There was no answer.

"Marta."

"Let me alone," grumbled a muffled voice.

"I'm not angry about the bicycle."

He walked to the hole and peered through the partition

into the next cell. She crouched in a corner, peering at him with frightened, tear-reddened eyes. He glanced at the opening in the rear wall.

"Why haven't you gone outside?" he asked.

She giggled hysterically. "Why don't you go look down?"

He stepped to the opening and glanced twenty feet down to a concrete sidewalk. He went back to stare at the girl.

"Where's your baby?"

"They took him away," she whimpered.

Mitch frowned and thought about it for a moment. "To the city nursery, probably—while you're in jail."

"They won't take care of him! They'll let him die!"

"Don't scream like that. He'll be all right."

"Robots don't give milk!"

"No but there are such things as bottles, you know," he chuckled.

"Are there?" Her eyes were wide with horror. "And what will they put in the bottles?"

"Why—" He paused. Central certainly wasn't running any dairy farms.

"Wait'll they bring you a meal," she said. "You'll see."

"Meal?"

"Empty tray," she hissed. "Empty tray, empty paper cup, paper fork, clean paper napkin. No food."

Mitch swallowed hard. Central's logic was sometimes hard to see. The servo-attendants probably went through the motions of ladling stew from an empty pot and drawing coffee from an empty urn. Of course, there weren't any truck farmers to keep the city supplied with produce.

"So that's why . . . the bones . . . in the other cells," he muttered.

"They'll starve us to death!"

"Don't scream so. We'll get out. All we need is something to climb down on."

"There isn't any bedding."

"There's our clothing. We can plait a rope. And if necessary, we can risk a jump."

She shook her head dully and stared at her hands. "It's no use. They'd catch us again."

Mitch sat down to think. There was bound to be a police arsenal somewhere in the building, probably in the basement. The robot cops were always unarmed. But, of

course, there had been a human organization for investigation purposes and to assume command in the event of
violence. When one of the traffic units faced a threat, it
could do nothing but try to handcuff the offender and call
for human help. There were arms in the building somewhere, and a well-placed rifle shot could penetrate the
thin sheet-steel bodies.

He deplored the thought of destroying any of the city's
service machinery, but if it became necessary to wreck a
few subunits, it would have to be done. He must somehow get access to the vaults where the central data tanks
and the co-ordinators were located—get to them before
Ferris' gang came to wreck them completely so that they
might be free to pick the city clean.

An hour later, he heard the cell block gate groan open,
and he arose quickly. Interrogation, he thought. They
were coming to question him about the plot to wreck Central. He paused to make a hasty decision, then scrambled
for the narrow opening and clambered through it into the
adjoining cell while the skater came rolling down the corridor.

The girl's eyes widened. "Wh-what are you—"

"*Shhh!*" he hissed. "This might work."

The skater halted before his cell while he crouched
against the wall beyond the opening.

"Willie Jesser, please," the robot croaked.

There was a silence. He heard the door swing open.
The robot rolled around inside his cell for a few seconds,
repeating his name and brushing rubble aside to make
way. If only he failed to look through the opening!

Suddenly a siren growled, and the robot went tearing
down the corridor again. Mitch stole a quick glance. The
robot had left the door ajar. He dragged the girl to her
feet and snapped, "Let's go."

They squeezed through the hole and raced out into the
corridor. The cell-block gate was closed. The girl moaned
weakly. There was no place to hide.

The door bolts were operated from remote boxes,
placed in the corridor so as to be beyond the reach of the
inmates. Mitch dragged the girl quickly toward another
cell, opened the control panel, and threw the bolt. He
closed the panel, leaving the bolt open. They slipped
quickly inside the new cell, and he pulled the door quietly

closed. The girl made a choking sound as she stumbled over the remains of a former inmate.

"Lie down in the corner," he hissed, "and keep still. They're coming back in force."

"What if they notice the bolt is open?"

"Then we're sunk. But they'll be busy down at our end of the hall. Now shut up."

They rolled under the steel cot and lay scarcely breathing. The robot was returning with others. The faint twitter of computer code echoed through the cell blocks. Then the skaters rushed past, and screeched to a stop before the escapee's cell. He heard them enter. He crawled to the door for a look, then pushed it open and stole outside.

He beckoned the girl to his side and whispered briefly. Then they darted down the corridor on tiptoe toward the investigators. They turned as he raced into view. He seized the bars and jerked the door shut. The bolt snapped in place as Marta tugged at the remote.

Three metal bodies crashed simultaneously against the door, and rebounded. One of them spun around three times before recovering.

"Release the lock, please."

Mitch grinned through the bars. "Why don't you try the hole in the wall?"

The robot who had spun crazily away from the door now turned. He went charging across the cell floor at full acceleration—and sailed out wildly into space.

An ear-splitting crash came from the street. Shattered metal skidded across pavement. A siren wailed, and brakes shrieked. The others went to look—and began twittering.

Then they turned. "You will surrender, please. We have summoned armed guards to seize you if you resist."

Mitch laughed and tugged at the whimpering girl.

"Wh-where—?"

"To the gate. Come on."

They raced swiftly along the corridor. And the gate was opening to admit the "armed guards." But, of course, no human bluecoats charged through. The girl muttered frightened bewilderment, and he explained on the run.

"Enforced habit pattern. Central has to do it, even when no guards are available."

Two repair units were at work on the damaged booking computer as the escapees raced past. The repair units paused, twittered a notation to Central, then continued with their work.

Minutes later they found the arsenal, and the mechanical attendant had set out a pair of .45s for the "armed guards." Mitch caught one of them up and fired at the attendant's sheet-metal belly. The robot careened crazily against the wall, emitted a shower of blue sparks, and stood humming while the metal around the hole grew cherry red. There was a dull cough. The machine smoked and fell silent.

Mitch vaulted across the counter and caught a pair of submachine guns from the rack. But the girl backed away, shaking her head.

"I couldn't even use your shotgun," she panted.

He shrugged and laid it aside. "Carry as much ammunition as you can, then," he barked.

Alarm bells were clanging continuously as they raced out of the arsenal, and a loud-speaker was thundering a request for all human personnel to be alert and assist in their capture. Marta was staggering against him as they burst out of the building into the street. He pushed her back against the wall and fired a burst at two skaters who raced toward them down the sidewalk. One crashed into a fire plug; the other went over the curb and fell in the street.

"To the parking lot!" he called over his shoulder.

But the girl had slumped in a heap on the sidewalk. He grumbled a curse and hurried to her side. She was semi-conscious, but her face was white and drawn. She shivered uncontrollably.

"What's wrong?" he snapped.

There was no answer. Fright had dazed her. Her lips moved, seemed to frame a soundless word: "George."

Muttering angrily, Mitch stuffed a fifty-round drum of ammunition in his belt, took another between his teeth, and lifted the girl over one shoulder. He turned in time to fire a one-handed burst at another skater. The burst went wide. But the skater stopped. Then the skater ran away.

He gasped, and stared after it. The blare of the loud-speaker was furnishing the answer.

". . . All human personnel. Central patrol service has reached the limit of permissible subunit expenditure. Responsibility for capture no longer applied without further orders to expend subunits. Please instruct. Commissioner of Police, please instruct. Waiting. Waiting."

Mitch grinned. Carrying the girl, he stumbled toward a car on the parking lot. He dumped her in the back seat and started in behind her, but a loud-speaker in the front protested.

"Unauthorized personnel. This is Mayor Sarquist's car. Unauthorized personnel. Please use an extra."

Mitch looked around. There were no extras on the lot. And if there had been one, it would refuse to carry him unless he could identify himself as authorized to use it.

Mayor Sarquist's car began twittering a radio protest to Central. Mitch climbed inside and wrenched loose the cable that fed the antenna. The loud-speaker began barking complaints about sabotage. Mitch found a toolbox under the back seat and removed several of the pilot-computer's panels. He tugged a wire loose, and the speaker ceased complaining. He ripped at another, and a bank of tubes went dead.

He drove away, using a set of dial controls for steering. The girl in the back seat began to recover her wits. She sat up and stared out the window at the thin traffic. The sun was sinking, and the great city was immersing itself in gloom.

"You're worthless!" he growled at Marta. "The world takes a poke at you, and you jump in your mental coffin and nail the lid shut. How do you expect to take care of your baby?"

She continued to stare gloomily out the window. She said nothing. The car screeched around a corner, narrowly missing a mechanical cop. The cop skated after them for three blocks, siren wailing; then it abandoned the chase.

"You're one of the machine-age's spoiled children," he fumed. "Technologists gave you everything you could possibly want. Push a button, and you get it. Instead of taking part in the machine age, you let it wait on you. You spoiled yourself. When the machine age cracks up, you crack up, too. Because you never made yourself its master; you just let yourself be mechanically pampered."

She seemed not to hear him. He swung around another corner and pulled to the curb. They were in front of a three-storey brick building set in the center of a green-

lawned block and surrounded by a high iron fence. The
girl stared at it for a moment, and raised her chin slowly
from her fist.

"The city orphanage!" she cried suddenly, and bounded
outside. She raced across the sidewalk and beat at the
iron gate with her fists.

Mitch climbed out calmly and opened it for her. She
darted up toward the porch, but a servo-attendant came
rolling out to intercept her. Its handcuff-hand was open
to grasp her wrist.

"Drop low!" he bellowed at her.

She crouched on the walkway, then rolled quickly aside
on the lawn. A burst of machine-gun fire brightened the
twilight. The robot spun crazily and stopped, hissing and
sputtering. Wrecking a robot could be dangerous. If a
bullet struck the tiny nuclear reactor just right, there
would be an explosion.

They skirted wide around it and hurried into the building. Somewhere upstairs, a baby was crying. A servo-nurse
sat behind a desk in the hall, and she greeted them as if
they were guests.

"Good evening, sir and madam. You wish to see one of
the children?"

Marta started toward the stairs, but Mitch seized her
arm. "No! Let *me* go up. It won't be pretty."

But she tore herself free with a snarl and bounded up
the steps toward the cry of her child. Mitch shrugged to
himself and waited. The robot nurse protested the illegal
entry, but did nothing about it.

"Noooo—!"

A horrified shriek from the girl! He glanced up the
staircase, knowing what was wrong, but unable to help
her. A moment later, he heard her vomiting. He waited.

A few minutes later, she came staggering down the
stairway, sobbing and clutching her baby tightly against
her. She stared at Mitch with tear-drenched eyes, gave
him a wild shake of her head, and babbled hysterically.

"Those cribs! They're full of little bones. Little bones—
all over the floor. Little bones—"

"Shut up!" he snapped. "Be thankful yours is all right.
Now let's get out of here."

After disposing of another robotic interferer, they
reached the car, and Mitch drove rapidly toward the out-

skirts. The girl's sobbing ceased, and she purred a little unsung lullaby to her child, cuddling it as if it had just returned from the dead. Remorse picked dully at Mitch's heart, for having growled at her. Motherwise, she was still a good animal, despite her lack of success in adjusting to the reality of a ruptured world.

"Marta—?"

"What?"

"You're not fit to take care of yourself."

He said it gently. She only stared at him as he piloted the car.

"You ought to find a big husky gal who wants a baby, and let her take care of it for you."

"No."

"It's just a suggestion. None of my business. You want your baby to live, don't you?"

"George promised he'd take care of us. George always took care of us."

"George killed himself."

She uttered a little whimper. "Why did he do it? Why? I went to look for food. I came back, and there he was. Why, *why?*"

"Possibly because he was just like you. What did he do—before the war?"

"Interior decorator. He was good, a real artist."

"Yeah."

"Why do you say it *that* way? He *was.*"

"Was he qualified to live in a mechanical culture?"

"I don't know what you mean."

"I mean—could he control his slice of mechanical civilization, or did it control him?"

"I don't see—"

"Was he a button-pusher and a switch-puller? Or did he care what made the buttons and switches work? Men misuse their tools because they don't understand the principles of the tools. A man who doesn't know how a watch works might try to fix it with a hammer. If the watch is communal property, he's got no right to fool with it. A nontechnologist has no right to take part in a technological civilization. He's a bull in a china shop. That's what happened to our era. Politicians were given powerful tools. They failed to understand the tools. They wrecked our culture with them."

"You'd have a scientist in the White House?"

"If all men were given a broad technical education, there could be nothing else there, could there?"

"Technocracy—"

"No. Simply a matter of education."

"People aren't smart enough."

"You mean they don't *care* enough. Any man above the level of a dullard has enough sense to grasp the principles of physics and basic engineering and mechanics. They just aren't motivated to grasp them. The brain is a tool, not a garbage can for oddments of information! Your baby there—he should learn the principles of logic and semantics before he's ten. He should be taught *how to use* the tool, the brain. We've just begun to learn how to think. If the common man were trained in scientific reasoning methods, we'd solve our problems in a hurry."

"What has this got to do with us?"

"Everything. Your George folded up because he couldn't control his slice of civilization, and he couldn't live without it. He couldn't fix the broken toy, but he suffered from its loss. And you're in the same fix. I haven't decided yet whether you're crazy or just neurotic."

She gave him an icy stare. "Let me know when you figure it out."

They were leaving the city, driving out through the suburbs again into the night-shrouded residential areas. He drove by streetlight, for the car—accustomed to piloting itself by radar—had no headlights. Mitch thought gloomily that he had stalked into the city without a plan, and had accomplished nothing. He had alerted Central, and had managed to get himself classified as a criminal in the central data tanks. Instead of simplifying his task, he had made things harder for himself.

Whenever they passed a cop at an intersection, the cop retreated to the curb and called Central to inform the Co-ordinator of their position. But no attempt was made to arrest the fugitives. Having reached her limit of subunit expenditures, Central was relying on the nonexistent human police force.

"Mayor Sarquist's house," the girl muttered suddenly.

"Huh? Where?"

"Just ahead. The big cut-stone house on the right—with part of the roof caved in."

Mitch twisted a dial in the heart of the pilot-computer,

and the car screeched to a stop at the curb. The girl lurched forward.

"You woke the baby," she complained. "Why stop here? We're still in the city limits."

"I don't know," he murmured, staring thoughtfully at the dark hulk of the two-story mansion set in a nest of oaks. "Just sort of a hunch."

There was a long silence while Mitch chewed his lip and frowned at the house.

"I hear a telephone ringing," she said.

"Central calling Mayor Sarquist. You can't tell. It might have been ringing for three years."

She was looking out the rear window. "Mitch—?"

"Huh?"

"There's a cop at the intersection."

He seemed not to hear her. He opened the door. "Let's go inside. I want to look around. Bring the gun."

They strolled slowly up the walkway toward the damaged and deserted house. The wind was breathing in the oaks, and the porch creaked loudly beneath their feet. The door was still locked. Mitch kicked the glass out of a window, and they slipped into an immense living room. He found the light.

"The cop'll hear that noise," she muttered, glancing at the broken glass.

The noisy clatter of the steelwheeled skater answered her. The cop was coming to investigate. Mitch ignored the sound and began prowling through the house. The phone was still ringing, but he could not answer it without knowing Sarquist's personal identifying code.

The girl called suddenly from the library. "What's this thing, Mitch?"

"What thing?" he yelled.

"Typewriter keyboard, but no type. Just a bunch of wires and a screen."

His jaw fell agape. He trotted quickly toward the library.

"A direct channel to the data tanks!" he gasped, staring at the metal wall-panel with its encoders and the keyboard.

"What's it doing here?"

He thought about it briefly. "Must be . . . I remember: just before the exodus, they gave Sarquist emergency powers in the defense setup. He could requisition whatever was needed for civil defense—draft workers for first aid, traffic direction, and so on. He had the power to draft anybody or anything during an air raid."

Mitch approached the keyboard slowly. He closed the main power switch, and the tubes came alive. He sat down and typed: *Central from Sarquist; You will completely clear the ordinance section of your data tanks and await revised ordinances. The entire city code is hereby repealed.*

He waited. Nothing happened. There was no acknowledgement. The typed letters had not even appeared on the screen.

"Broken?" asked the girl.

"Maybe," Mitch grunted. "Maybe not. I think I know."

The mechanical cop had lowered his retractable sprockets, climbed the porch steps, and was hammering at the door. "Mayor Sarquist, please!" he was calling. "Mayor Sarquist, please!"

"Let him rave," Mitch grunted, and looked around the library.

There was a mahogany desk, several easy-chairs, a solid wall of books, and a large safe in another wall. The safe—

"Sarquist should have some rather vital papers in there," he murmured.

"What do you want with papers?" the girl snapped. "Why don't we get out of the city while we can?"

He glanced at her coldly. "Like to go the rest of the way alone?"

She opened her mouth, closed it, and frowned. She was holding the tommy gun, and he saw it twitch slightly in her hand, as if reminding him that she didn't *have* to go alone.

He walked to the safe and idly spun the dial. "Locked," he muttered. "It'd take a good charge of T.N.T. . . . or—"

"Or what?"

"Central." He chuckled dryly. "Maybe she'll do it for us."

"Are you crazy?"

"Sure. Go unlock the door. Let the policeman in."

"No!" she barked.

Mitch snorted impatiently. "All right then, I'll do it. Pitch me the gun."

"No!" She pointed it at him and backed away.

"Give me the gun!"

"No!"

She had laid the baby on the sofa where it was now sleeping peacefully. Mitch sat down beside it.

"Trust your aim?"

She caught her breath. Mitch lifted the child gently into his lap.

"Give me the gun."

"You wouldn't!"

"I'll give the kid back to the cops."

She whitened, and handed the weapon to him quickly. Mitch saw that the safety was on, laid the baby aside, and stood up.

"Don't look at me like that!" she said nervously.

He walked slowly toward her.

"Don't you dare *touch me!*"

He picked up a ruler from Sarquist's desk, then dived for her. A moment later she was stretched out across his lap, clawing at his legs and shrieking while he applied the ruler resoundingly. Then he dumped her on the rug, caught up the gun, and went to admit the insistent cop.

Man and machine stared at each other across the threshold. The cop radioed a visual image of Mitch to Central, and got an immediate answer.

"Request you surrender immediately, sir."

"Am I now charged with breaking and entering?" he asked acidly.

"Affirmative."

"You planning to arrest me?"

Again the cop consulted Central. "If you will leave the city at once, you will be granted safe passage."

Mitch lifted his brows. Here was a new twist. Central was doing some interpretation, some slight modification of ordinance. He grinned at the cop and shook his head.

"I locked Mayor Sarquist in the safe," he stated evenly.

The robot consulted Central. There was a long twittering of computer code. Then it said, "This is false information."

"Suit yourself, tin-boy. I don't care whether you believe it or not."

Again there was a twittering of code. Then: "Stand aside, please."

Mitch stepped out of the doorway. The subunit bounced

over the threshold with the aid of the four-footed sprockets and clattered hurriedly toward the library. Mitch followed, grinning to himself. Despite Central's limitless "intelligence," she was as naive as a child.

He lounged in the doorway to watch the subunit fiddling with the dials of the safe. He motioned the girl down, and she crouched low in a corner. The tumblers clicked. There was a dull snap. The door started to swing.

"Just a minute!" Mitch barked.

The subunit paused and turned. The machine gun exploded, and the brief hail of bullets tore off the robot's antenna. Mitch lowered the gun and grinned. The cop just stood there, unable to contact Central, unable to decide. Mitch crossed the room through the drifting plaster dust and rolled the robot aside. The girl whimpered her relief, and came out of the corner.

The cop was twittering continually as it tried without success to contact the Co-ordinator. Mitch stared at it for a moment, then barked at the girl.

"Go find some tools. Search the garage, attic, basement. I want a screw driver, pliers, soldering iron, solder, whatever you can find."

She departed silently.

Mitch cleaned out the safe and dumped the heaps of papers, money, and securities on the desk. He began sorting them out. Among the various stacks of irrelevant records, he found a copy of the original specifications for the Central Co-ordinator vaults, dating from the time of installation. He found blue-prints of the city's network of computer circuits, linking the subunits into one. His hands became excited as he shuffled through the stacks. Here was data. Here was substance for reasonable planning.

Heretofore, he had gone off half-cocked, and quite naturally had met with immediate failure. No one ever won a battle by being good, pure, or ethically right, despite Galahad's claims to the contrary. Victories were won by intelligent planning, and Mitch felt ashamed for his previous impulsiveness. To work out a scheme for redirecting Central's efforts would require time.

The girl brought a boxful of assorted small tools. She set them on the floor and sat down to glower at him.

"More cops outside now," she said. "Standing and waiting. The place is surrounded."

He ignored her. Sarquist's identifying code—it had to be here somewhere.

"I tell you, we should get out of here!" she whined.

"Shut up."

Mitch occasionally plucked a paper from the stack and laid it aside while the girl watched.

"What are those?" she asked.

"Messages he typed into the unit at various times."

"What good are *they?*"

He showed her one of the slips of yellowed paper. It said: *Unit 67-BJ is retired for repairs.* A number was scrawled in one corner: 5.00326.

"So?"

"That number. It was his identifying code at the time."

"You mean it's different every day?"

"More likely, it's different every minute. The code is probably based on an equation whose independent variable is *time,* and whose dependent variable is the code number."

"How silly!"

"Not at all. It's just sort of a combination lock whose combination is continuously changing. All I've got to do is find the equation that describes the change. Then I can get to the Central Co-ordinator."

She paced restlessly while he continued the search. Half an hour later, he put his head in his hands and gazed despondently at the desk top. The key to the code was not there.

"What's the matter?" she asked.

"Sarquist. I figured he'd have to write it down somewhere. Evidently he memorized it. Or else his secretary did. I didn't figure a politician even had sense enough to substitute numbers in a simple equation."

The girl walked to the bookshelf and picked out a volume. She brought it to him silently. The title was *Higher Mathematics for Engineers and Physicists.*

"So I was wrong," he grunted.

"Now what?"

He shuffled the slips of paper idly while he thought about it. "I've got eleven code numbers here, and the corresponding times when they were good. I might be able to find it empirically."

"I don't understand."

"Find an equation that gives the same eleven answers

for the same eleven times and use it to predict the code number for now."

"Will it work?"

He grinned. "There are an infinite number of equations that would give the same eleven answers for the same eleven substitutions. But it might work, if I assume that the code equation was of a simple form."

She paced restlessly while he worked at making a graph with time as the abscissa and the code numbers for ordinates. But the points were scattered across the page, and there was no connecting them with any simple sort of curve. "It almost has to be some kind of repeating function," he muttered, "something that Central could check by means of an irregular cam. The normal way for setting a code into a machine is to turn a cam by clock motor, and the height of the cam's rider is the code number for that instant."

He tried it on polar co-ordinates, hoping to get the shape of such a cam, but the resulting shape was too irregular to be possible, and he had no way of knowing the period of the repeating function.

"That's the craziest clock I ever saw," the girl murmured.

"What?" He looked up quickly.

"That electric wall clock. Five minutes ahead of the electric clock in the living room. But when we first came, it was twenty minutes ahead."

"It's stopped, maybe."

"Look at the second hand."

The red sweep was running. Mitch stared at it for a moment, then came slowly to his feet and walked to her side. He took the small clock down from its hook and turned it over in his hands. Then he traced the cord to the wall outlet. The plug was held in place by a bracket so that it could not be removed.

The sweep hand moved slowly, it seemed. Silently he removed the screws from the case and stared inside at the works. Then he grunted surprise. "First clock I ever saw with elliptical gears!"

"What?"

"Look at these two gears in the train. Ellipses, mounted at the foci. That's the story. For a while the clock will run faster than the other one. Then it'll run slower." He handled it with growing excitement. "That's *it*, Marta—the key. Central must have another clock just like this one. The amount of lead or lag—in minutes, is probably the code!"

He moved quickly to the direct contact unit. "Tell me the time on the other clock!"

She hurried into the living room and called back, "Ten seventeen and forty seconds . . . forty-five . . . fifty—"

The other clock was leading by five minutes and fifteen seconds. He typed 5.250 on the keyboard. Nothing happened.

"You sure that's right?" he called.

"It's now 10:10 . . . fifteen . . . twenty."

The clock was still slowing down. He tried 5.230, but again nothing happened. The unit refused to respond. He arose with an angry grunt and began prowling around the library. "There's something else," he muttered. "There must be a modifying factor. That clock's too obvious anyway. But what else could they be measuring together except time?"

"Is that another clock on his desk?"

"No, it's a barometer. It doesn't—"

He paused to grin. "Could be! The barometric pressure-difference from the mean could easily be mechanically added or subtracted from the reading of that wacky clock. Visualize this, inside of Central: The two clock motors mounted on the same shaft, with the distance between their indicator needles as the code number. Except that the distance is modified by having a barometer rigged up to shift one of the clocks one way or the other on its axis when the pressure varies. It's simple enough."

She shook her head. Mitch took the barometer with him to the unit. The dial was calibrated in atmospheres, and the pressure was now 1.03. Surely, he thought, for simplicity's sake, there would be no other factor involved in the code. This way, Sarquist could have glanced at his watch and the wall clock and the barometer, and could have known the code number with only a little mental arithmetic. The wall time minus the wrist time plus the barometer's reading.

He called to the girl again, and the lag was now a little over four minutes. He typed again. There was a sharp click as the relays worked. The screen came alive, fluttered with momentary phosphorescence, then revealed the numbers in glowing type.

"We've got it!" he yelled at Marta.

She came to sit down on the rug. "I still don't see what we've got."

"Watch!" He began typing hurriedly, and the message flashed neatly upon the screen.

CENTRAL FROM SARQUIST. CLEAR YOUR TANKS OF ALL ORDINANCE DATA, EXCEPT ORDINANCES PERTAINING TO RECORDING OF INFORMATION IN YOUR TANKS. PREPARE TO RECORD NEW DATA.

He pressed the answer button, and the screen went blank, but the reply was slow to come.

"It won't work!" Marta snorted. "It knows you aren't Sarquist. The subunits in the street have seen us."

"What do you mean by 'know', and what do you mean by 'see'? Central isn't human."

"It *knows* and it *sees*."

He nodded. "Provided you mean those words in a mechanical sense. Provided you don't imply that she *cares* what she knows and sees, except where she's required to 'care' by enforced behavior-patterns—ordinances."

Then the reply began crawling across the screen. SARQUIST FROM CENTRAL. INCONSISTENT INSTRUCTIONS. ORDINANCE 36-J, PERTAINING TO THE RECORDING OF INFORMATION, STATES THAT ORDINANCE-DATA MAY NOT BE TOTALLY VOIDED BY YOU, EXCEPT DURING RED ALERT AIR WARNING.

"See?" the girl hissed.

DEFINE THE LIMITS OF MY AUTHORITY IN PRESENT CONDITIONS, he typed. MAY I TEMPORARILY SUSPEND SPECIFIC ORDINANCES?

YOU MAY SUSPEND SPECIFIC ORDINANCES FOR CAUSE, BUT THE CAUSE MUST BE RECORDED WITH THE ORDER OF SUSPENSION.

Mitch put on a gloating grin. READ ME THE SERIES NUMBERS OF ALL LAWS IN CRIMINAL AND TRAFFIC CODES.

The reaction was immediate. Numbers began flashing on the screen in rapid sequence. "Write these down!" he called to the girl.

A few moments later, the flashing numbers paused.

WAIT, EMERGENCY INTERRUPTION, said the screen.

Mitch frowned. The girl glanced up from her notes. "What's—"

Then it came. A dull booming roar that rattled the windows and shook the house.

"Not another raid!" she whimpered.

"It doesn't sound like—"

Letters began splashing across the screen. EMERGENCY ADVICE TO SARQUIST. MY CIVILIAN DEFENSE CO-ORDINATOR HAS BEEN DESTROYED. MY ANTI-AIRCRAFT CO-ORDINATOR HAS BEEN DESTROYED. ADVISE, PLEASE.

"What happened?"

"Frank Ferris!" he barked suddenly. "The Sugarton crowd—with their dynamite! They got into the city."

CENTRAL FROM SARQUIST, he typed. WHERE ARE THE DAMAGED CO-ORDINATORS LOCATED?

UNDERGROUND VAULT AT MAP CO-ORDINATES K-81.

"Outside the city," he breathed. "They haven't got to the main tanks yet. We've got a little time."

PROCEED WITH THE ORDINANCE LISTING, he commanded.

Half-an-hour later, they were finished. Then he began the long task of relisting each ordinance number and typing after it: REPEALED, CITY EVACUATED.

"I hear gunshots," Marta interrupted. She went to the window to peer up and down the dimly lighted streets.

Mitch worked grimly. It would take them a couple of hours to get into the heart of the city, unless they knew how to capture a robot vehicle and make it serve them. But with enough men and enough guns, they would wreck subunits until Central withdrew. Then they could walk freely into the heart of the city and wreck the main co-ordinators, with a consequent cessation of all city services. Then they would be free to pillage, to make a mechanical graveyard of the city that awaited the return of Man.

"They're coming down this street, I think," she called.

"Then turn out all the lights!" he snapped, "and keep quiet."

"They'll see all the cops out in the street. They'll wonder why."

He worked frantically to get all the codes out of the machine before the Sugarton crowd came past. He was destroying its duties, its habit-patterns, its normal functions. When he was finished, it would stand helplessly by and let Ferris' gang wreak their havoc unless he could replace the voided ordinances with new, more practical ones.

"Aren't you finished yet?" she called. "They're a couple of blocks away. The cops have quit fighting, but the men are still shooting them."

"I'm finished now!" He began rattling the keyboard frantically.

SUPPLEMENTAL ORDINANCES: #1, THERE IS NO LIMIT OF SUBUNIT EXPENDITURE.

#2, YOU WILL NOT PHYSICALLY INJURE ANY HUMAN BEING, EXCEPT IN DEFENSE OF CENTRAL CO-ORDINATOR UNITS.

#3, ALL MECHANICAL TRAFFIC WILL BE CLEARED FROM THE STREETS IMMEDIATELY.

#4, YOU WILL DEFEND CENTRAL CO-ORDINATOR AT ALL COSTS.

#5, THE HUMAN LISTED IN YOUR MEMORY UNITS UNDER THE NAME "WILLIE JESSER" WILL BE ALLOWED ACCESS TO CENTRAL DATA WITHOUT CHALLENGE.

#6, TO THE LIMIT OF YOUR ABILITY, YOU WILL SET YOUR OWN TASKS IN PURSUANCE OF THIS GOAL: TO KEEP THE CITY'S SERVICE INTACT AND IN GOOD REPAIR, READY FOR HUMAN USAGE.

#7, YOU WILL APPREHEND HUMANS ENGAGED IN ARSON, GRAND THEFT, OR PHYSICAL VIOLENCE, AND EJECT THEM SUMMARILY FROM THE CITY.

#8, YOU WILL OFFER YOUR SERVICE TO PROTECT THE PERSON OF WILLIE JESSER—

"They're here!" shouted the girl. "They're coming up the walk!"

. . . AND WILL ASSIST HIM IN THE TASK OF RENOVATING THE CITY, TOGETHER WITH SUCH PERSONS WILLING TO HELP REBUILD.

The girl was shaking him. "They're here, I tell you!"

Mitch punched a button labeled "commit to data," and the screen went blank. He leaned back and grinned at her. There was a sound of shouting in the street, and someone was beating at the door.

Then the skaters came rolling in a tide of sound two blocks away. The shouting died, and there were several bursts of gunfire. But the skaters came on, and the shouting grew frantic.

She muttered: "Now we're in for it."

But Mitch just grinned at her and lit a cigarette. Fifty men couldn't stand for long against a couple of thousand subunits who now had no expenditure limit.

He typed one last instruction into the unit. WHEN THE PLUNDERERS ARE TAKEN PRISONER, OFFER THEM THIS CHOICE: STAY AND HELP REBUILD, OR KEEP AWAY FROM THE CITY.

From now on, there weren't going to be any nonparticipators.

Mitch closed down the unit and went out to watch the waning fight.

A bigger job was ahead.

Blood Bank

THE COLONEL'S SECRETARY heard clomping footsteps in the corridor and looked up from her typing. The footsteps stopped in the doorway. A pair of jet-black eyes bored through her once, then looked away. A tall, thin joker in a space commander's uniform stalked into the reception room, sat in the corner, and folded his hands stiffly in his lap. The secretary arched her plucked brows. It had been six months since a visitor had done that—walked in without saying boo to the girl behind the rail.

"You have an appointment, sir?" she asked with a professional smile.

The man nodded curtly but said nothing. His eyes flickered toward her briefly, then returned to the wall. She tried to decide whether he was angry or in pain. The black eyes burned with cold fire. She checked the list of appointments. Her smile disappeared, to be replaced by a tight-lipped expression of scorn.

"You're Space Commander Eli Roki?" she asked in an icy tone.

Again the curt nod. She gazed at him steadily for several seconds. "Colonel Beth will see you in a few minutes." Then her typewriter began clattering with sharp sounds of hate.

The man sat quietly, motionlessly. The colonel passed through the reception room once and gave him a brief nod. Two majors came in from the corridor and entered the colonel's office without looking at him. A few moments later, the intercom crackled, "Send Roki in, Dela. Bring your pad and come with him."

The girl looked at Roki, but he was already on his feet, striding toward the door. Evidently he came from an unchivalrous planet; he opened the door without looking at her and let her catch in when it started to slam.

Chubby, elderly Colonel Beth sat waiting behind his desk, flanked by the pair of majors. Roki's bearing as he approached and saluted was that of the professional soldier, trained from birth for the military.

"Sit down, Roki."

The tall space commander sat at attention and waited, his face expressionless, his eyes coolly upon the colonel's forehead. Beth shuffled some papers on his desk, then spoke slowly.

"Before we begin, I want you to understand something, commander."

"Yes, sir."

"You are not being tried. This is not a court-martial. There are no charges against you. Is that clear?"

"Yes, sir."

The colonel's pale eyes managed to look at Roki's face without showing any contempt. "This investigation is for the record, and for the public. The incident has already been investigated, as you know. But the people are aroused, and we have to make a show of some kind."

"I understand, sir."

"Then let's begin. Dela, take notes, please." The colonel glanced at the papers before him. "Space Commander Roki, will you please tell us in your own words what happened during patrol flight Sixty-one on fourday sixmonth, year eighty-seven?"

There was a brief silence. The girl was staring at the back of Roki's neck as if she longed to attack it with a hatchet. Roki's thin face was a waxen mask as he framed his words. His voice came calm as a bell and clear.

"The flight was a random patrol. We blasted off Jod VII at thirteen hours, Universal Patrol Time, switched on the high-C drive, and penetrated to the ten-thousandth level of the C'th component. We re-entered the continuum on the outer patrol radius at thirty-six degrees theta and two-hundred degrees psi. My navigator threw the dice to select a random course. We were to proceed to a point on the same co-ordinate shell at thirty theta and one-fifty psi. We began—"

The colonel interrupted. "Were you aware at the time that your course would intersect that of the mercy ship?"

The girl looked up again. Roki failed to wince at the question. "I was aware of it, sir."

"Go on."

"We proceeded along the randomly selected course until the warp detectors warned us of a ship. When we came in range, I told the engineer to jockey into a parallel course and to lock the automatics to *keep* us parallel. When that was accomplished, I called the unknown freighter with the standard challenge."

"You saw its insignia?"

"Yes, sir. The yellow mercy star."

"Go on. Did they answer your challenge?"

"Yes, sir. The reply, decoded, was: Mercy liner Sol-G-6, departure Sol III, destination Jod VI, cargo emergency surgi-bank supplies, Cluster Request A-4-J."

Beth nodded and watched Roki with clinical curiosity. "You knew about the Jod VI disaster? That twenty thousand casualties were waiting in Suspendfreeze lockers for those supplies?"

"Yes, sir. I'm sorry they died."

"Go on with your account."

"I ordered the navigator to throw the dice again, to determine whether or not the freighter should be boarded for random cargo inspection. He threw a twelve, the yes-number. I called the freighter again, ordered the outer locks opened. It failed to answer, or respond in any way."

"One moment. You explained the reason for boarding? Sol is on the outer rim of the galaxy. It doesn't belong to any cluster system. Primitive place—or regressed. They wouldn't understand our ways."

"I allowed for that, sir," continued the cold-faced Roki. "I explained the situation, even read them extracts of our patrol regs. They failed to acknowledge. I thought perhaps they were out of contact, so I had the message repeated to them by blinker. I know they got it, because the blinker-operator acknowledged the message. Evidently carried it to his superiors. Apparently they told him to ignore us, because when we blinked again, he failed to acknowledge. I then attempted to pull alongside and attach to their hull by magnetic grapples."

"They resisted?"

"Yes, sir. They tried to break away by driving to a

higher C-level. Our warp was already at six-thousand C's. The mass-components of our star cluster at that level were just a collapsing gas cloud. Of course, with our automatic trackers, they just dragged us with them, stalled, and plunged the other way. They pulled us down to the quarter-C level; most of the galaxy was at the red-dwarf stage. I suppose they realized then that they couldn't get away from us like that. They came back to a sensible warp and continued on their previous course."

"And you did what?"

"We warned them by every means of communication at our disposal, read them the standard warning."

"They acknowledge?"

"Once, sir. They came back to say: This is an emergency shipment. We have orders not to stop. We are continuing on course, and will report you to authority upon arrival." Roki paused, eyeing the colonel doubtfully. "May I make a personal observation, sir?"

Beth nodded tolerantly. "Go ahead."

"They wasted more time dodging about in the C'th component than they would have lost if they had allowed us to board them. I regarded this behavior as highly suspicious."

"Did it occur to you that it might be due to some peculiarity in Sol III's culture? Some stubbornness, or resentment of authority?"

"Yes, sir."

"Did you ask opinions of your crew?"

A slight frown creased Roki's high forehead. "No, sir."

"Why not?"

"Regulation does not require it, sir. My personal reason —the cultural peculiarities of my planet."

The barb struck home. Colonel Beth knew the military culture of Roki's world—Coph IV. Military rank was inherited. On his own planet, Roki was a nobleman and an officer of the war-college. He had been taught to rely upon his own decisions and to expect crisp, quick obedience. The colonel frowned at his desk.

"Let's put it this way: Did you *know* the opinions of the crew?"

"Yes, sir. They thought that we should abandon the pursuit and allow the freighter to continue. I was forced to confine two of them to the brig for insubordination and attempted mutiny." He stopped and glanced at one of the majors. "All due apologies to you, sir."

The major flushed. He ranked Roki, but he had been with the patrol as an observer, and despite his higher rank, he was subject to the ship commander's authority while in space. He had also been tossed in the brig. Now he glared at the Cophian space commander without speaking.

"All right, commander, when they refused to halt, what did you do?"

"I withdrew to a safe range and fired a warning charge ahead of them. It exploded in full view of their scopes, dead ahead. They ignored the warning and tried to flee again."

"Go on."

Roki's shoulders lifted in the suggestion of a shrug. "In accordance with Article Thirty of the Code, I shot them out of space."

The girl made a choking sound. "And over ten thousand people died on Jod VI because you—"

"*That will do, Dela!*" snapped Colonel Beth.

There was a long silence. Roki waited calmly for further questioning. He seemed unaware of the girl's outburst. The colonel's voice came again with a forced softness.

"You examined the debris of the destroyed vessel?"

"Yes, sir."

"What did you find?"

"Fragments of quick-frozen bone, blood plasma, various bodily organs and tissues in cultured or frozen form, prepared for surgical use in transplanting operations; in other words, a complete stock of surgibank supplies, as was anticipated. We gathered up samples, but we had no facilities for preserving what was left."

The colonel drummed his fingers. "You said 'anticipated.' Then you knew full well the nature of the cargo, and you did not suspect contraband material of any kind?"

Roki paused. "I suspected contraband, colonel," he said quietly.

Beth lifted his eyebrows in surprise. "You didn't say that before."

"I was never asked."

"Why didn't you say it anyway?"

"I had no proof."

"Ah, yes," murmured the colonel. "The culture of Coph IV again. Very well, but in examining the debris, you found no evidence of contraband?" The colonel's distasteful expression told the room that he knew the answer, but only wanted it on the record.

But Roki paused a long time. Finally, he said, "No evidence, sir."

"Why do you hesitate?"

"Because I still suspect an illegality—without proof, I'm afraid."

This time, the colonel's personal feelings betrayed him in a snort of disgust. He shuffled his papers for a long time, then looked at the major who had accompanied the patrol. "Will you confirm Roki's testimony, major? Is it essentially truthful, as far as you know?"

The embarrassed officer glared at Roki in undisguised hatred. "For the record, sir—I think the commander behaved disgracefully and insensibly. The results of the stoppage of vitally needed supplies prove—"

"I didn't ask for a moral judgment!" Beth snapped. "I asked you to confirm what he has said here. Were the incidents as he described them?"

The major swallowed hard. "Yes, sir."

The colonel nodded. "Very well. I'll ask your opinions, gentlemen. Was there an infraction of regulations? Did Commander Roki behave as required by Space Code, or did he not? Yes or no, please. Major Tuli?"

"No direct infraction, sir, but—"

"No *buts!* Major Go'an?"

"Uh—no infraction, sir."

"I find myself in agreement." The colonel spoke directly at Dela's note pad. "The ultimate results of the incident were disastrous, indeed. And, Roki's action was unfortunate, ill-advised, and not as the Sixty Star Patrol would approve. Laws, codes, regulations are made for men, not men for regulations. Roki observed the letter of the law, but was perhaps forgetful of its spirit. However, no charge can be found against him. This investigating body recommends that he be temporarily grounded without prejudice, and given thorough physical and mental examinations before being returned to duty. That brings us to an end, gentlemen. Dela, you may go."

With another glare at the haughty Cophian, the girl stalked out of the room. Beth leaned back in his chair, while the majors saluted and excused themselves. His eyes kept Roki locked in his chair. When they were alone, Beth said:

"You have anything to say to me off the record?"

Roki nodded. "I can submit my resignation from the patrol through your office, can't I, sir?"

Beth smiled coldly. "I thought you'd do that, Roki." He opened a desk drawer and brought out a single sheet of paper. "I took the liberty of having it prepared for your signature. Don't misunderstand. I'm not urging you to resign, but we're prepared to accept it if you choose to do so. If you don't like this standard from, you may prepare your own."

The jet-eyed commander took the paper quickly and slashed his name quickly across the bottom. "Is this effective immediately, sir?"

"In this case, we can make it so."

"Thank you, sir."

"Don't regard it as a favor." The colonel witnessed the signature.

The Cophian could not be stung. "May I go now?"

Beth looked up, noticing with amusement that Roki— now a civilian—had suddenly dropped the "sir." And his eyes were no longer cold. They were angry, hurt, despairing.

"What makes you Cophians tick anyway?" he murmured thoughtfully.

Roki stood up. "I don't care to discuss it with you, colonel. I'll be going now."

"Wait, Roki." Beth frowned ominously to cover whatever he felt.

"I'm waiting."

"Up until this incident, I liked you, Roki. In fact, I told the general that you were the most promising young officer in my force."

"Kind of you," he replied tonelessly.

"And you could have been sitting at this desk, in a few years. You hoped to, I believe."

A curt nod, and a quick glance at Beth's shoulder insignia.

"You chose your career, and now you don't have it. I know what it means to you."

A tightening of the Cophian's jaw told the colonel that he wanted no sympathy, but Beth continued.

"Since this is the oldest, most established, most static planet in the Cluster, you're out of a job in a place where there's no work."

"That's none of your business, colonel," Roki said quietly.

"According to my culture's ethics it *is* my business," he bellowed. "Of course you Cophians think differently. But we're not quite so cold. Now you listen: I'm prepared to help you a little, although you're probably too pig-headed to accept. God knows, you don't deserve it anyway."

"Go on."

"I'm prepared to have a patrol ship take you to any planet in the galaxy. Name it, and we'll take you there." He paused. "All right, go ahead and refuse. Then get out."

Roki's thin face twitched for a moment. Then he nodded. "I'll accept. Take me to Sol III."

The colonel got his breath again slowly. He reddened and chewed his lip. "I did say galaxy, didn't I? I meant . . . well . . . you know we can't send a military ship outside the Sixty-Star Cluster."

Roki waited impassively, his dark eyes measuring the colonel.

"Why do you want to go *there?*"

"Personal reasons."

"Connected with the mercy ship incident?"

"The investigation is over."

Beth pounded his desk. "It's crazy, man! Nobody's been to Sol for a thousand years. No reason to go. Sloppy, decadent place. I never suspected *they'd* answer Jod VI's plea for surgibank supplies!"

"Why not? They were *selling* them."

"Of course. But I doubted that Sol still had ships, especially C-drive ships. Only contribution Sol ever made to the galaxy was to spawn the race of Man—if you believe that story. It's way out of contact with any interstellar nation. I just don't get it."

"Then you restrict your offer, colonel?" Roki's eyes mocked him.

Beth sighed. "No, no—I *said* it. I'll do it. But I can't send a patrol ship that far. I'll have to pay your way on a private vessel. We can find some excuse—exploration maybe."

Roki's eyes flickered sardonically. "Why not send a diplomatic delegation—to apologize to Sol for the blasting of their mercy ship."

"Uk! With YOU aboard?"

"Certainly. They won't know me."

Beth just stared at Roki as if he were of a strange species.

"You'll do it?" urged Roki.

"I'll think it over. I'll see that you get there, if you insist on going. Now get out of here. I've had enough of you, Roki."

The Cophian was not offended. He turned on his heel and left the office. The girl looked up from her filing cabinets as he came out. She darted ahead of him and blocked the doorway with her small tense body. Her face was a white mask of disgust, and she spoke between her teeth.

"How does it feel to murder ten thousand people and get away with it?" she hissed.

Roki looked at her face more closely and saw the racial characteristics of Jod VI—the slightly oversized irises of her yellow-brown eyes, the thin nose with flaring nostrils, the pointed jaw. Evidently some of her relatives had died in the disaster and she held him personally responsible. He had destroyed the help that was on its way to casualties.

"How does it feel?" she demanded, her voice going higher, and her hands clenching into weapons.

"Would you step aside please, Miss?"

A quick hand slashed out to rake his cheek with sharp nails. Pain seared his face. He did not move. Two bright stripes of blood appeared from his eye to the corner of his mouth. A drop trickled to the point of his chin and splattered down upon the girl's shoe.

"On my planet," he said, in a not unkindly tone, "when a woman insists on behaving like an animal, we assist her—by having her flogged naked in the public square. I see personal dignity is not so highly prized here. You do not regard it as a crime to behave like an alley cat?"

Her breath gushed out of her in a sound of rage, and she tore at the wounds again. Then, when he did nothing but look at her coldly, she fled.

Eli Roki, born to the nobility of Coph, dedicated to the service of the Sixty-Star Cluster, suddenly found himself something of an outcast. As he strode down the corridor away from Beth's office, he seemed to be walking into a thickening fog of desolation. He had no home now; for he had abdicated his hereditary rights on Coph in order to accept a commission with the SSC Patrol. That, too, was gone; and with it his career.

He had known from the moment he pressed the firing stud to blast the mercy freighter that unless the freighter proved to be a smuggler, his career would be forfeit. He was still morally certain that he had made no mistake. Had the freighter been carrying any other cargo, he would have been disciplined for *not* blasting it. And, if they had had nothing to hide, they would have stopped for inspection. Somewhere among Sol's planets lay the answer to the question—"What else was aboard besides the cargo of mercy?"

Roki shivered and stiffened his shoulders as he rode homeward in a heliocab. If the answer to the question were "Nothing," then according to the code of his planet, there was only one course left to follow. "The Sword of Apology" it was called.

He waited in his quarters for the colonel to fulfill his promise. On the following day, Beth called.

"I've found a Dalethian ship, Roki. Privately owned. Pilot's willing to fly you out of the Cluster. It's going as an observation mission—gather data on the Sol System. The commissioners vetoed the idea of sending a diplomatic delegation until we try to contact Solarians by high-C radio."

"When do I leave?"

"Be at the spaceport tonight. And good luck, son. I'm sorry all this happened, and I hope—"

"Yeah, thanks."

"Well—"

"Well?"

The colonel grunted and hung up. Ex-Commander

Roki gathered up his uniforms and went looking for a pawn shop. "Hock 'em, or sell 'em?" asked a bald man behind the counter. Then he peered more closely at Roki's face, and paused to glance at a picture on the front page of the paper. "Oh," he grunted, "you. You wanta sell 'em." With a slight sneer, he pulled two bills from his pocket and slapped them on the counter with a contemptuous take-it-or-leave-it stare. The clothing was worth at least twice as much. Roki took it after a moment's hesitation. The money just matched the price tag on a sleek, snub-nosed Multin automatic that lay in the display case.

"And three hundred rounds of ammunition," he said quietly as he pocketed the weapon.

The dealer sniffed. "It only takes one shot, bud—for what *you* need to do."

Roki thanked him for the advice and took his three hundred rounds.

He arrived at the spaceport before his pilot, and went out to inspect the small Dalethian freighter that would bear him to the rim of the galaxy. His face clouded as he saw the pitted hull and the glaze of fusion around the lips of the jet tubes. Some of the ground personnel had left a Geiger hanging on the stern, to warn wanderers to keep away. Its dial indicator was fluttering in the red. He carried it into the ship. The needle dropped to a safe reading in the control cabin, but there were dangerous spots in the reactor room. Angrily he went to look over the controls.

His irritation grew. The ship—aptly named the *Idiot* —was of ancient vintage, without the standard warning systems or safety devices, and with no armament other than its ion guns. The fifth dial of its position-indicator was calibrated only to one hundred thousand C's, and was redlined at ninety thousand. A modern service-ship, on the other hand, could have penetrated to a segment of five-space where light's velocity was constant at one hundred fifty thousand C's and could reach Sol in two months. The *Idiot* would need five or six, if it could make the trip at all. Roki dobted it. Under normal circumstances, he would hesitate to use the vessel even within the volume of the Sixty-Star Cluster.

He thought of protesting to Beth, but realized that the colonel had fulfilled his promise, and would do nothing more. Grumbling, he stowed his gear in the cargo hold, and settled down in the control room to doze in wait for the pilot.

A sharp whack across the soles of his boots brought him painfully awake. "Get your feet off the controls!" snapped an angry voice.

Roki winced and blinked at a narrow frowning face with a cigar clenched in its teeth. "And get out of that chair!" the face growled around its cigar.

His feet stung with pain. He hissed a snarl and bounded to his feet; grabbing a handful of the intruder's shirt-front, he aimed a punch at the cigar—then stayed the fist in midair. Something felt wrong about the shirt. Aghast, he realized there was a woman inside it. He let go and reddened. "I . . . I thought you were the pilot."

She eyed him contemptuously as she tucked in her shirt. "I am, Doc." She tossed her hat on the navigation desk, revealing a close-cropped head of dark hair. She removed the cigar from her face, neatly pinched out the fire, and filed the butt in the pocket of her dungarees for a rainy day. She had a nice mouth, with the cigar gone, but it was tight with anger.

"Stay out of my seat," she told him crisply, "and out of my hair. Let's get that straight before we start."

"This . . . this is *your* tub?" he gasped.

She stalked to a panel and began punching settings into the courser. "That's right. I'm Daleth Shipping Incorporated. Any comments?"

"You expect this wreck to make it to Sol?" he growled.

She snapped him a sharp, green-eyed glance. "Well listen to the free ride! Make your complaints to the colonel, fellow. I don't expect anything, except my pay. I'm willing to chance it. Why shouldn't you?"

"The existence of a fool is not necessarily a proof of the existence of two fools," he said sourly.

"If you don't like it, go elsewhere." She straightened and swept him with a clinical glance. "But as I understand it, *you* can't be too particular."

He frowned. "Are you planning to make *that* your business?"

"*Uh*-uh! You're nothing to me, fellow. I don't care *who* I haul, as long as it's legal. Now do you want a ride, or don't you?"

He nodded curtly and stalked back to find quarters. "Stay outa my cabin," she bellowed after him.

Roki grunted disgustedly. The pilot was typical of Daleth civilization. It was still a rough, uncouth planet with a thinly scattered population, a wild frontier, and growing pains. The girl was the product of a wildly expanding tough-fisted culture with little respect for authority. It occurred to him immediately that she might be thinking of selling him to the Solarian officials—as the man who blasted the mercy ship.

"Prepare to lift," came the voice of the intercom. "Two minutes before blast-off."

Roki suppressed an urge to scramble out of the ship and call the whole thing off. The rockets belched, coughed, and then hissed faintly, idling in wait for a command. Roki stretched out on his bunk, for some of these older ships were rather rough on blast-off. The hiss became a thunder, and the *Idiot* moved skyward—first slowly, then with a spurt of speed. When it cleared the atmosphere, there was a sudden lurch as it shed the now empty booster burners. There was a moment of dead silence, as the ship hovered without power. Then the faint shriek of the ion streams came to his ears—as the ion drive became useful in the vacuum of space. He glanced out the port to watch the faint streak of luminescence focus into a slender needle of high-speed particles, pushing the *Idiot* ever higher in a rush of acceleration.

He punched the intercom button. "Not bad, for a Dalethian," he called admiringly.

"Keep your opinions to yourself," growled Daleth Incorporated.

The penetration to higher C-levels came without subjective sensation. Roki knew it was happening when the purr from the reactor room went deep-throated and when the cabin lights went dimmer. He stared calmly out the port, for the phenomenon of penetration never ceased to thrill him.

The transition to high-C began as a blue-shift in the starlight. Distant, dull-red stars came slowly brighter, whiter—until they burned like myriad welding arcs in the black vault. They were not identical with the stars of the home continuum, but rather, projections of the same star-masses at higher C-levels of five-space, where the velocity of light was gradually increasing as the *Idiot* climbed higher in the C-component.

At last he had to close the port, for the starlight was becoming unbearable as its wave-length moved into the ultra-violet and the X-ray bands. He watched on a fluorescent viewing screen. The projective star-masses were flaring into supernovae, and the changing continuums seemed to be collapsing toward the ship in the blue-shift of the cosmos. As the radiant energy increased, the cabin became warmer, and the pilot set up a partial radiation screen.

At last the penetration stopped. Roki punched the intercom again. "What level are we on, Daleth?"

"Ninety thousand," she replied curtly.

Roki made a wry mouth. She had pushed it up to the red line without a blink. It was O.K.—if the radiation screens held out. If they failed to hold it, the ship would be blistered into a drifting dust cloud.

"Want me to navigate for you?" he called.

"I'm capable of handling my own ship," she barked.

"I'm aware of that. But I have nothing else to do. You might as well put me to work."

She paused, then softened a little. "O.K., come on forward."

She swung around in her chair as he entered the cabin, and for the first time he noticed that, despite the close-cropped hair and the dungarees and the cigar-smoking, she was quite a handsome girl—handsome, proud, and highly capable. Daleth, the frontier planet, bred a healthy if somewhat unscrupulous species.

"The C-maps are in that case," she said, jerking her thumb toward a filing cabinet. "Work out a course for maximum radiant thrust."

Roki frowned. "Why not a least-time course?"

She shook her head. "My reactors aren't too efficient. We need all the boost we can get from external energy. Otherwise we'll have to dive back down for fuel."

Worse and worse!—Roki thought as he dragged out the C-maps. Flying this boat to Sol would have been a feat of daring two centuries ago. Now, in an age of finer ships, it was a feat of idiocy.

Half an hour later, he handed her a course plan that would allow the *Idiot* to derive about half of its thrust

from the variations in radiation pressure from the roaring
inferno of the high-level cosmos. She looked it over without change of expression, then glanced at him curiously,
after noting the time.

"You're pretty quick," she said.

"Thank you."

"You're hardly stupid. Why did you pull such a stupid
boner?"

Roki stiffened. "I thought you planned to regard that
as none of your business."

She shrugged and began punching course-settings into
the courser. "Sorry, I forgot."

Still angry, he said, "I don't regard it as a boner. I'd do
it again."

She shrugged again and pretended a lack of interest.

"Space-smuggling could be the death of the galaxy,"
he went on. "That's been proven. A billion people once
died on Tau II because somebody smuggled in a load of
non-Tauian animals—for house pets. I did only what history has proven best."

"I'm trying to mind my own business," she growled,
eyeing him sourly.

Roki fell silent and watched her reshape the radiation
screen to catch a maximum of force from the flare of
energy that blazed behind them. Roki was not sure that
he wanted her to mind her own business. They would
have to bear each other's presence for several months,
and it would be nice to know how things stood.

"So you think it was a stupid boner," he continued at
last. "So does everyone else. It hasn't been very pleasant."

She snorted scornfully as she worked. "Where I come
from, we don't condemn fools. We don't need to. They
just don't live very long, not on Daleth."

"And I am a fool, by your code?"

"How should I know? If you live to a ripe old age and
get what you want, you probably aren't a fool."

And *that*, thought Roki, was the Dalethian golden rule.
If the universe lets you live, then you're doing all right.
And there was truth in it, perhaps. Man was born with
only one right—the right to a chance at proving his fitness. And that right was the foundation of every culture,
even though most civilized worlds tried to define "fitness"
in terms of cultural values. Where life was rough, it was
rated in terms of survival.

"I really don't mind talking about it," he said with some embarrassment. "I have nothing to hide."

"That's nice."

"Do you have a name—other than your firm name?"

"As far as you're concerned, I'm Daleth Incorporated." She gave him a suspicious look that lingered a while and became contemplative. "There's only one thing I'm curious about—why are you going to Sol?"

He smiled wryly. "If I told a Dalethian that, she would indeed think me a fool."

Slowly the girl nodded. "I see. I know of Cophian ethics. If an officer's blunder results in someone's death, he either proves that it was not a blunder or he cuts his throat—ceremonially, I believe. Will you do that?"

, Roki shrugged. He had been away from Coph a long time. He didn't know.

"A stupid custom," she said.

"It manages to drain off the fools, doesn't it? It's better than having society try them and execute them forcibly for their crimes. On Coph, a man doesn't need to be afraid of society. He needs only to be afraid of his own weakness. Society's function is to protect individuals against unfortunate accidents, but not against their own blunders. And when a man blunders, Coph simply excludes him from the protectorate. As an outcast, he sacrifices himself. It's not too bad a system."

"You can have it."

"Dalethian?"

"Yeah?"

"You have no personal anger against what I did?"

She frowned at him contemptuously. "Uh-uh! I judge no one. I judge no one unless I'm personally involved. Why are you worried about what others think?"

"In our more highly developed society," he said stiffly, "a man inevitably grows a set of thinking-habits called 'conscience.' "

"Oh—yeah." Her dull tone indicated a complete lack of interest.

Again Roki wondered if she would think of making a quick bit of cash by informing Solarian officials of his identity. He began a mental search for a plan to avoid such possible treachery.

They ate and slept by the ship's clock. On the tenth day, Roki noticed a deviation in the readings of the radiation-screen instruments. The shape of the screen shell was gradually trying to drift toward minimum torsion, and assume a spherical shape. He pointed it out to Daleth, and she quickly made the necessary readjustments. But the output of the reactors crept a notch higher as a result of the added drain. Roki wore an apprehensive frown as the flight progressed.

Two days later, the screen began creeping again. Once more the additional power was applied. And the reactor output needle hung in the yellow band of warning. The field-generators were groaning and shivering with threatening overload. Roki worked furiously to locate the trouble, and at last he found it. He returned to the control cabin in a cold fury.

"Did you have this ship pre-flighted before blast-off?" he demanded.

Her mouth fluttered with amusement as she watched his anger. "Certainly, commander."

He flushed at the worthless title. "May I see the papers?"

For a moment she hesitated, then fumbled in her pocket and displayed a folded pink paper.

"Pink!" he roared. "You had no business taking off!"

Haughtily, she read him the first line of the pre-flight report. " 'Base personnel disclaim any responsibility for accidents resulting from flight of Daleth Ship—' It doesn't say I can't take off."

"I'll see you banned from space!" he growled.

She gave him a look that reminded him of his current status. It was a tolerant, amused stare. "What's wrong, commander?"

"The synchronizers are out, that's all," he fumed. "Screen's getting farther and farther from resonance."

"So?"

"So the overload'll get worse, and the screen'll break down. You'll have to drop back down out of the C-component and get it repaired."

She shook her head. "We'll chance it like it is. I've always wanted to find out how much overload the reactor'll take."

Roki choked. There wasn't a chance of making it. "Are you a graduate space engineer?" he asked.

"No."

"Then you'd better take one's advice."

"Yours?"

"Yes."

"No! We're going on."

"Suppose I refuse to let you?"

She whirled quickly, eyes flashing. "I'm in command of my ship. I'm also armed. I suggest you return to your quarters, passenger."

Roki sized up the situation, measured the determination in the girl's eyes, and decided that there was only one thing to do. He shrugged and looked away, as if admitting her authority. She glared at him for a moment, but did not press her demand that he leave the control room. As soon as she glanced back at the instruments, Roki padded his rough knuckles with a handkerchief, selected a target at the back of her short crop of dark hair, and removed her objections with a short chopping blow to the head. "Sorry, friend," he murmured as he lifted her limp body out of the seat.

He carried her to her quarters and placed her on the bunk. After removing a small needle gun from her pocket, he left a box of headache tablets in easy reach, locked her inside, and went back to the controls. His fist was numb, and he felt like a heel, but there was no use arguing with a Dalethian. Clubbing her to sleep was the only way to avoid bloodier mayhem in which she might have emerged the victor—until the screen gave way.

The power-indication was threateningly high as Roki activated the C-drive and began piloting the ship downward through the fifth component. But with proper adjustments, he made the process analogous to freefall, and the power reading fell off slowly. A glance at the C-maps told him that the *Idiot* would emerge far beyond the limits of Sixty-Star Cluster. When it re-entered the continuum, it would be in the general volume of space controlled by another interstellar organization called The Viggern Federation. He knew little of its culture, but certainly it should have facilities for repairing a set of screen-synchronizers. He looked up its capitol planet, and began jetting toward it while the ship drifted downward in C. As he reached lower energy-levels, he cut out the screen altogether and went to look in on Daleth Incorporated who had made no sound for two hours.

He was surprised to see her awake and sitting up on

the bunk. She gave him a cold and deadly stare, but
displayed no rage. "I should've known better than to turn
my back on you."

"Sorry. You were going to—"

"Save it. Where are we?"

"Coming in on Tragor III."

"I'll have you jailed on Tragor III, then."

He nodded. "You *could* do that, but then you might
have trouble collecting my fare from Beth."

"That's all right."

"Suit yourself. I'd rather be jailed on your trumped-up
charges than be a wisp of gas at ninety-thousand C's."

"Trumped up?"

"Sure, the pink pre-flight. Any court will say that whatever happened was your own fault. You lose your authority if you fly pink, unless your crew signs a release."

"You a lawyer?"

"I've had a few courses in space law. But if you don't
believe me, check with the Interfed Service on Tragor III."

"I will. Now how about opening the door. I want out."

"Behave?"

She paused, then: "My promise wouldn't mean anything, Roki. I don't share your system of ethics."

He watched her cool green eyes for a moment, then
chuckled. "In a sense you *do*—or you wouldn't have said
that." He unlocked the cabin and released her, not trusting her, but realizing that the synchronizers were so bad
by now that she couldn't attempt to go on without repairs.
She could have no motive for turning on him—except
anger perhaps.

"My gun?" she said.

Again Roki hesitated. Then, smiling faintly, he handed
it to her. She took the weapon, sniffed scornfully, and
cocked it.

"Turn around, fool!" she barked.

Roki folded his arms across his chest, and remained
facing her. "Go to the devil," he said quietly.

Her fingers whitened on the trigger. Still the Cophian
failed to flinch, lose his smile, or move. Daleth Incorporated arched her eyebrows, uncocked the pistol, and returned it to her belt. Then she patted his cheek and
chuckled nastily. "Just watch yourself, commander. I
don't like you."

And he noticed, as she turned away, that she had a

"You are a well-traveled man, E Roki?" the bushy-browed man asked politely.

"Space has been my business."

"Then you need no warning about local customs." The captain bowed.

"I know enough to respect them and conform to them," Roki assured him. "That's a general rule. But I'm not familiar with Tragor III. Is there anything special I should know before we start out?"

"Your woman, E Roki. You might do well to inform her that she will have to wear a veil, speak to no man, and be escorted upon the streets at all times. Otherwise, she will be wise to remain on the ship, in her quarters."

Roki suppressed a grin. "I shall try to insure her good behavior."

The captain looked defensive. "You regard our customs as primitive?"

"Every society to its own tastes, captain. The wisdom of one society would be folly for another. Who is qualified to judge? Only the universe, which passes the judgment of survival on all peoples."

"Thank you. You are a wise traveler. I might explain that our purdah is the result of an evolutionary peculiarity. You will see for yourself, however."

"I can't *guarantee* my companion's behavior," Roki said before he went to join Daleth. "But I'll try my best to influence her."

Roki was grinning broadly as he went to the patrol vessel to wait. One thing was certain: the girl would have a rough time on Tragor if she tried to have him jailed for mutiny.

Her face reddened to forge-heat as he relayed the captain's warning.

"I shall do nothing of the sort," she said stiffly.

Roki shrugged. "You know enough to respect local customs."

"Not when they're personally humiliating!" She curled up on a padded seat in the visitor's room and began to pout. He decided to drop the subject.

Repairing the synchronizers promised to be a week-long job, according to the Tragorian inspector who accompanied the *Idiot* upon landing. "Our replacements are standardized, of course—within our own system. But parts for SSC ships aren't carried in stock. The synchronizers will have to be specially tailored."

"Any chance of rushing the job?"

"A week *is* rushing it."

"All right, we'll have to wait." Roki nudged the controls a bit, guiding the ship toward the landing site pointed out by the captain. Daleth was in her cabin, alone, to save herself embarrassment.

"May I ask a question about your mission, E Roki—or is it confidential in nature?"

Roki paused to think before answering. He would have to lie, of course, but he had to make it safe. Suddenly he chuckled. "I forgot for a moment that you weren't with Sixty-Star Cluster. So I'll tell you the truth. This is supposed to be an observation mission, officially—but actually, our superior sent us to buy him a holdful of a certain scarce commodity."

The captain grinned. Graft and corruption were apparently not entirely foreign to Tragor III. But then his grin faded into thoughtfulness. "On Sol's planets?"

Roki nodded.

"This scarce commodity—if I'm not too curious—is it surgibank supplies?"

Roki felt his face twitch with surprise. But he recovered from his shock in an instant. "Perhaps," he said calmly. He wanted to grab the man by the shoulders and shout a thousand questions, but he said nothing else.

The official squirmed in his seat for a time. "Does your federation buy many mercy cargoes from Sol?"

Roki glanced at him curiously. The captain was brimming with ill-concealed curiosity. Why?

"Occasionally, yes."

The captain chewed his lip for a moment. "Tell me," he blurted, "will the Solarian ships stop for your patrol inspections?"

Roki hesitated for a long time. Then he said, "I suppose that you and I could get together and share what we know about Sol without revealing any secrets of our own governments. Frankly, I, too, am curious about Sol."

The official, whose name was WeJan, was eager to accept. He scrawled a peculiar series of lines on a scrap of paper and gave it to Roki. "Show this to a heliocab driver. He will take you to my apartment. Would dinner be convenient?"

Roki said that it would.

The girl remained in her quarters when they landed. Roki knocked at the door, but she was either stubborn or asleep. He left the ship and stood for a moment on the ramp, staring at the hazy violet sky. Fine grit sifted against his face and stung his eyes.

"You will be provided goggles, suitable clothing, and an interpreter to accompany you during your stay," said WeJan as they started toward a low building.

But Roki was scarcely listening as he stared across the ramp. A thousand yards away was a yellow-starred mercy ship, bearing Solar markings. The most peculiar thing about it was the ring of guards that surrounded it. They apparently belonged to the ship, for their uniforms were different from those of the base personnel.

WeJan saw him looking. "Strange creatures, aren't they?" he whispered confidentially.

Roki had decided that in the long run he could gain more information by pretending to know more than he did. So he nodded wisely and said nothing. The mercy ship was too far away for him to decide whether the guards were human. He could make out only that they were bipeds. "Sometimes one meets strange ones all right. Do you know the Quinjori—from the other side of the galaxy?"

"No—no, I believe not, E Roki. Quinjori?"

"Yes. A very curious folk. Very curious indeed." He smiled to himself and fell silent. Perhaps, before his visit was over, he could trade fictions about the fictitious Quinjori for facts about the Solarians.

Roki met his interpreter in the spaceport offices, donned the loose garb of Tragor, and went to quibble with repair service. Still he could not shorten the promised-time on the new synchros. They were obviously stuck for a week on Tragor. He thought of trying to approach the Solarian ship, but decided that it would be better to avoid suspicion.

Accompanied by the bandy-legged interpreter, whose mannerisms were those of a dog who had received too many beatings, Roki set out for Polarin, the Tragorian capital, a few miles away. His companion was a small middle-aged man with a piping voice and flaring ears; Roki decided that his real job was to watch his alien charge for suspicious activities, for the little man was no expert linguist. He spoke two or three of the tongues used in the Sixty-Star Cluster, but not fluently. The Cophian decided to rely on the Esperanto of space, and let the interpreter translate it into native Tragorian wherever necessary.

"How would E Roki care to amuse himself?" the little man asked. "A drink? A pretty girl? A museum?"

Roki chuckled. "What do most of your visitors do while they're here?" He wondered quietly what, in particular, the *Solarian* visitors did. But it might not be safe to ask.

"Uh—that would depend on nationality, sir," murmured Pok. "The true-human foreigners often like to visit the Wanderer, an establishment which caters to their business. The evolved-human and the nonhuman visitors like to frequent The Court of Kings—a rather, uh, peculiar place." He looked at Roki, doubtfully, as if wondering about his biological status.

"Which is most expensive?" he asked, although he really didn't care. Because of the phony "observation mission papers," he could make Colonel Beth foot the bill.

"The Court of Kings is rather high," Pok said. "But so is the Wanderer."

"Such impartiality deserves a return. We will visit them both, E Pok. If it suits you."

"I am your servant, E Roki."

How to identify a Solarian without asking?—Roki wondered as they sat sipping a sticky, yeasty drink in the lounge of the Wanderer. The dimly lighted room was filled with men of all races—pygmies, giants, black, red, and brown. All appeared human, or nearly so. There were a few women among the crewmen, and most of them removed their borrowed veils while in the tolerant sanctuary of the Wanderer. The Tragorian staff kept stealing furtive glances at these out-system females, and the Cophian wondered about their covetousness.

"Why do you keep watching the strange women, E Pok?" he asked the interpreter a few minutes later.

The small man sighed. "Evidently you have not yet seen Tragorian women."

Roki had seen a few heavily draped figures on the street outside, clinging tightly to the arms of men, but there hadn't been much to look at. Still, Pok's hint was enough to give him an idea.

"You don't mean Tragor III is one of those places where evolution has pushed the sexes further apart?"

"I do," Pok said sadly. "The feminine I.Q. is seldom higher than sixty, the height is seldom taller than your jacket pocket, and the weight is usually greater than your own. As one traveler put it: 'short, dumpy, and dumb'. Hence, the Purdah."

"Because you don't like looking at them?"

"Not at all. Theirs is our standard of beauty. The purdah is because they are frequently too stupid to remember which man is their husband."

"Sorry I asked."

"Not at all," said Pok, whose tongue was being loosened by the yeasty brew. "It is our tragedy. We can bear it."

"Well, you've got it better than some planets. On Jevah, for instance, the men evolved into sluggish spidery little fellows, and the women are big husky brawlers."

"Ah yes. But Sol is the most peculiar of all, is it not?" said Pok.

"How do you mean?" Roki carefully controlled his voice and tried to look bored.

"Why, the Vamir, of course."

Because of the fact that Pok's eyes failed to move toward any particular part of the room, Roki concluded that there were no Solarians in the place. "Shall we visit the Court of Kings now, E Pok?" he suggested.

The small man was obviously not anxious to go. He murmured about ugly brutes, lingered over his drink, and gazed wistfully at a big dusky Sanbe woman. "Do you suppose she would notice me if I spoke to her?" the small interpreter asked.

"Probably. So would her five husbands. Let's go."

Pok sighed mournfully and came with him.

The Court of Kings catered to a peculiar clientele indeed; but not a one, so far as Roki could see, was completely inhuman. There seemed to be at least one common denominator to all intelligent life: it was bipedal and bimanual. Four legs was the most practical number for any animal on any planet, and it seemed that nature had nothing else to work with. When she decided to give intelligence to a species, she taught him to stand on his hind legs, freeing his forefeet to become tools of his intellect. And she usually taught him by making him use his hands to climb. As a Cophian biologist had said, "Life first tries to climb a tree to get to the stars. When it fails, it comes down and invents the high-C drive."

Again, Roki looked around for something that might be a Solarian. He saw several familiar species, some horned, some tailed, scaled, or heavily furred. Some stumbled and drooped as if Tragorian gravity weighted them down. Others bounced about as if floating free in space. One small creature, the native of a planet with an eight-hour rotational period, curled up on the table and fell asleep. Roki guessed that ninety per cent of the customers were of human ancestry, for at one time during the history of the galaxy, Man had sprung forth like a sudden blossom to inherit most of space. Some said they came from Sol III, but there was no positive evidence.

As if echoing his thoughts, Pok suddenly grunted, "I will never believe we are descended from those surly creatures."

Roki looked up quickly, wondering if the small interpreter was telepathic. But Pok was sneering toward the doorway. The Cophian followed his tipsy gaze and saw a man enter. The man was distinguished only by his height and by the fact that he appeared more human, in the classical sense, than most of the other customers. He wore a uniform—maroon jacket and gray trousers—and it matched the ones Roki had seen from a distance at the spaceport.

So this was a Solarian. He stared hard, trying to take in much at once. The man wore a short beard, but there seemed to be something peculiar about the jaw. It was—predatory, perhaps. The skull was massive, but plump and rounded like a baby's, and covered with sparse yellow fur. The eyes were quick and sharp, and seemed almost to leap about the room. He was at least seven feet tall, and there was a look of savagery about him that caused the Cophian to tense, as if sensing an adversary.

"What is it you don't like about them?" he asked, without taking his eyes from the Solarian.

"Their sharp ears for one thing," whispered Pok as the Solarian whirled to stare toward their table. "Their nasty tempers for another."

"Ah? Rage reactions show biologic weakness," said the Cophian in a mild tone, but as loud as the first time.

The Solarian, who had been waiting for a seat at the bar, turned and stalked straight toward them. Pok whimpered. Roki stared at him cooly. The Solarian loomed over them and glared from one to the other. He seemed to decide that Pok was properly cowed, and he turned his fierce eyes on the ex-patrolman.

"Would you like to discuss biology, manthing?" he growled like distant thunder. His speaking exposed his teeth—huge white chisels of heavy ivory. They were not regressed toward the fanged stage, but they suggested, together with the massive jaw, that nature might be working toward an efficient bone-crusher.

Roki swirled his drink thoughtfully. "I don't know you, Bristleface," he murmured. "But if your biology bothers you, I'd be glad to discuss it with you."

He watched carefully for the reaction. The Solarian went gray-purple. His eyes danced with fire, and his slit mouth quivered as if to bare the strong teeth. Just as he seemed about to explode, the anger faded—or rather, settled in upon itself to brood. "This is beneath me," the eyes seemed to be saying. Then he laughed cordially.

"My apologies. I thought to share a table with you."

"Help yourself."

The Solarian paused. "Where are you from, manthing?"

Roki also paused. They might have heard that a Cophian commander blasted one of their ships. Still he didn't care to be caught in a lie. "Sixty-Star Cluster," he grunted.

"Which sun?" The Solarian's voice suggested that he was accustomed to being answered instantly.

Roki glowered at him. "Information for information, fellow. And I don't talk to people who stand over me." He pointedly turned to Pok. "As we were saying—"

"I am of Sol," growled the big one.

"Fair enough. I am of Coph."

The giant's brows lifted slightly. "Ah, yes." He inspected Roki curiously and sat down. The chair creaked a warning. "Perhaps that explains it."

"Explains what?" Roki frowned ominously. He disliked overbearing men, and his hackles were rising. There was something about this fellow—

"I understand that Cophians are given to a certain ruthlessness."

Roki pretended to ponder the statement while he eyed the big man coldly. "True, perhaps. It would be dangerous for you to go to Coph, I think. You would probably be killed rather quickly."

The angry color reappeared, but the man smiled politely. "A nation of duelists, I believe, military in character, highly disciplined. Yes? They sometimes serve in the Sixty-Star Forces, eh?"

The words left no doubt in Roki's mind that the Solarian knew who had blasted their ship and why. But he doubted that the man had guessed his identity.

"I know less of your world, Solarian."

"Such ignorance is common. We are regarded as the galactic rurals, so to speak. We are too far from your dense star cluster." He paused. "You knew us once. We planted you here. And I feel sure you will know us again." He smiled to himself, finished his drink, and arose. "May we meet again, Cophian."

Roki nodded and watched the giant stride away. Pok was breathing asthmatically and picking nervously at his nails. He let out a sigh of relief with the Solarian's departure.

Roki offered the frightened interpreter a stiff drink, and then another. After two more, Pok swayed dizzily, then fell asleep across the table. Roki left him there. If Pok were an informer, it would be better to keep him out of the meeting with the patrol officer, Captain WeJan.

He hailed a cab and gave the driver the scrap of paper. A few minutes later, he arrived before a small building in the suburbs. WeJan's name was on the door—written in the space-tongue—but the officer was not at home. Frowning, he tried the door; locked. Then, glancing back toward the street, he caught a glimpse of a man standing in the shadows. It was a Solarian.

Slowly, Roki walked across the street. "Got a match, Bristleface?" he grunted.

In the light of triple-moons, he saw the giant figure swell with rage. The man looked quickly up and down the street. No one was watching. He emitted a low animal-growl, exposing the brutal teeth. His arms shot out to grasp the Cophian's shoulders, dragging him close.

Roki gripped the Multin automatic in his pocket and struggled to slip free. The Solarian jerked him up toward the bared teeth.

His throat about to be crushed, Roki pulled the trigger. There was a dull *chug*. The Solarian looked surprised. He released Roki and felt of his chest. There was no visible wound. Then, within his chest, the incendiary needle flared to incandescent heat. The Solarian sat down in the street. He breathed a frying sound. He crumpled. Roki left hastily before the needle burned its way out of the body.

He hadn't meant to kill the man, and it had been in self-defense, but he might have a hard time proving it. He hurried along back alleys toward the spaceport. If only they could leave Tragor immediately!

What had happened to WeJan? Bribed, beaten, or frightened away. Then the Solarians *did* know who he was and where he was going. There were half a dozen men around the spaceport who knew—and the information would be easy to buy. Pok had known that he was to meet with WeJan, and the Solarian had evidently been sent to watch the captain's quarters. It wasn't going to be easy now—getting to Sol III and landing.

What manner of creatures were these, he wondered. Men who supplied mercy cargoes to the galactic nations —as if charity were the theme and purpose of their culture—yet who seemed as arrogant as the warriors of some primitive culture whose central value was brutal power? What did they really want here? The Solarian had called him "manthing" as if he regarded the Cophian as a member of some lesser species.

The Solarians were definitely different. Roki could see it. Their heads were plump and soft like a baby's, hinting of some new evolutionary trend—a brain that could continue growing, perhaps. But the jaws, the teeth, the quick tempers, and the hypersensitive ears—what sort of animal developed such traits? There was only one answer: a nocturnal predator with the instincts of a lion. "You shall get to know us again," the man had said.

It spelled politico-galactic ambitions. And it hinted at something else—something that made the Cophian shiver, and shy away from dark shadows as he hurried shipward.

Daleth Incorporated was either asleep or out. He checked at the ship, then went to the Administration

bump on her head to prove it. He wondered how much the bump would cost him before it was over. Treachery on Sol, perhaps.

The pilot called Tragor III and received instructions to set an orbital course to await inspection. All foreign ships were boarded before being permitted to land. A few hours later, a small patrol ship winged close and grappled to the hull. Roki went to manipulate the locks.

A captain and two assistants came through. The inspector was a young man with glasses and oversized ears. His eyebrows were ridiculously bushy and extended down on each side to his cheekbones. The ears were also filled with yellow brush. Roki recognized the peculiarities as local evolutionary tendencies; for they were shared also by the assistants. Tragor III evidently had an exceedingly dusty atmosphere.

The captain nodded a greeting and requested the ship's flight papers. He glanced at the pink pre-flight, clucked to himself, and read every word in the dispatcher's forms. "Observation flight? To Sol?" He addressed himself to Roki, using the interstellar Esperanto.

The girl answered. "That's right. Let's get this over with."

The captain gave her a searing, head-to toe glance. "Are you the ship's owner, woman?"

Daleth Incorporated contained her anger with an effort. "I am."

The captain told her what a Tragorian thought of it by turning aside from her, and continuing to address Roki as if he were ship's skipper. "Please leave the ship while we fumigate and inspect. Wohr will make you comfortable in the patrol vessel. You will have to submit to physical examination—a contagion precaution."

Roki nodded, and they started out after the assistant. As they entered the corridor, he grinned at Daleth, and received a savage kick in the shin for his trouble.

"Oops, sorry!" she muttered.

"Oh—one moment, sir," the captain called after them. "May I speak to you a moment—"

They both stopped and turned.

"Privately," the captain added.

The girl marched angrily on. Roki stepped back in the cabin and nodded.

Building to inquire about her. The clerk seemed embarrassed.

"Uh . . . E Roki, she departed from the port about five."

"You've heard nothing of her since?"

"Well . . . there was a call from the police agency, I understand." He looked apologetic. "I assure you I had nothing to do with the matter."

"Police! What . . what's wrong, man?"

"I hear she went unescorted and unveiled. The police are holding her."

"How long will they keep her?"

"Until some gentleman signs for her custody."

"You mean I have to sign for her?"

"Yes, sir."

Roki smiled thoughtfully. "Tell me, young man—are Tragorian jails particularly uncomfortable?"

"I wouldn't know, personally," the clerk said stiffly. "I understand they conform to the intergalactic 'Code of Humanity' however."

"Good enough," Roki grunted. "I'll leave her there till we're ready to go."

"Not a bad idea," murmured the clerk, who had evidently encountered the cigar-chewing lady from Daleth.

Roki was not amused by the reversal of positions, but it seemed as good a place as any to leave her for safekeeping. If the Solarians became interested in him, they might also notice his pilot.

He spent the following day watching the Sol ship, and waiting fatalistically for the police to come and question him about the Solarian's death. But the police failed to come. A check with the news agencies revealed that the man's body had not even been found. Roki was puzzled. He had left the giant lying in plain sight where he had fallen. At noon, the Solarian crew came bearing several lead cases slung from the centers of carrying poles. They wore metal gauntlets and handled the cases cautiously. Roki knew they contained radioactive materials. So that was what they purchased with their surgibank supplies— nuclear fuels.

Toward nightfall, they loaded two large crates aboard. He noted the shape of the crates, and decided that one of them contained the body of the man he had killed. Why didn't they want the police to know? Was it possible that they wanted him free to follow them?

The Sol-ship blasted-off during the night. He was surprised to find it gone, and himself still unmolested by morning. Wandering around the spaceport, he saw WeJan, but the man had developed a sudden lapse of memory. He failed to recognize the Cophian visitor. With the Solarians gone, Roki grew bolder in his questioning.

"How often do the Solarians visit you?" he inquired of a desk clerk at Administration.

"Whenever a hospital places an order, sir. Not often. Every six months perhaps."

"That's all the traffic they have with Tragor?"

"Yes, sir. This is our only interstellar port."

"Do the supplies pass through your government channels?"

The clerk looked around nervously. "Uh, no sir. They refuse to deal through óur government. They contact their customers directly. The government lets them because the supplies are badly needed."

Roki stabbed out bluntly. "What do you think of the Solarians?"

The clerk looked blank for a moment, then chuckled. "I don't know, myself. But if you want a low opinion, ask at the spaceport cafe."

"Why? Do they cause trouble there?"

"No, sir. They bring their own lunches, so to speak. They eat and sleep aboard ship, and won't spend a thin galak around town."

Roki turned away and went back to the *Idiot*. Somewhere in his mind, an idea was refusing to let itself be believed. A mercy ship visited Tragor every six months. Roki had seen the scattered, ruined cargo of such a ship, and he had estimated it at about four thousand pints of blood, six thousand pounds of frozen bone, and seven thousand pounds of various replaceable organs and tissues. That tonnage in itself was not so startling, but if Sol III supplied an equal amount twice annually to even a third of the twenty-eight thousand civilized worlds in the galaxy, a numbing question arose: where did they get their raw material? Surgibank supplies were normally obtained by contributions from accident victims who lived long enough to voluntarily contribute their undamaged organs to a good cause.

Charitable organizations tried to secure pledges from men in dangerous jobs, donating their bodies to the planet's surgibank in the event of death. But no man felt easy about signing over his kidneys or his liver to the bank, and such recruiters were less popular than hangmen or life insurance agents. Mercy supplies were quite understandably scarce.

The grim question lingered in Roki's mind: where did the Sol III traders find between three and five million healthy accident victims annually? Perhaps they made the accidents themselves, accidents very similar to those occurring at the end of the chute in the slaughterhouse. He shook his head, refusing to believe it. No planet's population, however terrorized by its rulers, could endure such a thing without generating a sociological explosion that would make the world quiver in its orbit. There was a limit to the endurance of tyranny.

He spent the rest of the week asking innocent questions here and there about the city. He learned nearly nothing. The Solarians came bearing their peculiar cargo, sold it quickly at a good price, purchased fissionable materials, and blasted-off without a civil word to anyone. Most men seemed nervous in their presence, perhaps because of their bulk and their native arrogance.

When the base personnel finished installing the synchronizers, he decided the time had come to secure Daleth Incorporated from the local jail. Sometimes he had chided himself for leaving her there after the Solarians had blasted-off, but it seemed to be the best place to keep the willful wench out of trouble. Belatedly, as he rode toward the police station, he wondered what sort of mayhem she would attempt to commit on his person for leaving her to fume in a cell. His smile was rueful as he marched in to pay her fine. The man behind the desk frowned sharply.

"Who did you say?" he grunted.

"The foreign woman from the Dalethian Ship."

The officer studied his records. "Ah, yes—Talewa Walkeka the name?"

Roki realized he didn't know her name. She was still Daleth Incorporated. "From the Daleth Ship," he insisted.

"Yes. Talewa Walkeka—she was released into the custody of Eli Roki on twoday of last spaceweek."

"That's imposs—" Roki choked and whitened. "I am
Eli Roki. Was the man a Solarian?"

"I don't recall."

Why don't you? Didn't you ask him for identification?"

"Stop bellowing, please," said the official coldly. "And
get your fists off my desk."

The Cophian closed his eyes and tried to control himself. "Who is responsible for this?"

The officer failed to answer.

"You are responsible!"

"I cannot look out for all the problems of all the foreigners who—"

"Stop! You have let her die."

"She is only a female."

Roki straightened. "Meet me at any secluded place of
your choice and I will kill you with any weapon of your
choice."

The official eyed him coldly, then turned to call over
his shoulder. "Sergeant, escort this barbarian to his ship
and see that he remains aboard for the rest of his visit."

The Cophian went peacefully, realizing that violence
would gain him nothing but the iron hospitality of a cell.
Besides, he had only himself to blame for leaving her
there. It was obvious to him now—the contents of the
second crate the Solarians had carried aboard consisted
of Talewa Walkeka, lately of Daleth and high-C. Undoubtedly they had taken her alive. Undoubtedly she was
additional bait to bring him on to Sol. Why did they want
him to come? *I'll oblige them and find out for myself,* he
thought.

The ship was ready. The bill would be sent back to
Beth. He signed the papers, and blasted off as soon as
possible. The lonely old freighter crept upward into the
fifth component like a struggling old vulture, too ancient
to leave its sunny lair. But the snychros were working perfectly, and the screen held its shape when the ascent
ceased just below red-line level. He chose an evasive
course toward Sol and began gathering velocity.

Then he fed a message into the coder, to be broadcast
back toward the Sixty-Star Cluster: *Pilot abducted by
Solarians; evidence secured to indicate that Solarian
mercy-merchandise is obtained through genocide.* He recorded the coded message on tape and let it feed con-

tinuously into the transmitters, knowing that the carrier made him a perfect target for homing devices, if anyone chose to silence him.

And he knew it was a rather poor bluff. The message might or might not be picked up. A listening ship would have to be at the same C-level to catch the signal. Few ships, save the old freighters, lingered long at ninety-thousand C's. But if the Solarians let him live long enough, the message would eventually be picked up—but not necessarily believed. The most he could hope for was to arouse curiosity about Sol. No one would care much about the girl's abduction, or about his own death. Interstellar federations never tried to protect their citizens beyond the limits of their own volume of space. It would be an impossible task.

Unless the Solarians were looking for him however, they themselves would probably not intercept the call. Their ships would be on higher C. And since they knew he was coming, they had no reason to search for him. At his present velocity and energy-level, he was four months from Sol. The mercy ship on a higher level, would probably reach Sol within three weeks. He was a sparrow chasing a smug hawk.

But now there was more at stake than pride or reputation. He had set out to clear himself of a bad name, but now his name mattered little. If what he suspected were true, then Sol III was a potential threat to every world in the galaxy. Again he remembered the Solarian's form of address—"manthing"—as if a new race had arisen to inherit the places of their ancestors. If so, the new race had a right to bid for survival. And the old race called Man had a right to crush it if he could. Such was the dialectic of life.

Four months in the solitary confinement of a spaceship was enough to unnerve any man, however well-conditioned to it. He paced restlessly in his cell, from quarters to control to reactor room, reading everything that was aboard to read and devouring it several times. Sometimes he stopped to stare in Daleth's doorway. Her gear was still in the compartment, gathering dust. A pair of boots in the corner, a box of Dalethia cigars on the shelf.

"Maybe she has a book or two," he said once, and entered. He opened the closet and chuckled at the rough masculine clothing that hung there. But among the coarse fabrics was a wisp of pale green silk. He parted the dungarees to stare at the frail feminine frock, nestled toward the end and half-hidden like a suppressed desire. For a moment he saw her in it, strolling along the cool avenues of a Cophian city. But quickly he let the dungarees fall back, slammed the door, and stalked outside, feeling ashamed. He never entered again.

The loneliness was overpowering. After three months, he shut off the transmitters and listened on the space-frequencies for the sound of a human voice. There was nothing except the occasional twittering of a coded message. Some of them came from the direction of Sol.

Why were they letting him come without interference? Why had they allowed him to transmit the message freely? Perhaps they wanted him as a man who knew a great deal about the military and economic resources of the Sixty-Star Cluster, information they would need if they had high ambitions in space. And perhaps the message no longer mattered, if they had already acquired enough nuclear materials for their plans.

After a logical analysis of the situation, he hit upon a better answer. Their ships didn't have the warp-locking devices that permitted one ship to slip into a parallel C with an enemy and stay with that enemy while it maneuvered in the fifth component. The Solarians had proven that deficiency when the "mercy ship" had tried to escape him by evasive coursing. If their own ships were equipped with the warp lockers, they would have known better than to try. They wanted such equipment. Perhaps they thought that the *Idiot* possessed it, or that he could furnish them with enough information to let them build it.

After several days of correlating such facts as he already knew, Roki cut on his transmitters, fanned the beam down to a narrow pencil, and directed it toward Sol. "Blind Stab from Cluster-Ship *Idiot*," he called. "Any Sol Ship from *Idiot*. I have information to sell in exchange for the person of Talewa Walkeka. Acknowledge, please."

He repeated the message several times, and expected to wait a few days for an answer. But the reply came within three hours, indicating that a ship had been hovering just ahead of him, beyond the range of his own outmoded detectors.

"Cluster-Ship from Sol Seven," crackled the loud-speaker. "Do you wish to land on our planet? If so, please prepare to be boarded. One of our pilots will take you in. You are approaching our outer patrol zone. If you refuse to be boarded, you will have to turn back. Noncooperative vessels are destroyed upon attempting to land. Over."

There was a note of amusement in the voice. They knew he wouldn't turn back. They had a hostage. They were inviting him to surrender but phrasing the invitation politely.

Roki hesitated. Why had the man said—"destroyed upon attempting to land?" After a moment's thought, he realized that it was because they could not destroy a ship while manuevering in the fifth component. They could not even stay in the same continuum with it, unless they had the warp-locking devices. A vague plan began forming in his mind.

"I agree conditionally. Do you have Talewa Walkeka aboard? If so, prove it by asking her to answer the following request in her own voice: 'List the garments contained in the closet of her quarters aboard this ship.' If this is accomplished satisfactorily, then I'll tentatively assume intentions are not hostile. Let me remind you, however, that while we are grappled together, I can rip half your hull off by hitting my C-drive—unless you're equipped with warp-locking devices."

That should do it, he thought. With such a warning, they would make certain that they had him aboard their own ship as a captive before they made any other move. And he would do his best to make it easy for them. Two or three hours would pass before he could expect an answer, so he began work immediately, preparing to use every means at his disposal to make a booby trap of the *Idiot*, and to set the trap so that only his continued well-being would keep it from springing.

The *Idiot's* stock of spare parts was strictly limited, as he had discovered previously. There were a few spare selsyns, replacement units for the calculator and courser, radio and radar parts, control-mechanisms for the reactors, and an assortment of spare instruments and detectors. He augmented this stock by ruthlessly tearing into the calculator and taking what he needed.

He was hard at work when the answer came from the

Sol ship. It was Daleth's voice, crisp and angry, saying, "Six pair of dungarees, a jacket, a robe, and a silk frock. Drop dead, Roki."

The Solarian operator took over. "Expect a meeting in six hours. In view of your threat, we must ask that you stand in the outer lock with the hatch open, so that we may see you as we grapple together. Please acknowledge willingness to co-operate."

Roki grinned. They wanted to make certain that he was nowhere near the controls. He gave them a grumbling acknowledgment and returned to his work, tearing into the electronic control-circuits, the radio equipment, the reaction-rate limiters, and the controls of the C-drive. He wove a network of inter-dependency throughout the ship, running linking-circuits from the air-lock mechanisms to the reactors, and from the communication equipment to the C-drive. Gradually the ship became useless as a means of transportation. The jets were silent. He set time clocks to activate some of the apparatus, and keyed other equipment by relays set to trip upon the occurrence of various events.

It was not a difficult task, nor a long one. He added nothing really new. For example, it was easy to remove the wires from the air lock indicator lamp and feed their signal into a relay section removed from the calculator, a section which would send a control pulse to the reactors if the air locks were opened twice. The control pulse, if it came, would push the units past the red line. The relay sections were like single-task robots, set to obey the command: "If *this* happens, then push *that* switch."

When he was finished, the six hours were nearly gone. Pacing restlessly, he waited for them to come. Then, noticing a sudden flutter on the instruments, he glanced out to see the dark hulk slipping through his radiation screen. It came to a stop a short distance away.

Roki started the timers he had set, then donned a pressure suit. Carrying a circuit diagram of the changes he had wrought, he went to stand in the outer lock. He held open the outer hatch. The beam of a searchlight stabbed out to hold him while the Sol Ship eased closer. He could see another suited figure in its lock, calling guidance to the pilot. Roki glanced up at his own grapples; they were already energized and waiting for something to which they could cling.

The ships came together with a rocking jerk as both sets of grapples caught and clung. Roki swung himself across a gravityless space, then stood facing the burly figure of the Solarian. The man pushed him into the next lock and stepped after him.

"Search him for weapons," growled a harsh voice as Roki removed his helmet. "And get the boarding party through the locks."

"If you do that, you'll blow both ships to hell," the Cophian commented quietly. "The hatches are rigged to throw the reactors past red line."

The commander, a sharp-eyed oldster with a massive bald skull, gave him a cold stare that slowly became a sneer. "Very well, we can cut through the hull."

Roki nodded. "You can, but don't let any pressure escape. The throttles are also keyed to the pressure gauge."

The commander reddened slightly. "Is there anything else?"

"Several things." Roki handed him the circuit diagram. "Have your engineer study this. Until he gets the idea, anything you do may be dangerous, like trying to pull away from my grapples. I assure you we're either permanently grappled together, or permanently dead."

The Solarian was apparently his own engineer. He stared at the schematic while another relieved Roki of his weapon. There were four of them in the cabin. Three were armed and watching him carefully. He knew by their expressions that they considered him to be of a lesser species. And he watched them communicate silently among themselves by a soundless language of facial twitches and peculiar nods. Once the commander looked up to ask a question.

"When will this timer activate this network?"

Roki glanced at his watch. "In about ten minutes. If the transmitter's periodic signals aren't answered in the correct code, the signals serve to activate C-drive."

"I see that," he snapped. He glanced at a burly assistant. "Take him out. Skin him—from the feet up. He'll give you the code."

"I'll give it to you now," Roki offered calmly.

The commander showed faint surprise. "Do so then."

"The Cophian multiplication tables is the code. My

transmitter will send a pair of Cophian numbers every two minutes. If you fail to supply the product within one second, a relay starts the C-drive. Since you can't guarantee an exactly simultaneous thrust, there should be quite a crash."

"Very well, give us your Cophian number symbols."

"Gladly. But they won't help you."

"Why not?"

"Our numbers are to the base eighteen instead of base ten. You couldn't react quickly enough unless you've been using them since childhood."

The Solarian's lips pulled back from his heavy teeth and his jaw muscles began twitching. Roki looked at his watch.

"You have seven minutes to get your transmitter set up, with me at the key. We'll talk while I keep us intact."

The commander hesitated, then nodded to one of the guards who promptly left the room.

"Very well, manthing, we will set it up temporarily." He paused to smile arrogantly. "You have much to learn about our race. But you have little time in which to learn it."

"What do you mean?"

"Just this. This transmitter—and the whole apparatus—will be shut down after a certain period of time."

Roki stiffened. "Just how do you propose to do it?"

"Fool! By waiting until the signals stop. You obviously must have set a time limit on it. I would guess a few hours at the most."

It was true, but he had hoped to avoid mentioning it. The power to the control circuits would be interrupted after four hours, and the booby trap would be deactivated. For if he hadn't achieved his goal by then, he meant to neglect a signal during the last half-hour and let the C-ward lurch tear them apart. He nodded slowly.

"You're quiet right. You have four hours in which to surrender your ship into my control. Maybe. I'll send the signals until I decide you don't mean to co-operate. Then—" He shrugged.

The Solarian gave a command to his aides. They departed in different directions. Roki guessed that they had

"She is a mere incidental," he growled, fearful of choking on the words. "The price is surrender."

Hulgruv laughed heartily. It was obvious he had other plans. "Why do you deem us your enemy?"

"You heard the accusation I beamed back to my Cluster."

"Certainly. We ignored it, directly. Indirectly we made a fool of you by launching another, uh, mercy ship to your system. The cargo was labeled as to source, and the ship made a point of meeting one of your patrol vessels. It stopped for inspection. You're less popular at home than ever." He grinned. "I suggest you return to Sol with us. Help us develop the warp locks."

Roki hesitated. "You say the ship *stopped for inspection?*"

"Certainly."

"Wasn't it inconvenient? Changing your diet, leaving your 'livestock' at home—so our people wouldn't know you for what you really are."

Hulgruv stiffened slightly, then nodded. "Good guess."

"Cannibal!"

"Not at all. I am not a man."

They stared fixedly at one another. The Cophian felt the clammy cloak of hate creeping about him. The tone from the speaker suddenly stopped. A moment of dead silence. Roki leaned back in his chair.

"I'm not going to answer the first signal."

The commander glanced through the doorway and jerked his head. A moment later, Talewa Walkeka stepped proudly into the room, escorted by a burly guard. She gave him an icy glance and said nothing.

"Daleth—"

She made a noise like an angry cat and sat where the guard pushed her. They waited. The first signal suddenly screeched from the receiver: two series of short bleats of three different notes.

Involuntarily his hand leaped to the key. He bleated back the answering signal.

Daleth wore a puzzled frown. "Ilgen times ufneg is hork-segan," she muttered in translation.

A slow grin spread across Hulgruv's heavy face. He turned to look at the girl. "You're trained in the Cophian number system?"

"Don't answer that!" Roki bellowed.

"She *has* answered it, manthing. Are you aware of what your friend is doing, female?"

She shook her head. Hulgruv told her briefly. She frowned at Roki, shook her head, and stared impassively at the floor. Apparently she was either drugged or had learned nothing about the Solarians to convince her that they were enemies of the galaxy.

"Tell me, Daleth. Have they been feeding you well?"
She hissed at him again. "Are you crazy—"

Hulgruv chuckled. "He is trying to tell you that we are cannibals. Do you believe it?"

Fright appeared in her face for an instant, then disbelief. She stared at the commander, saw no guilt in his expression. She looked scorn at Roki.

"Listen, Daleth! That's why they wouldn't stop. Human livestock aboard. One look in their holds and we would have known, seen through their guise of mercy, recognized them as self-styled supermen, guessed their plans for galactic conquest. They breed their human cattle on their home planet and make a business of selling the parts. Their first weapon is infiltration into our confidence. They knew that if we gained an insight into their bloodthirsty culture, we would crush them."

"You're insane, Roki!" she snapped.

"No! Why else would they refuse to stop? Technical secrets? Baloney! Their technology is still inferior to ours. They carried a cargo of hate, our hate, riding with them unrecognized. They couldn't afford to reveal it."

Hulgruv laughed uproariously. The girl shook her head slowly at Roki, as if pitying him.

"It's true, I tell you! I guessed, sure. But it was pretty obvious they were taking their surgibank supplies by murder. And they contend they're not men. They guard their ships so closely, live around them while in port. And he admitted it to me."

The second signal came. Roki answered it, then began ignoring the girl. She didn't believe him. Hulgruv appeared amused. He hummed the signals over to himself —*without mistake*.

"You're using polytonal code for challenge, monotonal for reply. That makes it harder to learn."

The Cophian caught his breath. He glanced at the Solarian's huge, bald braincase. "You hope to learn some

three or four hundred sounds—and sound-combinations
within the time I allow you?"

"We'll see."

Some note of contempt in Hulgruv's voice gave Roki
warning.

"I shorten my ultimatum to one hour! Decide by then.
Surrender, or I stop answering. Learn it, if you can."

"He can, Roki," muttered Daleth. "They can memorize
a whole page at a glance."

Roki keyed another answer. "I'll cut it off if he tries it."

The commander was enduring the tension of the stale-
mate superbly. "Ask yourself, Cophian," he grunted with
a smile, "what would you gain by destroying the ship—
and yourself? We are not important. If we're destroyed,
our planet loses another gnat in space, nothing more. Do
you imagine we are incapable of self-sacrifice?"

Roki found no answer. He set his jaw in silence and
answered the signals as they came. He hoped the bluff
would win, but now he saw that Hulgruv would let him
destroy the ship. And—if the situation were reversed,
Roki knew that he would do the same. He had mistak-
enly refused to concede honor to an enemy. The commander seemed to sense his quiet dismay, and he leaned
forward to speak softly.

"We are a new race, Roki—grown out of man. We
have abilities of which you know nothing. It's useless to
fight us. Ultimately, your people will pass away. Or become stagnant. Already it has happened to man on
Earth."

"Then—there *are two* races on Earth."

"Yes, of course. Did apes pass away when man appeared? The new does not replace the old. It adds to it,
builds above it. The old species is the root of the new
tree."

"Feeding it," the Cophian grunted bitterly.

He noticed that Talewa was becoming disturbed. Her
eyes fluttered from one to the other of them.

"That was inevitable, manthing. There are no other
animal foodstuffs on Earth. Man exhausted his planet,
overpopulated it, drove lesser species into extinction. He
spent the world's resources getting your ancestors to the
denser star-clusters. He saw his own approaching stag-
nation on Earth. And, since Sol is near the rim of the

galaxy, with no close star-neighbors, he realized he could never achieve a mass-exodus into space. He didn't have the C-drive in its present form. The best he could do was a field-cancellation drive."

"But that's the heart of the C-drive."

"True. But he was too stupid to realize what he had. He penetrated the fifth component and failed to realize what he had done. His ships went up to five-hundred C's or so, spent a few hours there by the ship's clock, and came down to find several years had passed on Earth. They never got around that time-lag."

"But that's hardly more than a problem in five-space navigation!"

"True again. But they still thought of it in terms of field-cancellation. They didn't realize they'd actually left the four-space continuum. They failed to see the blue-shift as anything more than a field-phenomenon. Even in high-C, you measure light's velocity as the same constant —because your measuring instruments have changed proportionally. It's different, relative to the home continuum, but you can't know it except by pure reasoning. They never found out.

"Using what they had, they saw that they could send a few of their numbers to the denser star-clusters, if they wanted to wait twenty thousand years for them to arrive. Of course, only a few years would pass aboard ship. They knew they could do it, but they procrastinated. Society was egalitarian at the time. Who would go? And why should the planet's industry exhaust itself to launch a handful of ships that no one would ever see again? Who wanted to make a twenty thousand year investment that would impoverish the world? Sol's atomic resources were never plentiful."

"How did it come about then?"

"Through a small group of men who didn't *care* about the cost. They seized power during a 'population rebellion'—when the sterilizers were fighting the euthanasiasts and the do-nothings. The small clique came into power by the fantastic promise of draining off the population-surplus into space. Enough of the stupid believed it to furnish them with a strong backing. They clamped censorship on the news agencies and imprisoned everyone who said it couldn't be done. They put the planet to work building ships. Their fanatic personal philosophy was: 'We are giving the galaxy to Man. What does it matter if he perishes on Earth?' They put about twelve hundred ships into space before their slave-structure collapsed. Man never developed another technology on Sol III. He was sick of it."

"And *your* people?"

Hulgruv smiled. "A natural outgrowth of the situation. If a planet were glutted with rabbits who ate all the grass, a species of rabbits who learned to exploit other rabbits would have the best chance for survival. We are predators, Cophian. Nature raised us up to be a check on your race."

"You pompous fool!" Roki snapped. "Predators are specialists. What abilities do you have—besides the ability to prey on man?"

"I'll show you in a few minutes," the commander muttered darkly.

Daleth had lost color slowly as she listened to the Solarian's roundabout admission of Roki's charge. She suddenly moaned and slumped in a sick heap. Hulgruv spoke to the guard in the soundless facial language. The guard carried her away quickly.

"If you were an advanced species, Hulgruv—you would not have let yourself be tricked so easily, by me. And a highly intelligent race would discover the warp locks for themselves."

Hulgruv flushed. "We underestimated you, manthing. It was a natural mistake. Your race has sunk to the level of cattle on earth. As for the warp locks, we know their principles. We have experimental models. But we could short-circuit needless research by using your design. We are a new race, new to space. Naturally we cannot do in a few years what you needed centuries to accomplish."

"You'll have to look for help elsewhere. In ten minutes, I'm quitting the key—unless you change your mind."

Hulgruv shrugged. While Roki answered the signals, he listened for sounds of activity throughout the ship. He heard nothing except the occasional clump of boots, the brief mutter of a voice in the corridor, the intermittent rattling of small tools. There seemed to be no excitement or anxiety. The Solarians conducted themselves with quiet self-assurance.

"Is your crew aware of what is happening?"

"Certainly."

As the deadline approached, his fingers grew nervous on the key. He steeled himself, and waited, clutching at each second as it marched past. What good would it do to sacrifice Daleth and himself? He would succeed only in destroying one ship and one crew. But it was a good trade—two pawns for several knights and a rook. And, when the Solarians began their march across space, there would be many such sacrifices.

For the last time, he answered a signal, then leaned back to stare at Hulgruv. "Two minutes, Solarian. There's still time to change your mind."

Hulgruv only smiled. Roki shrugged and stood up. A pistol flashed into the commander's hand, warning him back. Roki laughed contemptuously.

"Afraid I'll try to take your last two minutes away?"

He strolled away from the table toward the door.

"Stop!" Hulgruv barked.

"Why? I want to see the girl."

"Very touching. But she's busy at the moment."

"What?" He turned slowly, and glanced at his watch. "You don't seem to realize that in fifty seconds—'"

"We'll see. Stay where you are."

The Cophian felt a sudden coldness in his face. Could they have found a flaw in his net of death?—a way to circumvent the sudden application of the *Idiot's* C-drive, with its consequent ruinous stresses to both ships? Or had they truly memorized the Cophian symbols to a one second reaction time?

He shrugged agreeably and moved in the general direction of the transmitter tuning units. There was one way to test the possibility. He stopped several feet away and turned to face Hulgruv's suspicious eyes. "You are braver than I thought," he growled.

The admission had the desired effect. Hulgruv tossed his head and laughed arrogantly. There was an instant of relaxation. The heavy automatic wavered slightly. Roki backed against the transmitters and cut the power switch. The hum died.

"Ten seconds, Hulgruv! Toss me your weapon. Shoot and you shatter the set. Wait and the tubes get cold. *Toss it!*"

Hulgruv bellowed, and raised the weapon to fire. Roki grinned. The gun quivered. Then with a choking sound, the Solarian threw it to him. "Get it on!" he howled. *"Get it on!"*

As Roki tripped the switch again, the signals were already chirping in the loud-speaker. He darted aside, out of view from the corridor. Footsteps were already racing toward the control room.

The signals stopped. Then the bleat of an answer! Another key had been set up in the adjoining room! With Daleth answering the challenges?

The pistol exploded in his hand as the first crewman came racing through the doorway. The others backed out of sight into the corridor. as the projectile-weapon knocked their comrade back in a bleeding sprawl. Hulgruv made a dash for the door. Roki cut him down with a shot at the knee.

"The next one takes the transmitter," he bellowed. "Stay back."

Hulgruv roared a command. "Take him! If you can't, let the trap spring!"

Roki stooped over him and brought the pistol butt crashing against his skull, meaning only to silence him. It was a mistake; he had forgotten about the structure of the Solarian skull. He put his foot on Hulgruv's neck and jerked. The butt came free with a wet *cluck.* He raced to the doorway and pressed himself against the wall to listen. The crewmen were apparently having a parley at the far end of the corridor. He waited for the next signal.

When it came, he dropped to the floor—to furnish an unexpected sort of target—and snaked into view. He shot twice at three figures a dozen yards away. The answering fire did something to the side of his face, blurring his vision. Another shot sprayed him with flakes from the deck. One crewman was down. The others backed through a door at the end of the corridor. They slammed it and a pressure seal tightened with a rubbery sound.

Roki climbed to his feet and slipped toward a doorway from which he heard the click of the auxiliary key. He felt certain someone was there besides Daleth. But when he risked a quick glance around the corner, he saw only the girl. She sat at a small desk, her hand frozen to the key, her eyes staring dazedly at nothing. He started to speak, then realized what was wrong. Hypnosis! Or a hypnotic drug. She sensed nothing but the key beneath her fingers, waiting for the next challenge.

The door was only half-open. He could see no one, but there had been another man; of that he was certain. Thoughtfully he took aim at the plastic door panel and fired. A gun skidded toward Daleth's desk. A heavy body sprawled across the floor.

The girl started. The dull daze left her face, to be replaced with wide-eyed shock. She clasped her hands to her cheeks and whimpered. A challenge bleated from the radio.

"Answer!" he bellowed.

Her hand shot to the key and just in time. But she seemed about to faint.

"Stay on it!" he barked, and dashed back to the control room. The crewmen had locked themselves aft of the bulkhead, and had started the ventilator fans. Roki heard their whine, then caught the faint odor of gas. His eyes were burning and he sneezed spasmodically.

"Surrender immediately, manthing!" blared the intercom.

Roki looked around, then darted toward the controls. He threw a damping voltage on the drive tubes, defocused the ion streams, and threw the reactors to full emission. The random shower of high-speed particles would spray toward the focusing coils, scatter like deflected buckshot, and loose a blast of hard X-radiation as they peppered the walls of the reaction chambers. Within a few seconds, if the walls failed to melt, the crewmen back of the bulkhead should recognize the possibility of being quickly fried by the radiant inferno.

The tear gas was choking him. From the next compartment, he could hear Daleth coughing and moaning. How could she hear the signals for her own weeping? He tried to watch the corridor and the reaction-chamber temperature at the same time. The needle crept toward the danger-point. An explosion could result, if the walls failed to melt.

Suddenly the voice of the intercom again: "Shut it off, you fool! You'll destroy the ship."

He said nothing, but waited in tense silence, watching the other end of the corridor. Suddenly the ventilator fans died. Then the bulkhead door opened a crack, and paused.

"Throw out your weapon first!" he barked.

A gun fell through the crack and to the floor. A Solarian slipped through, sneezed, and rubbed his eyes.

"Turn around and back down the corridor."

The crewman obeyed slowly. Roki stood a few feet behind him, using him for a shield while the others emerged. The fight was gone out of them. It was strange, he thought; they were willing to risk the danger of the *Idiot's* C-drive, but they couldn't stand being locked up with a runaway reactor. They could see death coming then. He throttled back the reactors, and prodded the men toward the storage rooms. There was only one door that suggested a lockup. He halted the prisoners in the hallway and tried the bolt.

"Not in there, manthing!" growled one of the Solarians.

"Why not?"

"There are—"

A muffled wail from within the compartment interrupted the explanation. It was the cry of a child. His hand trembled on the bolt.

"They are wild, and we are weaponless," pleaded the Solarian.

"How many are in there?"

"Four adults, three children."

Roki paused. "There's nowhere else to put you. One of you—*you* there—go inside, and we'll see what happens."

The man shook his head stubbornly in refusal. Roki repeated the order. Again the man refused. The predator, unarmed, was afraid of its prey. The Cophian aimed low and calmly shot him through the leg.

"Throw him inside," he ordered tonelessly.

With ill-concealed fright for their own safety, the other two lifted their screaming comrade. Roki swung open the door and caught a brief glimpse of several human shadows in the gloom. Then the Solarian was thrown through the doorway and the bolt snapped closed.

At first there was silence, then a bull-roar from some angry throat. Stamping feet—then the Solarian's shriek— and a body was being dashed against the inside walls while several savage voices roared approval. The two remaining crewmen stood in stunned silence.

"Doesn't work so well, does it?" Roki murmured with ruthless unconcern.

After a brief search, he found a closet to lock them in, and went to relieve Daleth at the key. When the last signal came, at the end of the four hours, she was asleep from exhaustion. And curled up on the floor, she looked less like a tough little frontier urchin than a frightened bedraggled kitten. He grinned at her for a moment, then went back to inspect the damage to the briefly overloaded reactors. It was not as bad as it might have been. He worked for two hours, replacing fused focusing sections. The jets would carry them home.

The *Idiot* was left drifting in space to await the coming of a repair ship. And Daleth was not anxious to fly it back alone. Roki set the Solarian vessel on a course with a variable C-level, so that no Sol ship could track them without warp lockers. As far as Roki was concerned the job was done. He had a shipful of evidence and two live Solarians who could be forced to confirm it.

"What will they do about it?" Daleth asked as the captured ship jetted them back toward the Sixty-Star Cluster.

"Crush the Solarian race immediately."

"I thought we were supposed to keep hands-off non-human races?"

"We are, unless they try to exploit human beings. That is automatically an act of war. But I imagine an ultimatum will bring a surrender. They can't fight without warp lockers."

"What will happen on Earth when they do surrender?"

Roki turned to grin. "Go ask the human Earthers. Climb in their cage."

She shuddered, and murmured, "Some day—they'll be a civilized race again, won't they?"

He sobered, and stared thoughtfully at the star-lanced cosmos. "Theirs is the past, Daleth. Theirs is the glory of having founded the race of man. They sent us into space. They gave the galaxy to man—in the beginning. We would do well to let them alone."

He watched her for a moment. She had lost cockiness, temporarily.

"Stop grinning at me like that!" she snapped.

Roki went to feed the Solarian captives: canned cabbage.

Big Joe and the Nth Generation

A THIEF, HE was about to die like a thief.

He hung from the post by his wrists. The wan sunlight glistened faintly on his naked back as he waited, eyes tightly closed, lips moving slowly as he pressed his face against the rough wood and stood on tiptoe to relieve the growing ache in his shoulders. When his ankles ached, he hung by the nails that pierced his forearms just above the wrists.

He was young, perhaps in his tenth Marsyear, and his crisp black hair was close-cropped in the fashion of the bachelor who had not yet sired a pup, or not yet admitted that he had. Lithe and sleek, with the quick knotty muscles and slender rawhide limbs of a wild thing, half-fed and hungry with a quick furious hunger that crouched in ambush. His face, though twisted with pain and fright, remained that of a cocky pup.

When he opened his eyes he could see the low hills of Mars, sun-washed and gray-green with trees, trees brought down from the heavens by the Ancient Fathers. But he could also see the executioner in the foreground, sitting spraddlelegged and calm while he chewed a blade of grass and waited. A squat man with a thick face, he occasionally peered at the thief with empty blue eyes—while he casually played mumblety-peg with the bleeding-blade. His stare was blank.

"Ready for me yet, Asir?" he grumbled, not unpleasantly.

The knifeman sat beyond spitting range, but Asir spat,

and tried to wipe his chin on the post. "Your dirty mother!" he mumbled.

The executioner chuckled and played mumblety-peg.

After three hours of dangling from the spikes that pierced his arms, Asir was weakening, and the blood throbbed hard in his temples, with each jolt of his heart a separate pulse of pain. The red stickiness had stopped oozing down his arms; they knew how to drive the spike just right. But the heartbeats labored in his head like a hammer beating at red-hot iron.

How many heartbeats in a lifetime—and how many left to him now?

He whimpered and writhed, beginning to lose all hope. Mara had gone to see the Chief Commoner, to plead with him for the pilferer's life—but Mara was about as trustworthy as a wild hüffen, and he had visions of them chuckling together in Tokra's villa over a glass of amber wine, while life drained slowly from a young thief.

Asir regretted nothing. His father had been a renegade before him, had squandered his last ritual formula to buy a wife, then impoverished, had taken her away to the hills. Asir was born in the hills, but he came back to the village of his ancestors to work as a servant and steal the rituals of his masters. No thief could last for long. A ritual-thief caused havoc in the community. The owner of a holy phrase, not knowing that it had been stolen, tried to spend it—and eventually counter-claims would come to light, and a general accounting had to be called. The thief was always found out.

Asir had stolen more than wealth, he had stolen the strength of their souls. For this they hung him by his wrists and waited for him to beg for the bleeding-blade.

Woman thirsts for husband,
Man thirsts for wife,
Baby thirsts for breast-milk
Thief thirsts for knife . . .

A rhyme from his childhood, a childish chant, an eenie-meenie-miney for determining who should drink first from a nectar-cactus. He groaned and tried to shift his weight more comfortably. Where was Mara?

"Ready for me yet, Asir?" the squat man asked.

Asir hated him with narrowed eyes. The executioner

was bound by law to wait until his victim requested his
fate. But Asir remained ignorant of what the fate would
be. The Council of Senior Kinsmen judged him in secret,
and passed sentence as to what the executioner would do
with the knife. But Asir was not informed of their judgment. He knew only that when he asked for it, the executioner would advance with the bleeding-blade and
exact the punishment—his life, or an amputation, depending on the judgment. He might lose only an eye or an ear
or a finger. But on the other hand, he might lose his life,
both arms, or his masculinity.

There was no way to find out until he asked for the
punishment. If he refused to ask, they would leave him
hanging there. In theory, a thief could escape by hanging
four days, after which the executioner would pull out the
nails. Sometimes a culprit managed it, but when the nails
were pulled, the thing that toppled was already a corpse.

The sun was sinking in the west, and it blinded him.
Asir knew about the sun—knew things the stupid council
failed to know. A thief, if successful, frequently became
endowed with wisdom, for he memorized more wealth
than a score of honest men. Quotations from the ancient
gods—Fermi, Einstein, Elgermann, Hanser and the rest
—most men owned scattered phrases, and scattered
phrases remained meaningless. But a thief memorized all
transactions that he overheard, and the countless phrases
could be fitted together into meaningful ideas.

He knew now that Mars, once dead, was dying again,
its air leaking away once more into space. And Man
would die with it, unless something were done, and done
quickly. The Blaze of the Great Wind needed to be rekindled under the earth, but it would not be done. The
tribes had fallen into ignorance, even as the holy books
had warned:

*It is realized that the colonists will be unable to main-
tain a technology without basic tools, and that a rebuilding
will require several generations of intelligently directed
effort. Given the knowledge, the colonists may be able to
restore a machine culture if the knowledge continues to be
bolstered by desire. But if the third, fourth, and Nth generations fail to further the gradual retooling process, the
knowledge will become worthless.*

The quotation was from the god Roggins, *Progress of
the Mars-Culture,* and he had stolen bits of it from various

sources. The books themselves were no longer in existence, remembered only in memorized ritual chants, the possession of which meant wealth.

Asir was sick. Pain and slow loss of blood made him weak, and his vision blurred. He failed to see her coming until he heard her feet rustling in the dry grass.

"Mara—"

She smirked and spat contemptuously at the foot of the post. The daughter of a Senior Kinsman, she was a tall, slender girl with an arrogant strut and mocking eyes. She stood for a moment with folded arms, eyeing him with amusement. Then, slowly, one eye closed in a solemn wink. She turned her back on him and spoke to the executioner.

"May I taunt the prisoner, Slubil?" she asked.

"It is forbidden to speak to the thief," growled the knifeman.

"Is he ready to beg for justice, Slubil?"

The knifeman grinned and looked at Asir. "Are you ready for me yet, thief?"

Asir hissed an insult. The girl had betrayed him.

"Evidently a coward," she said. "Perhaps he means to hang four days."

"Let him then."

"No—I think that I should *like* to see him beg."

She gave Asir a long searching glance, then turned to walk away. The thief cursed her quietly and followed her with his eyes. A dozen steps away she stopped again, looked back over her shoulder, and repeated the slow wink. Then she marched on toward her father's house. The wink made his scalp crawl for a moment, but then . . .

Suppose she hasn't betrayed me? Suppose she had wheedled the sentence out of Tokra, and knew what his punishment would be. *I think that I should like to see him beg.*

But on the other hand, the fickle she-devil might be tricking him into asking for a sentence that she *knew* would be death or dismemberment—just to amuse herself.

He cursed inwardly and trembled as he peered at the bored executioner. He licked his lips and fought against dizzyness as he groped for words. Slubil heard him muttering and looked up.

"Are you ready for me yet?"

Asir closed his eyes and gritted his teeth. "Give it to

me!" he yelped suddenly, and braced himself against the post.

Why not? The short time gained couldn't be classed as living. Have it done with. Eternity would be sweet in comparison to this ignominy. A knife could be a blessing.

He heard the executioner chuckle and stand up. He heard the man's footsteps approaching slowly, and the singing hiss of the knife as Slubil swung it in quick arcs. The executioner moved about him slowly, teasing him with the whistle of steel fanning the air about him. He was expected to beg. Slubil occasionally laid the knife against his skin and took it away again. Then Asir heard the rustle of the executioner's cloak as his arm went back. Asir opened his eyes.

The executioner grinned as he held the blade high— aimed at Asir's head! The girl had tricked him. He groaned and closed his eyes again, muttering a half-forgotten prayer.

The stroke fell—and the blade chopped into the post above his head. Asir fainted.

When he awoke he lay in a crumpled heap on the ground. The executioner rolled him over with his foot.

"In view of your extreme youth, thief," the knifeman growled, "the council has ordered you perpetually banished. The sun is setting. Let dawn find you in the hills. If you return to the plains, you will be chained to a wild hüffen and dragged to death."

Panting weakly, Asir groped at his forehead, and found a fresh wound, raw and rubbed with rust to make a scar. Slubil had marked him as an outcast. But except for the nail-holes through his forearms, he was still in one piece. His hands were numb, and he could scarcely move his fingers. Slubil had bound the spike-wounds, but the bandages were bloody and leaking.

When the knifeman had gone, Asir climbed weakly to his feet. Several of the townspeople stood nearby, snickering at him. He ignored their catcalls and staggered toward the outskirts of the village, ten minutes away. He had to speak to Mara, and to her father if the crusty oldster would listen. His thief's knowledge weighed upon him and brought desperate fear.

Darkness had fallen by the time he came to Welkir's house. The people spat at him in the streets, and some of them flung handfuls of loose dirt after him as he passed.

A light flickered feebly through Welkir's door. Asir rattled it and waited.

Welkir came with a lamp. He set the lamp on the floor and stood with feet spread apart, arms folded, glaring haughtily at the thief. His face was stiff as weathered stone. He said nothing, but only stared contemptuously.

Asir bowed his head. "I have come to plead with you, Senior Kinsman."

Welkir snorted disgust. "Against the mercy we have shown you?"

He looked up quickly, shaking his head. "No! For that I am grateful."

"What then?"

"As a thief, I acquired much wisdom. I know that the world is dying, and the air is boiling out of it into the sky. I wish to be heard by the council. We must study the words of the ancients and perform their magic, lest our children's children be born to strangle in a dead world."

Welkir snorted again. He picked up the lamp. "He who listens to a thief's wisdom is cursed. He who acts upon it is doubly cursed and a party to the crime."

"The vaults," Asir insisted. "The key to the Blaze of the Winds is in the vaults. The god Roggins tells us in the words—"

"Stop! I will not hear!"

"Very well, but the blaze can be rekindled, and the air renewed. The vaults—" He stammered and shook his head. "The council must hear me."

"The council will hear nothing, and you shall be gone before dawn. And the vaults are guarded by the sleeper called Big Joe. To enter is to die. Now go away."

Welkir stepped back and slammed the door. Asir sagged in defeat. He sank down on the doorstep to rest a moment. The night was black, except for lamp-flickers from an occasional window.

"Ssssst!"

A sound from the shadows. He looked around quickly, searching for the source.

"Ssssst! Asir!"

It was the girl Mara, Welkir's daughter. She had slipped out the back of the nouse and was peering at him around the corner. He arose quietly and went to her.

"What did Slubil do to you?" she whispered.

Asir gasped and caught her shoulders angrily. "Don't you *know?*"

"No! Stop! You're hurting me. Tokra wouldn't tell me. I made love to him, but he wouldn't tell."

He released her with an angry curse.

"You *had* to take it sometime," she hissed. "I knew if you waited you would be too weak from hanging to even run away."

He called her a foul name.

"Ingrate!" she snapped. "And I bought you a hüffen!"

"You *what?*"

"Tokra gave me a ritual phrase and I bought you a hüffen with it. You can't *walk* to the hills, you know."

Asir burned with full rage. "You slept with Tokra!" he snapped.

"You're jealous!" she tittered.

"How can I be jealous! I hate the sight of you!"

"Very well then, I'll keep the hüffen."

"*Do!*" he growled. "I won't need it, since I'm not going to the hills!"

She gasped. "You've got to go, you fool! They'll kill you!"

He turned away, feeling sick. She caught at his arm and tried to pull him back. "Asir! Take the hüffen and *go!*"

"I'll go," he growled. "But not to the hills. I'm going out to the vault."

He stalked away, but she trotted along beside him, trying to tug him back. "Fool! The vaults are sacred! The priests guard the entrance, and the Sleeper guards the inner door. They'll kill you if you try it, and if you linger, the council will kill you tomorrow."

"Let them!" he snarled. "I am no sniveling townsman! I am of the hills, and my father was a renegade. Your council had no right to judge me. Now *I* shall judge *them!*"

The words were spoken hotly, and he realized their folly. He expected a scornful rebuke from Mara, but she hung onto his arm and pleaded with him. He had dragged her a dozen doorways from the house of her father. Her voice had lost its arrogance and became pleading.

"Please, Asir! Go away. Listen! I will even go with you—if you want me."

He laughed harshly. "Tokra's leavings."

She slapped him hard across the mouth. "Tokra is an impotent old dodderer. He can scarcely move for arthritis. You're an idiot! I sat on his lap and kissed his bald pate for you."

"Then why did he give you a ritual phrase?" he asked stiffly.

"Because he likes me."

"You lie." He stalked angrily on.

"Very well! Go to the vaults. I'll tell my father, and they'll hunt you down before you get there."

She released his arm and stopped. Asir hesitated. She meant it. He came back to her slowly, then slipped his swollen hands to her throat. She did not back away.

"Why don't I just choke you and leave you lying here?" he hissed.

Her face was only a shadow in darkness, but he could see her cool smirk.

"Because you love me, Asir of Franic."

He dropped his hands and grunted a low curse. She laughed low and took his arm.

"Come on. We'll go get the hüffen," she said.

Why not? he thought. *Take her hüffen, and take her too.* He could dump her a few miles from the village, then circle back to the vaults. She leaned against him as they moved back toward her father's house, then skirted it and stole back to the field behind the row of dwellings. Phobos hung low in the west, its tiny disk lending only a faint glow to the darkness.

He heard the hüffen's breathing as they approached a hulking shadow in the gloom. Its great wings snaked out slowly as it sensed their approach, and it made a low piping sound. An native Martian species, it bore no resemblance to the beasts that the ancients had brought with them from the sky. Its back was covered with a thin shell like a bettle's, but its belly was porous and soft. It digested food by sitting on it, and absorbing it. The wings were bony—parchment stretched across a fragile frame. It was headless, and lacked a centralized brain, the nervous functions being distributed.

The great creature made no protest as they climbed up the broad flat back and strapped themselves down with the belts that had been threaded through holes cut in the hüffen's thin, tough shell. Its lungs slowly gathered a tremendous breath of air, causing the riders to rise up as the huge air-sacs became distended. The girth of an inflated hüffen was nearly four times as great as when deflated. When the air was gathered, the creature began to shrink again as its muscles tightened, compressing the breath until a faint leakage-hiss came from behind. It waited, wings taut.

The girl tugged at a ring set through the flesh of its flank. There was a blast of sound and a jerk. Nature's experiment in jet propulsion soared ahead and turned into the wind. Its first breath exhausted, it gathered another and blew itself ahead again. The ride was jerky. Each tailward belch was a rough lurch. They let the hüffen choose its own heading as it gained altitude. Then Mara tugged at the wing-straps, and the creature wheeled to soar toward the dark hills in the distance.

Asir sat behind her, a sardonic smirk on his face, as the wind whipped about them. He waited until they had flown beyond screaming distance of the village. Then he took her shoulders lightly in his hands. Mistaking it for affection, she leaned back against him easily and rested her dark head on his shoulder. He kissed her—while his hand felt gingerly for the knife at her belt. His fingers were numb, but he managed to clutch it, and press the blade lightly against her throat. She gasped. With his other hand, he caught her hair.

"Now guide the hüffen down!" he ordered.

"*Asir!*"

"Quickly!" he barked.

"What are you going to do?"

"Leave you here and circle back to the vaults."

"No! Not out here at night!"

He hesitated. There were slinking prowlers on the Cimerian plain, beasts who would regard the marooned daughter of Welkir a delicious bit of good fortune, a gustatory delight of a sort they seldom were able to enjoy. Even above the moan of the wind, he would hear an occasional howl-cry from the fanged welcoming committee that waited for its dinner beneath them.

"Very well," he growled reluctantly. "Turn toward the vaults. But one scream and I'll slice you." He took the blade from her throat but kept the point touching her back.

"Please, Asir, *no!*" she pleaded. "Let me go on to the

hills. Why do you want to go to the vaults? Because of Tokra?"

He gouged her with the point until she yelped. "Tokra be damned, and you with him!" he snarled. "Turn back."

"Why?"

"I'm going down to kindle the Blaze of the Winds."

"You're *mad! The spirits of the ancients live in the vaults.*"

"I am going to kindle the Blaze of the Winds," he insisted stubbornly. "Now either turn back, or go down and I'll turn back alone."

After a hesitant moment, she tugged at a wing rein and the hüffen banked majestically. They flew a mile to the south of the village, then beyond it toward the cloister where the priests of Big Joe guarded the entrance to the vaults. The cloister was marked by a patch of faint light on the ground ahead.

"Circle around it once," he ordered.

"You can't get in. They'll kill you."

He doubted it. No one ever tried to enter, except the priests who carried small animals down as sacrifices to the great Sleeper. Since no outsider ever dared go near the shaft, the guards expected no one. He doubted that they would be alert.

The cloister was a hollow square with a small stone tower rising in the center of the courtyard. The tower contained the entrance to the shaft. In the dim light of Phobos, assisted by yellow flickers from the cloister windows, he peered at the courtyard as they circled closer. It seemed to be empty.

"Land beside the tower!" he ordered.

"Asir—please—"

"Do it!"

The Hüffen plunged rapidly, soared across the outer walls, and burst into the courtyard. It landed with a rough jolt and began squeaking plaintively.

"Hurry!" he hissed. "Get your straps off and let's go."

"I'm not going."

A prick of the knife point changed her mind. They slid quickly to the ground, and Asir kicked the hüffen in the flanks. The beast sucked in air and burst aloft.

Startled faces were trying to peer through the lighted cloister windows into the courtyard. Someone cried a challenge. Asir darted to the door of the tower and

been sent to check for some way to enter the *Idiot* that would not energize a booby circuit.

His host waved him through a doorway, and he found himself in their control room. A glance told him that their science still fell short of the most modern cultures. They had the earmarks of a new race, and yet Sol's civilization was supposedly the oldest in the galaxy.

"There are the transmitters," the commander barked. "Say what you have to say, and we shall see who is best at waiting."

Roki sat down, fingered the key, and watched his adversary closely. The commander fell into a seat opposite him and gazed coolly through narrowed lids. He wore a fixed smile of amusement. "Your name is Eli Roki, I believe. I am Space Commander Hulgruv."

A blare of sound suddenly came from the receiver. Hulgruv frowned and lowered the volume. The sound came forth as a steady musical tone. He questioned the Cophian with his eyes.

"When the tone ceases, the signals will begin."

"I see."

"I warn you, I may get bored rather quickly. I'll keep the signals going only until I think you've had time to assure yourselves that this is not a bluff I am trying to put over on you."

"I'm sure it's not. It's merely an inconvenience."

"You know little of my home planet then."

"I know a little."

"Then you've heard of the 'Sword of Apology.' "

"How does that—" Hulgruv paused and lost his smirk for an instant. "I see. If you blunder, your code demands that you die anyway. So you think you wouldn't hesitate to neglect a signal."

"Try me."

"It may not be necessary. Tell me, why did you space them two minutes apart? Why not one signal every hour?"

"You can answer that."

"Ah yes. You think the short period insures you against any painful method of persuasion, eh?"

"Uh-huh. And it gives me a chance to decide frequently whether it's worth it."

"What is it you want, Cophian? Suppose we give you the girl and release you."

dragged it open. Now forced to share the danger, the girl came with him without urging. They stepped into a stair-landing. A candle flickered from a wall bracket. A guard, sitting on the floor beneath the candle glanced up in complete surprise. Then he reached for a short barbed pike. Asir kicked him hard in the temple, then rolled his limp from outside. Men with torches were running across the courtyard. He slammed the heavy metal door and bolted it.

Fists began beating on the door. They paused for a moment to rest, and Mara stared at him in fright. He expected her to burst into angry speech, but she only leaned against the wall and panted. The dark mouth of the stairway yawned at them—a stone throat that led into the bowels of Mars and the realm of the monster, Big Joe. He glanced at Mara thoughtfully, and felt sorry for her.

"I can leave you here," he offered, "but I'll have to tie you."

She moistened her lips, glanced first at the stairs, then at the door where the guards were raising a frantic howl. She shook her head.

"I'll go with you."

"The priests won't bother you, if they see that you were a prisoner."

"I'll go with you."

He was pleased, but angry with himself for the pleasure. An arrogant, spiteful, conniving wench, he told himself. She'd lied about Tokra. He grunted gruffly, seized the candle, and started down the stairs. When she started after him, he stiffened and glanced back, remembering the barbed pike.

As he had suspected, she had picked it up. The point was a foot from the small of his back. They stared at each other, and she wore her self-assured smirk.

"Here," she said, and handed it casually. "You might need this."

They stared at each other again, but it was different this time. Bewildered, he shook his head and resumed the descent toward the vaults. The guards were battering at the doors behind them.

The stairwell was damp and cold. Blackness folded about them like a shroud. They moved in silence, and after five thousand steps, Asir stopped counting.

Somewhere in the depths, Big Joe slept his restless

sleep. Asir wondered grimly how long it would take the guards to tear down the metal door. Somehow they had to get past Big Joe before the guards came thundering after them. There was a way to get around the monster: of that he was certain. A series of twenty-four numbers was involved, and he had memorized them with a stolen bit of ritual. How to use them was a different matter. He imagined vaguely that one must call them out in a loud voice before the inner entrance.

The girl walked beside him now, and he could feel her shivering. His eyes were quick and nervous as he scanned each pool of darkness, each nook and cranny along the stairway wall. The well was silent· except for the mutter of their footsteps, and the gloom was full of musty odors. The candle afforded little light.

"I told you the truth about Tokra," she blurted suddenly.

Asir glowered straight ahead and said nothing, embarrassed by his previous jealousy. They moved on in silence.

Suddenly she stopped. "Look," she hissed, pointing down ahead.

He shielded the candle with his hand and peered downward toward a small square of dim light. "The bottom of the stairs," he muttered.

The light seemed faint and diffuse—with a slight greenish cast. Asir blew out the candle, and the girl quickly protested.

"How will we see to climb again?"

He laughed humorlessly. "What makes you think we will?"

She moaned and clutched at his arm, but came with him as he descended slowly toward the light. The stairway opened into a long corridor whose ceiling was faintly luminous. White-faced and frightened, they paused on the bottom step and looked down the corridor. Mara gasped and covered her eyes.

"Big Joe!" she whispered in awe.

He stared through the stairwell door and down the corridor through another door into a large room. Big Joe sat in the center of the room, sleeping his sleep of ages amid a heap of broken and whitening bones. A creature of metal, twice the height of Asir, he had obviously been designed to kill. Tri-fingered hands with gleaming talons, and a monstrous head shaped like a Marswolf, with long silver fangs. Why should a metal-creature have fangs, unless he had been built to kill?

The behemoth slept in a crouch, waiting for the intruders.

He tugged the girl through the stairwell door. A voice droned out of nowhere: *"If you have come to plunder, go back!"*

He stiffened, looking around. The girl whimpered.

"Stay here by the stairs," he told her, and pushed her firmly back through the door.

Asir started slowly toward the room where Big Joe waited. Beyond the room he could see another door, and the monster's job was apparently to keep intruders back from the inner vaults where, according to the ritual chants, the Blaze of the Winds could be kindled.

Halfway along the corridor, the voice called out again, beginning a kind of sing-song chant: *"Big Joe will kill you, Big Joe will kill you, Big Joe will kill you—"*

He turned slowly, searching for the speaker. But the voice seemed to come from a black disk on the wall. The talking-machines perhaps, as mentioned somewhere in the ritual.

A few paces from the entrance to the room, the voice fell silent. He stopped at the door, staring in at the monster. Then he took a deep breath and began chanting the twenty-four numbers in a loud but quavering voice. Big Joe remained in his motionless crouch. Nothing happened. He stepped through the doorway.

Big Joe emitted a deafening roar, straightened with a metallic groan, and lumbered toward him, taloned hands extended and eyes blazing furiously. Asir shrieked and ran for his life.

Then he saw Mara lying sprawled in the stairway entrance. She had fainted. Blocking an impulse to leap over her and flee alone, he stopped to lift her.

But suddenly he realized that there was no pursuit. He looked back. Big Joe had returned to his former position, and he appeared to be asleep again. Puzzled, Asir stepped back into the corridor.

"If you have come to plunder, go back!"

He moved gingerly ahead again.

"Big Joe will kill you, Big Joe will kill you, Big Joe will kill—"

He recovered the barbed pike from the floor and stole into the zone of silence. This time he stopped to look around. Slowly he reached the pike-staff through the doorway. Nothing happened. He stepped closer and waved it around inside. Big Joe remained motionless.

Then he dropped the point of the pike to the floor. The monster bellowed and started to rise. Asir leaped back, scalp crawling. But Big Joe settled back in his crouch.

Fighting a desire to flee, Asir reached the pike through the door and rapped it on the floor again. This time nothing happened. He glanced down. The pike's point rested in the center of a gray floor-tile, just to the left of the entrance. The floor was a checkerboard pattern of gray and white. He tapped another gray square, and this time the monster started out of his drowse again.

After a moment's thought, he began touching each tile within reach of the door. Most of them brought a response from Big Joe. He found four that did not. He knelt down before the door to peer at them closely. The first was unmarked. The second bore a dot in the center. The third bore two, and the fourth three—in order of their distance from the door.

He stood up and stepped inside again, standing on the first tile. Big Joe remained motionless. He stepped diagonally left to the second—straight ahead to the third— then diagonally right to the fourth. He stood there for a moment, trembling and staring at the Sleeper. He was four feet past the door!

Having assured himself that the monster was still asleep, he crouched to peer at the next tiles. He stared for a long time, but found no similar markings. Were the dots coincidence?

He rached out with the pike, then drew it back. He was too close to the Sleeper to risk a mistake. He stood up and looked around carefully, noting each detail of the room— and of the floor in particular. He counted the rows and columns of tiles—twenty-four each way.

Twenty-four—and there were twenty-four numbers in the series that was somehow connected with safe passage through the room. He frowned and muttered through the series to himself——0,1,2,3,3,3,2,2,1 . . .

The first four numbers—0,1,2,3. And the tiles—the first with no dots, the second with one, the third with two, the fourth with three. But the four tiles were not in a straight line, and there were no marked ones beyond the fourth. He backed out of the room and studied them from the end of the corridor again.

Mara had come dizzily awake and was calling for him weakly. He replied reassuringly and turned to his task again. "First tile, then diagonally left, then straight, then diagonally right—"

0,1,2,3,3.

A hunch came. He advanced as far as the second tile, then reached as far ahead as he could and touched the square diagonally right from the fourth one. Big Joe remained motionless but began to speak. His scalp bristled at the growling voice.

"If the intruder makes an error, Big Joe will kill."

Standing tense, ready to leap back to the corridor, he touched the square again. The motionless behemoth repeated the grim warning.

Asir tried to reach the square diagonally right from the fifth, but could not without stepping up to the third. Taking a deep breath, he stepped up and extended the pike cautiously, keeping his eyes on Big Joe. The pike rapped the floor.

"If the intruder makes an error, Big Joe will kill."

But the huge figure remained in his place.

Starting from the first square, the path went left, straight, right, right, right. And after zero, the numbers went 1, 2, 3, 3, 3. Apparently he had found the key. One meant a square to the southeast; two meant south; and three southwest. Shivering, he moved up to the fifth square upon which the monster growled his first warning. He looked back at the door, then at Big Joe. The taloned hands could grab him before he could dive back into the corridor.

He hesitated. He could either turn back now, or gamble his life on the accuracy of the tentative belief. The girl was calling to him again.

"Come to the end of the corridor!" he replied.

She came hurriedly, to his surprise.

"No!" he bellowed. "Stay back of the entrance! Not on the tile! *No!"*

Slowly she withdrew the foot that hung poised over a trigger-tile.

"You can't come in unless you know how," he gasped.

She blinked at him and glanced nervously back over

her shoulder. "But I hear them. They're coming down the stairs."

Asir cursed softly. Now he *had* to go ahead.

"Wait just a minute," he said. "Then I'll show you how to come through."

He advanced to the last tile that he had tested and stopped. The next two numbers were two—for straight ahead. And they would take him within easy reach of the long taloned arms of the murderous sentinel. He glanced around in fright at the crushed bones scattered across the floor. Some were human. Others were animal-sacrifices tossed in by the priests.

He had tested only one two—back near the door. If he made a mistake, he would never escape; no need bothering with the pike.

He stepped to the next tile and closed his eyes.

"If the intruder makes an error, Big Joe will kill."

He opened his eyes again and heaved a breath of relief.

"Asir! They're getting closer! I can hear them!"

He listened for a moment. A faint murmur of angry voices in the distance. "All right," he said calmly. "Step only on the tiles I tell you. See the gray one at the left of the door?"

She pointed. "This one?"

"Yes, step on it."

The girl moved up and stared fearfully at the monstrous sentinel. He guided her up toward him. "Diagonally left —one ahead—diagonally right. Now don't be frightened when he speaks—"

The girl came on until she stood one square behind him. Her quick frightened breathing blended with the growing sounds of shouting from the stairway. He glanced up at Big Joe, noticing for the first time that the steel jaws were stained with a red-brown crust. He shuddered.

The grim chess-game continued a cautious step at a time, with the girl following one square behind him. What if she fainted again? And fell across a triggered tile? They passed within a foot of Big Joe's arm.

Looking up, he saw the monster's eyes move—following them, scrutinizing them as they passed. He froze.

"We want no plunder," he said to the machine.

The gaze was steady and unwinking.

"The air is leaking away from the world."

The monster remained silent.

"Hurry!" whimpered the girl. Their pursuers were gaining rapidly and they had crossed only half the distance to the opposing doorway. Progress was slower now, for Asir needed occasionally to repeat through the whole series of numbers, looking back to count squares and make certain that the next step was not a fatal one.

"They won't dare to come in after us," he said hopefully.

"And if they do?"

"If the intruder makes an error, Big Joe will kill," announced the machine as Asir took another step.

"Eight squares to go!" he muttered, and stopped to count again.

"Asir! They're in the corridor!"

Hearing the tumble of voices, he looked back to see blue-robed men spilling out of the stairway and milling down the corridor toward the room. But halfway down the hall, the priests paused—seeing the unbelievable: two intruders walking safely past their devil-god. They growled excitedly among themselves. Asir took another step. Again the machine voiced the monotonous warning.

"If the intruder makes an error . . ."

Hearing their deity speak, the priests of Big Joe babbled wildly and withdrew a little. But one, more impulsive than the rest, began shrieking.

"Kill the intruders! Cut them down with your spears!"

Asir glanced back to see two of them racing toward the room, lances cocked for the throw. If a spear struck a triger-tile—

"Stop!" he bellowed, facing around.

The two priests paused. Wondering if it would result in his sudden death, he rested a hand lightly against the huge steel arm of the robot, then leaned against it. The huge eyes were staring down at him, but Big Joe did not move.

The spearmen stood frozen, gaping at the thief's familiarity with the horrendous hulk. Then, slowly they backed away.

Continuing his bluff, he looked up at Big Joe and spoke in a loud voice. "If they throw their spears or try to enter, kill them."

He turned his back on the throng in the hall and continued the cautious advance. Five to go, four, three, two—

He paused to stare into the room beyond. Gleaming machinery—all silent—and great panels, covered with a multitude of white circles and dials. His heart sank. If here lay the magic that controlled the Blaze of the Great Wind, he could never hope to re-kindle it.

He stepped through the doorway, and the girl followed. Immediately the robot spoke like low thunder.

"The identity of the two technologists is recognized. Hereafter they may pass with impunity. Big Joe is charged to ask the following: why do the technologists come, when it is not yet time?"

Staring back, Asir saw that the robot's head had turned so that he was looking directly back at the thief and the girl. Asir also saw that someone had approached the door again. Not priests, but townspeople.

He stared, recognizing the Chief Commoner, and the girl's father Welkir, three other Senior Kinsmen, and— Slubil, the executioner who had nailed him to the post.

"Father! Stay back."

Welkir remained silentt, glaring at them. He turned and whispered to the Chief Commoner. The Chief Commoner whispered to Slubil. The executioner nodded grimly and took a short-axe from his belt thong. He stepped through the entrance, his left foot striking the zero-tile. He peered at Big Joe and saw that the monster remained motionless. He grinned at the ones behind him, then snarled in Asir's direction.

"Your sentence has been changed, thief."

"Don't try to cross, Slubil!" Asir barked.

Slubil spat, brandished the axe, and stalked forward. Big Joe came up like a resurrection of fury, and his elbow was explosive in the vaults. Slubil froze, then stupidly drew back his axe.

Asir gasped as the talons closed. He turned away quickly. Slubil's scream was cut off abruptly by a ripping sound, then a series of dull cracks and snaps. The girl shrieked and closed her eyes. There were two distinct thuds as Big Joe tossed Slubil aside.

The priests and the townspeople—all except Welkir— had fled from the corridor and up the stairway. Welkir was on his knees, his hands covering his face.

"Mara!" he moaned. "My daughter."

"Go back, Father," she called.

Dazed, the old man picked himself up weakly and staggered down the corridor toward the stairway. When he passed the place of the first warning voice, the robot moved again—arose slowly and turned toward Asir and Mara who backed quickly away, deeper into the room of strange machines. Big Joe came lumbering slowly after them.

Asir looked around for a place to flee, but the monster stopped in the doorway. He spoke again, a mechanical drone like memorized ritual.

Big Joe is charged with announcing his function for the intelligence of the technologists. His primary function is to prevent the entrance of possibly destructive organisms into the vaults containing the control equipment for the fusion reaction which must periodically renew atmospheric oxygen. His secondary function is to direct the technologists to records containing such information as they may need. His tertiary function is to carry out simple directions given by the technologists if such directions are possible to his limited design.

Asir stared at the lumbering creature and realized for the first time that it was not alive, but only a machine built by the ancients to perform specific tasks. Despite the fresh redness about his hands and jaws, Big Joe was no more guilty of Slubil's death than a grinding mill would be if the squat sadist had climbed into it while the Marsoxen were yoked to the crushing roller.

Perhaps the ancients had been unnecessarily brutal in building such a guard—but at least they had built him to *look* like a destroyer, and to give ample warning to the intruder. Glancing around at the machinery, he vaguely understood the reason for Big Joe. Such metals as these would mean riches for swordmakers and smiths and plunderers of all kinds.

Asir straightened his shoulders and addressed the machine.

"Teach us how to kindle the Blaze of the Great Wind."

"Teaching is not within the designed functions of Big Joe. I am charged to say: the renewal reaction should not be begun before the Marsyear 6,000, as the builders reckoned time."

Asir frowned. The years were not longer numbered,

but only named in honor of the Chief Commoners who ruled the villages. "How long until the year 6,000?" he asked.

Big Joe clucked like an adding machine. "Twelve Marsyears, technologist."

Asir stared at the complicated machinery. Could they learn to operate it in twelve years? It seemed impossible.

"How can we begin to learn?" he asked the robot.

"This is an instruction room, where you may examine records. The control mechanisms are installed in the deepest vault."

Asir frowned and walked to the far end of the hall where another door opened into—*another anteroom with another Big Joe!* As he approached the second robot spoke:

"If the intruder has not acquired the proper knowledge, Big Oswald will kill."

Thunderstruck, he leaped back from the entrance and swayed heavily against an instrument panel. The panel lit up and a polite recorded voice began reading something about "President Snell's role in the Eighth World War." He lurched away from the panel and stumbled back toward Mara who sat glumly on the foundation slap of a weighty machine.

"What are you laughing about?" she muttered.

"We're still in the first grade!" he groaned, envisioning a sequence of rooms. "We'll have to learn the magic of the ancients before we pass to the next."

"The ancients weren't so great," she grumbled. "Look at the mural on the wall."

Asir looked, and saw only a strange design of circles about a bright splash of yellow that might have been the sun. "What about it?" he asked.

"My father taught me about the planets," she said. "That is supposed to be the way they go around the sun."

"What's wrong with it?"

"One planet too many," she said. "Everyone knows that there is only an asteroid belt between Mars and Venus. The picture shows a planet there."

Asir shrugged indifferently, being interested only in the machinery. "Can't you allow them one small mistake?"

"I suppose." She paused, gazing miserably in the direction in which her father had gone. "What do we do now?"

Asir considered it for a long time. Then he spoke to Big Joe. "You will come with us to the village."

The machine was silent for a moment, then: *"There is an apparent contradiction between primary and tertiary functions. Request priority decision by technologist."*

Asir failed to understand. He repeated his request. The robot turned slowly and stepped through the doorway. He waited.

Asir grinned. "Let's go back up," he said to the girl.

She arose eagerly. They crossed the anteroom to the corridor and began the long climb toward the surface, with Big Joe lumbering along behind.

"What about your banishment, Asir?" she asked gravely.

"Wait and see." He envisioned the pandemonium that would reign when girl, man, and robot marched through the village to the council house, and he chuckled. "I think that I shall be the next Chief Commoner," he said. "And my councilmen will all be thieves."

"Thieves!" she gasped. "Why?"

"Thieves who are not afraid to steal the knowledge of the gods—and become technologists, to kindle the Blaze of the Winds."

"What is a 'technologist', Asir?" she asked worshipfully.

Asir glowered at himself for blundering with words he did not understand, but could not admit ignorance to Mara who clung tightly to his arm. "I think," he said, "that a technologist is a thief who tells the gods what to do."

"Kiss me, Technologist," she told him in a small voice.

Big Joe clanked to a stop to wait for them to move on. He waited a long time.

The Big Hunger

I AM BLIND, yet I know the road to the stars. Space is my harp, and I touch it lightly with fingers of steel. Space sings. Its music quivers in the flux patterns, comes creeping along the twitch of a positron stream, comes to whisper in glass ears. I hear. Aiee! Though I am without eyes, I see the stars tangled in their field-webs, tangled into One. I am the spider who runs over the web. I am the spider who spins, spinning a space where no stars are.

And I am Harpist to a pale, proud Master.

He builds me, and feeds me the fuel I eat, and leads me riding through the space I make, to the glare of another sun. And when he is done with me, I lie rusting in the rain. My metal rots with ages, and the sea comes washing over land to take me while I sleep. The Master forgets. The Master chips flint from a stone, leaving a stone-ax. He busies himself with drums and bloody altars; he dances with a writhing snake in his mouth, conjuring the rain.

Then—after a long time—he remembers. He builds another of me, and I am the same, for like the Soul of him who builds me, my principle lies beyond particular flesh. When my principle is clothed in steel, we go wandering again. I the minstrel, with Man the king.

Hear the song of his hunger, the song of his endless thirst.

There was a man named Abe Jolie, and he leaned against me idly with one hand in the gloom while he spoke quietly and laughed with a female of his species.

191

"It's finished, Junebug. We got it made," he said.

And the girl looked her green eyes over me while the crickets sang beyond the wall, and while the shuffling of their feet echoed faintly in the great hangar.

"Finished," she murmured. "It's your success, Abe."

"Mine, and a lot of others. And the government's money."

She toyed with the lapel of his coveralls, grinned, and said, "Let's steal it and run away."

"*Ssshh!*" He looked around nervously, but there were no guards in sight. "They can shoot you for less than that,' he warned. "The S.P. doesn't have a sense of humor."

"Abe—"

"What?"

"Kiss me."

He kissed her.

"When is that going to be illegal, too?" she whispered.

He looked at her grimly, and she answered her own question.

"As soon as the eugenics laws are passed, Abe. Abe Jolie, who built the spacedrive, a genetic undesirable."

"*Don't!*"

They stood there breathing quietly, and there was hate in their throats.

"Well?"

He looked around again, and whispered, "Meet me here at eleven o'clock, Junebug."

They parted to the sound of casual footsteps.

At eleven o'clock, a lion roared in the hangar. At eleven o'clock a steel juggernaut tore through the hangar wall and paused on a concrete ramp while bullets ricocheted off the hull. Then the first star-chariot burnt a verticle column of flame in the night. Thunder walked upward on fiery stilts, while men shouted angrily. When we were alone in the airless, star-stung, sun-torn blackness, I stroked the web of space, and listened to the muted notes. When the tune is memorized, I speak. I contradict. I refute the universe. We lived in a spaceless space beyond stars.

The man and the woman had gone. But the plan remained on Earth. My principle lingered on the drawing boards, and in the dreams of men—men who said they were sick of wars and politics and the braying of collectivist jackasses. Others were sick of petty peace and cheapness and Independence Day speeches and incorporated jackasses who blubbered disgustingly about various freedoms.

They wanted the one Big Freedom. They built me again, these pale, proud bipeds, these children of an Ape-Prince who walked like a god. They packed themselves in cylinders of steel and wandering, riding starward on a heart-tempest that had once sung them down from the trees to stalk the plains with club and torch. The pod of earth opened, scattered its seed spaceward. It was the time of the great bursting, the great birth-giving. Empires shivered in the storm.

Sky-chariots flung themselves upward to vanish beyond the fringes of the atmosphere. Prairie schooners of space bore the restless, the contemptuous, the hungry and the proud. And I led them along the self-road that runs around space. The world seethed, and empires toppled, and new empires arose whose purpose it was to build the sky-chariots.

Young men, young women, clamored at the gates of launching fields. Those who were chosen grinned expectantly at the stars. They climbed aboard in throngs and deserted Earth. They were hard laughers with red freckles and big fists. They wore slide rules at their belts like swords, and they spoke familiarly of Schwarzchild Line-Elements and Riemann-Christofel tensors. Their women were restless talkers, big women, with flashing white teeth. They teased the men, and their hands were strong and brown.

Poets came—and misfits, and saints, sinners, dirt-farmers. Engineers came and child-bearers, fighters, utopianists, and dreamers with the lights of God glowing in their starward eyes.

"Why were we taught to pray with *downcast* eyes?" they asked. "When you pray, look starward, look to the God at the north end of the Universe."

Man was a starward wind, a mustard seed, a wisp of Brahma's breath breathed across space.

They found two corpses in an orbit about Arcturus. The corpses were frozen and the ice was slowly sublimating into space-vapor. One of them had an Engineering Union card in his pocket. It gave his name as Abe Jolie. The other was a girl. And, because the corpse had given them the blueprints that led to space, they hauled him aboard with the girl. Somebody sang the *"Kyrie"* and somebody said, "I am the Resurrection and the Life." Then they cancelled. out the orbital velocity and let the corpses go toppling toward Arcturus, toward a burning sun-grave where their light would shine forever.

There were those who remained behind. There were those who made Earth their business and stayed at home. Their tribes were numbered at two billion souls. And they were somehow different from the spacers. They liked to sit in their rocking chairs. They liked prettiness and a one-hundred-cent dollar. They voted for the Conservative Party. They abolished centralization. Eventually they abolished government. And for the first time in anyone's memory, there was peace on Earth, good will among men.

My Master was hungry for land. My Master sought new worlds. And we found them.

There was a yellow sun in Serpens called 27 Lambda, lying eight parsecs inward toward the galactic heartland and seven parsecs north toward the galactic pole. A lush green planet drifted at one hundred twenty megamiles from the friendly sun-star, and it awoke in the wandering biped nostalgic thoughts. We paused in space-black, we looked, we came down on tongues of lightning from the clear sky to set jet-fires in the grassy plain near a river and a forest.

Man was a seed replanted.

He wandered away from the sky-chariot and drank from a pool in the jungle. A behemoth with several legs and a parasite-rider came roaring his appetite at the pale biped. And his bones lay whitening in the sun, and his descendants learned that it was easier to stay alive by ignoring the biped from the sky.

I lay rusting in the rain. Houses of log and stone grew up on the hillsides. They crumbled slowly into ruin. A man wearing a fur robe came and built an altar at my feet. He burnt his eldest daughter on it while he sang a battle song and danced, danced a victory under strange sky.

The sons of men molded clay and chipped arrowheads and built fires. The old men told them stories of a space-going god, and the stories became their legends. They kidnaped the daughters of neighbors, knew wives, and multiplied.

A glacier came and ground me into dust. Millenniums passed, and each Prophet had his Hazar.

One of the prophets wrote an energy equation. Men crucified an Agitator on a telegraph pole. They purged a minority-group. They split a uranium atom into atoms of strontium and xenon. They wrote immortal lines deploring war while they invented better ways to wage it. They refashioned a body for my life-principle, for the tensor-transformers that constitute my soul. They mounted me again in a sky-borne prairie schooner because they were weary of sanctified braying.

There were growling columns of blue-white fire in the night, and growling voices of restless masses of men. Men darted along the road around space.

Men departed for other stars. But after a thousand years, many remained on the planet of their birth—home-bodies and movie-idols and morticians, nembutal-addicts and advocates of world-government.

When the restless ones, the wild-eyed spacers were gone, the addicts got religion and the federalists became placid anarchists and the Parliaments voted themselves out of existence. There was peace of the third planet of 27 Lambda Serpentis, and good will among the inhabitants thereof. They made love and studied sociology under a friendly sun, under a pleasant blue sky forever.

On the road around space, my Master hungered for land.

And there was a yellow sun in the region of the Scorpion, and once it had been called 18 Scorpii, but now they named it Ba'Lagan. It was a little south of Serpens, a little nearer to the galactic nucleus. They named its planets Albrasa and Nynfi, and they were twins. Albrasa was already populated by a clan of hairy intellectuals with teeth and twittering voices. They liked the flavor of man-flesh, digested it easily.

Man came down on sky-lightning. Man came down to walk on the land and own it. I lay quietly rusting in the rain.

Man taught his grandson to hammer virgin copper into a vicious battle-ax, and taught him the mystic recipe for roasting a hairy intellectual. It was forbidden to boil a young intellectual in the milk of its mother, but it was

permissible to roast it alive and remind it that its fathers
had dared to attack a two-legged god.

Man's grandson waxed strong and malicious. He committed genocide on the furry natives and used their skins
for blankets. He shattered their braincases and erected
his own altars in their temples. He butchered an octo-
genarian on one of the altars, because the old man had
made the silly suggestion that they sacrifice a perfectly
healthy young virgin to their god. The young virgin
watched the ceremony with quietly triumphant eyes; then
she married the chief priest and bore him many children.

The biped bludgeoned the planet into submission. He
assured himself that he was the Chosen Child of the Most
High. He built himself a throne and sat upon it—while
he listened to a newscaster describe jet-battles over the
North Pole. Centuries wandered by, decked in gaudy
robes. And there was a war with Nynfi between the
worlds.

And then another Abraham Jolie bent over his drawing
board. Another crew of big-fisted men wrapped steel flesh
around my principle. Another race of men spat contempt
on the soil—the soil that had drunk the blood of their
fathers, felt the fire of the suns as the rockets heaved
skyward bearing my body and the bodies of my Master.

Men were steel-jacketed motes of flesh, scurrying
among the stars. Men were as dust, rolling across the
galactic prairie—bits of dandelion fluff whirling in a rising
tempest that bore them along the arm of the galactic
spiral and inward, ever inward. Their eyes were on Hercules and the fardistant globular clusters. He paused at
Nu Lupi and 15 Sagittea and a nameless yellow sun in
Ophiuchus where he met a native race who dared to be
bipeds. He crushed them quickly.

There were always those who remained behind, lingered on the planets where their ancestors had fought. I
watched them with my last eyes as the last ship hurtled
into space. I watched, and saw the lust go out of them,
saw them become as a cauldron removed from the fire.
Their boiling waned to a simmer, and they cooled. They
always found peace when the spacers were gone.

This I have never understood. I, the machine, the
space-spider, cannot understand. But I have seen it—the
exodus of the hungry, the settling of peace over those who
chose to linger. The hungry drink of the emptiness of

space, and their hunger grows. The placid eat of the
earth, and find peace, yet somehow—they seem to die a
little.

Ever deeper pressed the starships, deeper into Sagitta-
rius and Scorpius, and Lupus, Ophiuchus and Sagitta.
Now and then they paused to colonize and conquer. A
planet devoured a handful of men and tormented them
with its biological devices. But the men grew and beat the
savage planet into a slave after long ages, forced it to pay
tribute to its king. Once more they coveted the stars. Once
more they darted heavenward, leaving reluctant brothers
in peace.

They wrote a song. They called it "Ten Parsecs to Paradise." They sang the song as if they believed it. This I
have never understood.

It was always ten or twelve parsecs to another sun with
a class G spectrum, with a planet chastely clad in green
forests and white clouds. There he landed to rebuild, to
furrow the fertile earth, to rock in a porch swing at twilight sucking his pipe, and to thoughtfully stare at the
stars while his grandchildren romped like young chimpan-
zees on the cool lawn.

He had forgotten Earth—this old man—his race had
forgotten its history. But he knew a little. He knew the
star-going cycle—the landing of the starships, the re-
gression to savagery, the painful rebuilding, the cruelty,
the re-learning, the proud exodus. He knew these things
because Man had learned to keep a little of the past intact throughout a cycle. He no longer fell back to chipping
arrowheads. Now he managed to begin again in an age
of bronze or soft iron. And he knew in advance that he
would carve mighty industries out of savage wilderness.

But the old man was sad as he sat on his porch. He
knew so little of the Great Purpose. Why must his seed
fling itself starward? He knew that it must—but he lacked
a reason. His grandchildren played in the twilight, played
space-games, although there was not yet a starship on the
planet.

There was a small boy on the lawn who tried to tease
the girls, but the girls put on masks of superior sophisti-
cation and ignored the little man. Disgruntled, he looked
up and saw the old man dreaming on the porch.

"Gramp's got star-craze!" he shrieked. "Look at Gramp menting! Nnyahh! Gramp's got star-craze."

Musical laughter tittered over the lawn. Another voice took up the cry. The old man chuckled affectionately but wistfully. They were young, but they knew about the star-thirst. The planet was young, too young for star-ships, even though the priests preserved the records and scientific writings in the temples. The planet knew about space and coveted it. Yet, the children would all be dead before the first vessel was launched.

The laughter on the lawn subsided. The eldest child, a gawky and freckled girl of eight years came trudging up the steps to sit against the post and stare at him quietly in the gloom. He felt a question lurking in her silence. He nudged her ribs affectionately with his toe.

"What weighty matter worries you, Nari?" he asked pleasantly.

"Why is star-craze, Gramp?"

He rocked thoughtfully for a moment. "Why are there men to feel it?" he countered.

The child was silent.

"I know only what the priests say, Nari," he told her gently. "They say that man once owned a paradise planet, and that he ran away in search of a better one. They say he made the Lord Bion angry. And the lord hid the paradise, and condemned Man to forever wander, touched his heart with eternal hunger for the place he lost."

"Will people find it again, Gramp?"

"Never—so the priests say. The hunger is on him, Nari."

"It's not fair!" said the little girl.

"What isn't, my child?"

"Star-craze. Last night I saw a lady crying. She was just standing there crying at the sky."

"Where?"

"On the street. Waiting for a motor bus."

"How old was she?"

Nari scraped her heels and muttered doubtfully. "It was kind of dark."

Gramp chuckled reassuringly. "I bet she wasn't over fourteen. I bet she was still a kid. Star-craze comes to little girls about the time they start being interested in little boys. Works the other way, too. But you grow out of it, Nari. By the time you're twenty, it won't make you miserable any more. It gives you a goal. Gives everyone a goal. Something to work for. Something to long for and fight for. The stars—you'll want to give them to your grandchildren."

"Won't I get to go?"

"Not ever, Nari."

They fell silent again, and the old man peered up into the deepening blackness with its countless array of suns sitting like hens on their nests of planets. He scarely believed the legend of the lost paradise-planet, but it was a good story to tell little girls. It made him sad though, and revived a little of the forgotten restlessness of his youth. If only he could have lived two centuries later—

But then a gust of wind brought the sweet perfume of freshly cut hay from the field to the east of the farmhouse, and the odor made him smile. The field would have to be raked tomorrow, and the hay brought in to the barn. A lot of things like that needed to be done before the starships could rise again. And every straining muscle helped toward the ultimate goal. The hay fed the animals whose flesh fed the men who made the tools which built the factories which fashioned more complicated tools—and so the journey, down the long road to space again.

The old man didn't know why the road had to be traveled, nor did he really care. The road was there, and it beckoned, and it gave meaning to life, for surely the Lord Bion was less cruel a tempter than the priests sometimes proclaimed Him. Surely there was something more than despair at the end of the long, long road.

The old man grew older, and died peacefully, and his ashes were scattered across the fields he had tilled since boyhood. His children, and his grandchildren, followed in his patient steps, and their ashes were mingled with his own before the first gleaming sky craft burst star fire in the night.

When the skycraft at last rumbled upward, the crowd thundered a triumphant roar, the crowd gathered to witness the culmination of their labors, and the labors of their ancestors. Men walked with shoulders erect and with pride glowing in their faces. Again they triumphed over forces that held them bound to a grain of sand in the sky. Again they slashed through the knot that held them in

the web of the continuum, and shed the weights that
dragged at their feet.

I noticed a subtle difference in those who lingered behind. They no longer lingered of their own choosing.
They were no longer the peace-seekers and placid ones.
They were those who could not go because they were old,
or sick, or because the industries were half-deserted and
there was no one left to build the ships. They still stared
longingly upward on dark nights.

"We'll do it again," they promised. "We'll repopulate
and do it again."

But the bitterness of their plight was upon them, a
sense of defeat and doom. They fought savagely among
themselves. They fell in feudal wars, while the starward
wave receded.

I am the acolyte of the space-priest, the server of the
pale proud biped. I have taken him onward across the
void, to the Hercules Cluster, and beyond it to the un-
charted regions past the dust clouds of the Great Rift,
into the star-pact heartland of the galactic nucleus where
other races were testing their space wings and tasting of
the great freedom. I have watched him, and have felt the
life-aura of his longing. And I have wondered. What is his
goal? Where is an answer to his hunger?

My neural circuits are not of flesh. My circuits are of
glass and steel. My thought is a fanning electron stream.
But I have prayed. I, the spider who builds around space,
have prayed to the gods of the biped I serve. I have
prayed to the God of the North End of Space. I have
asked, "Where is his peace?"

No answer came.

I have seen my Master change.

The biped was thunder across the galaxy. The biped
was a swift and steel-clad spear hurtling ruthlessly onward. He made no friends; for he came as a being who
owned the stars, and he took what he wanted along the
way. He left his seed to grow anew. A creature of fierce
pride! And fiercer longing. He trampled hatelessly such
races as he encountered. He crushed them, or harnessed
them to his plow, or borrowed their neural circuits for his
bio-computers. Sometimes he fought against his own race,
men who had traveled other routes to the galactic heartland. When man battled against man, they fought with

hatred and cruelty and bitterness—but never with contempt. Man saw a rival king in man. Against other races, he waged only cool contempt and hot death.

Sometimes a thoughtful old man would say, "Seems to me they've got as much right to live as we have. Seems to me all intelligent creatures have got a common denominator. God, maybe." But he muttered it quietly, speculatively. Even if he believed it, he never objected to the swift ambush of the alien ship, nor to the razing of the alien city. For the biped stalked a new frontier. The ape-tribe stole across a field where danger lurked. He was fresh from the branches of the trees, not wise to the ways of the plains. How could he risk offering peace to the shaggy beast who crouched in the tall grass? He could only weigh the odds—then strike or run away.

He took the planets of the yellow suns—deep in the galactic heartland. He skipped from one to the next in jumps as long as his patience would last. He captured the globular clusters. He inhabited each planet for a few generations. He built ships, and battled with his brothers for the right to take them. Many were left behind. They repopulated after an exodus, rebuilt, launched a second flight, and a third—until those who finally remained at home were those who lacked the incentive of the big hunger.

Those who lacked incentive sought their peace. They molded a pleasant place to live in and infested it. Or else they scorned pleasantry and made themselves a battleground.

My Master is the Nomad, gaunt and tall. My Master grits his teeth in staring at the stars, and his eyes go narrow and moist. I have mirrored his hunger, have allowed his life-aura to seep into the cold steel and hot glass of me, have reflected his thoughts in my circuits. Sometimes he wonders if I am alive. But then he remembers that he built me. He built me to think, not to be alive. Perhaps I am not alive, but only a mirror that catches a little of my Master's life. I have seen him change.

The spearhead groups pushed relentlessly across the gleaming blackness, and each generation grew more restless than the one before it. The restless moved ahead. The contented remained at home. Each exodus was a separation, and a selection of the malcontent.

The biped came to believe his priests. He believed the

legend of the lost home. He believed that Bion had touched him with the hunger curse. How else could they explain the pressing cry of the heart? How could they interpret the clamor of the young, the tears—except as a Divine Thirst.

The star-craze. The endless search.

There was a green planet beyond the heartland, and it was ripe for bursting its human star-seed. There was a launching field, and a ship, and teeming crowd, and a fence with guards to keep the others out. A man and a girl stood at the fence, and it was nearly dawn.

He touched her arm and gazed at the shadows on the launching site.

"We won't find it, Marka," he said quietly. "We'll never find it."

"You believe the legend, Teris?" she whispered.

"The Planet of Heaven? It's up there. But we can never find it."

"Then why must you look?"

"We are damned, Marka."

There was a silence, then she breathed, "It *can* be found. The Lord Bion promised—"

"Where is *that* written, Marka?" he scoffed coldly.

"In a woman's heart."

Teris laughed loudly. "What does the heart-writing say?"

She turned to stare at the dark shadow of the ship against the graying sky. "It says: 'When Man is content —without his lost paradise—when he reconciles himself —Bion will forgive, and show us the road home.' "

He waved his hand fiercely at the fading stars in the west. "*Ours*, Marka. They're ours! We took them."

"Do you want them?"

He stiffened angrily and glared at the shadow of her face. "You . . . you make me sick. You're a hangbacker."

"No!" She shook her head wildly. "*No!*" She caught at his arm as he retreated a step. "I wish I could go! I want to go, do you hear?"

"I hear," he snapped. "But you can't, so there's no use talking about it. You're not well, Marka. The others wouldn't let you aboard." He backed away another step.

"I love you," she said frantically.

He turned and stumbled away toward the sky-chariot. *"I love you!"*

He began to trot, then burst into a wild sprint. Afraid, she thought in triumph. Afraid of turning back. Of loving her too much.

"*You'll never find it!*" she screamed after him. "*You can't find it up there! It's here—right here!*"

But he was lost in the crowd that milled about the ship. The ship had opened its hatches. The ship was devouring the people, two at a time. The ship devoured Teris and the space crew. Then it closed its mouth and belched flame from its rockets.

She gasped and slumped against a fencepost. She hung there sobbing until a guard drove her away.

A rocket bellowed the space song. The girl tore off her wedding bracelet and flung it in the gutter. Then she went home to fix breakfast for the children.

I am the Weaver of space. I am a Merchant of new fabrics in flux patterns for five-space continua. I serve the biped who built me, though his heart be steeped in hell.

Once in space, a man looked at me and murmured softly, "You are the cross on which we crucify ourselves."

But the big hunger pushed him on—on toward the ends of space. And he encountered worlds where his ancestors had lived, and where his peaceful cousins still dwelt in symbiosis with their neighbors. Some of the worlds were civilized, some barbaric, and some were archaeological graveyards. My nomads, they wore haunted faces as they re-explored the fringes of the galaxy where Man had walked before, leaving his footprints and his peace-seeking children. The galaxy was filled.

Where could he go now?

I have seen the frantic despair in their faces when, upon landing, natives appeared and greeted them politely, or tried to kill them, or worshiped them, or just ran away to hide. The nomads lurked near their ships. A planet with teeming cities was no place for a wanderer. They watched the multifaceted civilizations with bitter, lonely eyes.

Where were new planets?

Across the great emptiness to the Andromeda galaxy? Too far for the ships to go. Out to the Magellanic clouds? Already visited.

Where then?

He groped blindly, this biped. He had forgotten the

trail by which his ancestors had come, and he kept re-
crossing it, finding it winding everywhere. He could only
plunge aimlessly on, and when he reached the last limit of
his fuel—land. If the natives could not provide the fuel,
he would have to stay, and try to pass another cycle of
starward growth on the already inhabited world. But a
cycle was seldom completed. The nomads intermarried
with the local people; the children, the hybrid children,
were less steeped in hunger than their fathers. Sometimes
they built ships for economic purposes, for trade and commerce—but never for the hysterical starward sweep. They
heard no music from the North End of Space, no Lorelei
call from the void. The craving was slowly dying.

They came to a planet. The natives called it "Earth."
They departed again in cold fright, and a space commander blew out his brains to banish the memory. Then
they found another planet that called itself "Earth"—and
another and another. They smiled again, knowing that
they would never know which was the true home of Man.

They sensed the nearness of the end.

They no longer sang the old songs of a forgotten paradise. And there were no priests among them. They looked
back at the Milky Way, and it had been their royal road.
They looked ahead, where only scattered stars separated
them from the intergalactic wasteland—an ocean of emptiness and death. They could not consign themselves to its
ultimate embrace. They had fought too long, labored too
hard to surrender willingly to extinction.

But the cup of their life was broken.

And to the land's last limit they came.

They found a planet with a single moon, with green
forests, with thin clouds draping her gold and blue body in
the sunlight. The breath of the snowking was white on her
ice caps, and her seas were placid green. They landed.
They smiled when the natives called the planet "Earth."
Lots of planets claimed the distinction of being Man's
birthplace.

Among the natives there was a dumpy little professor—
still human, though slightly evolved. On the night following the nomad's landing, he sat huddled in an easy-chair,
staring at the gaunt nomadic giant whose bald head nearly
touched the ceiling of the professor's library. The professor slowly shook his head and sighed.

"I can't understand you people,"

"Nor I you," rumbled the nomad.

"Here is Earth—yet you won't believe it!"

The giant snorted contemptuously. "Who cares? Is this crumb in space the fulfillment of a dream?"

"You dreamed of a lost Earthparadise."

"So we thought. But who knows the real longing of a dream? Where is its end? Its goal?"

"We found ours here on Earth."

The giant made a wry mouth. "You've found nothing but your own smug existence. You're a snake swallowing its tail."

"Are you sure you're not the same?" purred the scholar.

The giant put his fists on his hips and glowered at him. The professor whitened.

"That's untrue," boomed the giant. "We've found nothing. And we're through. At least we went searching. Now we're finished."

"Not *you*. It's the *job* that's finished. You can live here. And be proud of a job well done."

The giant frowned. "Job? *What* job?"

"Why, fencing in the stars. Populating the galaxy."

The big man stared at him in horrified amazement.

"Well," the scholar insisted, "you did it, you know. Who populates the galaxy now?"

"People like you."

The impact of the searing words brought a sick gasp from the small professor. He was a long moment in realizing their full significance. He wilted. He sank lower in the chair.

The nomad's laughter suddenly rocked the room. He turned away from his victim and helped himself to a tumbler of liqueur. He downed it at a gulp and grinned at the professor. He tucked the professor's liqueur under his arm, waved a jaunty farewell, and lumbered out into the night.

"My decanter," protested the professor in a whisper.

He went to bed and lay whimpering slightly in drowsiness. He was afraid of the tomorrows that lay ahead.

The nomads settled on the planet for lack of fuel. They complained of the climate and steadfastly refused to believe that it was Earth. They were a troublesome, boisterous lot, and frequently needed psychoanalysis for their various crimes. A provisional government was set up to deal with the problem. The natives had forgotten about governments, and they called it a "welfare commission."

The nomads who were single kidnaped native wives. Sometimes they kidnaped several, being a prolific lot. They begot many children, and a third-generation hybrid became the first dictator of a northern continent.

I am rusting in the rain. I shall never serve my priest here on Earth again. Nuclear fuels are scarce. They are needed for the atomic warheads now zipping back and forth across the North Pole. A poet—one of the hybrids— has written immortal lines deploring war; and the lines were inscribed on the post-humous medal they gave his widow.

Three dumpy idealists built a spaceship, but they were caught and hung for treason. The eight-foot lawyer who defended them was also hung.

The world wears a long face; and the stars twinkle invitingly. But few men look upward now. Things are probably just as bad on the next inhabited planet.

I am the spider who walked around space. I, Harpist for a pale proud Master, have seen the big hunger, have tasted its red glow reflected in my circuits. Still I cannot understand.

But I feel there are some who understand. I have seen the pride in their faces. They walk like kings.

Conditionally Human

HE KNEW THERE was no use hanging around after breakfast, but he could not bear leaving her like this. He put on his coat in the kitchen, stood uncertainly in the doorway, and twisted his hat in his hands. His wife still sat at the table, fingered the handle of an empty cup, stared fixedly out the window at the kennels behind the house, and pointedly ignored his small coughings and scrapings. He watched the set of her jaw for a moment, then cleared his throat.

"Anne?"

"What?"

"I can't stand seeing you like this."

"Then go away."

"Can't I do anything—?"

"I've told you what to do."

Her voice was a monotone, full of hurt. He could neither endure the hurt nor remove it. He gingerly crossed the room to stand behind her, hoping she'd look up at him and let her face go soft, maybe even cry a little. But she kept gazing out the window in accusing silence. He chuckled suddenly and touched her silk-clad shoulder. The shoulder shivered away. Her dark hair quivered as she shuddered, and her arms were suddenly locked tightly about her breasts as if she were cold. He pulled back his hand; his big pliant face went slack. He gulped forlornly.

"Honeymoon's over, huh?"

"Ha!"

He backed a step away, paused again. "Hey, baby, you knew before you married me," he reminded her.

"I did not."

"You knew I was District Inspector for the F. B. A. You knew I had charge of a pound."

"I didn't know you *killed* them" she snapped, whirling.

"I don't have to kill many," he offered.

"That's like saying you don't kill them very dead."

"Look, honey, they're only animals."

"Intelligent animals!"

"Intelligent as a human imbecile, maybe."

"A baby is an imbecile. Would you kill a baby? Of course you would! You do! That's what they are: babies. I hate you."

He withered, groped desperately for a new approach. "Look, 'intelligence' is a word applicable only to humans. It's the name of a human function, and . . ."

"And that makes *them* human!" she finished. "Murderer!"

"Baby!"

"Don't call me baby! Call them baby!"

He made a miserable noise in his throat, backed a few steps toward the door, and beat down his better judgment against speaking again. "Anne, honey, look! Think of the good things about the job. Sure, everything has its ugly angle. But just think: we get this house rent-free; I've got my own district with no local boss to hound us; I make my own hours; you'll meet lots of people that stop in at the pound. It's a fine job, honey!"

Her face was a mask again. She sipped her coffee and seemed to be listening. He blundered hopefully on.

"And what can I do about it? I can't help my Placement Aptitude score. They say Bio-Authority is where I belong, and it's to Bio I have to go. Oh, sure, I don't *have* to work where they send me. You can always join the General Work Pool, but that's all the law allows, and GWP'ers don't have families. So I go where Placement Aptitude says I'm needed."

"You've got aptitudes for killing kids?"

He groaned and closed his eyes. "They gave me the job because I like kids. And because I have a biology degree, and a knack for being neighborly, maybe—with plain people. And because I'm not really brainy enough to be a scientists' scientist. Just a technician. Understand? And destroying the unclaimed animals is the smallest part of it. Honey, before the evolvotron, before anybody ever heard of Anthropos Incorporated, people used to have municipal officials for such things. Dogcatchers, I think they called them. Didn't have the Dog-R series then, of course—not mutants. But that's all it is. I'm just an up-to-date dogcatcher."

Ice-green eyes turned slowly to meet his gaze. Her face by window-light seemed delicately cut from dusty marble. A corner of her mouth twitched contempt. Then she looked out the window toward the kennels again.

He backed to the door, plucked nervously at a splinter on the woodwork, watched her hopefully for a moment.

"Work to do. Got to go."

"Do you need to be kissed?" Sweetly contemptuous.

He ripped the splinter loose. "See you tonight."

The front door slammed. She sat listening to his footsteps on the porch and down the walk. Then the kennel truck's starter grumbled, and its turbines whined to life. She choked back a sob and started after him, but by the time she got to the porch, the truck was already backed into the street. It lurched suddenly away with angry acceleration toward the highway that lay to the east. She stood blinking in the red morning sunlight, shoulders slumped. Things were wrong with the world.

A bell rang somewhere, rang again. She started slightly, shook herself, went to answer the telephone. A carefully enunciated voice that sounded chubby and professional called for Inspector Norris. She told it disconsolately that he was gone.

"Gone? Oh, you mean to work. I thought for a moment you meant . . . heh heh. Can this be the new Mrs. Norris?" The voice was hearty, greasy. She muttered affirmatively.

"Ah, yes. Norris told me. Ah, this is Doctor Georges, my dear. I have a rather urgent matter to talk over with your husband, but perhaps I can talk to you."

"You can probably get him on the highway. There's a phone in the truck." What sort of urgent matters, she wondered, did doctors discuss with dogcatchers.

"I'm afraid not, my dear. The inspector doesn't switch on his phone until office hours. I know him well."

"Can't you wait?"

"It's really an emergency, Mrs. Norris. I need an animal from the pound—a Chimp K-48-3, preferably a five-year-old."

"I know nothing about the kennels," she said rather stiffly. "You'll have to talk to him."

"Now see here, Mrs. Norris, this is an emergency, and I have to have . . ."

"Why don't you just do whatever you would have done if I hadn't answered the phone?" she said, and quietly hung up.

It began ringing again. She glanced back at it with a twings of guilt. Emergency? What sort of emergency would require a chimp K-48? "Butchery," she muttered vaguely, and let the phone ring. She was not not *not* going to get involved in his work. I'll leave him first, she told herself.

The truck whirred slowly along the suburban street that wound among nestled groups of pastel plastic cottages set approximately two to an acre on the lightly wooded land. With its population fixed by law at half a billion, the continent was one sprawling suburb, dotted with community centers, between the dense belts and blots of industrial development. There was no open country, had been none since the days of his grandparents. This was relative wilderness; he liked it, but there was still no place to be alone.

He approached an intersection. A small animal sat on the curb, wrapped in its own busy tail. The crown of its oversized head was bald, but its body was covered with gray-blue fur. A pink tongue licked daintily at small forepaws that were equipped with prehensile thumbs. It eyed the truck morosely as Norris drew to a halt and smiled down at it from the cab.

"Hi, kitten. What's *your* name?"

The Cat-Q-5 stared at him indifferently for a moment. *"Kiyi Rorry,"* it wailed at last.

"Kitty Rorry. That's a fine name. Where do you live, Rorry?"

The Cat-Q-5 ignored him.

"Whose child are you, Rorry? Will you tell me that?"

Rorry regarded him disgustedly. Norris glanced around. There were no houses near the intersection, and he feared the animal might be lost. It blinked at him sleepily, bored, then resumed its paw bath. He repeated the question.

"Mama kiyi, kiyi Mama," it finally reported.

"That's right, Mama's kitty. But where is Mama? Suppose she ran away?"

The Cat-Q-5 looked startled. It stuttered briefly. Its fur crept erect. It glanced both ways along the street, shot suddenly away at a fast scamper along the sidewalk. Norris followed it in the truck for two blocks, until it darted onto a porch and began wailing through the screen. "Mama no run ray! Mama no run ray!"

He chuckled and drove on. A couple who had failed to satisfy the genetic requirements for legal childbearing could become quite attached to a Cat-Q-5, but the cats were safer, emotionally safer, than any of the quasi-human models such as the Chimp-K, or neutroid. The death of a neutroid struck some families as hard as might the death of a child; most couples at least managed to endure the loss of a Cat-Q or Dog-F without formal mourning or quasi-religious rites. A genetic-C couple were permitted to own one neutroid, or two nonanthropic models whose daily food requirements would not exceed eight hundred calories. Many psychologists seemed to regard neutroids as dynamite, recommended pets with a lower love-demand potential.

What about Anne? Norris lost his vestigial smile. His own card was stamped "genetic-C." They had agreed to a childless marriage. Anne loved kids. But he had agreed to it. He had been thinking about the kennel animals: how she might help with them, direct her maternal feelings toward them, divert her basic need . . . But now, the hostility.

What if she wanted a pseudoparty, a neutroid for herself?

An invitation of a pseudoparty had come in yesterday's mail. He fumbled in his pocket for the battered card:

> You are cordially invited
> to attend the pseudoparturition
> and ensuing cocktail hour
> to celebrate the arrival of
> **HONEY BLOSSOM**

Cherished event to occur on
Twelveweek's Sixday of 2063 at
19:30 hours
Reception Room, Rockabye Hours Clinic

R.s.v.p.   Mr. & Mrs. John Hanley Slade

The invitation had come late, the party would be tonight. He had meant to call Slade today and say that he
and Anne would probably drop in for cocktails, but would
be unable to get there in time for the delivery. But now
that she had reacted so sharply to the less pleasant aspects
of his job, perhaps he had better keep her away from senti-
mental occasions involving neutroids.

Glancing at the card again reminded him to stop at
Sherman III Community Center for the mail. He turned
onto the shopping street that paralleled the great highway
and drove past several blocks of commercial buildings
that served the surrounding suburbs. At the down-ramp
he gave the attendant a four-bit bill and sent the truck
down to be parked under the street, then went to the message office. When he dropped his code-disk into the slot,
the feedway under his box number chattered out a yard
of paper tape. He scanned it slowly end to end—note from
Aunt Maye, bill from Synthamilk Products, letter from
Anne's mother. The only item of importance was the
memo from the chief: a troublesome tidbit, but he had
expected it:

*Attention All District Inspectors: Subject? Deviant
Neutroid. You will immediately initiate systematic
and thorough survey of all animals bearing serial
numbers in the Bermuda K-99 series for birth dates
during 26th through 32nd weeks of year 2062, in re
Delmont Negligency Case. Seize animals in this cate-
gory, impound, run applicable sections of normalcy
tests. Observe signs of endocrinal deviation and nonstandard response patterns. Delmont confessed to
passing only one nonstandard model, but suspect
others. He disclaims memory of deviant's serial number. Possible ruse to stop investigation after first animal found, if more than one.*

*If allowed to reach age-set or adulthood, such a
deviant could be dangerous to its owner or to others.*

Hold all seized K-99s who exhibit the slightest departure from standard. Forward to Central Lab. Return standard units to owners. Accomplish within seven days.

C. Franklin.

"Seven days," he remarked irritably, wadded the tape in his pocket, stalked out to get the truck.

The district covered two hundred square miles. With a replacement quota of seventy-five neutroids a week, the district would probably have picked up about forty K-99s from the Bermuda factory influx during the six-week period last year. Could he round them all up in a week? It seemed doubtful. And there were only eleven empty cages in the kennel. The other forty-nine were occupied by the previous inspector's unclaimed inventory, awaiting destruction. The crematorium behind the kennels appeared slated for a busy week. Anne, Anne.

He was halfway to Wylo City when the radiophone buzzed on the dash. He pulled into the slow lane and answered quickly, hoping for his wife's voice. Instead, there was a polite professional purr.

"Inspector Norris?"

Norris made a sour mouth. "Yes, Georges?"

"Are you extremely busy at the moment?"

"What rich bitch is your problem now, Doctor?"

"Now Norris!"

"Busy. Extremely busy."

"One of my patients, a Mrs. Sarah Glubbes, called a while ago and said her baby was sick."

"So?"

"She has no baby. I'm getting absent-minded; I forgot she's genetic-C until I got there."

"Let me guess. It turned out to be a neutroid."

"That's right."

"Why tell me?"

"It's dying. Eighteenth order virus. Naturally, I can't get it admitted to a hospital."

"Ever hear of vets?"

"You don't understand. She insists it's her baby, believes it's her own. How can I send it to a vet?"

"That's your worry. Is she an old patient of yours?"

"Why, yes, I've known Sarah since——"

"Since you presided at her pseudopart?"

"How did you know?"

"Just a guess. If you put her through pseudopart, then you deserve all the trouble you get."

"I take it you're an abolitionist."

"Skip it. What did you want from me?"

"A replacement neutroid. From the kennel."

"Baloney. You couldn't fool her. If she's blind, she'd still know her own animal."

"I'll have to take the chance. Listen, Norris, it's pathetic. She knows the disease can be cured—in humans —with hospitalization and expensive treatment that I can't get for a neutroid. No vet could get the drug either. Scarce. It's pathetic."

"I'm crying all over the steering wheel."

The doctor paused. "Sorry, Norris, I thought you were human."

"Not to the extent of doing half-legal favors that won't be appreciated for some rich neurotic dame and a doc who practices pseudopart."

"One correction," Georges said stiffly. "Sarah's not rich. She's a middle-aged widow and couldn't pay for treatment if she could get it. But thanks anyway, Norris."

"Hold it," he grunted. "What's the chimp's series?"

"It's a K-48, a five-year-old with a three-year age set."

Norris thought for a moment. It was a dirty deal, and it wouldn't work.

"I think I've got one in the kennel that's fairly close," he offered doubtfully.

"Good, good, I'll have Fred go over and—"

"Wait, now. This one'll be spooky, won't know her, and the serial number will be different."

"I know, I know," Georges sighed. "But it seems worth a try. An attack of V-18 can cause mild amnesia in humans; that might explain why it won't know her. About the serial number—"

"Don't try changing it," Norris growled.

"How about obliterating—"

"Don't, and I'll check on it a couple of weeks from now to make damn sure you don't. That's a felony, Georges."

"All right, all right, I'll just have to take the chance that she won't notice it. When can I pick it up?"

"Call my wife in fifteen minutes. I'll speak to her first."

"Uh, yes . . . Mrs. Norris. Uh, very well, thanks, Inspector." Georges hung up quickly.

Norris lit a cigarette, steeled himself, called Anne. Her voice was dull, depressed, but no longer angry.

"All right, Terry," she said tonelessly. "I'll go out to the kennel and get the one in cage thirty-one, and give it to Georges when he comes.

"Thanks, babe."

He heard her mutter, "And then I'll go take a bath," just before the circuit clicked off.

He flipped off the auto-driver, took control of the truck, slipped into the fast lane and drove furiously toward Wylo City and the district wholesale offices of Anthropos Incorporated to begin tracing down the suspected Bermuda K-99s in accordance with Franklin's memo. He would have to check through all incoming model files for the six-week period, go over the present inventory, then run down the Bermuda serial numbers in a mountain of invoices covering a thirty-week period, find the pet shops and retail dealers that had taken the doubtful models, and finally survey the retail dealers to trace the models to their present owners. With cooperation from wholesaler and dealers, he might get it down to the retail level by mid-afternoon, but getting the models away from their owners would be the nasty part of the job. He was feeling pretty nasty himself, he decided. The spat with Anne, the distasteful thoughts associated with Slade's pseudoparty, the gnawing remorse about collaborating with Dr. Georges in a doubtful maneuver to pacify one Sarah Glubbes, a grim week's work ahead, plus his usual charge of suppressed resentment toward Chief Franklin—it all added up to a mood that could turn either black or vicious, depending on circumstance.

If some doting Mama gave him trouble about impounding her darling tail-wagger, he was, he decided, in the right kind of mood to get a warrant and turn the job over to the sheriff.

The gasping neutroid lay on the examining table under the glaring light. The torso quivered and twitched as muscles contracted spasmodically, but the short legs were already limp and paralyzed, allowing the chubby man in the white coat to lift them easily by the ankles and retrieve the rectal thermometer. The neutroid wheezed and chattered plaintively as the nurse drew the blanket across its small body again.

"A hundred and nine," grunted the chubby man, his voice muffled by the gauze mask. His eyes probed the nurse's eyes for a moment. He jerked his head toward the door. "She still out there?"

The nurse nodded.

The doctor stared absently at the thermometer stem for a moment, looked up again, spoke quietly. "Get a hypo—necrofine."

She turned toward the sterilizer, paused briefly. "Three c.c.s?" she asked.

"Twelve," he corrected.

Her eyes locked with his for several seconds; then she nodded and went to the sterilizer.

"May I leave first?" she asked tonelessly while filling the syringe.

"Certainly."

"What'll I say to Mrs. Glubbes?" She crossed to the table again and handed him the hypo.

"Nothing. Use the back way. Go tell Fred to run over to the kennels and pick up the substitute. I've called Mrs. Norris. Oh yeah, and tell Fred to stop in here first. I'll have something for him to take out."

The nurse glanced down at the squirming, whimpering newt, shivered slightly, and left the room. When the door closed, Georges bent over the table with the hypo. When the door opened again, Georges looked up to see his son looking in.

"Take this along," he grunted, and handed Fred the bundle wrapped in newspapers.

"What'll I do with it?" the youth asked.

"Chuck it in Norris's incinerator."

Fred glanced at the empty examining table and nodded indifferently. "Can Miss Laskell come back now?" he asked in going.

"Tell her yeah. And hurry with that other newt."

"Sure, Pop. See you later."

The nurse looked in uncertainly before entering.

"Get cleaned up," he told her. "And go sit with Mrs. Glubbes."

"What'll I say?"

"The 'baby' will recover. She can take it home late this afternoon if she gets some rest first."

"What're you going to do—about the substitute?"

"Give it a shot to put it to sleep, give her some codeine to feed it."

"Why?"

"So it'll be too groggy for a few days to even notice her, so it'll get addicted and attached to her because she gives it the codeine."

"The serial number?"

"I'll put the tattooed foot in a cast. V-18 paralysis— you know."

"Smart," she muttered, but there was no approval in her voice.

When she had changed clothes in the anteroom, she unlocked the door to the office, but paused before passing on into the reception room. The door was ajar, and she gazed through the crack at the woman who sat on the sofa.

Sarah Glubbes was gray and gaunt and rigid as stone. She sat with her hands clenched in her lap, her wide empty eyes—dull blue spots on yellowed marble orbs— staring ceilingward while the colorless lips of a knife-slash mouth moved tautly in earnest prayer. The nurse's throat felt tight. She rubbed it for a moment. After all, the thing was only an animal.

She straightened her shoulders, put on a cheerful smile, and marched on into the reception room. The yellowed orbs snapped demandingly toward her.

"Everything's *all* right, Mrs. Glubbes," she began.

"Finished," Norris grunted at three o'clock that afternoon.

"Thirty-six K-99s," murmured the Anthropos file-clerk, gazing over Norris's shoulder at the clip-board with the list of doubtful newts and the dealers to whom they had been sent. "Lots of owners may be hard to locate."

"Yeah. Thanks, Andy, and you too Mabel."

The girl smiled and handed him a slip of paper. "Here's a list of owners for thirteen of them. I called the two local shops for you. Most of them live here close."

He glanced at the names, felt tension gathering in his stomach. It wasn't going to be easy. What could he say to them?

Howdy, ma'am, excuse me, but I've come to take your little boy away to jail. . . . Oh, yes ma'am, he'll have a place to stay—in a little steel cage with a forkful of straw, and he'll get vitaminized mush every day. What's that? His sleepy-time stories and his pink honey-crumbles? Sorry, ma'am, your little boy is only a mutated chimpanzee, you know, and not really human at all.

"That'll go over great," he grumbled, staring absently at the window.

"Beg pardon, sir?" answered the clerk.

"Nothing, Andy, nothing." He thanked them again and strode out into the late afternoon sunlight. Still a couple of hours working time left, and plenty of things to do. Checking with the other retail dealers would be the least unpleasant task, but there was no use saving the worst until last. He glanced at the list Mabel had given him, checked it for the nearest address, then squared his shoulders and headed for the kennel truck.

Anne met him at the door when he came home at six. He stood on the porch for a moment, smiling at her weakly. The smile was not returned.

"Doctor Georges' boy came," she told him. "He signed for the—"

She stopped to stare at him, then opened the screen, reached up quickly to brush light fingertips over his cheek.

"*Terry!* Those welts! What happened—get scratched by a Cat-Q?"

"No, by a human-F," he grumbled, and stepped past her into the hall; Anne followed, eyeing him curiously while he reached for the phone and dialed.

"Who're you calling?" she asked.

"Society's watchdog," he answered as the receiver buzzed in his ear.

"Your eye, Terry—it's all puffy. Will it turn black?"

"Maybe."

"Did the human-F do that too?"

"Uh-uh, Human-M—name of Pete Klusky . . ."

The phone craked at him suddenly. *"This is the record-voice of Sheriff Yates. I'll be out from five to seven. If it's urgent, call your constable."*

He hung up briefly, then irritably dialed the locator service.

"Mnemonic register, trail calls, and official locations," grated a mechanical voice. *"Your business, please."*

"This is T. Norris, Sherman-9-4566-78B, Official rating B, Priority B, code XT-88-U-Bio. Get Sheriff Yates for me."

"Nature of the call?"

"Offish biz."

"I shall record the call."

He waited. The robot found Yates on the first probability-trial attempt—in the local poolhall.

"I'm getting to hate that infernal gadget," Yates snapped. "Acts like it's got me psyched. Whattaya want, Norris?"

"Cooperation. I'm mailing you three letters charging three Wylo citizens with resisting a federal official— namely me—and charging one of them with assault. I tried to pick up their neutroids for a pound inspection, and—"

Yates bellowed lusty laughter in his ear.

"Not funny," he growled. "I've got to get those neutroids. It's connected with the Delmont case."

Yates stopped laughing. "Oh? Well . . . I'll take care of it."

"Rush order, Sheriff. Can you get the warrants tonight and pick up the animals in the morning?"

"Easy on those warrants, boy. Judge Charleman can't be bothered just any time. I can get the newts to you by noon, I guess, provided we don't have to get a helicopter posse to chase down the mothers."

"Well, okay. But listen—I want the charges dropped if they cooperate with you. And don't shake the warrants at them unless you have to. Just get those newts, that's all I want."

"Okay, boy. Give me the dope."

Norris read him the names and addresses of the three unwilling owners, and a precise account of what happened in each case. As soon as he hung up, Anne muttered "Sit still," perched on his knees, and began stroking chilly ointment across his burning cheek. He watched her cool eyes flicker from his cheek to his own eyes and down again. She was no longer angry, but only gloomy and withdrawn from him. He touched her arm. She seemed not to notice it.

"Hard day, Terry?"

"Slightly. I picked up nine newts out of thirteen, anyhow. They're in the truck now."

"Good thing you didn't get them all. There are only twelve empty cages."

"Twelve? Oh, Georges picked one up, didn't he?"

"And sent a package," she said, eyeing him soberly.

"Package? Where is it?"

"In the crematorium. The boy took it back there."

He swallowed a tight spot in his throat, said nothing.

"Oh, and darling—Mrs. Slade called. Why didn't you tell me we're going out tonight?"

"Going out?" It sounded a little weak.

"Well, she said she hadn't heard from you. I couldn't very well say no, so I told her I'd be there, at least."

"You—?"

"Oh, I didn't say about you, Terry. I said you'd like to go, but you might have to work. I'll go alone if you don't want to.

He stared at her with a puzzled frown. "*You* want to go to the psuedoparty?"

"Not particularly. But I've never been to one. I'm just curious."

He nodded, slowly, felt grim inside. She finished with the ointment, patted his cheek, managed a cheerful smile.

"Come on, Terry. Let's go unload your nine neutroids."

He stared at her dumbly.

"Let's forget about this morning, Terry."

He nodded. She averted her face suddenly, and her lip quivered. "I—I know you've got a job that's got to be—" She swallowed hard and turned away. "See you out in the kennels," she choked gaily, then hurried down the hall toward the door. Norris scratched his chin unhappily as he watched her go.

After a moment, he dialed the mnemonic register again. "Keep a line on this number," he ordered after identifying himself. "If Yates or Franklin calls, ring continuously until I can get in to answer. Otherwise, just memorize the call."

"Instructions acknowledged," answered the circuitry.

He went out to the kennels to help Anne unload the neutroids.

A sprawling concrete barn housed the cages, and the barn was sectioned into three large rooms, one housing the fragile, humanoid chimpanzee-mutants, and another for the lesser breeds such as Cat-Qs, Dog-Fs, dwarf bears, and foot-high lambs that never matured into sheep. The third room contained a small gas chamber, with a conveyor belt leading from it to the crematorium. He usually kept the third room locked, but he noticed in passing that it was open. Evidently Anne had found the keys in order to let Fred Georges dump his package.

A Noah's Ark chorus greeted him as he passed through the animal room, to be replaced by the mindless chatter of the doll-like neutroids as soon as he entered the air conditioned neutroid section. Dozens of blazing blond heads began dancing about their cages. Their bodies thwacked against the wire mesh as they leaped about their compartments with monkey grace, in recognition of their feeder and keeper.

Their human appearance was broken only by two distinct features: short beaver-like tails decorated with fluffy curls of fur, and an erect thatch of scalp hair that grew up into a bright candle-flame. Otherwise, they appeared completely human, with baby-pink skin, quick little smiles, and cherubic faces. They were sexually neuter and never grew beyond a predetermined age-set which varied for each series. Age-sets were available from one to ten years, human equivalent. Once a neutroid reached its age-set, it remained at this stage of retarded development until death.

"They must be getting to know you pretty well," Anne said as she came from behind a section of cages. "A big loud welcome for Pappa, huh?"

He frowned slightly as he glanced around the gloomy room and sniffed the animal odors. "That's funny. They don't usually get this excited."

She grinned. "Big confession: it started when *I* came in."

He shot her a quick suspicious glance, then walked slowly along a row of cages, peering inside. He stopped suddenly beside a three-year-old K-76 to stare.

"*Apple cores!*"

He turned slowly to face his wife, trying to swallow a sudden spurt of anger.

"*Well?*" he demanded.

Anne reddened. "I felt sorry for them, eating that goo from the mechanical feeders. So I drove down to Sherman III and bought six dozen cooking apples."

"That was a mistake."

She frowned irritably. "We can afford it."

"That's not the point. There's a reason for mechanical feedings."

"Oh? What is it?"

He hesitated, knowing she wouldn't like the answer. But she was already stiffening.

"Let me guess," she said coldly. "If you feed them yourself they get to love you. Right?"

"Uh, yeah. They even attach some affection to me because they know that right after I come in, the feeders get turned on."

"I see. And if they love you, you might get queasy about running them through Room 3's line, eh?"

"That's about the size of it," he admitted.

"Okay, Terry, I feed them apples, you run your production line," she announced firmly. "I can't see anything contradictory about that, can you?"

Her eyes told him that he had damn well better see something contradictory about it, whether he admitted it or not.

"Planning to get real chummy with them, are you?" he inquired stiffly.

"Planning to dispose of any soon?" she countered.

"Honeymoon's off again, eh?"

She shook her head slowly, came toward him a little, "I hope not, Terry—I hope not." She stopped again. They watched each other doubtfully amid the chatter of the neutroids.

After a time, he turned and walked to the truck, pulled out the snare pole and began fishing for the squealing, squeaking doll-things that bounded about- like frightened monkeys in the truck's wire mesh cage. They were one-family pets, always frightened of strangers, and these in the truck remembered him only as the villain who had dragged them away from Mama into a terrifying world of whirling scenery and roaring traffic.

They worked for a time without talking; then Anne asked casually: "What's the Delmont case, Terry?"

"Huh? What makes you ask?"

"I heard you mention it on the phone. Anything to do with a black eye and a scratched face?"

He nodded sourly. "Indirectly. It's a long story. Well— you know about the evolvotron."

"Only that Anthropos Incorporated uses it to induce mutation."

"It's sort of a sub-atomic surgical instrument—for doing 'plastic surgery' to reproductive cells— Here! Grab this chimp! Get him by the leg."

"Oops! Got him. . . . Go ahead, Terry."

"Using an evolvotron on the gene-structure of an ovum is like playing microscopic billiards—with protons and deuterons and alpha particles for cue balls. The operator takes the living ovum, mounts it in the device, gets a tremendously magnified image of it with the slow-neutrino shadowscope, compares the image with a gene-map, starts gouging out sub-molecular tidbits with single-particle shots. He juggles them around, hammers chunks in where nothing was before, plugs up gaps, makes new gaps. Catch?"

She looked thoughtful, nodded. "Catch. And the Lord Man made neutroid from the slime of an ape," she murmured.

"Heh? Here, catch this critter! Snare's choking him!"

"Okay—come to Mama. . . . Well, go on, tell me about Delmont."

"Delmont was a green evolvotron operator. Takes years of training, months of practice."

"Practice?"

"It's an art more than a science. Speed's the thing. You've got to perform the whole operation from start to finish in a few seconds. Ovum dies if you take too long."

"About Delmont—"

"Got through training and practice tryouts okay. Good rating, in fact. But he was just one of those people that blow up when rehearsals stop and the act begins. He spoiled over a hundred ova the first week. That's to be expected. One success out of ten tries is a good average. But he didn't get any successes."

"Why didn't they fire him?"

"Threatened to. Guess he got hysterical. Anyhow, he reported one success the next day. It was faked. The ovum had a couple of flaws—something wrong in the nervous system's determinants, and in the endocrinal setup. Not a standard neutroid ovum. He passed it on to the incubators to get a credit, knowing it wouldn't be caught until after birth."

"It wasn't caught at all?"

"Heh. He was afraid it might *not* be caught. So he

suppressed the testosterone flow to its incubator so that it *would* be—later on."

"Why that?"

"All the neutroids are potential females, you know. But male hormone is pumped to the foetus as it develops. Keeps female sexuality from developing, results in a neuter. He decided that the inspectors would surely catch a female, and that would be blamed on a malfunction of the incubator, not on him."

"So?"

Norris shrugged. "So inspectors are human. So maybe a guy came on the job with a hangover and missed a trick or two. Besides, they all *look* female. Anyhow, she didn't get caught."

"How did they ever find out Delmont did it?"

"He got caught last month—trying it again. Confessed to doing it once before. No telling how many times he *really* did it."

Norris held up the final kicking, squealing, tassel-haired doll from the back of the kennel truck. He grinned down at Anne.

"Now take this little yeep, for instance. Might be a potential she. Might also be a potential murderer. *All* these kiddos from the truck came from the machines in the section where Delmont worked last year when he passed that fake. Can't have nonstandard models on the loose. Can't have sexed models either—then they'd breed, get out of hand. The evolvotron could be shut down any time it became necessary, and when that generation of mutants died off . . ." He shrugged.

Anne caught the struggling baby-creature in her arms. It struggled and tried to bite, but subsided a little when she disentangled it from the snare.

"Kkr-r-reeee!" it cooed nervously. "Kree. Kkr-r-reeel!"

"You tell him you're no murderer," she purred to it.

He watched disapprovingly while she fondled it. One code he had accepted: steer clear of emotional attachment. It was eight months old and looked like a child of two years—a year short of its age-set. And it was designed to be as affectionate as a human child.

"Put it in the cage, Anne," he said quietly.

She looked up and shook her head.

"It belongs to somebody else. Suppose it transfers its

fixation to you? You'd be robbing its owners. They can't love many people at once."

She snorted, but installed the thing in its cage.

"Anne—" Norris hesitated, knowing that it was a bad time to approach the subject, but thinking about Slade's pseudoparty tonight, and wondering why she had accepted.

"What, Terry?"

He leaned on the snare pole and watched her. "Do you want one of them for yourself? I can sign an unclaimed one over to you. Wouldn't cost anything."

She stared at him evenly for a moment, glanced down at her feet, paced slowly to the window to stand hugging her arms and looking out into the twilight.

"With a pseudoparty, Terry?"

He swallowed a lump of anxiety, found his voice. "Whatever you want."

"I hear the phone ringing in the house."

He waited.

"It stopped," she said after a moment. -

"Well, babe?"

"Whatever I want, Terry?" She turned slowly to lean back against a patch of gray light and look at him.

He nodded. "Whatever you want."

"I want your child."

He stiffened with hurt, stared at her open-mouthed.

"I want your child."

He thrust his hand slowly in his hip pocket.

"Oh, don't reach for your social security card. I don't care if it's got 'genetic triple-Z' on it. I want your child."

"Uncle Federal says 'no,' babe."

"To hell with Uncle Federal! They can't send a human through your Room 3! Not yet, anyhow! If it's born, the world's stuck with it!"

"And the parents are forcibly separated, reduced to common-labor status. Remember?"

She stamped her foot and whirled to the window again. "Damn the whole hellish world!" she snarled.

Norris sighed heavily. He was sorry she felt that way. She was probably right in feeling that way, but he was still sorry. Righteous anger, frustrated, was no less searing a psychic acid than the unrighteous sort, nor did a stomach pause to weigh the moral worth of the wrath that drenched it before giving birth to an ulcer.

"Hey, babe, if we're going to the Slade affair—"

She nodded grimly and turned to walk with him toward the house. At least it was better having her direct her anger at the world rather than at him, he thought.

The expectant mother played three games of badminton before sundown, then went inside to shower and dress before the guests arrived. Her face was wreathed in a merry smile as she trotted downstairs in a fresh smock, her neck still pink from the hot water, her wake fragrant with faint perfume. There was no apparent need for the smock, nor was there any pregnant caution in the way she threw her arms around John's neck and kicked up her heels behind her.

"Darling," she chirped. "There'll be plenty of milk. I never believed in bottle-feeding. Isn't it wonderful?"

"Great. The injections are working, I guess."

She looked around. "It's a lovely resort hotel. I'm glad you didn't pick Angel's Haven."

"So am I," he grunted. "We'll have the reception room all to ourselves tonight."

"What time is it?"

"Seven ten. Oh, the doc called to say he'd be a few minutes late. He was busy all day with a sick baby."

She licked her lips and glanced aside uneasily. "Class A couple?"

"No, doll. Class C—and a widow."

"Oh." She brightened and watched his face teasingly. "Will you pace and chain-smoke while I'm in delivery?"

He snorted amusement. "Hey, it's not as if you were really . . ." He stopped amid a fit of coughing.

"Not as if I were really what?"

"Now look, I didn't mean . . ."

"Not as if I were really what?" she demanded, eyes beginning to brim.

"Listen, darling, I'll pace and I'll chain-smoke."

A nurse came clicking across the floor. "Mrs. Slade, it's time for your first injection. Doctor Georges just called. Will you come with me, please?"

"Not as if I what, John?" she insisted, ignoring the nurse.

He lit a cigarette from the butt of the last and looked around nervously. "She'll be all right?" he asked the nurse.

"Mrs. Slade, will you please . . ."

"All right, nurse, I'm coming." She tossed her husband a hurt glance, walked away dabbing at her eyes.

"Expectant dames are always cranky," sympathized an attendant who sat on a bench nearby. "Take it easy. She won't be so touchy after it comes."

John Hanley Slade shot an irritable glare at the eavesdropper, saw a friendly comedian-face grinning at him, returned the grin uneasily, and went over to sit down.

"Your first?"

John Hanley nodded, stroked nervously at his thin hair.

"I see 'em come, I see 'em go. It's always the same."

"Whattaya mean?" John grunted.

"Same expressions, same worries, same attitudes, same conversation, same questions. The guy always makes some remark about how it's not *really* having a baby, and the dame always gets sore. Happens every time."

"It's all pretty routine for you, eh?" he muttered stiffly.

The attendant nodded. He watched the expectant father for several seconds, then grunted: "Go ahead, ask me."

"Ask you what?"

"If I think all this is silly. They always do."

John stared at the attendant irritably. "Well—?"

"Do I think it's silly? No, I don't."

"Fine. That's settled, then."

"No, I don't think it's silly, because for a dame it ain't satisfying if she plunks down the dough, buys a newt, and lets it go at that. There's something missing between bedroom and baby."

"That so?"

John's sarcastic tone was apparently lost on the man. "It's so," he announced. "Physiological change—that's what's missing. For a newt to really take the place of a baby, the mother's got to go through the whole build-up. Doc gives her injections, she craves pickles and mangoes. More injections for morning sickness. More injections, she gets chubby. And finally shots to bring mild labor and false delivery. So then she gets the newt, and everything's right with the world."

"Mmmph."

"Ask me something else," the attendant offered.

John looked around helplessly, spied an elderly woman near the entrance. She had just entered, and stood looking around as if lost or confused. He did not recognize her, but he got up quickly.

"Excuse me, chum. Probably one of my guests."

"Sure, sure. I gotta get on the job anyhow."

The woman turned to stare at him as he crossed the floor to meet her. Perhaps one of Mary's friends, he thought. There were at least a dozen people coming that he hadn't met. But his welcoming smile faded slightly as he approached her. She wore a shabby dress, her hair was disheveled in a gray tangle, her matchstick legs were without makeup, and there were fierce red lines around her eyelids. She stared at him with wide wild eyes—dull orbs of dirty marble with tiny blue patches for pupils. And her mouth was a thin slash between gaunt leathery cheeks.

"Are—are you here for the party?" he asked doubtfully.

She seemed not to hear him, but continued to stare at or through him. Her mouth made words out of a quivering hiss of a voice. "I'm looking for *him*."

"Who?"

"The doctor."

He decided from her voice that she had laryngitis. "Doctor Georges? He'll be here soon, but he'll be busy tonight. Couldn't you consult another physician?"

The woman fumbled in her bag and brought out a small parcel to display. "I want to give him this," she hissed.

"I could—"

"I want to give it to him myself," she interrupted.

Two guests that he recognized came through the entrance. He glanced toward them nervously, returned their grins, glanced indecisively back at the haggard woman.

"I'll wait," she croaked, turned her back, and marched to the nearest chair where she perched like a sick crow, eyes glued to the door.

John Hanley Slade felt suddenly chilly. He shrugged it off and went to greet the Willinghams, who were the first arrivals.

Anne Norris, with her husband in tow, zig-zagged her

way through a throng of chattering guests toward the hostess, who now occupied a wheel chair near the entrance to the delivery room. They were a few minutes late, but the party had not yet actually begun.

"Why don't you go join the father's sweating circle?" Anne called over her shoulder. "The men are all over with John."

Norris glanced at the group that had gathered under a cloud of cigar smoke over by the portable bar. John Slade stood at the focus of it and looked persecuted.

"Job's counselors," Terry grunted.

A hand reached out from a nearby conversation-group and caught his arm. "Norris," coughed a gruff voice.

He glanced around. "Oh—Chief Franklin. Hello!"

Anne released his hand and said, "See you later," then wound her way out of sight in the milling herd.

Franklin separated himself from the small congregation and glanced down coolly at his district inspector. He was a tall man, with shoulders hunched up close to his head, long spindly legs, a face that was exceedingly wide across the cheekbones but narrow at the jaw. Black eyes gazed from under heavy brows, and his unruly black hair was badly cut. His family tree had a few Cherokee Indians among its branches, Norris had heard, and they were frequently on the warpath.

Franklin gulped his drink casually and handed the glass to a passing attendant. "Thought you'd be working tonight, Norris," he said.

"I got trapped into coming, Chief," he replied amiably.

"How're you doing with the Delmont pickup?"

"Nearly finished with record-tracing. I took a break today and picked up nine of them."

"Mmmph. I *wondered* why you plastipainted that right eye." Franklin rolled back his head and laughed loudly toward the ceiling. "Newts' mama tossed the crockery at you, did she?"

"Her husband," he corrected a little stiffly.

"Well—get them in a hurry, Norris. If the newt's owner knows it's a deviant, he might hear we're after something and hide it somewhere. I want them rounded up quickly."

"Expect to find the one?"

Franklin nodded grimly. "It's somewhere in this part of the country—or *was*. It narrows down to about six or eight districts. Yours has a good chance of being it. If I had my way, we'd destroy every Bermuda K-99 that came out during that period. That way, we'd be sure— in case Delmont faked more than one."

"Be pretty tough on dames like Mary," Norris reminded him, glancing toward Mrs. Slade.

"Yeah, yeah, five hundred Rachels blubbering for their children, and all on my neck. I'd almost rather let the deviant get away than have to put up with the screaming mommies."

"The burdens of office, Chief. Bear up under the brickbats. Herod did."

Franklin glowered at him suspiciously, noticed Norris's bland expression, muttered "eh heh heh," and glanced around the room.

"Who's presiding over the whelping tonight?" Norris asked.

"Local doctor. Georges. You ought to know him."

Terry's eyebrows went up. He nodded.

"He's already here. Saw him come in the doctor's entrance a few minutes ago. He's probably getting ready. Well, Norris . . . if you'll excuse me . . ."

Norris wandered toward the bar. He had been to several pseudoparties before. There was nothing to it, really. After the guests had gathered, the medics rolled the mother into delivery, and everyone paced restlessly and talked in hushed voices while she re-enacted the age-old drama of Birth—in a way that was only mildly uncomfortable and did nothing to aggravate the population problem. Then, when they rolled her out again— fatigued and emotionally spent—the nurse brought out a newly purchased neutroid, only a few days out of the incubator, and presented it to the mother. When the oohs and aahs were finished, the mother went home with her child to rest, and the father whooped it up with the guests. Norris hoped to get away early. He had things to do before dawn.

"Who's that hag by the door?" a guest grunted in his ear.

Norris glanced incuriously at the thin-lipped woman who sat stiffly with her hands in her lap, not gazing at the guests but looking through and beyond them. He shook his head and moved on to shake hands with his host.

"Glad you came, Norris!" Slade said with a grin, then leaned closer. "Your presence could be embarrassing at a time like this, though."

"How's that?"

"You should have brought your net and snare pole, Norris," said a man at Slade's elbow. "Then when they bring the baby out, go charging across the room yelling: 'That's it! That's the one I'm after!' "

The men laughed heartily. Norris grinned weakly and started away.

"Hey, Slade," a voice called. "They're coming after Mary."

Norris stood aside to let John hurry toward his wife. Most of the crowd stopped milling about to watch Dr. Georges, a nurse and an attendant coming from a rear door to take charge of Mary.

"Stop! Stop right there!"

The voice came from near the front entrance. It was a choked and hoarse gasp of sound, not loud, but somehow penetrating enough to command the room. Norris glanced aside during the sudden lull to see the thin-lipped woman threading her way through the crowd, and the crowd folded back to clear a way. The farther she walked, the quieter the room became, and Norris suddenly realized that somehow the center of the room was almost clear of people so that he could see Mary and John and the medics standing near the delivery room door. They had turned to stare at the intruder. Georges' mouth fell open slightly. He spoke in a low voice, but the room was suddenly silent enough so that Norris could hear.

"Why, Sarah—what're you doing here?"

The woman stopped six feet away from him. She pulled out a small parcel and reached it toward him. "This is for you," she croaked.

When Georges did not advance to take it, she threw it at his feet. "Open it!" she commanded.

Norris expected him to snort and tell the attendants to toss the nutty old dame out. Instead, he stooped, very slowly, keeping his eyes on the woman, and picked up the bundle.

"Unwrap it!" she hissed when he paused.

His hands fumbled with it, but his eyes never left her face. The package came open. Georges glanced down. He dropped it quickly to the floor.

"An amputated—"

Chubby mouth gaping, he stared at the gaunt woman.

"My Primrose had a black cowlick in her tail!"

The doctor swallowed and continued to stare.

"Where is my Primrose?"

The woman had her hand in her purse. The doctor retreated a step.

"Where is my baby?"

"Really, Sarah, there was nothing to do but—"

Her hand brought a heavy automatic out of the purse. It wavered and moved uncertainly, too weighty for her scrawny wrist and arm. The room was suddenly a scramble and a babble.

"You killed my baby!"

"The first shot riocheted from the ceiling and shattered a window," said the television announcer. "The second shot went into the wall. The third shot struck Doctor Georges in the back of the head as he ran toward the delivery room door. He died instantly. Mrs. Glubbes fled from the room before any of the guests could stop her, and a dragnet is now combing . . ."

Norris shuddered and looked away from the television screen that revealed the present state of the reception room where they had been not more than two hours ago. He turned off the set, nervously lit a cigarette, and glanced at Anne who sat staring at nothing at the other end of the sofa.

"How do you feel?" he murmured.

She looked at him dumbly, shook her head. Norris got up, paced to the magazine rack, thumbed idly through its contents, glanced back at her nervously, walked to the window, stood smoking and staring toward the street for a time, moved to the piano, glanced back at her nervously again, tried to play a few bars of *Beethoven's Fifth* with one finger, hit a foul note after the opening ta-ta-ta-taaaahh, grunted a curse, banged a crashing discord with his fist, and leaned forward with a sigh to press his forehead against the music rack and close his eyes.

"Don't blame yourself, Terry," she said softly.

"If I hadn't let him have that impounded newt, it wouldn't have happened."

She thought that over briefly. "And if my maternal grandfather hadn't lied to his wife back in 2013, I would never have been born."

"Why not?"

"Because if he'd told her the truth, she'd have up and left him, and Mother wouldn't have been born."

"Oh. Nevertheless—"

"Nevertheless nothing!" She shook herself out of the blue mood. "You come here, Terry Norris!"

He came, and there was comfort in holding her. She was prepared to blame the world all right, but he was in the world, and a part of it, and so was she. And there was no sharing of guilt, but only the whole weight of it on the shoulders of each of them. He thought of the Delmont case, and the way Franklin talked casually of slaughtering five hundred K-99s just to be sure, and how he continued to hate Franklin's guts for no apparent reason. Franklin was not a pleasant fellow, to be sure, but he had done nothing to Norris personally. He wondered if he hated what Franklin represented, but directed the hate at Franklin's person because he, Norris, represented it *too*. Franklin, however, liked the world as he found it, and was glad to help keep it that way.

If I think something's wrong with the setup, but keep on being a part of it, then the wrongness is not part mine, he thought, it's *all* mine, because I bought it.

"It's hard to decide," he murmured.

"What's that, Terry?"

"Whether it's all wrong, dead wrong—or whether it's the best that can be done under the circumstances."

"Whatever are you talking about?"

He shook himself and yawned. "About going to bed," he grunted.

They went to bed at midnight. At one o'clock, he became certain she was asleep. He lay in darkness for a time, listening to her even breathing. Then he sat up and eased himself out of bed. There was work to be done. He tiptoed quietly out of the bedroom, carrying his shoes and his trousers. He dressed in the kitchen by the glow of a cigarette ember and stole quietly out into the chilly night. A half-moon hung low in a misty sky, and the wind was sharp out of the north. He walked quietly toward the kennels. There were only three empty cages. He needed twenty-seven to accommodate the doubtful K-99s that were to be picked up during the next few days. There was work to be done.

He went into the neutroid room and flicked a switch. A few sleepy chatters greeted the light.

One at a time he awoke twenty-four of the older creatures and carried them to a large glass-walled compartment. These were the longtime residents; they knew him well, and they came willingly, snuggling sleepily against his chest. He whistled tunelessly while he worked, began carrying them by the tails, two in each hand, to speed the chore.

When he had gotten them in the glass chamber, he sealed the door and turned on the gas. Then he switched off the lights, locked up for the night again, and walked back toward the house through the crisp grass. The conveyor belt from the chamber to the crematorium would finish the job unaided.

Norris felt suddenly ill. He sank down on the back steps and laid his head on his arms across his knees. His eyes burned, but thought of tears made him sicker. When the low *chug* of the crematorium's igniter coughed quietly from the kennels, he staggered hurriedly away from the steps to retch.

She was waiting for him in the bedroom. She sat on the windowseat, her small figure silhouetted against the paleness of the moonlit yard.

She was staring silently out at the dull red tongue of exhaust gas from the crematorium chimney when he tiptoed down the hall and paused in the doorway. She looked around. Dead silence between them, then:

"Out for a walk, eh, Terry?"

A resumption of the dead silence. He backed quietly away without speaking. He went to the parlor and lay down on the couch.

After a time, he heard her puttering around in the kitchen, and saw a light. A little later, he opened his eyes to see her dark shadow over him, surrounded by an aura of negligee. She sat down on the edge of the couch and offered him a glass.

"Drink it. Make your stomach rest easy."

"Alcoholic?"

"Yeah."

He tasted it: milk, egg yolk, honey, and rum.

"No arsenic?"

She shook her head. He drank it quickly, lay back with a grunt, took her hand. They were silent for a time.

"I—I guess every new wife thinks her husband's flawless, for awhile," she murmured absently. . "Silly, how it's such a shock to find out the obvious: that he's not much different from other bull humans of the tribe."

Norris stiffened, rolled his face away from her. After a moment her hand crept out to touch his cheek. Her fingertips traced a soft line up and along his temple.

"It's all right, Terry," she whispered.

He kept his face averted. Her fingers stroked for a moment more, as if she were feeling something new and different in the familiar texture of his hair. Then she arose and padded quietly back to the bedroom.

Norris lay awake until dawn, knowing that it would never be all right Terry, nor all right World—never, as long as the prohibiting, the creating, the killing, the mockery, the falsification of birth, death, and life continued.

Dawn inherited the night mist, gathered it into clouds, and made a gloomy gray morning of it.

Anne was still asleep when he left for work. He backed out the kennel truck, meaning to get the rest of the Bermuda K-99s as quickly as possible so that he could begin running the normalcy tests and get the whole thing over with. The night's guilt was still with him as he drove away, a sticky dew that refused to depart with morning. Why should he have to kill the things? Why couldn't Franklin arrange for a central slaughter house for destroying neutroids that had been deserted, or whose owners could not be located, or that found themselves unclaimed for any other reason? But Franklin would purple at the notion. It was only a routine part of the job. Why shouldn't it be routine? Why were neutroids manufactured anyhow? Obviously, because they were disposable—an important feature which human babies unfortunately lacked. When the market became glutted with humans, the merchandise could not be dumped in the sea.

Anthropos' mutant pets fulfilled a basic biological need of Man—of all life, for that matter—the need to have young, or a reasonable facsimile, and care for them. Neutroids kept humanity satisfied with the restricted birth rate, and if it were not satisfied, it would breed itself into famine, epidemic, and possible extinction. With the population held constant at five billions, the Federation could insure a decent living standard for everyone. And as long as birth must be restricted, why not restrict it logically and limit it to genetic desirables?

Why not? Norris felt no answer, but he was acutely aware of the "genetic-C" on his social security card.

The world was a better place, wasn't it? Great strides since the last century. Science had made life easier to live and harder to lose. The populace thoughtlessly responded by pouring forth a flood of babies and doddering old codgers to clutter the earth and make things tougher again by eating and not producing; but again science increased the individual's chances to survive and augmented his motives for doing so—and again the populace responded with fecundity and long white beards, making more trouble for science again. So it had continued until it became obvious that progress wasn't headed toward "The Good Life" but toward more lives to continue the same old meager life as always. What could be done? Inpede science? Unthinkable! Chuck the old codgers into the sea? Advance the retirement age to ninety and work them to death? The old codgers still had the suffrage, and plenty of time to go to the polls.

The unborn, however, were not permitted to vote.

Man's technology had created little for the individual. Man used his technology to lengthen his life and sweeten it, but something had to be subtracted somewhere. The lives of the unborn were added onto the years of the aged. A son of Terry Norris might easily live till 110, but he would have damn little chance of being born to do it.

Neutroids filled the cradles. Neutroids never ate much, nor grew up to eat more or be on the unemployment roles. Neutroids could be bashed with a shovel and buried in the back yard when hard times came. Neutroids could satisfy a woman's longing for something small and lovable, but they never got in the economic way.

It was no good thinking about it, he decided. It was a Way Of Doing Things, and most people accepted it, and if it sometimes yielded heartache and horrors such as had occurred at Slade's pseudoparty, it was still an Accepted Way, and he couldn't change it, even if he knew what to do about it. He was already adjusted to the world-as-it-was, a world that loved the artificial mutants as children, looked the other way when crematorium flames licked in the night. He had been brought up in such a world, and it was only when emotion conflicted with the grim necessity of his job that he thought to question the world. And Anne? Eventually, he supposed, she would have her pseudoparty, cuddle a neutroid, forget about romantic notions like having a kid of her own.

At noon he brought home another dozen K-99s and installed them in the cages. Two reluctant mothers had put up a howl, but he departed without protest and left seizure of animals to the local authorities. Yates had already delivered the three from yesterday.

"What, no more scratches, bruises, broken bones?" Anne asked at lunch.

He smiled mechanically. "If Mama puts up a squawk, I go. Quietly."

"Learned your lesson yesterday?"

"Mmm! One dame pulled a fast one on me, though. I think. Told her what I wanted. She started moaning, but she let me in. I got her newt, started out with it. She wanted a receipt. So, I took the newt's serial number off the check list, made out the receipt. She took one look and squealed, 'That's not Chichi's number!' and grabbed for her tail-wagger. I looked at its foot-tattoo. Sure enough—wrong number. Had to leave it. A K-99 all right, but not even from Bermuda Plant."

"I thought they were all registered."

"They are, babe. Wires get crossed sometimes. I told her she had the wrong newt, and she started boiling. Got the sales receipt and showed it to me. Number checked with the newt's. Something's fouled up somewhere."

"Where'd she get it?"

"O'Reilley's pet shop—over in Sherman II. Right place, wrong serial number."

"Anything to worry about, Terry?"

"Well, I've got to track down that doubtful Bermuda model."

"Oh."

"And—well—" He frowned out the window at the kennels. "Ever think what'd happen if somebody started a black market in neutroids?"

They finished the meal in silence. Apparently there was going to be no further mention of last night's mass disposal, nor any rehash of the nightmare at Slade's party. He was thankful.

The afternoon's work yielded seven more Bermuda neutroids for the pound. Except for the missing newt that was involved in the confusion of serial numbers, the rest of them would have to be collected by Yates or his deputies, armed with warrants. The groans and the tears of the owners left him in a gloomy mood, but the pick-up phase of the operation was nearly finished. The normalcy tests, however, would consume the rest of the week and leave little time for sleeping and eating. If Delmont's falsification proved extensive, it might be necessary to deliver several of the animals to Central Lab for dissection and complete analysis, thus bringing the murderous wrath of the owners upon his head. He had a hunch about why bio-inspectors were frequently shifted from one territory to another.

On the way home, he stopped in Sherman II to check with the dealer about the confusion of serial numbers. Sherman II was the largest of the Sherman communities, covering fifty blocks of commercial buildings. He parked in the outskirts and took a sidewalk escalator toward O'Reilley's address. He had spoken to O'Reilley on the phone, but had not yet visited the dealer's shop.

It lay on a dingy side street that was reminiscent of centuries past, a street of small bars and bowling alleys and cigar stores. There was even a shop with three gold balls above the entrance, but the place was now an antique store. A light mist was falling when he stepped off the escalator and stood in front of the pet shop. A sign hung out over the sidewalk, announcing:

J."DOGGY" O'REILLEY

PETS FOR SALE

DUMB BLONDES AND GOLDFISH

MUTANTS FOR THE CHILDLESS

BUY A BUNDLE OF JOY

He frowned at the sign for a moment, then wandered

through the entrance into a warm and gloomy shop, wrinkling his nose at the strong musk of animal odors. O'Reilley's was no shining example of cleanliness.

Somewhere a puppy was yapping, and a parrot croaked the lyrics of *A Chimp To Call My Own*—theme song of a soap opera about a lady evolvotron operator, Norris recalled.

He paused briefly by a tank of silk-draped goldfish. The shop had a customer. An elderly lady haggled with the wizened manager over the price of a half-grown second-hand Dog-F. She shook her last dog's death certificate under his nose and demanded a guarantee of the dog's alleged F-5 intelligence. The old man offered to swear on a Bible that the dog was more knowledgeable than some humans, but he demurred when asked to swear by his ledger.

The dog was lamenting, "Don' sell me, Dada, don' sell me," and punctuating the pleas with mournful trainwhistle howls.

Norris smiled quietly. The nonhuman pets were brighter than the neutroids. A K-108 could speak a dozen words, but a K-99 never got farther than "mama," "papa," and "cookie." Anthropos feared making quasihumans too intelligent, lest sentimentalists proclaim them really human.

He wandered on toward the rear of the building, pausing briefly by the cash register to inspect O'Reilley's license which hung in a dusty frame on the wall behind the counter: "James Fallon O'Reilley . . . authorized dealer in mutant animals . . . all nonpredatory mammals including Chimpanzee-K series . . . license expires 15w 3d 2063y. . . ."

Expiration date approaching, he noticed, but otherwise okay. He headed for a bank of neutroid cages along the opposite wall, but O'Reilley minced across the floor to meet him. The elderly lady was leaving. O'Reilley's face wore a v-shaped smirk on a loose-skinned face, and his bald head bobbled professionally.

"And a good afternoon to ye, sir. What'll it be this foine drizzlin' afternoon? A dwarf kangaroo perhaps, or a—" He paused to adjust his spectacles as Norris flashed a badge and presented his card. O'Reilley's smile waned. "Inspector Norris is it," he muttered at the card, then looked up. "What'd they do with the last 'un, flay him alive?"

"My predecessor was transferred to the Montreal area."

"And *I* thought that I spoke to him only yesterday!"

"On the phone? That was me, O'Reilley. About the rundown on the K-99 sales."

"I gave it to you properly, did I not?" the oldster demanded.

"You gave it to me. Maybe properly."

O'Reilley seemed to puff up slightly and glower. "Meaning?"

"There's a mix-up in serial numbers on one of them. May not be your mistake."

"No mistakes, no mistakes."

"Okay, we'll see." Norris glanced at his list. "Let's check this number again—K-99-LJZ-351."

"It's nearly closing time," the oldster protested. "Come back some other day, Norris."

"Sorry, this one's rush. It'll only take a minute. Where's your book?"

The oldster began to quiver angrily. "Are you suggestin', sir, that I falsely—"

"No," he growled, "I'm suggesting that there was a mistake. Maybe *my* mistake, maybe yours, maybe Anthropos', maybe the owner's. I've got to find out, that's all. Let's have the book."

"What kind of a mistake? I gave you the owner's name!"

"She has a different newt."

"Can I help it if she traded with somebody?"

"She didn't. She bought it here. I saw the receipt." Norris was beginning to become impatient, tried to suppress it.

"Then she traded with one of my other customers!" O'Reilley insisted.

Norris snorted irritably. "You got two customers named Adelia Schultz? Come on, pop, let's look at the duplicate receipt. *Now.*"

"Doubt if it's still around," O'Reilley grumbled, refusing to budge.

Norris suddenly erupted. He turned away angrily and began pacing briskly around the shop, looking under cages, inspecting fixtures, probing into feeding troughs with a pencil, looking into feed bags, examining a Dog-F's wiry coat.

"Here there! What do you think you're doing?" the owner demanded.

Norris began barking off check-points in a loud voice. "Dirty cat-cage . . . inadequate ventilation . . . food trough not clean . . . no water in the newt cages . . ."

"I water them twice a day!" O'Reilley raged.

". . . mouldy rabbit-meal . . . no signs of disinfectant . . . What kind of disease-trap are you running here?"

He came back to face O'Reilley who stood trembling with rage and cursing him with his eyes.

"Not to mention that sign outside," Norris added casually. "'Dumb blondes'—they outlawed that one the year Kleyton got sent up for using hormones on K-108s, trying to grow himself a harem. Well?"

"Doubt if it's still around," O'Reilley repeated.

"Look, pop!" Norris snapped. "You're required to keep sales receipts until they're microfilmed. There hasn't been a microfilming for over a year . . ."

"Get out of my shop!"

"If I go, you won't *have* a shop after tomorrow."

"Are you threatening me?"

"Yeah."

For a moment, Norris thought the old man would attack him. But O'Reilley spat a sudden curse, scurried toward the counter, grabbed a fat book from beneath the cash register, then hurried away toward the stairs at the rear of the shop.

"Hey, pop! Where you going?"

"Get me glasses!"

"You're wearing your glasses!" Norris started after him.

"New ones. Can't see through them." O'Reilley bounded upstairs.

"Leave the book *here* and *I'll* check it!'

Norris stopped with his foot on the bottom step. O'Reilley slammed the door at the head of the stairs, locked it behind him. Grumbling suspiciously, the inspector went back to the counter to wait.

Five minutes passed. The door opened. O'Reilley came downstairs, looking less angry but decidedly nervous. He slammed the book on the counter, riffled its pages,

found a place, muttered, "Here it is, see for yourself," and
held it at a difficult angle.

"Give it here."

O'Reilley reluctantly released it, began babbling
about bureaucracy and tin-horn inspectors who acted
like dictators and inspection codes that prescribed and
circumscribed and prohibited. Norris ignored him and
stared at the duplicate receipt.

"Adelia Schultz . . . received Chimpanzee-K-99-LJZ-
351 on . . ."

It was the number on the list from Anthropos. It was
the number of the animal he wanted for normalcy tests.
But it was not the number of Mrs. Schultz's neutroid, nor
was it the number written on Mrs. Schultz's copy *of this
very same invoice*.

"O'Reilley was still babbling at him. Norris held the
book up to his eye, took aim at the bright doorway
across the surface of the page. O'Reilley stopped babbling.

"Rub marks," the inspector grunted. "Scrape marks
on the paper."

O'Reilley's breathing sounded asthmatic. Norris lowered the book.

"Nice erasure job—for a carbon copy. Do it while
you were upstairs?"

O'Reilley said nothing. Norris took a scrap of paper,
folded his handkerchief over the point of his pocketknife
blade, used the point to clean out the eraser dust from
between the receipts, emptied the dust on the paper,
folded it and put it in his pocket.

"Evidence."

O'Reilley said nothing.

Norris tore out the erased receipt, pocketed it, put on
his hat and started for the door.

"See you in court, O'Reilley."

"Wait!"

He turned. "Okay—I'm waiting."

"Let's go sit down first," the deflated oldster muttered
weakly.

"Sure."

They walked up the flight of stairs and entered a
dingy parlor. He glanced around, sniffed at the smell of
cabbage boiling and sweaty bedclothing. An orange-
haired neutroid lay sleeping on a dirty rug in the corner.

Norris stared down at it curiously. O'Reilley made a whining sound and slumped into a chair, his breath coming in little whiffs that suggested inward sobbing. Norris gazed at him expressionlessly for a moment, then went to kneel beside the newt.

"K-99-LJZ-351," he read aloud, peering at the sole of the tattooed foot. The newt stirred in its sleep at the sound of a strange voice. When Norris looked at O'Reilley again, the old man was staring at his feet, his forehead supported by a leathery old hand that shielded his eyes.

"Lots of good explanations, O'Reilley?"

"Ye've seen what ye've seen; now do what ye must. I'll say nothing to ye."

"Look, O'Reilley, the newt is what I'm after. So I found it. I don't know what else I've found, but juggling serial numbers is a serious offense. If you've got a story, you better tell it. Otherwise, you'll be telling it behind bars. I'm willing to listen here and now. You'd better grab the chance.

O'Reilley sighed, looked at the sleeping newt in the corner. "What'll ye do with her?"

"The newt? Take her in."

O'Reilley sat in gloomy silence while he thought things over. "We were class-B, me and the missus," he mumbled suddenly, "allowed a child of our own if we could have 'um. Fancy that, eh? Ugly old coot like me —class-B."

"So?"

"The government said we could have a child, but Nature said we couldn't."

"Tough."

"But since we were class-B, we weren't entitled to own a newt. See?"

"Yeah. Where's your wife?"

"With the saints, let's hope."

Norris wondered what sort of a sob-story this was getting to be. The oldster went on quietly, all the while staring at the sleeping figure in the corner.

"Couldn't have a kid, couldn't own a newt either— so we opened the pet shop. It wasn't like havin' yer own, though. Missus always blubbered when I sold a newt she'd got to feeling like a mother to. Never swiped one, though—not till Peony came long. Last year this Bermuda shipment come in, and I sold most of 'em pretty quick, but Peony here was puny. People afraid she'd not last long. Couldn't sell her. Kept her around so long thet we both loved her. Missus died last year. 'Don't let anybody take Peony,' she kept saying afore she passed on. I promised I wouldn't. So I switched 'em around and moved her up here."

"That's all?"

O'Reilley hesitated, then nodded.

"Ever done this before?"

O'Reilley shook his head.

There was a long silence while Norris stared at the child-thing. "Your license could be revoked," he said absently.

"I know."

He ground his fist thoughtfully in his palm, thought it over some more. If O'Reilley told the truth, he couldn't live with himself if he reported the old man . . . unless it wasn't the whole truth.

"I want to take your books home with me tonight."

"Help yourself."

"I'm going to make a complete check, investigate you from stem to stern."

He watched O'Reilley closely. The oldster was unaffected. He seemed concerned—grief-stricken—only by the thought of losing the neutroid.

"If plucking a newt out of stock to keep your company was the only thing you did, O'Reilley, I won't report you."

O'Reilley was not consoled. He continued to gaze hungrily at the little being on the rug.

"And if the newt turns out not to be a deviant," he added gently, "I'll send it back. We'll have to attach a correction to that invoice, of course, and you'll just have to take your chances about somebody wanting to buy it, but . . ." he paused. O'Reilley was staring at him strangely.

"And if she *is* a deviant, Mr. Norris?"

He started to reply, hesitated.

"*Is* she, O'Reilley?"

The oldster said nothing. His face tightened slowly. His shoulders shook slightly, and his squinted eyes were brimming. He choked.

"I see."

O'Reilley shook himself, produced a red bandanna,

dabbed at his eyes, blew his nose loudly, regathered his composure.

"How do you know she's deviant?"

O'Reilley gave him a bitter glance, chuckled hoarsely, shuffled across the room and sat on the floor beside the sleeping newt. He patted a small bare shoulder.

"Peony? . . . Peony-girl . . . wake up, me child, wake up."

Its fluffy tail twitched for a moment. It sat up, rubbed its eyes, and yawned. There was a lazy casualness about its movements that caused Norris to lean closer to stare. Neutroids usually moved in bounces and jerks and scrambles. This one stretched, arched its back, and smiled —like a two-year-old with soft brown eyes. It glanced at Norris. The eyes went wider for a moment, then it studiously ignored him.

"Shall I play bouncey, Daddy?" it piped.

Norris sucked in a long slow breath and sat frozen.

"No need to, Peony." O'Reilley glanced at the inspector. "Bouncey's a game we play for visitors," he explained. "Making believe we're a neutroid."

The inspector could find nothing to say.

Peony licked her lips. "Wanna glass of water, Daddy."

O'Reilley nodded and hobbled away to the kitchen, leaving the man and the neutroid to stare at each other in silence. She was quite a deviant. Even a fully age-set K-108 could not have spoken the two sentences that he had heard, and Peony was still a long way from age-set and a K-99 at that.

O'Reilley came back with the water. She drank it greedily, holding the glass herself while she peered up at the old man.

"Daddy's eyes all wet," she observed.

O'Reilley began trembling again. "Never mind, child. You go get your coat."

"Whyyyy?"

"You're going for a ride with Mr. Norris."

She whirled to stare hostilely at the stunned visitor. "I don't *want* to!"

The old man choked out a sob and flung himself down to seize her in his arms and hug her against his chest. He tearfully uttered a spasmodic bubble of reassurances that would have frightened even a human child.

The deviant neutroid began to cry. Standard neutroids never cried, they whimpered and yeeped. Norris felt weak inside. Slowly, the old man lifted his head to peer at the inspector, blinking away tears. He began loosening Peony from the embrace. Suddenly he put her down and stood up.

"Take her quickly," he hissed, and strode away to the kitchen. He slammed the door behind him. The latch clicked.

Peony scampered to the door and began beating on it with tiny fists. "Daddy . . . *Daddy! ! !* Open 'a door!" she wailed.

Norris licked his lips and swallowed a dry place. Still he did not budge from the sofa, his gaze fastened on the child-thing. Disjointed phrases tumbled through his mind . . . what Man hath wrought . . . out of the slime of an ape . . . fat legs and baby fists and a brain to know . . . and the State spoke to Job out of a whirlwind, saying . . .

"Take her!" came a roaring bellow from the kitchen. *"Take her before I lose me wits and kill ye!"*

Norris got unsteadily to his feet and advanced toward the frightened child-thing. He carried her, kicking and squealing, out into the early evening. By the time he turned into his own driveway, she had subsided a little, but she was still crying.

He saw Anne coming down from the porch to meet him. She was staring at the neutroid who sat on the front seat beside him, while seven of its siblings chattered from their cages in the rear of the truck. She said nothing, only stared through the window at the small tear-stained face.

"Home! I want to go home!" it whined.

Norris lifted the newt and handed it to his wife. "Take it inside. Keep your mouth shut about it. I'll be in as soon as I chuck the others in their cages."

She seemed not to notice his curtness as she cradled the being in her arms and walked away. The truck lurched on to the kennels.

He thought the whole thing over while he worked. When he was finished, he went back in the house and stopped in the hall to call Chief Franklin. It was the only thing to do: get it over with as quickly as possible.

The operator said, "His office fails to answer. No taped readback. Shall I give you the locator?"

Anne came into the hall and stood glaring at him, her arms clenched across her bosom, one foot tapping the floor angrily. Peony stood behind her, no longer crying, and peering at him curiously around Anne's skirt.

"Are you doing what I think you're doing, Terry?"

He gulped. "Cancel the call," he told the operator. "It'll wait till tomorrow." He dropped the phone hard and sank down in the straight chair. It was the only thing to do: delay it as long as he could.

"We'd better have a little talk," she said.

"Maybe we'd better," he admitted.

They went into the living room. Peony's world had evidently been restricted to the pet shop, and she seemed awed by the clean, neat house, no longer frightened, and curious enough about her surroundings to forget to cry for O'Reilley. She sat in the center of the rug, occasionally twitching her tail as she blinked around at the furniture and the two humans who sat in it.

"The deviant?"

"A deviant."

"Just what are you going to do?"

He squirmed. "You know what I'm supposed to do."

"What you were going to do in the hall?"

"Franklin's bound to find out anyway."

"How?"

"Do you imagine that Franklin would trust *anybody?*"

"So?"

"So, he's probably already got a list of all serial numbers from the District Anthropos Wholesalers. As a double-check on *us*. And we'd better deliver."

"I see. That leaves you in a pinch, doesn't it?"

"Not if I do what I'm supposed to."

"By whose law?"

He tugged nervously at his collar, stared at the child-thing who gazed at him fixedly. "Heh heh," he said weakly, waggled a finger at it, held out his hands invitingly. The child-thing inched away nervously.

"Don't evade, Terry."

"I wanna go home . . . I want Dada."

"I gotta think. Gotta have time to think."

"Listen, Terry, you know what calling Franklin would be? It would be M, U, R, D, E, R."

"She's just a newt."

"*She?*"

"Probably. Have to examine her to make sure."

"Great. Intelligent, capable of reproduction. Just great."

"Well, what they do with her after I'm finished with the normalcy tests is none of my affair."

"It's not? *Look* at me, Terry. . . . No, not with that patiently suffering . . . *Terry!*"

He stopped doing it and sat with his head in his hands, staring at the patterns in the rug, working his toes anxiously. "Think—gotta think."

"While you're thinking, I'll feed the child," she said crisply. "Come on, Peony."

"How'd you know her name?"

"*She* told me, naturally."

"Oh." He sat trying grimly to concentrate, but the house was infused with Anne-ness, and it influenced him. After a while, he got up and went out to the kennels where he could think objectively. But that was wrong too. The kennels were full of Franklin and the system he represented. Finally he went out into the back yard and lay on the cool grass to stare up at the twilight sky. The problem shaped up quite formidably. Either he turned her over to Franklin to be studied and ultimately destroyed, or he didn't. If he didn't, he was guilty of Delmont's crime. Either he lost Anne and maybe something of himself, or his job and maybe his freedom.

A big silence filled the house during dinner. Only Peony spoke, demanding at irregular intervals to be taken home. Each time the child-thing spoke, Anne looked at him, and each time she looked at him, her eyes said "See?"—until finally he slammed down his fork and marched out to the porch to sulk in the gloom. He heard their voices faintly from the kitchen.

"You've got a good appetite, Peony."

"I like Dada's cooking better."

"Well, maybe mine'll do for awhile."

"I wanna go home."

"I know—but I think your dada wants you to stay with us for awhile."

"I don't want to."

"Why don't you like it here?"

"I want Dada."

"Well maybe we can call him on the phone, eh?"

"Phone?"

"After you get some sleep."

The child-thing whimpered, began to cry. He heard Anne walking with it, murmuring softly. When he had heard as much as he could take, he trotted down the steps and went for a long walk in the night, stalking slowly along cracked sidewalks beneath overhanging trees, past houses and scattered lights of the suburbs. Suburbs hadn't changed much in a century, only grown more extensive. Some things underwent drastic revision with the passing years, other things—like walking sticks and garden hoes and carving knives and telephones and bicycles—stayed pretty much as they were. Why bother the established system?

He eyed the lighted windows though the hedges as he wandered past. Flourescent lights, not much different from those of a century ago. But once they had been campfires, the fires of shivering hunters in the forest, when man was young and the world was sparsely planted with his seed. Now the world was choked with his riotous growth, glittering with his lights and his flashing signs, full of the sound of his engines and the roar of his rockets. He had inherited it and filled it—filled it too full, perhaps.

There was no escaping from the past. The last century had glutted the Earth with its children and grandchildren, had strained the Earth's capacity to feed, and the limit had been reached. It had to be guarded. There was no escape into space, either. Man's rockets had touched two planets, but they were sorry worlds, and even if he made them better, Earth could beget children —if allowed—faster than ships could haul them away. The only choice: increase the death rate, or decrease the birth rate—or, as a dismal third possibility—do nothing, and let Nature wield the scythe as she had once done in India and China. But letting-Nature-do-it was not in the nature of Man, for he could always do it better. If his choice robbed his wife of a biological need, then he would build her a disposable baby to pacify her. He would give it a tail and only half a mind, so that she would not confuse it with her own occasional children.

Peony, however, was a grim mistake. The mistake had to be quickly corrected before anyone noticed.

What was he, Norris, going to do about it, if anything? Defy the world? Outwit the world? The world was made in the shape of Franklin, and it snickered at him out of the shadows. He turned and walked back home.

Anne was rocking on the porch with Peony in her arms when he came up the sidewalk. The small creature dozed fitfully, muttered in its sleep.

"How old is she, Terry?" Anne asked.

"About nine months, or about two years, depending on what you mean."

"Born nine months ago?"

"Mmm. But two years by the development scale, human equivalent. Newts would be fully mature at nine or ten, if they didn't stop at an age-set. Fast maturation."

"But she's brighter than most two-year-olds."

"Maybe."

"You've heard her talk."

"You can't make degree-comparisons between two species, Anne. Not easily anyhow. 'Bright'—signifying I.Q.—by what yardstick?"

"Bright—signifying on-the-ball—by my yardstick. And if you turn her over to Franklin, I'll leave you."

"Car coming," he grunted tonelessly. "Get in the house. It's slowing down."

Anne slipped out of her chair and hurried inside. Norris lingered only a moment, then followed. The headlights paused in front of a house down the block, then inched ahead. He watched from deep in the hall.

"Shall I take her out to the kennels right quick?" Anne called tensely.

"Stick where you are," he muttered, and a moment later regretted it. The headlights stopped in front. The beam of a powerful flashlight played over the porch, found the house number, winked out. The driver cut the engine. Norris strode to the living room.

"Play bouncey!" he growled to Peony.

"Don't want to," she grumbled back.

"There's a man coming, and you'd better play bouncey if you ever want to see your Dada again!" he hissed.

Peony yeeped and backed away from him, whimpering.

"Terry! What're you talking about! You should be ashamed!"

"Shut up. . . . Peony, play bouncey."

Peony chattered and leaped to the back of the sofa with monkeylike grace.

"She's frightened! She's acting like a common newt!"

"That's bouncey," he grunted. "That's good."

The car door slammed. Norris went to put on the porch light and watch the visitor come up the steps—a husky, bald gentleman in a black suit and Roman collar. He blinked and shook his head. Clergyman? The fellow must have the wrong house.

"Good evening."

"Uh—yeah."

"I'm Father Mulreany. Norris residence?" The priest had a slight brogue; it stirred a vague hunch in Norris' mind, but failed to clear it.

"I'm Norris. What's up?"

"Uh, well, one of my parishioners—I think you've met him—"

"Countryman of yours?"

"Mmm."

"O'Reilley?"

"Yes."

"What'd he do, hang himself?"

"Nothing that bad. May I come in?"

"I doubt it. What do you want?"

"Information."

"Personal or official?"

The priest paused, studied Norris' silhouette through the screen. He seemed not taken aback by the inspector's brusqueness, perhaps accepting it as normal in an era that had little regard for the cloth.

"O'Reilley's in bad shape, Inspector," Mulreany said quietly. "I don't know whether to call a doctor, a psychiatrist, or a cop."

Norris stiffened. "A cop?" He hesitated, feeling a vague hostility, and a less vague suspicion. He opened the screen, let the priest in, led him to the living room. Anne muttered half-politely, excused herself, snatched Peony, and headed for the rear of the house. The priest's eyes followed the neutroid intently.

"So O'Reilley did something?"

"Mmm."

"What's it to you?"

Mulreany frowned. "In addition to things you wouldn't understand—he was my sister's husband."

Norris waved him into a chair. "Okay, so—?"

"He called me tonight. He was loaded. Just a senseless babble, but I knew something was wrong. So I went over to the shop." Mulreany stopped to light a cigarette and frown at the floor. He looked up suddenly. "You see him today?"

Norris could think of no reason not to admit it. He nodded irritably.

Mulreany leaned forward curiously. "Was he sober?"

"Yeah."

"Sane?"

"How should I know?"

"Did he impress you as the sort of man who would suddenly decide to take a joint of pipe and a meat cleaver and mass-slaughter about sixty helpless animals?"

Norris felt slightly dazed. He sank back, shaking his head and blinking. There was a long silence. Mulreany was watching him carefully.

"I can't help you," Norris muttered. "I've got nothing to say."

"Look, Inspector, forget this, will you?" He touched his collar.

Norris shook his head, managed a sour smile. "I can't help you."

"All right," Mulreany sighed, starting to his feet. "I'm just trying to find out if what he says . . ."

"Men talking about Dada?" came a piping voice from the kitchen.

Mulreany shot a quick glance toward it. ". . . is true," he finished softly.

There was a sudden hush. He could hear Anne whispering in the kitchen, saw her steal a glance through the door.

"So it *is* true," Mulreany murmured.

Face frozen, Norris came to his feet. "Anne," he called in a bitter voice. "Bouncey's off."

She came in carrying Peony and looking murderous. "Why did you ask him in?" she demanded in a hiss.

Mulreany stared at the small creature. Anne stared at the priest.

"It's poison to you isn't it!" she snapped, then held

Peony up toward him. "Here! Look at your enemy. Offends your humanocentrism, doesn't she?"

"Not at all," he said rather wistfully.

"You condemn them."

He shook his head. "Not *them*. Only what they're used for by society." He looked at Norris, a bit puzzled. "I'd better leave."

"Maybe not. Better spill it. What do you want?"

"I told you. O'Reilley went berserk, made a butcher shop out of his place. When I got there, he was babbling about a talking neutroid—'his baby'—said you took it to the pound to destroy it. Threatened to kill you. I got a friend to stay with him, came over to see if I could find out what it's all about."

"The newt's a deviant. You've heard of the Delmont case?"

"Rumors."

"She's it."

"I see." Mulreany looked glum, grim, gloomy. "Nothing more I need to know I guess. Well—"

Norris grabbed his arm as he turned. "Sit a spell," he grunted ominously.

The priest looked puzzled, let himself be guided back to the chair. Norris stood looking down at him.

"What's the matter with Dada?" Peony chirped. "I wanna go see Dada."

"Well?" Norris growled. "What about her?"

"I don't understand."

"You people are down on Anthropos, aren't you?"

Mulreany kept patience with an effort. "To make nitroglycerine for curing heart trouble is good, to make it for blowing open safes is bad. The stuff itself is morally neutral. The same goes for mutant animals. As pets, okay; as replacements for humans, no."

"Yeah, but you'd just as soon see them dead, eh?"

Mulreany hesitated. "I admit a personal dislike for them."

"This one?"

"What about her?"

"Better dead, eh?"

"I didn't say that."

"You couldn't admit she might be human?"

"Don't know her that well. Human? How do you

mean—biologically? Obviously not. Theologically? Why should *you* care?"

"I'm interested in your particular attitude, buster."

Mulreany gazed at him, gathering a glower. "I'm a little doubtful about my status here," he growled. "I came for information; the roles got switched somewhere. Okay, Norris, but I'm sick of neopagan innocents like you. Now sit down, or show me the door."

Norris sat down slowly.

The priest watched the small neutroid for a moment before speaking. "She's alive, performs the function of living, is evidently aware. Life—a kind of functioning. A specific life—an invariant kind of functioning—with sameness-of-self about it. Invariance of functioning—a principle. Self, soul, call it what you like. Whatever's alive has it." He paused to watch Norris doubtfully.

Norris nodded curtly. "Go on."

"Doesn't have to be anything immortal about it. Not unless she were known to be human. Or intelligent."

"You heard her," Anne snapped.

"I've heard metal boxes speak with great wisdom," Mulreany said sourly. "And if I were a Hottentot, a vocalizing computer would . . ."

"Skip the analogies. Go on."

"What's intelligence? A function of Man, immortal. What's Man? An intelligent immortal creature, capable of choice."

"Quit talking in circles."

"That's the point. I can't—not where Peony's concerned. What do you want to know? If I think she's equal to Man? Give me all the intelligence test results, and all the data you can get—I still couldn't decide."

"Whattaya need? Mystic writings in the sky?"

"Precisely."

"I feel a bush being beat about," Anne said suddenly. "Is this guy going to make things tough, or isn't he?"

Mulreany looked puzzled again.

"To the point, then," Norris said. "Would you applaud if she gets the gasser?"

"Hardly."

"If you had to decide for yourself—"

"What? Whether to destroy her or not?" Mulreany snorted irritably. "Not if there was the least doubt in my mind about her. She's a shadow in the brush. Maybe it's ten to one that the shadow's a bear and not a man—but on the one chance, don't shoot, son, don't shoot."

"You think the authorities have the right to kill her, maybe?" Anne asked.

"Who, him?" Mulreany jerked his head toward Norris.

"Well *say* him."

"I'd have to think about it. But I don't think so."

"Why? The government made her. Why can't it un-make her?"

"Made her? *Did* it now?"

"Delmont did," Norris corrected.

"*Did* he now?" said Mulreany.

"Why not?" Anne snorted.

"I, the state, am Big Fertility," Norris said sourly; then baiting Mulreany: "Thou shalt accept no phallus but the evolvotron."

Mulreany reddened, slapped his knee, and chortled. The Norrises exchanged puzzled glances.

"I feel an affinity," Anne murmured suspiciously.

Norris came slowly to his feet. "If you talk to any-body about Peony, you may be responsible for her death."

"I don't quite see—"

"You don't need to."

Mulreany shrugged.

"Tell O'Reilley the same."

Mulreany nodded. "You've got my word."

"Your which?"

"Sorry, I forgot. Ancient usage. I won't mention Peony. I'll see that O'Reilley doesn't."

Norris led him to the door. The priest was obviously suppressing large quantities of curiosity, but contained it well. On the steps, he paused to look back, wearing a curious smirk.

"It just occurred to me—if the child is 'human' in the broad sense, she's rather superior to you and me."

"Why?"

"Hasn't picked an apple yet."

Norris shrugged slightly.

"And Inspector—if Delmont made her—ask yourself: Just what was it that he 'made'?" He nodded quickly. "Good night."

"What do you make of him?" Anne hissed nervously.

"Backworldsman. Can't say."

"Fool, why'd you bring him in?"

"I'm no good at conspiracies."

"Then you *will* do it?"

"What?"

"Hide her, or something."

He stared at her doubtfully. "The only thing I can hope to do is falsify the test reports and send her back to O'Reilley as a standard model."

"That's better than nothing."

"And then spend the rest of our days waiting for it to be uncovered," he added grimly.

"You've got to, Terry."

Maybe, he thought, maybe.

If he gave her back to O'Reilley, there was a good chance she'd be discovered when the auditor came to microfilm the records and check inventory. He certainly couldn't keep her himself—not with other bio agents wandering in and out every few days. She could not be hidden.

He sat down for a smoke and watched Anne tiptoe to the sofa with the sleeping Peony. It would be easy to obey the law, turn her over to Franklin, and tell Anne that he had done something else with her, something like . . .

He shuddered and chopped the thought off short. She glanced at him curiously.

"I don't like the way you're looking at me," she muttered.

"You imagine things."

"Uh-uh. Listen to me, Terry, if you let that baby . . ."

"I'm sick of your ifs!" he barked. "If I hear another goddam threat of your leaving *if*, then to hell with it, you can leave any time!"

"Terry!"

She stared, puzzled, in his direction for a moment, then slowly wandered out, still puzzling. He sank lower in the chair, brooding. Then it hit him. It wasn't Anne that worried him; it was a piece of himself. It was a piece of himself that threatened to go, and if he let Peony be packed off to Central Lab, it *would* go, and thereafter he would not be able to stomach anything, even himself.

The morning news from the Scriber was carefully folded beside his plate when he came to the table for breakfast. It was so deliberately folded that he bothered to notice the advertisement in the center of the displayed portion.

"You lay this out for my benefit?" he asked.

"Not particularly," she said casually.

He read it with a suspicious frown:

BIOLOGISTS WANTED
by
ANTHROPOS INCORPORATED
for
Evolvotron Operators
Incubator Tenders
Nursery Supervisors
Laboratory Personnel
in
NEW ATLANTA PLANT
Call or write
Personnel Manager
ANTHROPOS INCORPORATED
Atlanta, Ga.
Note: Secure Labor Dept.
release from present job
before applying.

"What's this supposed to mean to me?" he demanded.

"Nothing in particular. Why? Does it mean something to you?"

He brushed the paper aside and decided to ignore the subtlety, if any. She picked it up, glanced at it as if she had not seen it before. "New jobs, new places to live," she murmured.

After breakfast, he went down to police headquarters to sign a statement concerning the motive in Doctor Georges' murder. Sarah Glubbes had been stashed away in a psychopathic ward, according to Chief Miler, and would probably stay awhile.

"Funny thing, Norris," the cop said. "What people won't do over a newt! You know, it's a wonder you don't get your head blown off. I don't covet your job."

"Good." He signed the paper and glanced at Miler coolly.

"Must take an iron gut, huh, Norris?"

"Sure. Just a matter of adaptation."

"Guess so." Miler patted his paunch and yawned.

"How you coming on this Delmont business? Picked up any deviants yet?"

Norris pitched the fountain pen on the desk, splattering ink. "What made you ask that?" he said stiffly.

"Nothing *made* me. I did it myself. Touchy today?"

"Maybe."

Miler shrugged. "Something made you jump when I said 'deviants.' "

"Nothing made me. I—"

"Ya, ya, sure, but—"

"Save it for a suspect, Fat." He stalked out of the office, leaving Miler tapping his pencil and gazing curiously after him. A phone rang somewhere behind him. He hurried on—angry with himself for jumpiness and for indecisiveness. He had to make a choice, and make it soon. It was the lack of a choice that left him jumpy, susceptible to a jolt from either side.

"Norris . . . Hey, Norris . . ."

Miler's voice. He whirled to see the cop trotting down the steps behind him, his pudgy face glistening in the morning sun.

"Your wife's on the phone, Norris. Says it's urgent."

When he got back to the office, he heard the faint, "Hello, *hello!*" coming from the receiver on the desk, caught it up quickly.

"Anne? What's wrong?"

Her voice was low and strained beneath a cheerful overnote. "Nothing's wrong, darling. We have a visitor. Come right home. Chief Franklin's here."

It knocked the breath out of him. He felt himself going white. He glanced at Chief Miler, sitting calmly nearby.

"Can you tell me about it now?" he asked her.

"Not very well. Please hurry home. He wants to talk to you about the K-99s."

"Have the two of them met?"

"Yes, they have." She paused, as if waiting for him to speak, then said, "Oh, *that!* Bouncey, honey—remember bouncey?"

"Good, I'll be right home." He hung up and started out.

"Troubles?" the chief called after him.

"Just a sick newt, if it's any of your business," he called back.

Franklin's helicopter was parked in the empty lot next

door when Norris drove up in front of the house. The departmental chief heard the truck and came out on the porch to watch his agent walk up the path. His bulky body was loosely draped in gray tweeds, and his hawk face was a dark, solemn mask. He greeted Norris with a slow, almost sarcastic mood.

"I see you don't read your mail. If you'd looked at it, you'd have known I was coming. I wrote you yesterday."

"Sorry Chief, I didn't have a chance to stop by the message office this morning."

Franklin grunted. "Then you don't know why I'm here?"

"No, sir."

"Let's sit out on the porch," Franklin said, and perched his bony frame on the railing. "We've got to get busy on these Bermuda K-99s, Norris. How many have you got?"

"Thirty-four, I think."

"I counted thirty-five."

"Maybe you're right. I—I'm not sure."

"Found any deviants yet?"

"Uh—I haven't run any tests yet, sir."

Franklin's voice went sharp. "Do you need a test to know when a neutroid is talking a blue streak?"

"What do you mean?"

"Just this. We've found at least a dozen of Delmont's units that have mental ages that correspond to their physical age. What's more, they're functioning females, and they have normal pituitaries. Know what that means?"

"They won't take an age-set then," Norris said. "They'll grow to adulthood."

"And have children."

Norris frowned. "How can they have children? There aren't any males."

"No? Guess what we found in one of Delmont's incubators."

"Not a—"

"Yeah. And it's probably not the first. This business about padding his quota is baloney! Hell, man, he was going to start his own black market! He finally admitted it, after twenty hours' questioning without a letup. He was going to raise them, Norris. He was stealing them right out of the incubators before an inspector ever saw

them. The K-99s—the numbered ones—are just the ones
he couldn't get back. Lord knows how many males he's
got hidden away someplace!"

"What're you going to do?"

"Do! What do you *think* we'll do? Smash the whole
scheme, that's what! Find the deviants and kill them.
We've got enough now for lab work."

Norris felt sick. He looked away. "I suppose you'll
want me to handle the destruction, then."

Franklin gave him a suspicious glance. "Yes, but why
do you ask? You *have* found one, haven't you?"

"Yes, sir," he admitted.

A moan came from the doorway. Norris looked up to
see his wife's white face staring at him in horror, just
before she turned and fled into the house. Franklin's
bony head lifted.

"I see," he said. "We have a fixation on our deviant.
Very well, Norris, I'll take care of it myself. Where is
it?"

"In the house, sir. My wife's bedroom."

"Get it."

Norris went glumly in the house. The bedroom door
was locked.

"Honey," he called softly. There was no answer. He
knocked gently.

A key turned in the lock, and his wife stood facing him.
Her eyes were weeping ice.

"Stay back!" she said. He could see Peony behind her,
sitting in the center of the floor and looking mystified.

Then he saw his own service revolver in her trembling
hand.

"Honey, look—it's *me.*"

She shook her head. "No, it's not you. It's a man that
wants to kill a little girl. Stay back."

"You'd shoot, wouldn't you?" he asked softly.

"Try to come in and find out," she invited.

"Let me have Peony."

She laughed, her eyes bright with hate. "I wonder
where Terry went. I guess he died. Or adapted. I guess
I'm a widow now. Stay back, mister, or I'll kill you."

Norris smiled. "Okay, I'll stay back. But the gun isn't
loaded."

She tried to slam the door; he caught it with his foot.
She struck at him with the pistol, but he dragged it out

of her hand. He pushed her aside and held her against the wall while she clawed at his arm.

"Stop it!" he said. "Nothing will happen to Peony, I promise you!" He glanced back at the child-thing, who had begun to cry.

Anne subsided a little, staring at him angrily.

"There's no other way out, honey. Just trust me. She'll be all right."

Breathing quickly, Anne stood aside and watched him. "Okay, Terry. But if you're lying—tell me, is it murder to kill a man to protect a child?"

Norris lifted Peony in his arms. Her wailing ceased, but her tail switched nervously.

"In whose law book?" he asked his wife. "I was wondering the same thing." Norris started toward the door. "By the way—find my instruments while I'm outside, will you?"

"The dissecting instruments?" she gasped. "If you intend—"

"Let's call them surgical instruments, shall we? And get them sterilized."

He went on outside, carrying the child. Franklin was waiting for him in the kennel doorway.

"Was that Mrs. Norris I heard screaming?"

Norris nodded. "Let's get this over with. I don't stomach it so well." He let his eyes rest unhappily on the top of Peony's head.

Franklin grinned at her and took a bit of candy out of his pocket. She refused it and snuggled closer to Norris.

"When can I go home?" she piped. "I want Dada."

Franklin straightened, watching her with amusement. "You're going home in a few minutes, little newt. Just a few minutes."

They went into the kennels together, and Franklin headed straight for the third room. He seemed to be enjoying the situation. Norris, hating him silently, stopped at a workbench and pulled on a pair of gloves. Then he called after Franklin.

"Chief, since you're in there, check the outlet pressure while I turn on the main line, will you?"

Franklin nodded assent. He stood outside the gas chamber, watching the dials on the door. Norris could see his back while he twisted the main-line valve.

"Pressure's up!" Franklin called.

"Okay. Leave the hatch ajar so it won't lock, and crack the intake valves. Read it again."

"Got a mask for me?"

Norris laughed. "If you're scared, there's one on the shelf. But just open the hatch, take a reading, and close it. There's no danger."

Franklin frowned at him and cracked the intakes. Norris quietly closed the main valve again.

"Drops to zero!" Franklin called.

"Leave it open, then. Smell anything?"

"No. I'm turning it off, Norris." He twisted the intakes. Simultaneously, Norris opened the main line.

"Pressure's up again!"

Norris dropped his wrench and walked back to the chamber, leaving Peony perched on the workbench.

"Trouble with the intakes," he said gruffly. "It's happened before. Mind getting your hands dirty with me, Chief?"

Franklin frowned irritably. "Let's hurry this up, Norris. I've got five territories to visit."

"Okay, but we'd better put on our masks." He climbed a metal ladder to the top of the chamber, leaned over to inspect the intakes. On his way down, he shouldered a light-bulb over the door, shattering it. Franklin cursed and stepped back, brushing glass fragments from his head and shoulders.

"Good thing the light was off," he snapped.

Norris handed him the gas mask and put on his own. "The main switch is off," he said. He opened the intakes again. This time the dials fell to normal open-line pressure. "Well, look—it's okay," he called through the mask. "You sure it was zero before?"

"Of course I'm sure!" came the muffled reply.

"Leave it on for a minute. We'll see. I'll go get the newt. Don't let the door close, sir. It'll start the automatics and we can't get it open for half an hour."

"I know, Norris. Hurry up."

Norris left him standing just outside the chamber, propping the door open with his foot. A faint wind was coming through the opening. It should reach an explosive mixture quickly with the hatch ajar.

He stepped into the next room, waited a moment, and jerked the switch. The roar was deafening as the exposed tungsten filament flared and detonated the escaping anesthetic vapor. Norris went to cut off the main line. Peony was crying plaintively. He moved to the door and glanced at the smouldering remains of Franklin.

Feeling no emotion whatever, Norris left the kennels, carrying the sobbing child under one arm. His wife stared at him without understanding.

"Here, hold Peony while I call the police," he said.

"Police? What's happened?"

He dialed quickly. "Chief Miler? This is Norris. Get over here quick. My gas chamber exploded—killed Chief Agent Franklin. Man, it's awful! Hurry!"

He hung up and went back to the kennels. He selected a normal Bermuda K-99 and coldly killed it with a wrench. "You'll serve for a deviant," he said, and left it lying in the middle of the floor.

Then he went back to the house, mixed a sleeping capsule in a glass of water, and forced Peony to drink it.

"So she'll be out when the cops come," he explained to Anne.

She stamped her foot. "Will you tell me what's happened?"

"You heard me on the phone. Franklin accidentally died. That's all you have to know."

He carried Peony out and locked her in a cage. She was too sleepy to protest, and she was dozing when the police came.

Chief Miler strode about the three rooms like a man looking for a burglar at midnight. He nudged the body of the neutroid with his foot. "What's this, Norris?"

"The deviant we were about to destroy. I finished her with a wrench."

"I thought you said there weren't any deviants."

"As far as the public's concerned, there aren't. I couldn't see that it was any of your business. It still isn't."

"I see. It may become my business, though. How'd the blast happen?"

Norris told him the story up to the point of the detonation. "The light over the door was loose. Kept flickering on and off. Franklin reached up to tighten it. Must have been a little gas in the socket. Soon as he touched it—wham!"

"Why was the door open with the gas on?"

"I told you—we were checking the intakes. If you close

the door, it starts the automatics. Then you can't get it open till the cycle's finished."

"Where were you?"

"I'd gone to cut off the gas again."

"Okay, stay in the house until we're finished out here."

When Norris went back in the house, his wife's white face turned slowly toward him.

She sat stiffly by the living room window, looking sick. Her voice was quietly frightened.

"Terry, I'm sorry about everything."

"Skip it."

"What did you do?"

He grinned sourly. "I adapted to an era. Did you find the instruments?"

She nodded. "What are they for?"

"To cut off a tail and a skin-tattooed foot. Go to the store and buy some brown hair-dye and a pair of boy's trousers, age two. Peony's going to get a crew cut. From now on, she's Mike."

"We're class-C, Terry! We can't pass her off as our own."

"We're class-A, honey. I'm going to forge a heredity certificate."

Anne put her face in her hands and rocked slowly to and fro.

"Don't feel bad, baby. It was Franklin or a little girl. And from now on, it's society or the Norrises."

"What'll we do?"

"Go to Atlanta and work for Anthropos. I'll take up where Delmont left off."

"Terry!"

"Peony will need a husband. They may find all of Delmont's males. I'll *make* her one. Then we'll see if a pair of Chimp-Ks can do better than their makers."

Wearily, he stretched out on the sofa.

"What about the priest? Suppose he tells about Peony. Suppose he guesses about Franklin and tells the police?"

"The police," he said, "would then smell a motive. They'd figure it out and I'd be finished. We'll wait and see. Let's don't talk; I'm tired. We'll just wait for Miler to come in."

She began rubbing his temples gently, and he smiled.

"So we wait," she said. "Shall I read to you, Terry?"

"That would be pleasant," he murmured, closing his eyes.

She slipped away, but returned quickly. He heard the rustle of dry pages and smelled musty leather. Then her voice came, speaking old words softly. And he thought of the small child-thing lying peacefully in her cage while angry men stalked about her. A small life with a mind; she came into the world as quietly as a thief, a burglar in the crowded house of Man.

"I will send my fear before thee, and I will destroy the peoples before whom thou shalt come, sending hornets to drive out the Hevite and the Canaanite and the Hethite before thou enterest the land. Little by little, I will drive them out before thee, till thou be increased, and dost possess the land. Then shalt thou be to me a new people, and I to thee a God . . ."

And on the quiet afternoon in May, while he waited for the police to finish puzzling in the kennels, it seemed to Terrell Norris that an end to scheming and pushing and arrogance was not too far ahead. It should be a pretty good world then.

He hoped Man could fit into it somehow.

The Darfsteller

"JUDAS, JUDAS" WAS playing at the Universal on Fifth Street, and the cast was entirely human. Ryan Thornier had been saving up for it for several weeks, and now he could afford the price of a matinée ticket. It had been a race for time between his piggy bank and the wallets of several "public-spirited" angels who kept the show alive, and the piggy bank had won. He could see the show before the wallets went flat and the show folded, as any such show was bound to do after a few limping weeks. A glow of anticipation suffused him. After watching the wretched mockery of dramaturgical art every day at the New Empire Theater where he worked as janitor, the chance to see real theater again would be like a breath of clean air.

He came to work an hour early on Wednesday morning and sped through his usual chores on overdrive. He finished his work before one o'clock, had a shower backstage, changed to street clothes, and went nervously upstairs to ask Imperio D'Uccia for the rest of the day off.

D'Uccia sat enthroned at a rickety desk before a wall plastered with photographs of lightly clad female stars of the old days. He heard the janitor's petition with a faint, almost oriental smile of apparent sympathy, then drew himself up to his full height of sixty-five inches, leaned on the desk with chubby hands to study Thornier with beady eyes.

"Off? So you wanna da day off? Mmmph—" He shook

his head as if mystified by such an incomprehensible request.

The gangling janitor shifted his feet uneasily. "Yes, sir. I've finished up, and Jigger'll come over to stand by in case you need anything special." He paused. D'Uccia was studying his nails, frowning gravely. "I haven't asked for a day off in two years, Mr. D'Uccia," he added, "and I was sure you wouldn't mind after all the overtime I've—"

"Jigger," D'Uccia grunted. "Whoosa t'is Jigger?"

"Works at the Paramount. It's closed for repairs, and he doesn't mind—"

The theater manager grunted abruptly and waved his hands. "I don' pay no Jigger, I pay you. Whassa this all about? You swip the floor, you putsa things away, you all finish now, ah? You wanna day off. Thatsa whass wrong with the world, too mucha time loaf. Letsa machines work. More time to mek trouble." The theater manager came out from behind his desk and waddled to the door. He thrust his fat neck outside and looked up and down the corridor, then waddled back to confront Thornier with a short fat finger aimed at the employee's long and majestic nose.

"Whensa lass time you waxa the upstairs floor, hah?"

Thornier's jaw sagged forlornly. "Why, I—"

"Don't tell me no lie. Looka that hall. Sheeza feelth. *Look!* I want you to look." He caught Thornier's arm, tugged him to the doorway, pointed excitedly at the worn and ancient oak flooring. "Sheeza feelth ground in! See? When you wax, hah?"

A great shudder seemed to pass through the thin elderly man. He sighed resignedly and turned to look down at D'Uccia with weary gray eyes.

"Do I get the afternoon off, or don't I?" he asked hopelessly, knowing the answer in advance.

But D'Uccia was not content with a mere refusal. He began to pace. He was obviously deeply moved. He defended the system of free enterprise and the cherished traditions of the theater. He spoke eloquently of the golden virtues of industriousness and dedication to duty. He bounced about like a furious Pekingese yapping happily at a scarecrow. Thornier's neck reddened, his mouth went tight.

"Can I go now?"

"When you waxa da floor? Palisha da seats, fixa da lights? When you clean op the dressing room, hah?" He stared up at Thornier for a moment, then turned on his heel and charged to the window. He thrust his thumb into the black dirt of the window box, where several prize lilies were already beginning to bloom. *Ha!*" he snorted. "Dry like I thought! You think the bulbs a don't need a drink, hah?"

"But I watered them this morning. The sun—"

"Hah! You letsa little *fiori* wilt and die, hah? And you wanna the day off?"

It was hopeless. When D'Uccia drew his defensive mantle of calculated deafness or stupidity about himself, he became impenetrable to any request or honest explanation. Thornier sucked in a slow breath between his teeth, stared angrily at his employer for a moment, and seemed briefly ready to unleash an angry blast. Thinking better of it, he bit his lip, turned, and stalked wordlessly out of the office. D'Uccia followed him triumphantly to the door.

"Don' you go sneak off, now!" he called ominously, and stood smiling down the corridor until the janitor vanished at the head of the stairs. Then he sighed and went back to get his hat and coat. He was just preparing to leave when Thornier came back upstairs with a load of buckets, mops, and swabs.

The janitor stopped when he noticed the hat and coat, and his seamed face went curiously blank. "Going home, Mr. D'Uccia?" he asked icily.

"Yeh! I'ma worka too hard, the doctor say. I'ma need the sunshine. More fresh air. I'ma go relax on the beach a while."

Thornier leaned on the mop handle and smiled nastily. "Sure," he said. "Letsa machines do da work."

The comment was lost on D'Uccia. He waved airily, strode off toward the stairway, and called an airy *"A rivederci!"* over his shoulder.

"A rivederci, padrone," Thornier muttered softly, his pale eyes glittering from their crow's-feet wrappings. For a moment his face seemed to change—and once again he was Chaubrec's Adolfo, at the exit of the Commandant, Act II, scene *iv*, from "A Canticle for the Marsman."

Somewhere downstairs, a door slammed behind D'Uccia.

"Into death!" hissed Adolfo-Thornier, throwing back his head to laugh Adolfo's laugh. It rattled the walls. When its reverberations had died away, he felt a little better. He picked up his buckets and brooms and walked on down the corridor to the door of D'Uccia's office.

Unless "Judas-Judas" hung on through the weekend, he wouldn't get to see it, since he could not afford a ticket to the evening performance, and there was no use asking D'Uccia for favors. While he waxed the hall, he burned. He waxed as far as D'Uccia's doorway, then stood staring into the office for several vacant minutes.

"I'm fed up," he said at last.

The office remained silent. The window-box lilies bowed to the breeze.

"You little creep!" he growled. "I'm through!"

The office was speechless. Thornier straightened and tapped his chest.

"I, Ryan Thornier, am walking out, you hear? The show is finished!"

When the office failed to respond, he turned on his heel and stalked downstairs. Minutes later, he came back with a small can of gold paint and a pair of artists' brushes from the storeroom. Again he paused in the doorway.

"Anything else I can do, Mr. D'Uccia?" he purred.

Traffic murmured in the street; the breeze rustled the lilies; the building creaked.

"Oh? You want me to wax in the wall-cracks, too? How could I have forgotten!"

He clucked his tongue and went over to the window. Such lovely lilies. He opened the paint can, set it on the window ledge, and then very carefully he glided each of the prize lilies, petals, leaves, and stalks, until the flowers glistened like the work of Midas' hands in the sun-light. When he finished, he stepped back to smile at them in admiration for a moment, then went to finish waxing the hall.

He waxed it with particular care in front of D'Uccia's office. He waxed under the throw rug that covered the worn spot on the floor where D'Uccia had made a sharp left turn into his sanctum every morning for fifteen years,

and then he turned the rug over and dusted dry wax
powder into the pile. He replaced it carefully and pushed
at it a few times with his foot to make certain the lubri-
cation was adequate. The rug slid about as if it rode on
a bed of bird-shot.

Thornier smiled and went downstairs. The world was
suddenly different somehow. Even the air smelled different. He paused on the landing to glance at himself in the
decorative mirror.

Ah! the old trouper again. No more of the stooped
and haggard menial. None of the wistfulness and weariness of self-perpetuated slavery. Even with the gray at
the temples and the lines in the face, here was something
of the old Thornier—or one of the *many* old Thorniers
of earlier days. Which one? Which one'll it be? Adolfo?
Or Hamlet? Justin, or J.J. Jones, from "The Electrocu-
tioner"? Any of them, all of them; for he was Ryan
Thornier, star, in the old days.

"Where've you been, baby?" he asked his image with
a tight smile of approval, winked, and went on home for
the evening. Tomorrow, he promised himself, a new life
would begin.

"But you've been making that promise for years,
Thorny," said the man in the control booth, his voice
edged with impatience. "What do you mean, 'you quit?'
Did you tell D'Uccia you quit?"

Thornier smiled loftily while he dabbed with his broom
at a bit of dust in the corner. "Not exactly, Richard,"
he said. "But the *padrone* will find it out soon enough."

The technician grunted disgust. "I don't understand
you, Thorny. Sure, if you *really* quit, that's swell—if you
don't just turn around and get another job like this one."

"Never!" the old actor proclaimed resonantly, and
glanced up at the clock. Five till ten. Nearly time for
D'Uccia to arrive for work. He smiled to himself.

"If you really quit, what are you doing here today?"
Rick Thomas demanded, glancing up briefly from the
Maestro. His arms were thrust deep into the electronic
entrails of the machine, and he wore a pencil-sized screwdriver tucked behind one ear. "Why don't you go home,
if you quit?"

"Oh, don't worry, Richard. This time it's for real."

"Pssss!" An amused hiss from the technician. "Yeah,
it was for real when you quit at the Bijou, too. Only then

a week later you came to work here. So what now, Mercutio?"

"To the casting office, old friend. A bit part somewhere, perhaps." Thornier smiled on him benignly. "Don't concern yourself about me."

"Thorny, can't you get it through your head that theater's *dead?* There isn't any theater! No movies, no television either—except for dead men and the Maestro here." He slapped the metal housing of the machine.

"I *meant,*" Thorny explained patiently, " 'employment office,' and 'small job,' you . . . you machine-age flintsmith. Figures of speech, solely."

"Yah."

"I thought you *wanted* me to resign my position, Richard."

"Yes! If you'll do something worthwhile with yourself. Ryan Thornier, star of 'Walkaway,' playing martyr with a scrub-bucket! Aaaak! You give me the gripes. And you'll do it again. You can't stay away from the stage, even if all you can do about it is mop up the oil drippings."

"You couldn't possibly understand," Thornier said stiffly.

Rick straightened to look at him, took his arms out of the Maestro and leaned on top of the cabinet. "I dunno, Thorny," he said in a softer voice. "Maybe I do. You're an actor, and you're always playing roles. Living them, even. You can't help it, I guess. But you *could* do a saner job of picking the parts you're going to play."

"The world has cast me in the role I play," Thornier announced with a funereal face.

Rick Thomas clapped a hand over his forehead and drew it slowly down across his face in exasperation. "I give up!" he groaned. "Look at you! Matinée idol, pushing a broom. Eight years ago, it made sense—*your* kind of sense, anyhow. Dramatic gesture. Leading actor defies autodrama offer, takes janitor's job. Loyal to tradition, and the guild —and all that. It made small headlines, maybe even helped the legit stage limp along a little longer. But the audiences stopped bleeding for you after a while, and then it stopped making even *your* kind of sense!"

Thornier stood wheezing slightly and glaring at him. "What would *you* do," he hissed, "if they started making a little black box that could be attached to the wall up there"

—he waved to a bare spot above the Maestro's bulky housing—"that could repair, maintain, operate, and adjust —do all the things you do to that . . . that contraption. Suppose nobody needed electronicians any more."

Rick Thomas thought about it a few moments, then grinned. "Well, I guess I'd get a job making the little black boxes, then."

"You're not funny, Richard!"

"I didn't intend to be."

"You're . . . you're not an artist." Flushed with fury, Thornier swept viciously at the floor of the booth.

A door slammed somewhere downstairs, far below the above-stage booth. Thorny set his broom aside and moved to the window to watch. The *clop, clop, clop* of bustling footsteps came up the central aisle.

"Hizzoner, da Imperio," muttered the technician, glancing up at the clock. "Either that clock's two minutes fast, or else this was his morning to take a bath."

Thornier smiled sourly toward the main aisle, his eyes traveling after the waddling figure of the theater manager. When D'Uccia disappeared beneath the rear balcony, he resumed his sweeping.

"I don't see why you don't get a sales job, Thorny," Rick ventured, returning to his work. "A good salesman is just an actor, minus the temperament. There's *lots* of demand for good actors, come to think of it. Politicians, top executives, even generals—some of them seem to make out on *nothing but* dramatic talent. History affirms it."

"Bah! I'm no schauspieler." He paused to watch Rick adjusting the Maestro, and slowly shook his head. "Ease your conscience, Richard," he said finally.

Startled, the technician dropped his screwdriver, looked up quizzically. "*My* conscience? What the devil is uneasy about my conscience?"

"Oh, don't pretend. That's why you're always so concerned about me. I know *you* can't help it that your . . . your trade has perverted a great art."

Rick gaped at him in disbelief for a moment. "*You* think *I*—" He choked. He colored angrily. He stared at the old ham and began to curse softly under his breath.

Thornier suddenly lifted a finger to his mouth and went *shhhh!* His eyes roamed toward the back of the theater.

"That was only D'Uccia on the stairs," Rick began.
"What—?"

"*Shhhh!*"

They listened. The janitor wore a rancid smile. Seconds later it came—first a faint yelp, then—

Bbbrroom*mmpb!*

It rattled the booth windows. Rick started up frowning.

"What the—?"

"*Shhhh!*"

The jolting jar was followed by a faint mutter of profanity.

"That's D'Uccia. What happened?"

The faint mutter suddenly became a roaring stream of curses from somewhere behind the balconies.

"Hey!" said Rick. "He must have hurt himself."

"Naah. He just found my resignation, that's all. See? I told you I'd quit."

The profane bellowing grew louder to the accompaniment of an elephantine thumping on carpeted stairs.

"He's not *that* sorry to see you go," Rick grunted, looking baffled.

D'Uccia burst into view at the head of the aisle. He stopped with his feet spread wide, clutching at the base of his spine with one hand and waving a golden lily aloft in the other.

"Lily gilder!" he screamed. "Pansy painter! You fancy-pantsy bom! Come out, you fonny fonny boy!"

Thornier thrust his head calmly through the control-booth window, stared at the furious manager with arched brows. "You calling me, Mr. D'Uccia?"

D'Uccia sucked in two or three gasping breaths before he found his bellow again.

"*Thornya!*"

"Yes, sir?"

"Itsa finish, you hear?"

"What's finished, boss?"

"Itsa finish. I'ma go see the servo man. I'ma go get me a swip-op machine. You gotta two wiks notice."

"Tell him you don't want any notice," Rick grunted softly from nearby. "Walk out on him."

"All right, Mr. D'Uccia," Thornier called evenly.

D'Uccia stood there sputtering, threatening to charge,

waving the lily helplessly. Finally he threw it down in the
aisle with a curse and whirled to limp painfully out.

"*Whew!*" Rick breathed. "What did you do?"

Thornier told him sourly. The technician shook his
head.

"He won't fire you. He'll change his mind. It's too hard
to hire anybody to do dirty-work these days."

"You heard him. He can buy an autojan installation.
'Swip-op' machine."

"Baloney! Dooch is too stingy to put out that much
dough. Besides, he can't get the satisfaction of screaming
at a machine."

Thornier glanced up wryly. "Why *can't* he?"

"Well—" Rick paused. "Ulp! . . . You're right. He can.
He came up here and bawled out the Maestro once.
Kicked it, yelled at it, shook it—like a guy trying to get
his quarter back out of a telephone. Went away looking
pleased with himself, too."

"Why not?" Thorny muttered gloomily. "People are
machines to D'Uccia. And he's *fair* about it. He's willing
to treat them all alike."

"But you're not going to stick around two weeks, are
you?"

"Why not? It'll give me time to put out some feelers for
a job."

Rick grunted doubtfully and turned his attention back
to the machine. He removed the upper front panel and set
it aside. He opened a metal canister on the floor and lifted
out a foot-wide foot-thick roll of plastic tape. He mounted
it on a spindle inside the Maestro, and began feeding the
end of the tape through several sets of rollers and guides.
The tape appeared wormeaten—covered with thousands
of tiny punch-marks and wavy grooves. The janitor paused
to watch the process with cold hostility.

"Is that the script-tape for the 'Anarch?' " he asked
stiffly.

The technician nodded. "Brand new tape, too. Got to
be careful how I feed her in. It's still got fuzz on it from
the recording cuts." He stopped the feed mechanism
briefly, plucked at a punchmark with his awl, blew on it,
then started the feed motor again.

"What happens if the tape gets nicked or scratched?"
Thorny grunted curiously. "Actor collapse on stage?"

Rick shook his head. "Naa, it happens all the time. A

scratch or a nick'll make a player muff a line or maybe stumble, then the Maestro catches the goof, and compensates. Maestro gets feedback from the stage, continuously directs the show. It can do a lot of compensating, too."

"I thought the whole show came from the tape."

The technician smiled. "It does, in a way. But it's more than a recorded mechanical puppet show, Thorny. The Maestro watches the stage . . . no, more than that . . . the Maestro *is* the stage, an electronic analogue of it." He patted the metal housing. "All the actors' personality patterns are packed in here. It's more than a remote controller, the way most people think of it. It's a creative directing machine. It's even got pickups out in the audience to gauge reactions to——"

He stopped suddenly, staring at the old actor's face. He swallowed nervously. "Thorny *don't* look that way. I'm sorry. Here, have a cigarette."

Thorny accepted it with trembling fingers. He stared down into the gleaming maze of circuitry with narrowed eyes, watched the script-belt climb slowly over the rollers and down into the bowels of the Maestro.

"Art!" he hissed. "Theater! What'd they give you your degree in, Richard? Dramaturgical engineering?"

He shuddered and stalked out of the booth. Rick listened to the angry rattle of his heels on the iron stairs that led down to stage level. He shook his head sadly, shrugged, went back to inspecting the tape for rough cuts.

Thorny came back after a few minutes with a bucket and a mop. He looked reluctantly repentant. "Sorry, lad," he grunted. "I know you're just trying to make a living, and——"

"Skip it," Rick grunted curtly.

"It's just . . . well . . . this particular show. It gets me."

"This——? 'The Anarch,' you mean? What about it, Thorny? You play in it once?"

"Uh-uh. It hasn't been on the stage since the Nineties, except—well, it was almost revived ten years ago. We rehearsed for weeks. Show folded before opening night. No dough."

"You had a good part in it?"

'I was to play Andreyev," Thornier told him with a faint smile.

Rick whistled between his teeth. "The lead. That's too

bad." He hoisted his feet to let Thorny mop under them. "Big disappointment, I guess."

"It's not that. It's just . . . well . . . 'The Anarch' rehearsals were the last time Mela and I were on stage together. That's all."

"Mela?" The technician paused, frowning. "Mela *Stone?*"

Thornier nodded.

Rick snatched up a copy of the uncoded script, waved it at him. "But she's in *this* version, Thorny! Know that! She's playing Marka."

Thornier's laugh was brief and brittle.

Rick reddened slightly. "Well, I mean her mannequin's playing it."

Thorny eyed the Maestro distastefully. "Your mechanical Svengali's playing its airfoam zombies in *all* roles, you mean."

"Oh, cut it out, Thorny. Be sore at the world if you want to, but don't blame me for what audiences want. And I didn't invent autodrama anyhow."

"I don't blame anybody. I merely detest that . . . that—" He punched at the base of the Maestro with his wet mop.

"You and D'Uccia," Rick grunted disgustedly. "Except —D'Uccia loves it when it's working O.K. It's just a machine, Thorny. Why hate it?"

"Don't need a reason to hate it," he said, snarly-petulant. "I hate air-cabs, too. It's a matter of taste, that's all."

"All right, but the public likes autodrama—whether it's by TV, stereo, or on stage. And they get what they want."

"Why?"

Rick snickered. "Well, it's their dough. Autodrama's portable, predictable, duplicatable. And flexible. You can run 'Macbeth' tonight, the 'Anarch' tomorrow night, and 'King of the Moon' the next night—in the same house. No actor-temperament problems. No union problems. Rent the packaged props, dolls, and tapes from Smithfield. Packaged theater. Systematized, mass-produced. In Coon Creek, Georgia, yet."

"Bah!"

Rick finished feeding in the script tape, closed the panel, and opened an adjacent one. He ripped the lid from a cardboard carton and dumped a heap of smaller tape-spools on the table.

"Are *those* the souls they sold to Smithfield?" Thornier asked, smiling at them rather weirdly.

The technician's stool scraped back and he exploded: "You know what they are!"

Thornier nodded, leaned closer to stare at them as if fascinated. He plucked one of them out of the pile, sighed down at it.

"If you say 'Alas, poor Yorick,' I'll heave you out of here!" Rick grated.

Thornier put it back with a sigh and wiped his hand on his coveralls. Packaged personalities. Actor's egos, analogized on tape. Real actors, once, whose dolls were now cast in the roles. The tapes contained complex psycho-physiological data derived from months of psychic and somatic testing, after the original actors had signed their Smithfield contracts. Data for the Maestro's personality matrices. Abstractions from the human psyche, incarnate in glass, copper, chromium. The souls they rented to Smithfield on a royalty basis, along with their flesh and blood likenesses in the dolls.

Rick loaded a casting spool onto its spindle, started it feeding through the pickups.

"What happens if you leave out a vital ingredient? Such as Mela Stone's tape, for instance," Thornier wanted to know.

"The doll'd run through its lines like a zombie, that's all." Rick explained. "No zip. No interpretation. Flat, deadpan, like a robot."

"They are robots."

"Not exactly. Remote marionettes for the Maestro, but interpreted. We did a run-through on 'Hamlet' once, without any actor tapes. Everybody talked in flat monotones, no expressions. It was a scream."

"Ha, ha," Thornier said grimly.

Rick slipped another tape on the spindle, clicked a dial to a new setting, started the feed again. "This one's Andreyev, Thornier—played by Peltier." He cursed suddenly, stopped the feed, inspected the tape anxiously, flipped open the pickup mechanism, and inspected it with a magnifier.

"What's wrong?" asked the janitor.

"Take-off's about worn out. Hard to keep its spacing

right. I'm nervous about it getting hung up and chewing up the tape."

"No duplicate tapes?"

"Yeah. One set of extras. But the show opens tonight." He cast another suspicious look at the pickup glideway, then closed it and switched the feed again. He was replacing the panel when the feed mechanism stalled. A ripping sound came from inside. He muttered fluent profanity, shut off the drive, jerked away the panel. He held up a shredded ribbon of tape for Thorny to see, then flung it angrily across the booth. "Get out of here! You're a jinx!"

"Not till I finish mopping."

"Thorny, get D'Uccia for me, will you? We'll have to get a new pickup flown in from Smithfield before this afternoon. This is a helluva mess."

"Why not hire a human stand-in?" he asked nastily, then added: "Forgive me. That would be a perversion of your art, wouldn't it? Shall I get D'Uccia?"

Rick threw the Peltier spool at him. He ducked out with a chuckle and went to find the theater manager. Halfway down the iron stairs, he paused to look at the wide stage that spread away just beyond the folded curtains. The footlights were burning, and the gray-green floor looked clean and shimmering, with its checkerboard pattern of imbedded copper strips. The strips were electrified during the performance, and they fed the mannequins' energy-storage packs. The dolls had metallic disks in their soles, and rectifiers in their insteps. When batteries drained low, the Maestro moved the actor's foot an inch or so to contact the floor electrodes for periodic recharging during the play, since a doll would grow wobbly and its voice indistinct after a dozen minutes on internal power alone.

Thorny stared at the broad expanse of stage where no humans walked on performance night. D'Uccia's Siamese tomcat sat licking itself in the center of the stage. It glanced up at him haughtily, seemed to sniff, began licking itself again. He watched it for a moment, then called back upstairs to Rick.

"Energize the floor a minute, will you, Rick?"

"Huh? Why?"—a busy grunt.

"Want to check something."

"O.K., but then fetch D'Uccia."

He heard the technician snap a switch. The cat's calm hauteur exploded. The cat screamed, scrambled, barrel-rolled, amid a faint sputter of sparks. The cat did an Immelmann turn over the footlights, landed in the pit with a clawing crash, then scampered up the aisle with fur erect toward its haven beneath Imperio's desk.

"Whatthehell?" Rick growled, and thrust his head out of the booth.

"Shut it off now," said the janitor. "D'Uccia'll be here in a minute."

"With fangs showing!"

Thornier went to finish his routine clean-up. Gloom had begun to gather about him. He was leaving—leaving even this last humble role in connection with the stage. A fleeting realization of his own impotence came to him. Helpless. Helpless enough to seek petty revenges like vandalizing D'Uccia's window box and tormenting D'Uccia's cat, because there was not any real enemy at which he could strike out.

He put the realization down firmly, and stamped on it. *He* was Ryan Thornier, and never helpless, unless he willed it so. I'll make them know who I am just *once,* he thought, before I go. I'll make them remember, and they won't ever forget.

But that line of thought about playing one last great role, one last masterful interpretation, he knew was no good. "Thorny, if you ever played a one-last-great," Rick had said to him once, "there wouldn't be a thing left to live for, would there?" Rick had said cynically, but it was true anyhow. And the pleasant fantasy was somehow alarming as well as pleasant.

The chic little woman in the white-plumed hat was explaining things carefully—with round vowels and precise enunciation—to the Playwright of the Moment, up-and-coming, with awed worshipfulness in his gaze as he listened to the pert little producer. "Stark realism, you see, is the milieu of autodrama," she said. "Always remember, Bernie, that consideration for the actors is a thing of the past. Study the drama of Rome—ancient Rome. If a play had a crucifixion scene, they got a slave for the part and crucified him. On stage, but *really!*"

The Playwright of the Moment laughed dutifully around his long cigarette holder. "So that's where they got the

line: 'It's superb, but it's hell on the actors.' I must re-
write the murder scene in my 'George's Wake.' Do it with
a hatchet, this time."

"Oh, now, *Bernie!* Mannequins don't bleed."

They both laughed heartily. "And they *are* expensive.
Not hell on the actors, but hell on the budget."

"The Romans probably had the same problem. I'll bear
it in mind."

Thornier saw them—the producer and the Playwright
of the Moment—standing there in the orchestra when he
came from backstage and across toward the center aisle.
They lounged on the arms of their seats, and a crowd of
production personnel and technicians milled about them.
The time for the first run-through was approaching.

The small woman waved demurely to Thorny when she
saw him making his way slowly through the throng, then
turned to the playwright again. "Bernie, be a lamb and get
me a drink, will you? I've got a butterfly."

"Surely. Hard, or soft?"

"Oh, hard. Scotch mist in a paper cup, please. There's a
bar next door."

The playwright nodded a nod that was nearly a bow
and shuffled away up the aisle. The woman caught at the
janitor's sleeve as he passed.

"Going to snub me, Thorny?"

"Oh, hello, Miss Ferne," he said politely.

She leaned close and muttered: "Call me 'Miss Ferne'
again and I'll claw you." The round vowels had vanished.

"O.K., Jade, but—" He glanced around nervously.
Technicians milled about them. Ian Feria, the producer,
watched them curiously from the wings.

"What's been doing with you, Thorny? Why haven't I
seen you?" she complained.

He gestured with the broom handle, shrugged. Jade
Ferne studied his face a moment and frowned. "Why the
agonized look, Thorny? Mad at me?"

He shook his head. "This play, Jade—'The Anarch,'
well—" He glanced miserably toward the stage.

Memory struck her suddenly. She breathed a compas-
sionate *ummm.* "The attempted revival, ten years ago—
you were to be Andreyev. Oh, Thorny, I'd forgotten."

"It's all right." He wore a carefully tailored martyr's
smile.

She gave his arm a quick pat. "I'll see you after the

run-through, Thorny. We'll have a drink and talk old times."

He glanced around again and shook his head. "You've got new friends now, Jade. They wouldn't like it."

"The crew? Nonsense! They're not snobs."

"No, but they want your attention. Feria's trying to catch your eye right now. No use making them sore."

"All right, but after the run-through I'll see you in the mannequin room. I'll just slip away."

"If you want to."

"I do, Thorny. It's been so long."

The playwright returned with her Scotch mist and gave Thornier a hostilely curious glance.

"Bless your heart, Bernie," she said, the round vowels returning, then to Thornier: "Thorny, would you do me a favor? I've been trying to corner D'Uccia, but he's tied up with a servo salesman somewhere. Somebody's got to run and pick up a mannequin from the depot. The shipment was delivered, but the trucker missed a doll crate. We'll need it for the runthrough. Could you—"

"Sure, Miss Ferne. Do I need a requisition order?"

"No, just sign the delivery ticket. And Thorny, see if the new part for the Maestro's been flown in yet. Oh, and one other thing—the Maestro chewed up the Peltier tape. We've got a duplicate, but we should have two, just to be safe."

"I'll see if they have one in stock," he murmured, and turned to go.

D'Uccia stood in the lobby with the salesman when he passed through. The theater manager saw him and smirked happily.

". . . Certain special features, of course," the salesman was saying. "It's an old building, and it wasn't designed with autojanitor systems in mind, like buildings are now. But we'll tailor the installation to fit your place, Mr. D'Uccia. We want to do the job *right,* and a packaged unit wouldn't do it."

"Yah, you gimme da price, hah?"

"We'll have an estimate for you by tomorrow. I'll have an engineer over this afternoon to make the survey, and he'll work up a layout tonight."

"Whatsa 'bout the demonstration, uh? Whatsa 'bout you show how da swhip-op machine go?"

The salesman hesitated, eying the janitor who waited

nearby. "Well, the floor-cleaning robot is only a small part of the complete service, but . . . I tell you what I'll do. I'll bring a packaged char-all over this afternoon, and let you have a look at it."

"Fine. Datsa fine. You bring her, den we see."

They shook hands. Thornier stood with his arms folded, haughtily inspecting a bug that crawled across the frond of a potted palm, and waiting for a chance to ask D'Uccia for the keys to the truck. He felt the theater manager's triumphant gaze, but gave no indication that he heard.

"We can do the job for you all right, Mr. D'Uccia. Cut your worries in half. And that'll cut your doctor bills in half, too, like you say. Yes, sir! A man in your position gets ground down with just plain human inefficiency—other people's inefficiency. You'll never have to worry about that, once you get the building autojanitored, no sir!"

"T'ank you kindly."

"Thank *you*, Mr. D'Uccia, and I'll see you later this afternoon."

The salesman left.

"Well, bom?" D'Uccia grunted to the janitor.

"The keys to the truck. Miss Ferne wants a pickup from the depot."

D'Uccia tossed them to him. "You hear what the man say? Letsa machines do alla work, hah? Always you wantsa day off. O.K., you takka da day off, ever'day pretty soon. Nice for you, hah, ragazzo?"

Thornier turned away quickly to avoid displaying the surge of unwanted anger. "Be back in an hour," he grunted, and hurried away on his errand, his jaw working in sullen resentment. Why wait around for two humiliating weeks? Why not just walk out? Let D'Uccia do his own chores until the autojan was installed. He'd never be able to get another job around the theater anyhow, so D'Uccia's reaction wouldn't matter.

I'll walk out now, he thought—and immediately knew that he wouldn't. It was hard to explain to himself, but—when he thought of the final moment when he would be free to look for a decent job and a comfortable living—he felt a twinge of fear that was hard to understand.

The janitor's job had paid him only enough to keep him alive in a fourth floor room where he cooked his own

meager meals and wrote memoirs of the old days, but it
had kept him close to the lingering remnants of something
he loved.

"Theater," they called it. Not *the* theater—as it was to
the scalper's victim, the matinée housewife, or the awe-
struck hick—but just "theater." It wasn't a place, wasn't a
business, wasn't the name of an art. "Theater" was a condition of the human heart and soul. Jade Ferne was theater. So was Ian Feria. So was Mela, poor kid, before her
deal with Smithfield. Some had it, others didn't. In the
old days, the ones that didn't have it soon got out. But the
ones that had it, still had it, even after *the* theater was
gobbled up by technological change. And they hung
around. Some of them, like Jade and Ian and Mela,
adapted to the change, profited by the prostitution of the
stage, and developed ulcers and a guilty conscience. Still,
they were theater, and because they were, he, Thornier,
hung around, too, scrubbing the floors they walked on,
and feeling somehow that he was still in theater. Now he
was leaving. And now he felt the old bitterness boiling up
inside again. The bitterness had been chronic and passive,
and now it threatened to become active and acute.

If I could only give them one last performance! he
thought. One last great role—

But *that* thought led to the fantasy-plan for revenge,
the plan that came to him often as he wandered about the
empty theater. Revenge was no good. And the plan was
only a daydream. And yet—he wasn't going to get another chance.

He set his jaw grimly and drove on to the Smithfield depot.

The depot clerk had hauled the crated mannequin to
the fore, and it was waiting for Thornier when he entered
the stockroom. He rolled it out from the wall on a dolly,
and the janitor helped him wrestle the coffin-sized packing
case onto the counter.

"Don't take it to the truck yet," the clerk grunted
around the fat stub of a cigar. "It ain't a new doll, and
you gotta sign a release."

"What kind of a release?"

"Liability for malfunction. If the doll breaks down during the show, you can't sue Smithfield. It's standard prack
for used-doll rentals."

"Why didn't they send a new one, then?"

"Discontinued production on this model. You want it, you take a used one, and sign the release."

"Suppose I don't sign?"

"No siggy, no dolly."

"Oh." He thought for a moment. Obviously, the clerk had mistaken him for production personnel. His signature wouldn't mean anything—but it was getting late, and Jade was rushed. Since the release wouldn't be valid anyhow he reached for the form.

"Wait," said the clerk. "You better look at what you're signing for." He reached for a wrecking claw and slipped it under a metal binding strap. The strap broke with a screechy snap. "It's been overhauled," the clerk continued. "New solenoid fluid injected, new cosmetic job. Nothing really wrong. A few fatigue spots in the padding, and one toe missing. But you oughta have a look, anyhow."

He finished breaking the lid-fastenings loose and turned to a wall-control board. "We don't have a complete Maestro here," he said as he closed a knife switch, "but we got the control transmitters, and some taped sequences. It's enough to pre-flight a doll."

Equipment hummed to life somewhere behind the panel. The clerk adjusted several dials while Thornier waited impatiently.

"Let's see—" muttered the clerk. "Guess we'll start off with the Frankenstein sequence." He flipped a switch.

A purring sound came faintly from within the coffin-like box. Thornier watched nervously. The lid stirred, began to rise. A woman's hands came into view, pushing the lid up from within. The purring increased. The lid clattered aside to hang by the metal straps.

The woman sat up and smiled at the janitor.

Thornier went white. "Mela!" he hissed.

"Ain't that a chiller?" chuckled the clerk. "Now for the hoochy-coochy sequence—"

"No—"

The clerk flipped another switch. The doll stood up slowly, chastely nude as a window-dummy. Still smiling at Thorny, the doll did a bump and a grind.

"Stop it!" he yelled hoarsely.

"Whassa matter, buddy?"

Thorny heard another switch snap. The doll stretched gracefully and yawned. It stretched out in its packing case again, closed its eyes and folded its hands over its bosom. The purring stopped.

"What's eating you?" the clerk grumbled, slapping the lid back over the case again. "You sick or something?"

"I . . . I knew her," Ryan Thornier wheezed. "I used to work—" He shook himself angrily and seized the crate.

"Wait, I'll give you a hand."

Fury awakened new muscles. He hauled the crate out on the loading dock without assistance and dumped it in the back of the truck, then came back to slash his name across the release forms.

"You sure get sore easy," the clerk mumbled. "You better take it easy. You sure better take it easy."

Thorny was cursing softly as he nosed the truck out into the river of traffic. Maybe Jade thought it was funny, sending him after Mela's doll. Jade remembered how it had been between them—if she bothered to think about it. Thornier and Stone—a team that had gotten constant attention from the gossip columnists in the old days. Rumors of engagement, rumors of secret marriage, rumors of squabbles and reunions, break-ups and patch-ups, and some of the rumors were almost true. Maybe Jade thought it was a howl, sending him to fetch the mannequin.

But no—his anger faded as he drove along the boulevard—she hadn't thought about it. Probably she tried hard not to think of old times any more.

Gloom settled over him again, replacing rage. Still it haunted him—the horrified shock of seeing her sit up like an awakened corpse to smile at him. *Mela . . . Mela*—

They'd had it good together and bad together. Bit parts and beans in a cold-water flat. Starring roles and steaks at Sardi's. And—love? Was that what it was? He thought of it uneasily. Hypnotic absorption in each other, perhaps, and in the mutual intoxication of their success—but it wasn't necessarily love. Love was calm and even and lasting, and you paid for it with a dedicated lifetime, and Mela wouldn't pay. She'd walked out on them. She'd walked to Smithfield and bought security with sacrifice of principle. There'd been a name for what she'd done. "Scab," they used to say.

He shook himself. It was no good, thinking about those times. Times died with each passing minute. Now they paid $8.80 to watch Mela's figurine move in her stead, wearing Mela's face, moving with Mela's gestures, walking with the same lilting walk. And the doll was still young, while Mela had aged ten years, years of collecting quarterly royalties from her dolls and living comfortably.

Great Actors Immortalized—that was one of Smithfield's little slogans. But they had discontinued production on Mela Stone, the depot clerk had said. Overstocked.

The promise of relative immortality had been quite a bait. Actors unions had resisted autodrama, for obviously the bit players and the lesser-knowns would not be in demand. By making dozens—even hundreds—of copies of the same leading star, top talent could be had for every role, and the same actor-mannequin could be playing simultaneously in dozens of shows all over the country. The unions had resisted—but only a few were wanted by Smithfield anyhow, and the lure was great. The promise of fantastic royalties was enticing enough, but in addition —immortality for the actor, through duplication of mannequins. Authors, artists, playwrights had always been able to outlive the centuries, but actors were remembered only by professionals, and their names briefly recorded in the annals of the stage. Shakespeare would live another thousand years, but who remembered Dick Burbage who trouped in the day of the bard's premiers? Flesh and bone, heart and brain, these were the trouper's media, and his art could not outlive them.

Thorny knew the yearnings after lastingness, and he could no longer hate the ones who had gone over. As for himself, the autodrama industry had made him a tentative offer, and he had resisted—partly because he was reasonably certain that the offer would have been withdrawn during testing procedures. Some actors were not "cybergenic"—could not be adequately sculptured into electronic-robotic analogues. These were the portrayers, whose art was inward, whose roles had to be lived rather than played. No polygraphic analogue could duplicate their talents, and Thornier knew he was one of them. It had been easy for him to resist.

At the corner of Eighth Street, he remembered the spare tape and the replacement pickup for the Maestro. But if he turned back now, he'd hold up the run-through, and Jade would be furious. Mentally he kicked himself, and drove on to the delivery entrance of the theater. There he

left the crated mannequin with the stage crew, and headed
back for the depot without seeing the producer.

"Hey, bud," said the clerk, "your boss was on the
phone. Sounded pretty unhappy."

"Who . . . D'Uccia?"

"No . . . well, yeah, D'Uccia, too. He wasn't unhappy,
just having fits. I meant Miss Ferne."

"Oh . . . where's your phone?"

"Over there. The lady was near hysterical."

Thorny swallowed hard and headed for the booth. Jade
Ferne was a good friend, and if his absent-mindedness had
goofed up her production—

"I've got the pickup and the tape ready to go," the clerk
called after him. "She told me about it on the phone. Boy,
you're sure on the ball today, ain't ya—the greasy eight
ball."

Thorny reddened and dialed nervously.

"Thank God!" she groaned. "Thorny, we did the run-
through with Andreyev a walking zombie. The Maestro
chewed up our duplicate Peltier tape, and we're running
without an actor-analogue in the starring role. Baby, I
could murder you!"

"Sorry, Jade. I slipped a cog, I guess."

"Never mind! Just get the new pickup mechanism over
here for Thomas. And the Peltier tape. And don't have a
wreck. It's two o'clock, and tonight's opening, and we're
still short our leading man. And there's no time to get
anything else flown in from Smithfield."

"In some ways, nothing's changed, has it, Jade?" he
grunted, thinking of the eternal backstage hysteria that
lasted until the lights were low and beauty and calm order
somehow emerged miraculously out of the prevailing
chaos.

"Don't philosophize, just *get* here!" she snapped, and
hung up.

The clerk had the cartons ready for him as he emerged.
"Look, chum, better take care of that Peltier tape," the
clerk advised. "It's the last one in the place. I've got more
on order, but they won't be here for a couple of days."

Thornier stared at the smaller package thoughtfully.
The last Peltier?

The plan, he remembered the plan. *This* would make it
easy. Of course, the plan was only a fantasy, a vengeful

dream. He couldn't go through with it. To wreck the show
would be a stab at Jade—

He heard his own voice like a stranger's, saying; "Miss
Ferne also asked me to pick up a Wilson Granger tape,
and a couple of three-inch splices."

The clerk looked surprised. "Granger? He's not in 'The
Anarch,' is he?"

Thornier shook his head. "No—guess she wants it for a
trial casting. Next show, maybe."

The clerk shrugged and went to get the tape and the
splices. Thornier stood clenching and unclenching his
fists. He wasn't going to go through with it, of course. Only
a silly fantasy.

"I'll have to make a separate ticket on these," said the
clerk, returning.

He signed the delivery slips in a daze, then headed for
the truck. He drove three blocks from the depot, then
parked in a loading zone. He opened the tape cartons
carefully with his penknife, peeling back the glued flaps so
that they could be sealed again. He removed the two rolls
of pattern perforated tape from their small metal canisters,
carefully plucked off the masking-tape seals and stuck
them temporarily to the dashboard. He unrolled the first
half-yard of the Peltier tape; it was unperforated, and
printed with identifying codes and manufacturer's data.
Fortunately, it was not a brand-new tape; it had been
used before, and he could see the wear-marks. A splice
would not arouse suspicion.

He cut off the identifying tongue with his knife, laid it
aside. Then he did the same to the Granger tape.

Granger was fat, jovial, fiftyish. His mannequin played
comic supporting roles.

Peltier was young, gaunt, gloomy—the intellectual villain, the dedicated fanatic. A fair choice for the part of
Andreyev.

Thornier's hands seemed to move of their own volition,
playing reflexively in long-rehearsed roles. He cut the tapes.
He took out one of the hot-splice packs and jerked the tab
that started the chemical action. He clocked off fifteen
seconds by his watch, then opened the pack and fitted into
it the cut ends of the Granger tape and the Peltier identifying tongue, butted them carefully end to end, and
closed the pack. When it stopped smoking, he opened it
to inspect the splice. A neat patch, scarcely visible on the

slick plastic tape. Granger's analogue, labeled as Peltier's. And the body of the mannequin was Peltier's. He resealed it in its canister.

He wadded the Peltier tape and the Granger label and the extra delivery receipt copy into the other box. Then he pulled the truck out of the loading zone and drove through the heavy traffic like a racing jockey, trusting the anti-crash radar to see him safely through. As he crossed the bridge, he threw the Peltier tape out the window into the river. And then there was no retreat from what he had done.

Jade and Feria sat in the orchestra, watching the final act of the run-through with a dud Andreyev. When Thorny slipped in beside them, Jade wiped mock sweat from her brow.

"Thank God you're back!" she whispered as he displayed the delayed packages. "Sneak backstage and run them up to Rick in the booth, will you? Thorny, I'm out of my mind!"

"Sorry, Miss Ferne." Fearing that his guilty nervousness hung about him like a ragged cloak, he slipped quickly backstage and delivered the cartons to Thomas in the booth. The technician hovered over the Maestro as the play went on, and he gave Thornier only a quick nod and a wave.

Thorny retreated into misty old corridors and unused dressing rooms, now heaped with junk and remnants of other days. He had to get a grip on himself, had to quit quaking inside. He wandered alone in the deserted sections of the building, opening old doors to peer into dark cubicles where great stars had preened in other days, other nights. Now full of trunks and cracked mirrors and tarpaulins and junked mannequins. Faint odors lingered— nervous smells—perspiration, make-up, dim perfume that pervaded the walls. Mildew and dust—the aroma of time. His footsteps sounded hollowly through the unpeopled rooms, while muffled sounds from the play came faintly through the walls—the hysterical pleading of Marka, the harsh laughter of Piotr, the marching boots of the revolutionist guards, a burst of music toward the end of the scene.

He turned abruptly and started back toward the stage. It was no good, hiding away like this. He must behave normally, must do what he usually did. The falsified Peltier tape would not wreak its havoc until after the first run-through, when Thomas fed it into the Maestro, reset the machine, and prepared to start the second trial run. Until then, he must remain casually himself, and afterwards—?

Afterwards, things would have to go as he had planned. Afterwards, Jade would have to come to him, as he believed she would. If she didn't, then he had bungled, he had clumsily wrecked, and to no avail.

He slipped through the power-room where converters hummed softly, supplying power to the stage. He stood close to the entrance, watching the beginnings of scene *iii,* of the third act. Andreyev—the Peltier doll—was on alone, pacing grimly in his apartment while the low grumble of a street mob and the distant rattle of machine-gun fire issued from the Maestro-managed sound effect system. After a moment's watching, he saw that Andreyev's movements were not "grim" but merely methodical and lifeless. The tapeless mannequin, going through the required motions, robotlike, without interpretation of meaning. He heard a brief burst of laughter from someone in the production row, and after watching the zombie-like rendering of Andreyev in a suspenseful scene, he, too, found himself grinning faintly.

The pacing mannequin looked toward him suddenly with a dead-pan face. It raised both fists toward its face. "Help," it said in a conversational monotone. "Ivan, where are you? Where? Surely they've come; they must come." It spoke quietly, without inflection. It ground its fists casually against its temples, paced mechanically again.

A few feet away, two mannequins that had been standing frozen in the off-stage lineup, clicked suddenly to life. As ghostly calm as display window dummies, they galvanized suddenly at a signal pulse command from the Maestro. Muscles—plastic sacs filled with oil-suspended magnetic powder and wrapped with elastic coils of wire, like flexible solenoids—tightened and strained beneath the airfoam flesh, working spasmodically to the pulsing rhythms of the polychromatic u.h.f. commands of the Maestro. Expressions of fear and urgency leaped to their faces. They crouched, tensed, looked around, then burst on stage, panting wildly.

"Comrade, she's come, she's come!" one of them screamed. "She's come with *him,* with Boris!"

"What? She has him prisoner?" came the casual reply. "No, no, comrade. We've been betrayed. She's with him. She's a traitor, she's sold out to them."

There was no feeling in the uninterpreted Andreyev's responses, even when he shot the bearer of bad tidings through the heart.

Thornier grew fascinated with watching as the scene progressed. The mannequins moved gracefully, their movements sinuous and more evenly flowing than human, they seemed boneless. The ratio of mass-to-muscle power of their members was carefully chosen to yield the flow of a dance with their every movement. Not clanking mechanical robots, not stumbling puppets, the dolls sustained patterns of movement and expression that would have quickly brought fatigue to a human actor, and the Maestro coördinated the events on stage in a way that would be impossible to a group of humans, each an individual and thinking independently.

It was as always. First, he looked with a shudder at the Machine moving in the stead of flesh and blood, at Mechanism sitting in the seat of artistry. But gradually his chill melted away, and the play caught him, and the actors were no longer machines. He lived in the role of Andreyev, and breathed the lines off-stage, and he knew the rest of them: Mela and Peltier, Sam Dion and Peter Repplewaite. He tensed with them, gritted his teeth in anticipation of difficult lines, cursed softly at the dud Andreyev, and forgot to listen for the faint crackle of sparks as the mannequins' feet stepped across the copper-studded floor, drinking energy in random bites to keep their storage packs near full charge.

Thus entranced, he scarcely noticed the purring and brushing and swishing sounds that came from behind him, and grew louder. He heard a quiet mutter of voices nearby, but only frowned at the distraction, kept his attention rooted to the stage.

Then a thin spray of water tickled his ankles. Something soggy and spongelike slapped against his foot. He whirled.

A gleaming metal spider, three feet high came at him slowly on six legs, with two grasping claws extended. It clicked its way toward him across the floor, throwing out a thin spray of liquid which it promptly sucked up with the spongelike proboscis. With one grasping claw, it lifted a ten-gallon can near his leg, sprayed under it, swabbed, and set the can down again.

Thornier came unfrozen with a howl, leaped over the thing, hit the wet-soapy deck off balance. He skidded and sprawled. The spider scrubbed at the floor toward the edge of the stage, then reversed directions and came back toward him.

Groaning, he pulled himself together, on hands and knees. D'Uccia's cackling laughter spilled over him. He glanced up. The chubby manager and the servo salesman stood over him, the salesman grinning, D'Uccia chortling.

"Datsa ma boy, datsa ma boy! Always, he watcha the show, then he don't swip-op around, then he wantsa day off. Thatsa ma boy, for sure." D'Uccia reached down to pat the metal spider's chassis. "Hey, *ragazzo*," he said again to Thornier, "want you should meet my new *boy* here. This one, he don't watcha the show like you."

He got to his feet, ghost-white and muttering. D'Uccia took closer note of his face, and his grin went sick. He inched back a step. Thornier glared at him briefly, then whirled to stalk away. He whirled into near collision with the Mela Stone mannequin, recovered, and started to pass in back of it.

Then he froze.

The Mela Stone mannequin was on stage, in the final scene. And this one looked older, and a little haggard. It wore an expression of shocked surprise as it looked him up and down. One hand darted to its mouth.

"Thorny—!" A frightened whisper.

"*Mela!*" Despite the play, he shouted it, opening his arms to her. "Mela, how *wonderful!*"

And then, he noticed she winced away from his sodden coveralls. And she wasn't glad to see him at all.

"Thorny, how nice," she managed to murmur, extending her hand gingerly. The hand flashed with jewelry.

He took it for an empty second, stared at her, then walked hurriedly away, knots twisting up inside him. Now he could play it through. Now he could go on with it, and even enjoy executing his plan against all of them.

Mela had come to watch opening night for her doll in "The Anarch," as if its performance were her own. *I'll arrange,* he thought, *for it not to be a dull show*.

"No, no, *nooo!*" came the monotone protest of the dud Andreyev, in the next-to-the-last scene. The bark of

Marka's gun, and the Peltier mannequin crumpled to the stage; and except for a brief triumphant denouement, the play was over.

At the sound of the gunshot, Thornier paused to smile tightly over his shoulder, eyes burning from his hawklike face. Then he vanished into the wings.

She got away from them as soon as she could, and she wandered around backstage until she found him in the storage room of the costuming section. Alone, he was sorting through the contents of an old locker and muttering nostalgically to himself. She smiled and closed the door with a thud. Startled, he dropped an old collapsible top-hat and a box of blank cartridges back into the trunk. His hand dived into his pocket as he straightened.

"Jade! I didn't expect—"

"Me to come?" She flopped on a dusty old chaise lounge with a weary sigh and fanned herself with a program, closing her eyes. She kicked off her shoes and muttered: "Infuriating bunch. I hate 'em!"—made a retching face, and relaxed into little-girlhood. A little girl who had trouped with Thornier and the rest of them—the *actress* Jade Ferne, who had begged for bit parts and haunted the agencies and won the roles through endless rehearsals and shuddered with fright before opening curtain like the rest of them. Now she was a pert little woman with shrewd eyes; streaks of gray at the temples, and hard lines around her mouth. As she let the executive cloak slip away, the shrewdness and the hard lines melted into weariness.

"Fifteen minutes to get my sanity back, Thorny," she muttered, glancing at her watch as if to time it.

He sat on the trunk and tried to relax. She hadn't seemed to notice his uneasiness, or else she was just too tired to attach any significance to it. If she found him out, she'd have him flayed and pitched out of the building on his ear, and maybe call the police. She came in a small package, but so did an incendiary grenade. *It won't hurt you, Jade, what I'm doing,* he told himself. *It'll cause a big splash, and you won't like it, but it won't hurt you, nor even wreck the show.*

He was doing it for show business, the old kind, the kind they'd both known and loved. And in that sense, he told himself further, he was doing it as much for her as he was for himself.

"How was the run-through, Jade?" he asked casually. "Except for Andreyev, I mean."

"Superb, simply superb," she said mechanically.

"I mean *really*."

She opened her eyes, made a sick mouth. "Like always, Thorny, like always. Nauseating, overplayed, perfectly directed for a gum-chewing bag-rattling crowd. A crowd that wants it overplayed so that it won't have to think about what's going on. A crowd that doesn't want to reach *out* for a feeling or a meaning. It wants to be clubbed on the head with the meaning, so it doesn't have to reach. I'm sick of it."

He looked briefly surprised. "That figures," he grunted wryly.

She hooked her bare heels on the edge of the lounge, hugged her shins, rested her chin on her knees, and blinked at him. "Hate me for producing the stuff, Thorny?"

He thought about it for a moment, shook his head. "I get sore at the setup sometimes, but I don't blame you for it."

"That's good. Sometimes I'd trade places with you. Sometimes I'd rather be a charwoman and scrub D'Uccia's floors instead."

"Not a chance," he said sourly. "The Maestro's relatives are taking *that* over, too."

"I know. I heard. You're out of a job, thank God. Now you can get somewhere."

He shook his head. "I don't know where. I can't do anything but act."

"Nonsense. I can get you a job tomorrow."

"Where?"

"With Smithfield. Sales promotion. They're hiring a number of old actors in the department."

"No." He said it flat and cold.

"Not so fast. This is something new. The company's expanding."

"Ha."

"Autodrama for the home. A four-foot stage in every living room. Miniature mannequins, six inches high. Centralized Maestro service. Great plays piped to your home by concentric table. Just dial Smithfield, make your request. Sound good?"

He stared at her icily. "Greatest thing in show business since Sarah Bernhardt," he offered tonelessly.

"Thorny! Don't get nasty with me!"

"Sorry. But what's so new about having it in the home? Autodrama took over TV years ago."

"I know, but this is different. Real miniature theater. Kids go wild for it. But it'll take good promotion to make it catch on."

"Sorry, but you know me better than that."

She shrugged, sighed wearily, closed her eyes again. "Yes, I do. You've got portrayer's integrity. You're a darfsteller. A director's ulcer. You can't play a role without living it, and you won't live it unless you believe it. So go ahead and starve." She spoke crossly, but he knew there was grudging admiration behind it.

"I'll be O.K.," he grunted, adding to himself: *after tonight's performance.*

"Nothing I can do for you?"

"Sure. Cast me. I'll stand in for dud mannequins."

She gave him a sharp glance, hesitated. "You know, I believe you *would?*"

He shrugged. "Why not?"

She stared thoughtfully at a row of packing cases, waggled her dark head. "Hmmp! What a spectacle that'd be—a human actor, incognito, playing in an autodrama."

"It's been done—in the sticks."

"Yes, but the audience knew it was being done, and that always spoils the show. It creates contrasts that don't exist or wouldn't be noticed otherwise. Makes the dolls seem snaky, birdlike, too rubbery quick. With no humans on stage for contrast, the dolls just seem wistfully graceful, ethereal."

"But if the audience didn't know—"

Jade was smiling faintly. "I wonder," she mused. "I wonder if they'd guess. They'd notice a difference, of course—in one mannequin."

"But they'd think it was just the Maestro's interpretation of the part."

"Maybe—if the human actor were careful."

He chuckled sourly. "If it fooled the critics—"

"Some ass would call it 'an abysmally unrealistic interpretation' or 'too obviously mechanical.' " She glanced at her watch, shook herself, stretched wearily, and slipped into her shoes again. "Anyway," she added, "there's no reason to do it, since the Maestro's *really* capable of rendering a better-than-human performance anyhow."

The statement brought an agonized gasp from the janitor. She looked at him and giggled. "Don't be shocked, Thorny. I said *'capable* of'—not 'in the habit of.' Autodrama entertains audiences on the level they *want* to be entertained on."

"But—"

"Just," she added firmly, "as show business has always done."

"But—"

"Oh, retract your eyeballs, Thorny. I didn't mean to blaspheme." She preened, began slipping back into her producer's mold as she prepared to return to her crowd. "The only thing wrong with autodrama is that it's scaled down to the moron-level—but show business always has been, and probably should be. Even if it gives us kids a pain." She smiled and patted his cheek. "Sorry I shocked you. Au 'voir, Thorny. And luck."

When she was gone, he sat fingering the cartridges in his pocket and staring at nothing. Didn't any of them have any sensibilities? Jade too, a seller of principle. And he had always thought of her as having merely compromised with necessity, against her real wishes. The idea that she could really believe autodrama capable of rendering a better-than-human performance—

But she didn't. Of course she needed to rationalize, to excuse what she was doing—

He sighed and went to lock the door, then to recover the old "Anarch" script from the trunk. His hands were trembling slightly. Had he planted enough of an idea in Jade's mind; would she remember it later? Or perhaps remember it too clearly, and suspect it?

He shook himself sternly. No apprehensions allowed. When Rick rang the bell for the second run-through, it would be his entrance-cue, and he must be in-character by then. Too bad he was no schauspieler, too bad he couldn't switch himself on-and-off the way Jade could do, but the necessity for much inward preparation was the burden of the darfsteller. He could not change into a role without first changing himself, and letting the revision seep surfaceward as it might, reflecting the inner state of the man.

Strains of Moussorgsky pervaded the walls. He closed his eyes to listen and feel. Music for empire. Music at once brutal and majestic. It was the time of upheaval, of vengeance, of overthrow. Two times, superimposed. It was the time of opening night, with Ryan Thornier—ten years ago—cast in the starring role.

He fell into a kind of trance as he listened and clocked the pulse of his psyche and remembered. He scarcely noticed when the music stopped, and the first few lines of the play came through the walls.

"*Cut! Cut!*" A worried shout. Feria's.

It had begun.

Thornier took a deep breath and seemed to come awake. When he opened his eyes and stood up, the janitor was gone. The janitor had been a nightmare role, nothing more.

And Ryan Thornier, star of "Walkaway," favored of the critics, confident of a bright future, walked out of the storage room with a strange lightness in his step. He carried a broom, he still wore the dirty coveralls, but now as if to a masquerade.

The Peltier mannequin lay sprawled on the stage in a grostesque heap. Ryan Thornier stared at it calmly from behind the set and listened intently to the babble of stage hands and technicians that milled about him:

"Don't know. Can't tell yet. It came out staggering and gibbering—like it was drunk. It reached for a table, then it fell on its face—"

"Acted like the trouble might be a mismatched tape, but Rick rechecked it. Really Peltier's tape—"

"Can't figure it out. Miss Ferne's having kittens."

Thornier paused to size up his audience. Jade, Ian, and their staff milled about in the orchestra section. The stage was empty, except for the sprawled mannequin. Too much frantic conversation, all around. His entrance would go unnoticed. He walked slowly on-stage and stood over the fallen doll with his hands in his pockets and his face pulled down in a somber expression. After a moment, he nudged the doll with his toe, paused, nudged it again. A faint giggle came from the orchestra. The corner of his eye caught Jade's quick glance toward the stage. She paused in the middle of a sentence.

Assured that she watched, he played to an imaginery audience-friend standing just off stage. He glanced toward the friend, lifted his brows questioningly. The friend apparently gave him the nod. He looked around warily, then knelt over the fallen doll. He took its pulse, nodded eagerly to the offstage friend. Another giggle came from orchestra. He lifted the doll's head, sniffed its breath, made a face. Then, gingerly, he rolled it.

He reached deep into the mannequin's pocket, having palmed his own pocket watch beforehand. His hand paused there, and he smiled to his offstage accomplice and nodded eagerly. He withdrew the watch and held it up by its chain for his accomplice's approval.

A light burst of laughter came from the production personnel. The laughter frightened the thief. He shot an apprehensive glance around the stage, hastily returned the watch to the fallen dummy, felt its pulse again. He traded a swift glance with his confederate, whispered "Aha!" and smiled mysteriously. Then he helped the doll to its feet and staggered away with it—a friend leading a drunk home to its family. In the doorway, he paused to frame his exit with a wary backward glance that said he was taking it to a dark alley where he could rob it in safety.

Jade was gaping at him.

Three technicians had been watching from just off the set, and they laughed heartily and clapped his shoulder as he passed, providing the offstage audience to which he had seemed to be playing.

Good-natured applause came from Jade's people out front, and as Thorny carried the doll away to storage, he was humming softly to himself.

At five minutes till six, Rick Thomas and a man from the Smithfield depot climbed down out of the booth, and Jade pressed forward through the crowd to question him with her eyes.

"The tape," he said. "Defective."

"But it's too late to get another!" she squawked.

"Well, it's the tape, anyway."

"How do you *know?*"

"Well—trouble's bound to be in one of three places. The doll, the tape, or the analogue tank where the tape-data gets stored. We cleared the tank and tried it with another actor. Worked O.K. And the doll works O.K. on an uninterpreted run. So, by elimination, the tape."

She groaned and slumped into a seat, covering her face with her hands.

"No way at *all* to locate another tape?" Rick asked.

"We called every depot within five hundred miles. They'd have to cut one from a master. Take too long."

"So we call off the show!" Ian Feria called out resignedly, throwing up his hands in disgust. "Refund on tickets, open tomorrow."

"Wait!" snapped the producer, looking up suddenly. "Dooch—the house is sold out, isn't it?"

"Yah," D'Uccia grunted irritably. "She'sa filled op. Wassa matter with you pipple, you don' getsa Maestro fix? Wassa matter? We lose the money, hah?"

"Oh, shut up. Change curtain time to nine, offer refunds if they won't wait. Ian, keep at it. Get things set up for tonight." She spoke with weary determination, glancing around at them. "There may be a slim chance. Keep at it. I'm going to try something." She turned and started away.

"Hey!" Feria called.

"Explain later," she muttered over her shoulder.

She found Thornier replacing burned-out bulbs in the wall fixtures. He smiled down at her while he reset the clamps of an amber glass panel. "Need mè for something, Miss Ferne?" he called pleasantly from the stepladder.

"I might," she said tersely. "Did you mean that offer about standing in for dud mannequins?"

A bulb exploded at her feet after it slipped from his hand. He came down slowly, gaping at her.

"You're not serious!"

"Think you could try a run-through as Andreyev?"

He shot a quick glance toward the stage, wet his lips, stared at her dumbly.

"Well—*can* you?"

"It's been ten years, Jade . . . I—"

"You can read over the script, and you can wear an earplug radio—so Rick can prompt you from the booth." She made the offer crisply and matter-of-factly, and it made Thorny smile inwardly. It was theater—calmly asking the outrageously impossible, gambling on it, and getting it.

"The customers—they're expecting Peltier."

"Right now I'm only asking you to try a runthrough,

Thorny. After that, we'll see. But remember it's our only chance of going on tonight."

"Andreyev," he breathed. "The lead."

"Please, Thorny, will you try?"

He looked around the theater, nodded slowly. "I'll go study my lines," he said quietly, inclining his head with what he hoped was just the proper expression of humble bravery.

I've got to make it good, I've got to make it great. The last chance, the last great role—

Glaring footlights, a faint whisper in his ear, and the cold panic of the first entrance. It came and passed quickly. Then the stage was a closed room, and the audience—of technicians and production personnel—was only the fourth wall, somewhere beyond the lights. He was Andreyev, commissioner of police, party whip, loyal servant of the regime, now tottering in the revolutionary storm of the Eighties. The last Bolshevik, no longer a rebel, no longer a radical, but now the loyalist, the conservatist, the defender of the status quo, champion of the Marxist ruling classes. No longer conscious of a self apart from that of the role, he lived the role. And the others, the people he lived it with, the people whose feet crackled faintly as they stepped across the floor, he acted and reacted with them and against them as if they, too, shared life, and while the play progressed he forgot their lifelessness for a little time.

Caught up by the magic, enfolded in scheme of the inevitable, borne along by the tide of the drama, he felt once again the sense of belonging as a part in a whole, a known and predictable whole that moved as surely from scene *i* to the final curtain as man from womb to tomb, and there were no lost years, no lapse or sense of defeated purpose between the rehearsals of those many years ago and this the fulfillment of opening night. Only when at last he muffed a line, and Rick's correction whispered in his ear did the spell that was gathered about him briefly break—and he found himself unaccountably frightened, frightened by the sudden return of realization that all about him was Machine, and frightened, too, that he had forgotten. He had been conforming to the flighty mechanical grace of the others, reflexively imitating the characteristic lightness of the mannequins' movements, the dancelike qualities of their playing. To know suddenly, having forgotten it, that the mouth he had just kissed was not a woman's, but the rubber mouth of a doll, and that dancing patterns of high frequency waves from the Maestro had controlled the solenoid currents that turned her face lovingly up toward his, had lifted the cold soft hands to touch his face. The faint rubbery smell-taste hung about his mouth.

When his first exit came, he went off trembling. He saw Jade coming toward him, and for an instant, he felt a horrifying certainty that she would say, "Thorny, you were almost as good as a mannequin!" Instead, she said nothing, but only held out her hand to him.

"Was it too bad, Jade?"

"Thorny, you're in! Keep it up, and you might have more than a one-night stand. Even Ian's convinced. He squealed at the idea, but now he's sold."

"No kicks? How about the lines with Piotr."

"Wonderful. Keep it up. Darling, you were marvelous."

"It's settled, then?"

"Darling, it's *never* settled until the curtain comes up. You know that." She giggled. "We had one *kick* all right —or maybe I shouldn't tell you."

He stiffened slightly. "Oh? Who from?"

"Mela Stone. She saw you come on, turned white as a sheet, and walked out. I can't imagine!"

He sank slowly on a haggard looking couch and stared at her. "The hell you can't," he grated softly.

"She's here on a personal appearance contract, you know. To give an opening and an intermission commentary on the author and the play." Jade smirked at him gleefully. "Five minutes ago she called back, tried to cancel her appearance. Of course, she can't pull a stunt like that. Not while Smithfield owns her."

Jade winked, patted his arm, tossed an uncoded copy of the script at him, then headed back toward the orchestra. Briefly he wondered what Jade had against Mela. Nothing serious, probably. Both had been actresses. Mela got a Smithfield contract; Jade didn't get one. It was enough.

By the time he had reread the scene to follow, his second cue was approaching, and he moved back toward the stage.

Things went smoothly. Only three times during the first act did he stumble over lines he had not rehearsed in ten years. Rick's prompting was in his ear, and the Maestro could compensate to some extent for his minor deviations from the script. This time he avoided losing himself so completely in the play; and this time the weird realization that he had become one with the machine-set pattern did not disturb him. This time he remembered, but when the first break came—

"Not quite so good, Thorny," Ian Feria called. "Whatever you were doing in the first scene, do it again. That was a little wooden. Go through that last bit again, and play it down. Andreyev's no mad bear from the Urals. It's Marka's moment, anyhow. Hold in."

He nodded slowly and looked around at the frozen dolls. He had to forget the machinery. He had to lose himself in it and live it, even if it meant being a replacement link in the mechanism. It disturbed him somehow, even though he was accustomed to subordinating himself to the total gestalt of the scene as in other days. For no apparent reason, he found himself listening for laughter from the production people, but none came.

"All right," Feria called. "Bring 'em alive again."

He went on with it, but the uneasy feeling nagged at him. There was self-mockery in it, and the expectation of ridicule from those who watched. He could not understand why, and yet—

There was an ancient movie—one of the classics—in which a man named Chaplin had been strapped into a seat on a production line where he performed a perfectly mechanical task in a perfectly mechanical fashion, a task that could obviously have been done by a few cams and a linkage or two, and it was one of the funniest commedies of all times—yet tragic. A task that made him a part in an over-all machine.

He sweated through the second and third acts in a state of compromise with himself—overplaying it for purposes of self-preparation, yet trying to convince Feria and Jade that he could handle it and handle it well. Overacting was necessary in spots, as a learning technique. Deliberately ham up the rehearsal to impress lines on memory, then underplay it for the real performance —it was an old trick of troupers who had to do a new show each night and had only a few hours in which to rehearse and learn lines. But would they know why he was doing it?

When it was finished, there was no time for another run-through, and scarcely time for a nap and a bite to eat before dressing for the show.

"It was terrible, Jade," he groaned. "I muffed it. I know I did."

"Nonsense. You'll be in tune tonight, Thorny. I knew what you were doing, and I can see past it."

"Thanks. I'll try to pull in."

"About the final scene, the shooting—"

He shot her a wary glance. "What about it?"

"The gun'll be loaded tonight, blanks, of course. And this time you'll have to fall."

"So?"

"So be careful where you fall. Don't go down on the copper bus-lugs. A hundred and twenty volts mightn't kill you, but we don't want a dying Andreyev bouncing up and spitting blue sparks. The stagehands'll chalk out a safe section for you. And one other thing—"

"Yes?"

"Marka fires from close range. Don't get burned."

"I'll watch it."

She started away, then paused to frown back at him steadily for several seconds. "Thorny, I've got a queer feeling about you. I can't place it exactly."

He stared at her evenly, waiting.

"Thorny, are you going to wreck the show?"

His face showed nothing, but something twisted inside him. She looked beseeching, trusting, but worried. She was counting on him, placing faith in him—

"Why should I botch up the performance, Jade? Why should I do a thing like that?"

"I'm asking you."

"O.K. I promise you—you'll get the best Andreyev I can give you."

She nodded slowly. "I believe you. I didn't doubt *that*, exactly."

"Then what worries you?"

"I don't know. I know how you feel about auto-drama. I just got a shuddery feeling that you had something up your sleeve. That's all. I'm sorry. I know you've got too much integrity to wreck your own performance, but—" She stopped and shook her head, her dark eyes searching him. She was still worried.

"Oh, all right. I was going to stop the show in the third act. I was going to show them my appendectomy scar, do a couple of card tricks, and announce that I was on strike. I was going to walk out." He clucked his tongue at her, looked hurt.

She flushed slightly, and laughed. "Oh, I know you wouldn't pull anything shabby. Not that you wouldn't do anything you *could* to take a swat at autodrama generally, but . . . there's nothing you could do tonight that would accomplish anything. Except sending the customers home mad. That doesn't fit you, and I'm sorry I thought of it."

"Thanks. Stop worrying. If you lose dough, it won't be my fault."

"I believe you, but—"

"But what?"

She leaned close to him. "But you look too triumphant, that's what!" she hissed, then patted his cheek.

"Well, it's my last role. I—"

But she had already started away, leaving him with his sandwich and a chance for a nap.

Sleep would not come. He lay fingering the .32 caliber cartridges in his pocket and thinking about the impact of his final exit upon the conscience of the theater. The thoughts were pleasant.

It struck him suddenly as he lay drowsing that they would call it suicide. How silly. Think of the jolting effect, the dramatic punch, the audience reaction. Mannequins don't bleed. And later, the headlines: Robot Player Kills Old Trouper, Victim of Mechanized Stage. Still, they'd call it suicide. How silly.

But maybe that's what the paranoid on the twentieth story window ledge thought about, too—the audience reaction. Wasn't every self-inflicted wound really aimed at the conscience of the world?

It worried him some, but—

"Fifteen minutes until curtain," the sound system was croaking. *"Fifteen minutes—"*

"Hey, Thorny!" Feria called irritably. "Get back to the costuming room. They've been looking for you."

He got up wearily, glanced around at the backstage

bustle, then shuffled away toward the makeup department. One thing was certain: he had to go on.

The house was less than packed. A third of the customers had taken refunds rather than wait for the postponed curtain and a substitute Andreyev, a substitute unknown or ill-remembered at best, with no Smithy index rating beside his name in lights. Nevertheless, the bulk of the audience had planned their evenings and stayed to claim their seats with only suppressed bad humor about the delay. Scalpers' customers who had overpaid and who could not reclaim more than half the bootleg price from the boxoffice were forced to accept the show or lose money and get nothing. They came, and shifted restlessly, and glanced at their watches while an m.c.'s voice made apologies and introduced orchestral numbers, mostly from the Russian composers. Then, finally—

"Ladies and gentlemen, tonight we have with us one of the best loved actresses of stage, screen, and autodrama, co-star of our play tonight, as young and lovely as she was when first immortalized by Smithfield—Mela Stone!"

Thornier watched tight-lipped from shadows as she stepped gracefully into the glare of the footlights. She seemed abormally pale, but makeup artistry had done a good job; she looked only slightly older than her doll, still lovely, though less arrogantly beautiful. Her flashing jewelry was gone, and she wore a simple dark gown with a deep-slit neck, and her tawny hair was wrapped high in a turbanlike coiffure that left bare a graceful neck.

"Ten years ago," she began quietly, "I rehearsed for a production of 'The Anarch' which never appeared, rehearsed it with a man named Ryan Thornier in the starring role, the actor who fills that role tonight. I remember with a special sort of glow the times—"

She faltered, and went on lamely. Thorny winced. Obviously the speech had been written by Jade Ferne and evidently the words were like bits of poisoned apples in Mela's mouth. She gave the impression that she was speaking them only because it wasn't polite to retch them. Mela was being punished for her attempt to back out, and Jade had forced her to appear only by threatening to fit out the Stone mannequin with a gray wig and have the doll read her curtain speeches. The small producer had a vicious streak, and she exercised it when crossed.

Mela's introductory lines were written to convince the audience that it was indeed lucky to have Thornier instead of Peltier, but there was nothing to intimate his flesh-and-blood status. She did not use the words "doll" or "mannequin," but allowed the audience to keep its preconceptions without confirming them. It was short. After a few anecdotes about the show's first presentation more than a generation ago, she was done.

"And with no further delay, my friends, I give you— Pruchev's 'The Anarch.' "

She bowed away and danced behind the curtains and came off crying. A majestic burst of music heralded the opening scene. She saw Thornier and stopped, not yet off stage. The curtain started up. She darted toward him, hesitated, stopped to stare up at him apprehensively. Her eyes were brimming, and she was biting her lip.

On stage, a telephone jangled on the desk of Commissioner Andreyev. His cue was still three minutes away. A lieutenant came on to answer the phone.

"Nicely done, Mela," he whispered, smiling sourly.

She didn't hear him. Her eyes drifted down to his costume—very like the uniform he'd worn for a dress rehearsal ten years ago. Her hand went to her throat. She wanted to run from him, but after a moment she got control of herself. She looked at her own mannequin waiting in the line-up, then at Thornier.

"Aren't you going to say something appropriate?" she hissed.

"I—" His icy smile faded slowly. The first small triumph—triumph over Mela, a sick and hag-ridden Mela who had bought security at the expense of integrity and was still paying for it in small installments like this, Mela whom he once had loved. The first small "triumph" coiled into a sick knot in his throat.

She started away, but he caught her arm.

"I'm sorry, Mela," he muttered hoarsely. "I'm really sorry."

"It's not your fault."

But it was. She didn't know what he'd done, of course; didn't know he'd switched the tapes and steered his own selection as a replacement for the Peltier doll, so that she'd have to watch him playing opposite the doll-image of a Mela who had ceased to exist ten years ago, watch him relive a mockery of something.

"I'm sorry," he whispered again.

She shook her head, pulled her arm free, hurried away. He watched her go and went sick inside. Their frigid meeting earlier in the day had been the decisive moment, when in a surge of bitterness he'd determined to go through with it and even excuse himself for doing it. Maybe bitterness had fogged his eyesight, he thought. Her reaction to bumping into him that way hadn't been snobbery; it had been horror. An old ghost in dirty coveralls and motley, whose face she'd probably fought to forget, had sprung up to confront her in a place that was too full of memories anyhow. No wonder she seemed cold. Probably he symbolized some of her own self-accusations, for he knew he had affected others that way. The successful ones, the ones who had profited by autodrama—they often saw him with mop and bucket, and if they remembered Ryan Thornier, turned quickly away. And at each turning away, he had felt a small glow of satisfaction as he imagined them thinking: *Thornier wouldn't compromise*—and hating him, because they had compromised and lost something thereby. But being hated by Mela—was different somehow. He didn't want it.

Someone nudged his ribs. "Your cue, Thorny!" hissed a tense voice. "You're *on!*"

He came awake with a grunt. Feria was shoving him frantically toward his entrance. He made a quick grab for his presence of mind, straightened into character, and strode on.

He muffed the scene badly. He knew that he muffed it even before he made his exit and saw their faces. He had missed two cues and needed prompting several times from Rick in the booth. His acting was wooden—he felt it.

"You're doing fine, Thorny, just fine!" Jade told him, because there was nothing else she *dared* tell him during a performance. Shock an actor's ego during rehearsal, and he had time to recover; shock it during a performance, and he might go sour for the night. He knew, though, without being told, the worry that seethed behind her mechanical little smile. "But just calm down a little, eh?" she advised. "It's going fine."

She left him to seethe in solitude. He leaned against the wall and glowered at his feet and flagellated himself. *You failure, you miserable crumb, you janitor-at-heart, you stage-struck charwoman—*

He had to straighten out. If he ruined this one, there'd never be another chance. But he kept thinking of Mela, and how he had wanted to hurt her, and how now that she was being hurt he wanted to stop.

"Your cue, Thorny—wake up!"

And he was on again, stumbling over lines, being terrified of the sea of dim faces where a fourth wall should be.

She was waiting for him after his second exit. He came off pale and shaking, perspiration soaking his collar. He leaned back and lit a cigarette and looked at her bleakly. She couldn't talk. She took his arm in both hands and kneaded it while she rested her forehead against his shoulder. He gazed down at her in dismay. She'd stopped feeling hurt; she couldn't feel hurt when she watched him make a fool of himself out there. She might have been vengefully delighted by it, and he almost wished that she were. Instead, she was pitying him. He was numb, sick to the core. He couldn't go on with it.

"Mela, I'd better tell *you;* I can't tell Jade what I—"

"Don't talk, Thorny. Just do your best." She peered up at him. "Please do your best?"

It startled him. Why should she feel that way?

"Wouldn't you really rather see me flop?" he asked.

She shook her head quickly, then paused and nodded it. "Part of me would, Thorny. A vengeful part. I've got to believe in the automatic stage. I . . . I do believe in it. But I don't want you to flop, not really." She put her hands over her eyes briefly. "You don't know what it's like seeing you out there . . . in the middle of all that . . . that—" She shook herself slightly. "It's a mockery, Thorny, you don't belong out there, but—as long as you're there, don't muff it. Do your best?"

"Yeah, sure."

"It's a precarious thing. The effect, I mean. If the audience starts realizing you're not a doll—" She shook her head slowly.

"What if they do?"

"They'll laugh. They'll laugh you right off the stage."

He was prepared for anything but that. It confirmed the nagging hunch he'd had during the run-through.

"Thorny, that's all I'm really concerned about. I don't care whether you play it well or play it lousy, as long as they don't find out what you are. I don't want them to laugh at you; you've been hurt enough."

"They wouldn't laugh if I gave a good performance."

"But they *would!* Not in the same way, but they would. Don't you see?"

His mouth fell open. He shook his head. It wasn't true. "Human actors have done it before," he protested. "In the sticks, on small stages with undersized Maestros."

"Have you ever seen such a play?"

He shook his head.

"I have. The audience knows about the human part of the cast in advance. So it doesn't strike them as funny. There's no jolt of discovering an incongruity. Listen to me Thorny—do your best, but you don't dare make it *better* than a doll could do."

Bitterness came back in a flood. Was this what he had hoped for? To give as machinelike a performance as possible, to do as good a job as the Maestro, but no better, and above all, no *different?* So that they wouldn't find out?

She saw his distressed expression and felt for his hand. "Thorny, don't you hate me for telling you. I want you to bring it off O.K., and I thought you ought to realize. I think I know what's been wrong. You're afraid—down deep—that they *won't* recognize you for who you are, and that makes your performance un-doll-like. You better start being afraid they will recognize you, Thorny."

As he stared at her, it began to penetrate that she was still capable of being the woman he'd once known and loved. Worse, she wanted to save him from being laughed at. Why? If she felt motherly, she might conceivably want to shield him against wrath, criticism, or rotten tomatoes, but not against loss of dignity. Motherliness thrived on the demise of male dignity, for it sharpened the image of the child in the man.

"Mela—?"

"Yes, Thorny."

"I guess I never quite got over you." She shook her head quickly, almost angrily.

"Darling, you're living ten years ago. I'm not, and I won't. Maybe I don't like the present very well, but I'm in it, and I can only change it in little ways. I can't make it the past again, and I won't try." She paused a moment, searching his face. "Ten years ago, we weren't living in the present either. We were living in a mythical, magic, wonderful future. Great talent, just starting to bloom. We were living in dream-plans in those days. The future we lived in never happened, and you can't go back and make it happen. And when a dream-plan stops being possible, it turns into a pipe dream. I won't live in a pipe dream. I want to stay sane, even if it hurts."

"Too bad you had to come tonight," he said stiffly.

She wilted. "Oh, Thorny, I didn't mean that the way it sounded. And I wouldn't say it that strongly unless"— she glanced through the soundproof glass toward the stage where her mannequin was on in the scene with Piotr—"unless I had trouble too, with too much wishing."

"I wish you were with me out there," he said softly. "With no dolls and no Maestro. I know how it'd be then."

"Don't! Please, Thorny, don't."

"Mela, I loved you—"

"No!" She got up quickly. "I . . . I want to see you after the show. Meet me. But don't talk that way. Especially not here and not now."

"I can't help it."

"Please! Good-by for now, Thorny, and—do your best."

My best to be a mechanism, he thought bitterly as he watched her go.

He turned to watch the play. Something was wrong out there on the stage. Badly wrong. The Maestro's interpretation of the scene made it seem unfamiliar somehow. He frowned. Rich had spoken of the Maestro's ability to compensate, to shift interpretations, to redirect. Was that what was happening? The Maestro compensating—for *his* performance?

His cue was approaching. He moved closer to the stage.

Act I had been a flop. Feria, Ferne, and Thomas conferred in an air of tension and a haze of cigarette smoke.

He heard heated muttering, but could not distinguish words. Jade called a stagehand, spoke to him briefly, and sent him away. The stagehand wandered through the group until he found Mela Stone, spoke to her quickly and pointed. Thorny watched her go to join the production group, then turned away. He slipped out of their line of sight and stood behind some folded backdrops, waiting for the end of a brief intermission and trying not to think.

"Great act, Thorny," a costumer said mechnically, and clapped his shoulder in passing.

He suppressed an impulse to kick the costumer. He got out a copy of the script and pretended to read his lines. A hand tugged at his sleeve.

"Jade!" He looked at her bleakly, started to apologize.

"Don't," she said. "We've talked it over. Rick, you tell him."

Rick Thomas who stood beside her grinned ruefully and waggled his head. "It's not altogether your fault, Thorny. Or haven't you noticed?"

"What do you mean?" he asked suspiciously.

"Take scene five, for example," Jade put in. "Suppose the cast had been entirely human. How would you feel about what happened?"

He closed his eyes for a moment and relived it. "I'd probably be sore," he said slowly. "I'd probably accuse Kovrin of jamming my lines and Aksinya of killing my exit—as an excuse," he added with a lame grin. "But I can't accuse the dolls. They can't steal."

"As a matter of fact, old man, they *can*," said the technician. "And your excuse is exactly right."

"Whh—what?"

"Sure. You *did* muff the first scene or two. The audience reacted to it. And the Maestro reacts to audience-reaction—by compensating through shifts in interpretation. It sees the stage as a whole, you included. As far as the Maestro's concerned, you're an untaped dud—like the Peltier doll we used in the first run-through. It sends you only the script-tape signals, uninterpreted. Because it's got no analogue tape on you. Now without an audience, that'd be O.K. But with an audience reaction to go by, it starts compensating, and since it can't compensate through *you*, it works on the others."

"I don't understand."

"Bluntly, Thorny, the first scene or two stunk. The audience didn't like you. The Maestro started compensating by emphasizing other roles—and recharacterizing *you*, through the others."

"Recharacterize? How can it do that."

"Easily, darling," Jade told him. "When Marka says 'I hate him; he's a beast'—for example—she can say it like it's true, or she can say it like she's just temporarily furious with Andreyev. And it affects the light in which the audience see you. Other actors affect *your* role. You know that's true of the old stage. Well, it's true of autodrama, too."

He stared at them in amazement. "Can't you stop it? Readjust the Maestro, I mean?"

"Not without clearing the whole thing out of the machine and starting over. The effect is cumulative. The more it compensates, the tougher it gets for you. The tougher it gets for you, the worse you look to the crowd. And the worse you look to the crowd, the more it tries to compensate."

He stared wildly at the clock. Less than a minute until the first scene of Act II. "What'll I do?"

"Stick it," said Jade. "We've been on the phone to Smithfield. There's a programming engineer in town, and he's on his way over in a heliocab. Then we'll see."

"We may be able to nurse it back in tune," Rick added, "a little at a time—by feeding in a fake set of audience-restlessness factors, and cutting out its feeler circuits out in the crowd. We'll try, that's all.

The light flashed for the beginning of the act.

"Good luck, Thorny."

"I guess I'll need it." Grimly he started toward his entrance.

The thing in the booth was watching him. It watched and measured and judged and found wanting. *Maybe,* he thought wildly, *it even hated him.* It watched, it planned, it regulated, and it was wrecking him.

The faces of the dolls, the hands, the voices—belonged to *it*. The wizard circuitry in the booth rallied them against him. It saw him, undoubtedly, as one of them, but not answering to its pulsing commands. It saw him, perhaps, as a malfunctioning doll, and it tried to correct the effects of his misbehavior. He thought of the old conflict between director and darfstellar, the self-directed actor—and it was the same conflict, aggravated by an electronic director's inability to understand that such things could be. The darfsteller, the undirectable portrayer whose acting welled from unconscious sources with no external strings—directors were inclined to hate them, even when the portrayal was superb. A mannequin, however, was the perfect schauspieler, the actor that a director could play like an instrument.

It would have been easier for him now had he been a schauspieler, for perhaps he could adapt. But he was Andreyev, *his* Andreyev, as he had prepared himself for the role. Andreyev was incarnate as an *alter anima* within him. He had never "played" a role. He had always become the role. And now he could adapt to the needs of the moment on stage only as Andreyev, in and through his identity with Andreyev, and without changing the feel of his portrayal. To attempt it, to try to fall into conformity with what the Maestro was doing, would mean utter confusion. Yet, the machine was forcing him —through the others.

He stood stonily behind his desk, listening coldly to the denials of the prisoner—a revolutionary, an arsonist associated with Piotr's guerrila band.

"I tell you, comrade, I had nothing to do with it!" the prisoner shouted. *"Nothing!"*

"Haven't you questioned him thoroughly?" Andreyev growled at the lieutenant who guarded the man. "Hasn't he signed a confession?"

"There was no need, comrade. His accomplice confessed," protested the lieutenant.

Only it wasn't supposed to be a protest. The lieutenant made it sound like a monstrous thing to do—to wring another confession, by torture perhaps, from the prisoner, when there was already sufficient evidence to convict. The words were right, but their meaning was wrenched. It should have been a crisp statement of fact: No need, comrade; his accomplice confessed.

Thorny paused, reddening angrily. His next line was, "See that this one confesses, too." But he wasn't going to speak it. It would augment the effect of the lieutenant's tone of shocked protest. He thought rapidly. The lieutenant was a bit-player, and didn't come back on until the third act. It wouldn't hurt to jam him.

He glowered at the doll, demanded icily: "And what have you done with the accomplice?"

The Maestro could not invent lines, nor comprehend an ad lib. The Maestro could only interpret a deviation as a malfunction, and try to compensate. The Maestro backed up a line, had the lieutenant repeat his cue.

"I told you—he *confessed.*"

"*So!*" roared Andreyev. "You killed him, eh? Couldn't survive the questioning, eh? And you killed him."

"*Thorny, what are you doing?*" came Rick's frantic whisper in his earplug.

"He confessed," repeated the lieutenant.

"You're under arrest, Nichol!" Thorny barked. "Report to Major Malin for discipline. Return the prisoner to his cell." He paused. The Maestro couldn't go on until he cued it, but now there was no harm in speaking the line. "Now—see that this one confesses, too."

"Yes, sir," the lieutenant replied stonily, and started off-stage with the prisoner.

Thorny took glee in killing his exit by calling after him: "And see that he lives through it!"

The Maestro marched them out without looking back, and Thorny was briefly pleased with himself. He caught a glimpse of Jade with her hands clasped over her head, giving him a "the-winnah" signal from concealment. But he couldn't keep ad libbing his way out of it every time.

Most of all, he dreaded the entrance of Marka, Mela's doll. The Maestro was playing her up, ennobling her, subtly justifying her treachery, at the expense of Andreyev's character. He didn't want to fight back. Marka's role was too important for tampering, and besides, it would be like slapping at Mela to confuse the performance of her doll.

The curtain dipped. The furniture revolved. The stage became a living room. And the curtain rose again.

He barked: "No more arrests; after curfew, shoot on sight!" at the telephone, and hung up.

When he turned, she stood in the doorway, listening. She shrugged and entered with a casual walk while he watched her in suspicious silence. It was the consummation of her treachery. She had come back to him, but as a spy for Piotr. He suspected her only of infidelity and not of treason. It was a crucial scene, and the Maestro could play her either as a treacherous wench, or a reluctant traitor with Andreyev seeming a brute. He watched her warily.

"Well—hello," she said petulantly, after walking around the room.

He grunted coldly. She stayed flippant and aloof. So far, it was as it should be. But the vicious argument was yet to come.

She went to a mirror and began straightening her wind-blown hair. She spoke nervously, compulsively, rattling about trivia, concealing her anxiety in his presence after her betrayal. She looked furtive, haggard, somehow more like the real Mela of today; the Maestro's control of expression was masterful.

"What are you doing here?" he exploded suddenly, interrupting her disjointed spiel.

"I still live here, don't I?"

"You got out."

"Only because you ordered me out."

"You made it clear you wanted to leave."

"Liar!"

"Cheat!"

It went on that way for a while; then he began dumping the contents of several drawers into a suitcase.

"I live here, and I'm staying," she raged.

"Suit yourself, comrade."

"What're you doing?"

"Moving out, of course."

The battle continued. Still there was no attempt by the Maestro to revise the scene. Had the trouble been corrected? Had his exchange with the lieutenant somehow affected the machine? Something was different. It was becoming a good scene, his best so far.

She was still raving at him when he started for the door. She stopped in mid-sentence, breathless—then shrieked his name and flung herself down on the sofa, sobbing violently. He stopped. He turned and stood with his fists on his hips staring at her. Gradually, he melted. He put the suitcase down and walked back to stand over her, still gruff and glowering.

Her sobbing subsided. She peered up at him, saw his inability to escape, began to smile. She came up slowly, arms sliding around his neck.

"Sasha . . . oh, my Sasha—"

The arms were warm, the lips moist, the woman alive

in his embrace. For a moment he doubted his senses. She giggled at him and whispered, "You'll break a rib."

"Mela—"

"Let go, you fool—the scene!" Then, aloud: "Can I stay, darling?"

"Always," he said hoarsely.

"And you won't be jealous again?"

"Never."

"Or question me every time I'm gone an hour or two?"

"Or sixteen. It *was* sixteen hours."

"I'm sorry." She kissed him. The music rose. The scene ended.

"How did you swing it?" he whispered in the clinch. "And why?"

"They asked me to. Because of the Maestro." She giggled. "You looked devastated. Hey, you can let go now. The curtain's down."

The mobile furniture had begun to rearrange itself. They scurried offstage, side-stepping a couch as it rolled past. Jade was waiting for them.

"Great!" she whispered, taking their hands. "That was just great."

"Thanks . . . thanks for sliding me in," Mela answered.

"Take it from here out, Mela—the scenes with Thorny, at least."

"I don't know," she muttered. "It's been so long. Anybody could have ad libbed through that fight scene."

"You can do it. Rick'll keep you cued and prompted. The engineer's here, and they're fussing around with the Maestro. But it'll straighten *itself* out, if you give it a couple more scenes like that to watch."

The second act had been rescued. The supporting cast was still a hazard, and the Maestro still tried to compensate according to audience reaction during Act I, but with a human Marka, the compensatory attempts had less effect, and the interpretive distortions seemed to diminish slightly. The Maestro was piling up new data as the play continued, and reinterpreting.

"It wasn't great," he sighed as they stretched out to relax between acts. "But it was passable."

"Act Three'll be better, Thorny," Mela promised. "We'll rescue it yet. It's just too bad about the first act."

"I wanted it to be tops," he breathed. "I wanted to

give them something to think about, something to remember. But now we're fighting to rescue it from being
a total flop."

"Wasn't it always like that? You get steamed up to
make history, but then you wind up working like crazy
just to keep it passable."

"Or to keep from ducking flying groceries sometimes."
She giggled. "Jiggie used to say, 'I went on like the
main dish and came off like the toss salad.' " She paused,
then added moodily: "The *tough* part of it is—you've
got to aim high just to hit anywhere at all. It can get to
be heartbreaking, too—trying for the sublime every
time, and just escaping the ridiculous, or the mediocre."

"No matter how high you aim, you can't hit escape
velocity. Ambition is a trajectory with its impact point
in oblivion, no matter how high the throw."

"Sounds like a quote."

"It is. From the Satyricon of an ex-Janitor."

"Thorny—?"

"What?"

"I'm going to be sorry tomorrow—but I *am* enjoying
it tonight—going through it all again I mean. Living it
like a pipe dream. It's no good though. It's opium."

He stared at her for a moment in surprise, said nothing. Maybe it was opium for Mela, but she hadn't started
out with a crazy hope that tonight would be the climax
and the highpoint of a lifetime on the stage. She was
filling in to save the show, and it meant nothing to her
in terms of a career she had deliberately abandoned. He,
however, had hoped for a great portrayal. It *wasn't* great,
though. If he worked hard at Act III, it might—as a
whole—stand up to his performances of the past. Unless—

"Think anybody in the audience has guessed yet?
About us, I mean?"

She shook her head. "Haven't seen any signs of it,"
she murmured drowsily. "People see what they expect to
see. But it'll leak out tomorrow."

"Why?"

"Your scene with the lieutenant. When you ad libbed
out of a jam. There's bound to be a drama critic or
maybe a professor out there who read the play ahead of
time, and started frowning when you pulled that off.

He'll go home and look up his copy of the script just to make sure, and then the cat's out."

"It won't matter by then."

"No."

She wanted a nap or a drowse, and he fell silent. As he watched her relax, some of his bitter disappointment slipped away. It was good just to be acting again, even for one opiate evening. And maybe it was best that he wasn't getting what he wanted. He was even ready to admit to a certain insanity in setting out on such a course.

Perfection and immolation. Now that the perfection wasn't possible, the whole scheme looked like a sick fanatic's nightmare, and he was ashamed. Why had he done it—given in to what had always been only a petulant fantasy, a childish dream? The wish, plus the opportunity, plus the impulse, in a framework of bitterness and in a time of personal transition—it had been enough to bring the crazy yearning out of its cortical wrinkle and start him acting on a dream. A child's dream.

And then the momentum had carried him along. The juggled tapes, the loaded gun, the dirty trick on Jade— and now fighting to keep the show from dying. He had gone down to the river and climbed up on the bridge rail and looked down at the black and swirling tide—and finally climbed down again because the wind would spoil his swan dive.

He shivered. It scared him a little, to know he could lose himself so easily. What had the years done to him, or what had he done to himself?

He had kept his integrity maybe, but what good was integrity in a vacuum? He had the soul of an actor, and he'd hung onto it when the others were selling theirs, but the years had wiped out the market and he was stuck with it. He had stood firm on principle, and the years had melted the cold glacier of reality from under the principle; still, he stood on it, while the reality ran on down to the sea. He had dedicated himself to the living stage, and carefully tended its grave, awaiting the resurrection.

Old ham, he thought, you've been flickering into mad warps and staggering into dimensions of infrasanity. You took unreality by the hand and led her gallantly through peril and confusion and finally married her be-

fore you noticed that she was dead. Now the only decent
thing to do was bury her, but her interment would do
nothing to get him back through the peril and confusion
and on the road again. He'd have to hike. Maybe it was
too late to do anything with the rest of a lifetime. But
there was only one way to find out. And the first step
was to put some mileage between himself and the stage.

If a little black box took over my job, Rich had said,
I'd go to work making little black boxes.

Thorny realized with a slight start that the technician
had meant it. Mela had done it, in a sense. So had Jade.
Especially Jade. But that wasn't the answer for him, not
now. He'd hung around too long mourning the dead, and
he needed a clean, sharp break. Tomorrow he'd fade out
of sight, move away, pretend he was twenty-one again,
and start groping for something to do with a lifetime.
How to keep eating until he found it—that would be the
pressing problem. Unskilled laborers were hard to find
these days, but so were unskilled jobs. Selling his acting
talent for commercial purposes would work only if he
could find a commercial purpose he could believe in and
live for, since his talent was not the surface talent of a
schauspieler. It would be a grueling search, for he had
never bothered to believe in anything but theater.

Mela stirred suddenly. "Did I hear somebody call
me?" she muttered. "This racket—!" She sat up to look
around.

He grunted doubtfully. "How long till curtain?" he
asked.

She arose suddenly and said, "Jade's waving me over.
See you in the act, Thorny."

He watched Mela hurry away, he glanced across the
floor at Jade who waited for her in the midst of a small
conference, he felt a guilty twinge. He'd cost them
money, trouble, and nervous sweat, and maybe the performance endangered the run of the show. It was a rotten thing to do, and he was sorry, but it couldn't be
undone, and the only possible compensation was to deliver
a best-possible Act III and then get out. Fast. Before
Jade found him out and organized a lynch mob.

After staring absently at the small conference for a
few moments, he closed his eyes and drowsed again.

Suddenly he opened them. Something about the conference group—something peculiar. He sat up and

frowned at them again. Jade, Mela, Rick, and Feria, and three strangers. Nothing peculiar about that. Except . . . let's see . . . the thin one with the scholarly look—that would be the programming engineer, probably. The beefy, healthy fellow with the dark business suit and the wandering glance—Thorny couldn't place him—he looked out of place backstage. The third one seemed familiar somehow, but he, too, looked out of place—a chubby little man with no necktie and a fat cigar, he seemed more interested in the backstage rush than in the proceedings of the group. The beefy gent kept asking him questions, and he muttered brief answers around his cigar while watching the stagehands' parade.

Once when answering he took his cigar out of his mouth and glanced quickly across the floor in Thorny's direction. Thorny stiffened, felt bristles rise along his spine. The chubby little gent was—

—The depot clerk!

Who had issued him the extra tape and the splices. Who could put the finger on the trouble right away, and was undoubtedly doing it.

Got to get out. Got to get out fast. The beefy fellow was either a cop or a private investigator, one of several hired by Smithfield. Got to run, got to hide, got to— Lynch mob.

"Not through that door, buddy, that's the stage; what're you— Oh, Thorny! It's not time to go on."

"Sorry," he grunted at the prop man and turned away. The light flashed, the buzzer sounded faintly.

"Now it's time," the prop man called after him.

Where was he going? And what good would it do?

"Hey, Thorny! The buzzer. Come back. It's line-up. You're on when the curtain lifts . . . *hey!"*

He paused, then turned around and went back. He went on-stage and took his place. She was already there, staring at him strangely as he approached.

"You didn't do it, did you, Thorny?" she whispered.

He gazed at her in tight-lipped silence, then nodded.

She looked puzzled. She looked at him as if he were no longer a person, but a peculiar object to be studied. Not scornful, nor angry, nor righteous—just puzzled.

"Guess I was nuts," he said lamely.

"Guess you were."

"Not too much harm done, though," he said hopefully.

"The wrong people saw the first act, Thorny. They walked out."

"Wrong people?"

"Two backers and a critic."

"Oh?"

He stood stunned. She stopped looking at him then and just stood waiting for the curtain to rise, her face showing nothing but a puzzled sadness. It wasn't her show, and she had nothing in it but a doll that would bring a royalty check or two, and now herself as a temporary substitute for the doll. The sadness was for him. Contempt he could have understood.

The curtain lifted. A sea of dim faces beyond the footlights. And he was Andreyev, chief of a Soviet police garrison, loyalist servant of a dying cause. It was easy to stay in the role this time, to embed his ego firmly in the person of the Russian cop and live a little of the last century. For the ego was more comfortable there than in the skin of Ryan Thornier—a skin that might soon be sent to the tannery, judging the furtive glances that were coming from backstage. It might even be comfortable to remain Andreyev after the performance, but that was a sure way to get Napoleon Bonaparte for a roommate.

There was no change of setting between scenes *i* and *ii*, but only a dip of the curtain to indicate a time-lapse and permit a change of cast. He stayed on-stage, and it gave him a moment to think. The thoughts weren't pleasant.

Backers had walked out. Tomorrow the show would close unless the morning teleprint of the *Times* carried a rave review. Which seemed wildly improbable. Critics were jaded. Jaded tastes were apt to be impatient. They would not be eager to forgive the first act. He had wrecked it, and he couldn't rescue it.

Revenge wasn't sweet. It tasted like rot and a sour stomach.

Give them a good third act. There's nothing more you can do. But even that wouldn't take away the rotten taste.

Why did you do it, Thorny? Rick's voice, whispering from the booth and in his earplug prompter.

He glanced up and saw the technician watching him from the small window of the booth. He spread his hands in a wide shrugging gesture, as if to ask: How can I tell you, what can I do?

Go on with it, what else? Rick whispered, and withdrew from the window.

The incident seemed to confirm that Jade intended for him to finish it, anyhow. She could scarcely intend otherwise. She was in it with him, in a sense. If the audience found out the play had a human stand-in, and if the critics didn't like the show, they might pounce on the producer who "perpetrated such an impossible substitution" —even harder than they'd pounce on him. She had gambled on him, and in spite of his plot to force her into such a gamble, it was her show, and her responsibility, and she'd catch the brunt of it. Critics, owners, backers, and public—they didn't care about "blame," didn't care about excuses or reasons. They cared about the finished product, and if they didn't like it, the responsibility for it was clear.

As for himself? A cop waiting backstage. Why? He hadn't studied the criminal code, but he couldn't think of any neat little felonious label that could be pinned on what he'd done. Fraud? Not without an exchange of money or property, he thought. He'd been after intangibles, and the law was an earthy thing; it became confused when motives carried men beyond assaults on property or person, into assaults on ideas or principles. Then it passed the buck to psychiatry.

Maybe the beefy gent wasn't a cop at all. Maybe he was a collector of maniacs.

Thorny didn't much care. The dream had tumbled down, and he'd just have to let the debris keep falling about him until he got a chance to start climbing out of the wreckage. It was the end of something that should have ended years ago, and he couldn't get out until it finished collapsing.

The curtain lifted. Scene *ii* was good. Not brilliant, but good enough to make them stop snapping their gum and hold them locked in their seats, absorbed in their identity with Andreyev.

Scene *iii* was his Gethsemane—when the mob besieged the public offices while he waited for word of Marka and an answer to his offer of a truce with the guerrilla forces. The answer came in one word.

"Nyet."

His death sentence. The word that bound him over to

the jackals in the streets, the word that cast him to the ravening mob. The mob had a way: the mob was collecting officials and mounting them. He could see their collection from the window, looking across the square, and he discussed it with an aide. Nine men impaled on the steel spikes of the heavy grillwork fence in front of the Regional Soviet offices. The mob seized another specimen with its thousand hands and mounted it carefully. It lifted the specimen into a sitting position over a two-foot spike, then dropped him on it. Two specimens still squirmed.

He'd cheat the mob, of course. There were the barricades in the building below, and there would be plenty of time to meet death privately and chastely before the mob tore its way inside. But he delayed. He waited for word from Marka.

Word came. Two guards burst in.

"She's here, comrade, she's come!"

Come with the enemy, they said. Come betraying him, betraying the state. *Impossible!* But the guard insisted.

Berserk fury, and refusal to believe. With a low snarl, he drew the automatic, shot the bearer of bad tidings through the heart.

With the crash of the gunshot, the mannequin crumpled. The explosion startled a sudden memory out of hiding, and he remembered: the second cartridge in the clip—*not a blank!* He had forgotten to unload the deadly round.

For an instant he debated firing it into the fallen mannequin as a way to get rid of it, then dismissed the notion and obeyed the script. He stared at his victim and wilted, letting the gun slip from his fingers and fall to the floor. He staggered to the window to stare out across the square. He covered his face with his hands, awaited the transition curtain.

The curtain came. He whirled and started for the gun.

No, Thorny, no! came Rick's frantic whisper from the booth. *To the ikon . . . the ikon!*

He stopped in mid-stage. No time to retrieve the gun and unload. The curtain had only dipped and was starting up again. Let Mela get rid of the round, he thought. He crossed to the shrine, tearing open his collar, rumpling his hair. He fell to his knees before the ancient ikon, in dereliction before the God of an older Russia, a Russia that survived as firmly in fierce negation as it had survived in fierce affirmation. The cultural soul was a living thing, and it survived as well in downfall as in victory; it could never be excised, but only eaten away or slowly transmuted by time and gentle pressures of rain wearing the rock.

There was a bust of Lenin beneath the ikon. And there was a bust of Harvey Smithfield beneath the Greek players' masks on the wall of D'Uccia's office. The signs of the times, and the signs of the timeless, and the cultural heartbeat pulsed to the rhythm of centuries. He had resisted the times as they took a sharp turn in direction, but no man could swim long against the tide as it plodded its zigzag course into timelessness. And the sharp deflections in the course were deceptive—for all of them really wound their way downstream. No man ever added his bit to the flow by spending all his effort to resist the current. The tide would tire him and take him into oblivion while the world flowed on.

Marka, Boris, Poitr had entered, and he had turned to start at them without understanding. The mockery followed and the harsh laughter, as they pushed the once haughty but now broken chieftain about the stage like a dazed animal unable to respond. He rebounded from one to another of them, as they prodded him to dispel the trancelike daze.

"Finish your prayer, comrade," said Mela, picking up the gun he'd dropped.

As he staggered close to Mela, he found his chance, and whispered quickly: "The gun, Mela—eject the first cartridge. Eject it, quickly."

He was certain she heard him, although she showed no reaction—unless the slight flicker of her eyes had been a quick glance at the gun. Had she understood? A moment later, another chance to whisper.

"The next bullet's real. Work the slide. Eject it."

He stumbled as Piotr pushed him, fell against a heavy couch, slid down, and stared at them. Poitr went to open the window and shout an offer to the mob below. A bull-roar arose from the herd outside. They hauled him to the window as a triumphal display.

"See, comrade?" growled the guerrilla. "Your faithful congregation awaits you."

Marka closed the windows. "I can't stand that sight!" she cried.

"Take him to his people," the leader ordered.

"No—" Marka brought up the gun, shook her head fiercely. "I won't let you do that. Not to the mob."

Poitr growled a curse. "They'll have him anyway. They'll be coming up here to search."

Thorny stared at the actress with a puzzled frown. Still she hadn't ejected the cartridge. And the moment was approaching—a quick bullet to keep him from the mob, a bit of hot mercy flung hastily to him by the woman who had enthralled him and used him and betrayed him.

She turned toward him with the gun, and he began to back away.

"All right, Poitr—if they'll get him anyway—"

She moved a few steps toward him as he backed to a corner. *The live round, Mela, eject it!*

Then her foot brushed a copper bus-lug, and he saw the faint little jet of sparks. Eyes of glass, flesh of airfoam plastic, nerves of twitching electron streams.

Mela was gone. This was her doll. Maybe the real Mela couldn't stomach it after she'd found what he'd done, or maybe Jade had called her off after the first scene of the third act. A plastic hand held the gun, and a tiny flexible solenoid awaited the pulse that would tighten the finger on the trigger. Terror lanced through him.

Cue, Thorny, *cue!* whispered his earplug.

The doll had to wait for his protest before it could fire. It had to be cued. His eyes danced about the stage, looking for a way out. Only an instant to decide.

He could walk over and take the gun out of the doll's hand without giving it a cue—betraying himself to the audience and wrecking the final moment of the show.

He could run for it, cue her, and hope she missed, falling after the shot. But he'd fall on the lugs that way, and come up shrieking.

For God's sake, Thorny! Rick was howling. *The cue, the cue!*

He stared at the gun and swayed slightly from side to side. The gun swayed with him—slightly out of phase. A second's delay, no more—

"Please, Marka—" he called, swaying faster.

The finger tensed on the trigger. The gun moved in a search pattern, as he shifted to and fro. It was risky. It had to be precisely timed. It was like dancing with a cobra. He wanted to flee.

You faked the tape, you botched the show, you came out second best to a system you hated, he reminded himself. *And you even loaded the gun. Now if you can't risk it—*

He gritted his teeth, kept up the irregular weaving motion, then—

"Please, Marka . . . no, no, *nooo!*"

A spiked fist hit him somewhere around the belt, spun him around, and dropped him. The sharp cough of the gun was only a part of the blow. Then he was lying crumpled on his side in the chalked safety area, bleeding and cursing softly. The scene continued. He started to cry out, but checked the shout in his throat. Through a haze, he watched the others move on toward the finale, saw the dim sea of faces beyond the lights. Bullet punched through his side somewhere.

Got to stop squirming. Can't have a dead Andreyev floundering about like a speared fish on the stage. Wait a minute—just another minute—hang on.

But he couldn't. He clutched at his side and felt for the wound. Hard to feel through all the stickiness. He wanted to tear his clothes free to get at it and stop the bleeding, but that was no good either. They'd accept a mannequin fumbling slightly in a death agony, but the blood wouldn't go over so well. Mannequins didn't bleed. Didn't they see it anyway? They had to see it. Clever gimmick, they'd think. Tube of red ink, maybe. Realism is the milieu of—

He twisted his hand in his belt, drew it up strangle-tight around his waist. The pain got worse for a moment, but it seemed to slow the flow of blood. He hung onto it, gritting his teeth, waiting.

He knew about where it hit him, but it was harder to tell where it had come out. And what it had taken with it on the way. Thank God for the bleeding. Maybe he wasn't doing much of it inside.

He tried to focus on the rest of the stage. Music was rising somewhere. Had they all walked off and left him? But no—there was Piotr, through the haze. Piotr approached his chair of office—heavy, ornate, antique. Once it had belonged to a noble of the czar. Piotr, perfectly cold young machine, in his triumph—inspecting the chair.

A low shriek came from backstage somewhere. Mela. Couldn't she keep her mouth shut for half a minute? Probably spotted the blood. Maybe the music drowned the squeal.

Piotr mounted the single step and turned. He sat down gingerly in the chair of empire, testing it, and smiling victory. He seemed to find the chair comfortable.

"I must keep this, Marka," he said.

Thorny wheezed a low curse at him. He'd keep it all right, until the times went around another twist in the long old river. And welcome to it—judging by the thundering applause.

And the curtain fell slowly to cover the window of the stage.

Feet trouped past him, and he croaked "Help!" a couple of times, but the feet kept going. The mannequins, marching off to their packing cases.

He got to his feet alone, and went black. But when the blackness dissolved, he was still standing there, so he staggered toward the exit. They were rushing toward him —Mela and Rick and a couple of the crew. Hands grabbed for him, but he fought them off.

"I'll walk by myself now!" he growled.

But the hands took him anyway. He saw Jade and the beefy gent, tried to lurch toward them and explain everything, but she went even whiter and backed away. *I must look a bloody mess*, he thought.

"I was trying to duck. I didn't want to—"

"Save your breath," Rick told him. "I saw you. Just hang on."

They got him onto a doll packing case, and he heard somebody yelling for a doctor from the departing audience, and then a lot of hands started scraping at his side and tugging at him.

"Mela—"

"Right here, Thorny. I'm here."

And after a while she was still there, but sunlight was spilling across the bed, and he smelled faint hospital odors. He blinked at her for several seconds before he found a voice.

"The show?" he croaked.

"They panned it," she said softly.

He closed his eyes again and groaned.

"But it'll make dough."

He blinked at her and gaped.

"Publicity. Terrific. Shall I read you the reviews?"

He nodded, and she reached for the papers. All about the madman who bled all over the stage. He stopped her halfway through the first article. It was enough. The audience had begun to catch on toward the last lines of the play, and the paging of a surgeon had confirmed the suspicion.

"You missed the bedlam backstage," she told him. "It was quite a mess."

"But the show won't close?"

"How can it? With all the morbidity for pulling power. If it closes, it'll be with the Peltier performance to blame."

"And Jade—?"

"Sore. Plenty sore. Can you blame her?"

He shook his head. "I didn't want to hurt anybody. I'm sorry."

She watched him in silence for a moment, then: "You can't flounder around like you've been doing, Thorny without somebody getting hurt, without somebody hating your guts, getting trampled on. You just can't."

It was true. When you hung onto a piece of the past, and just hung onto it quietly, you only hurt yourself. But when you started trying to bludgeon a place for it in the present, you began knocking over the bystanders.

"Theater's dead, Thorny. Can't you believe that now?"

He thought about it a little, and shook his head. It wasn't dead: Only the form was changed, and maybe not permanently at that. He'd thought of it first last night, before the ikon. There were things of the times, and a few things that were timeless. The times came as a result of a particular human culture. The timeless came as a result of any human culture at all. And Cultural Man was a showman. He created display windows of culture for an audience of men, and paraded his aspirations and ideals and purposes thereon, and the displays were necessary to the continuity of the culture, to the purposeful orientation of the species.

Beyond one such window, he erected an altar, and placed a priest before it to chant a liturgical description of the heart-reasoning of his times. And beyond another window, he built a stage and set his talking dolls upon it to live a dramaturgical sequence of wishes and woes of his times.

True, the priests would change, the liturgy would change, and the dolls, the dramas, the displays—but the windows would never—no never—be closed as long as Man outlived his members, for only through such windows could transient men see themselves against the background of a broader sweep, see man encompassed by Man. A perspective not possible without the windows.

Dramaturgy. Old as civilized Man. Outlasting forms and techniques and applications. Outlasting even current popular worship of the Great God Mechanism, who was temporarily enshrined while still being popularly misunderstood. Like the Great God Commerce of an earlier century, and the God Agriculture before him.

Suddenly he laughed aloud. "If they used human actors today, it would be a pretty moldy display. Not even *true*, considering the times."

By the time another figure lounged in his doorway, he had begun to feel rather expansive and heroic about it all. When a small cough caused him to glance up, he stared for a moment, grinned broadly, then called: "Ho, Richard! Come in. Here . . . sit down. Help me decide on a career, eh? Heh heh——" He waved the classified section and chuckled. "What kind of little black boxes can an old ham——"

He paused. Rick's expression was chilly, and he made no move to enter. After a moment he said: "I guess there'll always be a sucker to rerun this particular relay race."

"Race?" Thorny gathered a slow frown.

"Yeah. Last century, it was between a Chinese abacus operator and an IBM machine. They really had a race, you know."

"Now see here——"

"And the century before that, it was between a longhand secretary and a typewriting machine."

"If you came here to——"

"And before that, the hand-weavers against the automatic looms."

"Nice to have seen you, Richard. On your way out, would you ask the nurse to—"

"Break up the looms, smash the machines, picket the offices with typewriters, keep adding machines out of China! So then what? Try to be a better tool than a tool?"

Thorny rolled his head aside and glowered at the wall. "All right. I was wrong. What do you want to do? Gloat? Moralize?"

"No. I'm just curious. It keeps happening—a specialist trying to compete with a higher-level specialist's tools. Why?"

"*Higher* level?" Thorny sat up with a snarl, groaned, caught at his side and sank back again, panting.

"Easy, old man," Rick said quietly. "Sorry. Higher organizational-level, I meant. Why do you keep on doing it?"

Thorny lay silent for a few moments, then: "Status jealousy. Even hawks try to drive other hawks out of their hunting grounds. Fight off competition."

"But you're no hawk. And a machine isn't competition."

"Cut it out, Rick. What did you come here for?"

Rick glanced at the toe of his shoe, snickered faintly, and came on into the room. "Thought you might need some help finding a job," he said. "When I looked in the door and saw you lying there looking like somebody's King Arthur, I got sore again." He sat restlessly on the edge of a chair and watched the old man with mingled sadness, irritation, and affection.

"You'd help me . . . find a job?"

"Maybe. A job, not a permanent niche."

"It's too late to find a permanent niche."

"It was too late when you were born, old man! There isn't any such thing—hasn't been, for the last century. Whatever you specialize in, another specialty will either gobble you up, or find a way to replace you. If you get what looks like a secure niche, somebody'll come along and wall you up in it and write your epitaph on it. And the more specialized a society gets, the more dangerous it is for the pure specialist. You think an electronic engineer is any safer than an actor? Or a ditch-digger?"

"I don't know. It's not fair. A man's career—"

"You've always got one specialty that's safe."

"What's that?"

"The specialty of creating new specialties. Continuously. Your own."

"But that's—" He started to protest, to say that such a concept belonged to the highly trained few, to the technical elite of the era, and that it wasn't specialization, but generalization. But why to the few? The specialty of creating new specialties—

"But that's—"

"More or less a definition of Man, isn't it?" Rick finished for him. "Now about the job—"

"Yes, about the job—"

So maybe you don't start from the bottom after all, he decided. You start considerably above the lemur, the chimpanzee, the orangutan, the Maestro—if you ever start at all.

Dark Benediction

ALWAYS FEARFUL OF being set upon during the night, Paul slept uneasily despite his weariness from the long trek southward. When dawn broke, he rolled out of his blankets and found himself still stiff with fatigue. He kicked dirt over the remains of the campfire and breakfasted on a tough forequarter of cold boiled rabbit which he washed down with a swallow of earthy-tasting ditchwater. Then he buckled the cartridge belt about his waist, leaped the ditch, and climbed the embankment to the trafficless four-lane highway whose pavement was scattered with blown leaves and unsightly debris dropped by a long-departed throng of refugees whose only wish had been to escape from one another. Paul, with characteristic independence, had decided to go where the crowds had been the thickest—to the cities—on the theory that they would now be deserted, and therefore noncontagious.

The fog lay heavy over the silent land, and for a moment he paused groping for cognizance of direction. Then he saw the stalled car on the opposite shoulder of the road—a late model convertible, but rusted, flat-tired, with last year's license plates, and most certainly out of fuel. It obviously had been deserted by its owner during the exodus, and he trusted in its northward heading as he would have trusted the reading of a compass. He turned right and moved south on the empty highway. Somewhere just ahead in the gray vapor lay the outskirts of Houston. He had seen the high skyline before the setting of yester-

332

day's sun, and knew that his journey would soon be drawing to a close.

Occasionally he passed a deserted cottage or a burned-out roadside tavern, but he did not pause to scrounge for food. The exodus would have stripped such buildings clean. Pickings should be better in the heart of the metropolitan area, he thought—where the hysteria had swept humanity away quickly.

Suddenly Paul froze on the highway, listening to the fog. Footsteps in the distance—footsteps and a voice singing an absent-minded ditty to itself. No other sounds penetrated the sepulchral silence which once had growled with the life of a great city. Anxiety caught him with clammy hands. An old man's voice it was, crackling and tuneless. Paul groped for his holster and brought out the revolver he had taken from a deserted police station.

"Stop where you are, dermie!" he bellowed at the fog. "I'm armed."

The footsteps and the singing stopped. Paul strained his eyes to penetrate the swirling mist-shroud. After a moment, the oldster answered: "Sure foggy, ain't it, sonny? Can't see ya. Better come a little closer. I ain't no dermie."

Loathing choked in Paul's throat. "The hell you're not. Nobody else'd be crazy enough to sing. Get off the road! I'm going south, and if I see you I'll shoot. Now move!"

"Sure, sonny. I'll move. But I'm no dermie. I was just singing to keep myself company. I'm past caring about the plague. I'm heading north, where there's people, and if some dermie hears me a'singing . . . why, I'll tell him t'come jine in. What's the good o' being healthy if yer alone?"

While the old man spoke, Paul heard his sloshing across the ditch and climbing through the brush. Doubt assailed him. Maybe the old crank wasn't a dermie. An ordinary plague victim would have whimpered and pleaded for satisfaction of his strange craving—the laying-on of hands, the feel of healthy skin beneath moist gray palms. Nevertheless, Paul meant to take no chances with the oldster.

"Stay back in the brush while I walk past!" he called.

"Okay, sonny. You go right by. I ain't gonna touch you. You aiming to scrounge in Houston?"

Paul began to advance. "Yeah, I figure people got out

so fast that they must have left plenty of canned goods
and stuff behind."

"Mmmm, there's a mite here and there," said the
cracked voice in a tone that implied understatement.
"Course, now, you ain't the first to figure that way,
y'know."

Paul slacked his pace, frowning. "You mean . . . a lot
of people are coming back?"

"Mmmm, no—not a lot. But you'll bump into people
every day or two. Ain't my kind o' folks. Rough charac-
ters, mostly—don't take chances, either. They'll shoot first,
then look to see if you was a dermie. Don't never come
busting out of a doorway without taking a peek at the
street first. And if two people come around a corner in
opposite directions, somebody's gonna die. The few that's
there is trigger happy. Just thought I'd warn ya."

"Thanks."

"D'mention it. Been good t'hear a body's voice again, tho
I can't see ye."

Paul moved on until he was fifty paces past the voice.
Then he stopped and turned. "Okay, you can get back on
the road now. Start walking north. Scuff your feet until
you're out of earshot."

"Taking no chances, are ye?" said the old man as he
waded the ditch. "All right, sonny." The sound of his
footsteps hesitated on the pavement. "A word of advice—
your best scrounging'll be around the warehouses. Most of
the stores are picked clean. Good luck!"

Paul stood listening to the shuffling feet recede northward. When they became inaudible, he turned to continue
his journey. The meeting had depressed him, reminded
him of the animal-level to which he and others like him
had sunk. The oldster was obviously healthy; but Paul
had been chased by three dermies in as many days. And
the thought of being trapped by a band of them in the fog
left him unnerved. Once he had seen a pair of the grinning, maddened compulsives seize a screaming young child
while each of them took turns caressing the youngster's
arms and face with the gray and slippery hands that
spelled certain contraction of the disease—if disease it
was. The dark pall of neuroderm was unlike any illness
that Earth had ever seen.

The victim became the eager ally of the sickness that

gripped him. Caught in its demoniac madness, the stricken human searched hungrily for healthy comrades, then set upon them with no other purpose than to paw at the clean skin and praise the virtues of the blind compulsion that drove him to do so. One touch, and infection was insured. It was as if a third of humanity had become night-prowling maniacs, lurking in the shadows to seize the unwary, working in bands to trap the unarmed wanderer. And two-thirds of humanity found itself fleeing in horror from the mania, seeking the frigid northern climates where, according to rumor, the disease was less infectious. The normal functioning of civilization had been dropped like a hot potato within six months after the first alarm. When the man at the next lathe might be hiding gray discolorations beneath his shirt, industrial society was no place for humanity.

Rumor connected the onslaught of the plague with an unpredicted swarm of meteorites which had brightened the sky one October evening two weeks before the first case was discovered. The first case was, in fact, a machinist who had found one of the celestial cannon balls, handled it, weighed it, estimated its volume by fluid-displacement, then cut into it on his lathe because its low density suggested that it might be hollow. He claimed to have found a pocket of frozen jelly, still rigid from deep space, although the outershell had been heated white-hot by atmospheric friction. He said he let the jelly thaw, then fed it to his cat because it had an unpleasant fishy odor. Shortly thereafter, the cat disappeared.

Other meteorites had been discovered and similarly treated by university staffs before there was any reason to blame them for the plague. Paul, who had been an engineering student at Texas U at the time of the incident, had heard it said that the missiles were purposefully manufactured by parties unknown, that the jelly contained micro-organisms which under the microscope suggested a cross between a sperm-cell (because of a similar tail) and a Pucini Corpuscle (because of a marked resemblance to nerve tissue in subcellular detail).

When the meteorites were connected with the new and mushrooming disease, some people started a panic by theorizing that the meteor-swarm was a pre-invasion artillery attack by some space-horde lurking beyond telescope range, and waiting for their biological bombardment to wreck civilization before they moved in upon Earth. The government had immediately labeled all investigations "top-secret," and Paul had heard no news since the initial speculations. Indeed, the government might have explained the whole thing and proclaimed it to the country for all he knew. One thing was certain: the country had not heard. It no longer possessed channels of communication.

Paul thought that if any such invaders were coming, they would have already arrived—months ago. Civilization was not truly wrecked; it had simply been discarded during the crazed flight of the individual away from the herd. Industry lay idle and unmanned, but still intact. Man was fleeing from Man. Fear had destroyed the integration of his society, and had left him powerless before any hypothetical invaders. Earth was ripe for plucking, but it remained unplucked and withering. Paul, therefore, discarded the invasion hypothesis, and searched for nothing new to replace it. He accepted the fact of his own existence in the midst of chaos, and sought to protect that existence as best he could. It proved to be a full-time job, with no spare time for theorizing.

Life was a rabbit scurrying over a hill. Life was a warm blanket, and a secluded sleeping place. Life was ditchwater, and an unbloated can of corned beef, and a suit of clothing looted from a deserted cottage. Life, above all else, was an avoidance of other human beings. For no dermie had the grace to cry "unclean!" to the unsuspecting. If the dermie's discolorations were still in the concealable stage, then concealed they would be, while the lost creature deliberately sought to infect his wife, his children, his friends—whoever would not protest an idle touch of the hand. When the grayness touched the face and the backs of the hands, the creature became a feverish night wanderer, subject to strange hallucinations and delusions and desires.

The fog began to part toward midmorning as Paul drove deeper into the outskirts of Houston. The highway was becoming a commercial subcenter, lined with businesses and small shops. The sidewalks were showered with broken glass from windows kicked in by looters. Paul kept to the center of the deserted street, listening and watching cautiously for signs of life. The distant barking of a dog was the only sound in the once-growling metropolis. A flight of sparrows winged down the street, then darted in through a broken window to an inside nesting place.

He searched a small grocery store, looking for a snack, but the shelves were bare. The thoroughfare had served as a main avenue of escape, and the fugitives had looted it thoroughly to obtain provisions. He turned onto a side street, then after several blocks turned again to parallel the highway, moving through an old residential section. Many houses had been left open, but few had been looted. He entered one old frame mansion and found a can of tomatoes in the kitchen. He opened it and sipped the tender delicacy from the container, while curiosity sent him prowling through the rooms.

He wandered up the first flight of stairs, then halted with one foot on the landing. A body lay sprawled across the second flight—the body of a young man, dead quite a while. A well-rusted pistol had fallen from his hand. Paul dropped the tomatoes and bolted for the street. Suicide was a common recourse, when a man learned that he had been touched.

After two blocks, Paul stopped running. He sat panting on a fire hydrant and chided himself for being overly cautious. The man had been dead for months; and infection was achieved only through contact. Nevertheless, his scalp was still tingling. When he had rested briefly, he continued his plodding course toward the heart of the city. Toward noon, he saw another human being.

The man was standing on the loading dock of a warehouse, apparently enjoying the sunlight that came with the dissolving of the fog. He was slowly and solemnly spooning the contents of a can into a red-lipped mouth while his beard bobbled with appreciative chewing. Suddenly he saw Paul who had stopped in the center of the street with his hand on the butt of his pistol. The man backed away, tossed the can aside, and sprinted the length of the platform. He bounded off the end, snatched a bicycle away from the wall, and pedalled quickly out of sight while he bleated shrill blasts on a police whistle clenched between his teeth.

Paul trotted to the corner, but the man had made another turn. His whistle continued bleating. A signal? A dermie summons to a touching orgy? Paul stood still while he tried to overcome an urge to break into panicked flight.

After a minute, the clamor ceased; but the silence was ominous.

If a party of cyclists moved in, he could not escape on foot. He darted toward the nearest warehouse, seeking a place to hide. Inside, he climbed a stack of boxes to a horizontal girder, kicked the stack to topple it, and stretched out belly-down on the steel eye-beam to command a clear shot at the entrances. He lay for an hour, waiting quietly for searchers. None came. At last he slid down a vertical support and returned to the loading platform. The street was empty and silent. With weapon ready, he continued his journey. He passed the next intersection without mishap.

Halfway up the block, a calm voice drawled a command from behind him: "Drop the gun, dermie. Get your hands behind your head."

He halted, motionless. No plague victim would hurl the dermie-charge at another. He dropped the pistol and turned slowly. Three men with drawn revolvers were clambering from the back of a stalled truck. They were all bearded, wore blue jeans, blue neckerchiefs, and green woolen shirts. He suddenly recalled that the man on the loading platform had been similarly dressed. A uniform?

"Turn around again!" barked the speaker.

Paul turned, realizing that the men were probably some sort of self-appointed quarantine patrol. Tow ropes suddenly skidded out from behind and came to a stop near his feet on the pavement—a pair of lariat loops.

"One foot in each loop, dermie!" the speaker snapped.

When Paul obeyed, the ropes were jerked taut about his ankles, and two of the men trotted out to the sides, stood thirty feet apart, and pulled his legs out into a wide straddle. He quickly saw that any movement would cost him his balance.

"Strip to the skin."

"I'm no dermie," Paul protested as he unbuttoned his shirt.

"We'll see for ourselves, Joe," grunted the leader as he moved around to the front. "Get the top off first. If your chest's okay, we'll let your feet go."

When Paul had undressed, the leader walked around him slowly, making him spread his fingers and display the soles of his feet. He stood shivering and angry in the chilly winter air while the men satisfied themselves that he wore no gray patches of neuroderm.

"You're all right, I guess," the speaker admitted; than as Paul stooped to recover his clothing, the man growled, "Not those! Jim, get him a probie outfit."

Paul caught a bundle of clean clothing, tossed to him from the back of the truck. There were jeans, a woolen shirt, and a kerchief, but the shirt and kerchief were red. He shot an inquiring glance at the leader, while he climbed into the welcome change.

"All newcomers are on two weeks probation," the man explained. "If you decide to stay in Houston, you'll get another exam next time the uniform code changes. Then you can join our outfit, if you don't show up with the plague. In fact, you'll have to join if you stay."

"What is the outfit?" Paul asked suspiciously.

"It just started. Schoolteacher name of Georgelle organized it. We aim to keep dermies out. There's about six hundred of us now. We guard the downtown area, but soon as there's enough of us we'll move out to take in more territory. Set up road blocks and all that. You're welcome, soon as we're sure you're clean . . . and can take orders."

"Whose orders?"

"Georgelle's. We got no room for goof-offs, and no time for argument. Anybody don't like the setup, he's welcome to get out. Jim here'll give you a leaflet on the rules. Better read it before you go anywhere. If you don't, you might make a wrong move. Make a wrong move, and you catch a bullet."

The man called Jim interrupted, "Reckon you better call off the other patrols, Digger?" he said respectfully to the leader.

Digger nodded curtly and turned to blow three short blasts and a long with his whistle. An answering short-long-short came from several blocks away. Other posts followed suit. Paul realized that he had been surrounded by a ring of similar ambushes.

"Jim, take him to the nearest water barrel, and see that he shaves." Digger ordered, then: "What's your name, probie? Also your job, if you had one."

"Paul Harris Oberlin. I was a mechanical engineering student when the plague struck. Part-time garage mechanic while I was in school."

Digger nodded and jotted down the information on a scratchpad. "Good, I'll turn your name in to the registrar. Georgelle says to watch for college men. You might get a good assignment, later. Report to the Esperson Building on the seventeenth. That's inspection day. If you don't show up, we'll come looking for you. All loose probies'll get shot. Now Jim here's gonna see to it that you shave. Don't shave again until your two-weeker. That way, we can estimate how long you been in town—by looking at your beard. We got other ways that you don't need to know about. Georgelle's got a system worked out for everything, so don't try any tricks."

"Tell me, what do you do with dermies?"

Digger grinned at his men. "You'll find out, probie."

Paul was led to a rain barrel, given a basin, razor, and soap. He scraped his face clean while Jim sat at a safe distance, munching a quid of tobacco and watching the operation with tired boredom. The other men had gone.

"May I have my pistol back?"

"Uh-uh! Read the rules. No weapons for probies."

"Suppose I bump into a dermie?"

"Find yourself a whistle and toot a bunch of short blasts. Then run like hell. We'll take care of the dermies. Read the rules."

"Can I scrounge wherever I want to?"

"Probies have their own assigned areas. There's a map in the rules."

"Who wrote the rules, anyhow?"

"Jeezis!" the guard grunted disgustedly. "Read 'em and find out."

When Paul finished shaving, Jim stood up, stretched, then bounded off the platform and picked up his bicycle.

"Where do I go from here?" Paul called.

The man gave him a contemptuous snort, mounted the bike, and pedalled leisurely away. Paul gathered that he was to read the rules. He sat down beside the rain barrel and began studying the mimeographed leaflet.

Everything was cut and dried. As a probie, he was confined to an area six blocks square near the heart of the city. Once he entered it, a blue mark would be stamped on his forehead. At the two-week inspection, the indelible brand would be removed with a special solution. If a branded probie were caught outside his area, he would be forcibly escorted from the city. He was warned against attempting to impersonate permanent personnel, because a system of codes and passwords would ensnare him. One full page of the leaflet was devoted to propaganda. Houston was to become a "Bulwark of health in a stricken world, and the leader of a glorious recovery." The paper was signed by Dr. Georgelle, who had given himself the title of Director.

The pamphlet left Paul with a vague uneasiness. The uniforms—they reminded him of neighborhood boys' gangs in the slums, wearing special sweaters and uttering secret passwords, whipping intruders and amputating the tails of stray cats in darkened garages. And, in another way, it made him think of frustrated little people, gathering at night in brown shirts around a bonfire to sing the *Horst Wessel Leid* and listen to grandiose oratory about glorious destinies. *Their* stray cats had been an unfavored race.

Of course, the dermies were not merely harmless alley prowlers. They were a real menace. And maybe Georgelle's methods were the only ones effective.

Whil Paul sat with the pamphlet on the platform, he had been gazing absently at the stalled truck from which the men had emerged. Suddenly it broke upon his consciousness that it was a diesel. He bounded off the platform, and went to check its fuel tank, which had been left uncapped.

He knew that it was useless to search for gasoline, but diesel fuel was another matter. The exodus had drained all existing supplies of high octane fuel for the escaping motorcade, but the evacuation had been too hasty and too fear-crazed to worry with out-of-the-ordinary methods. He sniffed tank. It smelled faintly of gasoline. Some unknowing fugitive had evidently filled it with ordinary fuel, which had later evaporated. But if the cylinders had not been damaged by the trial, the truck might be useful. He checked the engine briefly, and decided that it had not been tried at all. The starting battery had been removed.

He walked across the street and looked back at the warehouse. It bore the sign of a trucking firm. He walked around the block, eyeing the streets cautiously for other patrolmen. There was a fueling platform on the opposite side of the block. A fresh splash of oil on the concrete told him that Georgelle's crew was using the fuel for some purpose—possibly for heating or cooking. He entered the building and found a repair shop, with several dismantled engines lying about. There was a rack of batteries in the corner, but a screwdriver placed across the terminals brought only a weak spark.

The chargers, of course, drew power from the city's electric service, which was dead. After giving the problem some thought, Paul connected five of the batteries in series, then placed a sixth across the total voltage, so that it would collect the charge that the others lost. Then he went to carry buckets of fuel from the pumps to the truck. When the tank was filled, he hoisted each end of the truck with a roll-under jack and inflated the tires with a hand-pump. It was a long and laborious job.

Twilight was gathering by the time he was ready to try it. Several times during the afternoon, he had been forced to hide from cyclists who wandered past, lest they send him on to the probie area and use the truck for their own purposes. Evidently they had long since decided that automotive transportation was a thing of the past.

A series of short whistle-blasts came to his ears just as he was climbing into the cab. The signals were several blocks away, but some of the answering bleats were closer. Evidently another newcomer, he thought. Most new arrivals from the north would pass through the same area on their way downtown. He entered the cab, closed the door softly, and ducked low behind the dashboard as three cyclists raced across the intersection just ahead.

Paul settled down to wait for the all-clear. It came after about ten minutes. Apparently the newcomer had tried to run instead of hiding. When the cyclists returned, they were moving leisurely, and laughing among themselves. After they had passed the intersection, Paul stole quietly out of the cab and moved along the wall to the corner, to assure himself that all the patrolmen had gone. But the sound of shrill pleading came to his ears.

At the end of the building, he clung close to the wall and risked a glance around the corner. A block away, the nude figure of a girl was struggling between taut ropes held by green-shirted guards. She was a pretty girl, with a tousled mop of chestnut hair and clean white limbs—clean except for her forearms, which appeared dipped in dark stain. Then he saw the dark irregular splotch across

her flank, like a splash of ink not quite washed clean.
She was a dermie.

Paul ducked close to the ground so that his face was
hidden by a clump of grass at the corner. A man—the
leader of the group—had left the girl, and was advancing
up the street toward Paul, who prepared to roll under the
building out of sight. But in the middle of the block, the
man stopped. He lifted a manhole cover in the pavement,
then went back for the girl's clothing, which he dragged
at the end of a fishing pole with a wire hook at its tip.
He dropped the clothing, one piece at a time into the
manhole. A cloud of white dust arose from it, and the
man stepped back to avoid the dust. Quicklime, Paul
guessed.

Then the leader cupped his hands to his mouth and
called back to the others. "Okay, drag her on up here!"
He drew his revolver and waited while they tugged the
struggling girl toward the manhole.

Paul felt suddenly ill. He had seen dermies shot in
self-defense by fugitives from their deathly gray hands,
but here was cold and efficient elimination. Here was
Dachau and Buchenwald and the nameless camps of
Siberia. He turned and bolted for the truck.

The sound of its engine starting brought a halt to the
disposal of the pest-girl. The leader appeared at the intersection and stared uncertainly at the truck, as Paul
nosed it away from the building. He fidgeted with his revolver doubtfully, and called something over his shoulder
to the others. Then he began walking out into the street
and signaling for the truck to stop. Paul let it crawl slowly
ahead, and leaned out the window to eye the man questioningly.

"How the hell you get that started?" the leader called
excitedly. He was still holding the pistol, but it dangled
almost unnoticed in his hand. Paul suddenly fed fuel to
the diesel and swerved sharply toward the surprised
guardsman.

The leader yelped and dived for safety, but the fender
caught his hips, spun him off balance, and smashed him
down against the pavement. As the truck thundered
around the corner toward the girl and her captors, he
glanced in the mirror to see the hurt man weakly trying to
crawl out of the street. Paul was certain that he was not
mortally wounded.

As the truck lumbered on, the girl threw herself prone before it, since the ropes prevented any escape. Paul swerved erratically, sending the girl's captors scurrying for the alley. Then he aimed the wheels to straddle her body. She glanced up, screamed, then hugged the pavement as the behemoth thundered overhead. A bullet ploughed a furrow across the hood. Paul ducked low in the seat and jammed the brake pedal down, as soon as he thought she was clear.

There were several shots, but apparently they were shooting at the girl. Paul counted three seconds, then gunned the engine again. If she hadn't climbed aboard, it was just tough luck, he thought grimly. He shouldn't have tried to save her anyway. But continued shooting told him that she had managed to get inside. The trailer was heaped with clothing, and he trusted the mound of material to halt the barrage of bullets. He heard the explosion of a blowout as he swung around the next corner, and the trailer lurched dangerously. It swayed from side to side as he gathered speed down the wide and trafficless avenue. But the truck had double wheels, and soon the dangerous lurching ceased.

He roared on through the metropolitan area, staying on the same street and gathering speed. An occasional scrounger or cyclist stopped to stare, but they seemed too surprised to act. And they could not have known what had transpired a few blocks away.

Paul could not stop to see if he had a passenger, or if she was still alive. She was more dangerous than the gunmen. Any gratitude she might feel toward her rescuer would be quickly buried beneath her craving to spread the disease. He wished fervently that he had let the patrolmen kill her. Now he was faced with the problem of getting rid of her. He noticed, however, that mirrors were mounted on both sides of the cab. If he stopped the truck, and if she climbed out, he could see, and move away again before she had a chance to approach him. But he decided to wait until they were out of the city.

Soon he saw a highway marker, then a sign that said "Galveston—58 miles." He bore ahead, thinking that perhaps the island-city would provide good scrounging, without the regimentation of Doctor Georgelle's efficient system with its plans for "glorious recovery."

Twenty miles beyond the city limits, he stopped the

truck, let the engine idle, and waited for his passenger to climb out. He locked the doors and laid a jack-handle across the seat as an added precaution. Nothing happened. He rolled down the window and shouted toward the rear.

"All passengers off the bus! Last stop! Everybody out!"

Still the girl did not appear. Then he heard something —a light tap from the trailer, and a murmur . . . or a moan. She was there all right. He called again, but she made no response. It was nearly dark outside.

At last he seized the jack-handle, opened the door, and stepped out of the cab. Wary of a trick, he skirted wide around the trailer and approached it from the rear. One door was closed, while the other swung free. He stopped a few yards away and peered inside. At first he saw nothing.

"Get out, but keep away or I'll kill you."

Then he saw her move. She was sitting on the floor, leaning back against a heap of clothing, a dozen feet from the entrance. He stepped forward cautiously and flung open the other door. She turned her head to look at him peculiarly, but said nothing. He could see that she had donned some of the clothing, but one trouser-leg was rolled up, and she had tied a rag tightly about her ankle.

"Are you hurt?"

She nodded. "Bullet . . ." She rolled her head dizzily and moaned.

Paul went back to the cab to search for a first aid kit. He found one, together with a flashlight and spare batteries in the glove compartment. He made certain that the cells were not corroded and that the light would burn feebly. Then he returned to the trailer, chiding himself for a prize fool. A sensible human would haul the dermie out at the end of a towing chain and leave her sitting by the side of the road.

"If you try to touch me, I'll brain you!" he warned, as he clambered into the trailer.

She looked up again. "Would you feel . . . like enjoying anything . . . if you were bleeding like this?" she muttered weakly. The flashlight beam caught the glitter of pain in her eyes, and accentuated the pallor of her small face. She was a pretty girl—scarcely older than twenty— but Paul was in no mood to appreciate pretty women, especially dermies.

"So that's how you think of it, eh? Enjoying yourself!"

She said nothing. She dropped her forehead against her knee and rolled it slowly.

"Where are you hit? Just the foot?"

"Ankle . . ."

"All right, take the rag off. Let's see."

"The wound's in back."

"All right, lie down on your stomach, and keep your hands under your head."

She stretched out weakly, and he shone the light over her leg, to make certain its skin was clear of neuroderm. Then he looked at the ankle, and said nothing for a time. The bullet had missed the joint, but had neatly severed the Achilles' tendon just above the heel.

"You're a plucky kid," he grunted, wondering how she had endured the self-torture of getting the shoe off and clothing herself.

"It was cold back here—without clothes," she muttered.

Paul opened the first aid packet and found an envelope of sulfa powder. Without touching her, he emptied it into the wound, which was beginning to bleed again. There was nothing else he could do. The tendon had pulled apart and would require surgical stitching to bring it together until it could heal. Such attention was out of the question.

She broke the silence. "I . . . I'm going to be crippled, aren't I?"

"Oh, not crippled," he heard himself telling her. "If we can get you to a doctor, anyway. Tendons can be sutured with wire. He'll probably put your foot in a cast, and you might get a stiff ankle from it."

She lay breathing quietly, denying his hopeful words by her silence.

"Here!" he said. "Here's a gauze pad and some tape. Can you manage it yourself?"

She started to sit up. He placed the first aid pack beside her, and backed to the door. She fumbled in the kit, and whimpered while she taped the pad in place.

"There's a tourniquet in there, too. Use it if the bleeding's worse."

She looked up to watch his silhouette against the darkening sky. "Thanks . . . thanks a lot, mister. I'm grateful. I promise not to touch you. Not if you don't want me to."

Shivering, he moved back to the cab. Why did they always get that insane idea that they were doing their victims a favor by giving them the neural plague? *Not if you don't want me to.* He shuddered as he drove away. She felt that way now, while the pain robbed her of the craving, but later—unless he got rid of her quickly—she would come to feel that she owed it to him—as a favor. The disease perpetuated itself by arousing such strange delusions in its bearer. The micro-organisms' methods of survival were indeed highly specialized. Paul felt certain that such animalicules had not evolved on Earth.

A light gleamed here and there along the Alvin-Galveston highway—oil lamps, shining from lonely cottages whose occupants had not felt the pressing urgency of the crowded city. But he had no doubt that to approach one of the farmhouses would bring a rifle bullet as a welcome. Where could he find help for the girl? No one would touch her but another dermie. Perhaps he could unhitch the trailer and leave her in downtown Galveston, with a sign hung on the back—"Wounded dermie inside." The plague victims would care for their own—if they found her.

He chided himself again for worrying about her. Saving her life didn't make him responsible for her . . . did it? After all, if she lived, and the leg healed, she would only prowl in search of healthy victims again. She would never be rid of the disease, nor would she ever die of it —so far as anyone knew. The death rate was high among dermies, but the cause was usually a bullet.

Paul passed a fork in the highway and knew that the bridge was just ahead. Beyond the channel lay Galveston Island, once brightly lit and laughing in its role as seaside resort—now immersed in darkness. The wind whipped at the truck from the southwest as the road led up onto the wide causeway. A faint glow in the east spoke of a moon about to rise. He saw the wide structure of the drawbridge just ahead.

Suddenly he clutched at the wheel, smashed furiously down on the brake, and tugged the emergency back. The tires howled ahead on the smooth concrete, and the force threw him forward over the wheel. Dusty water swirled far below where the upward folding gates of the drawbridge had once been. He skidded to a stop ten feet from the end. When he climbed out, the girl was calling weakly

from the trailer, but he walked to the edge and looked
over. Someone had done a job with dynamite.

Why, he wondered. To keep islanders on the island, or
to keep mainlanders off? Had another Doctor Georgelle
started his own small nation in Galveston? It seemed
more likely that the lower island dwellers had done the
demolition.

He looked back at the truck. An experienced truckster
might be able to swing it around all right, but Paul was
doubtful. Nevertheless, he climbed back in the cab and
tried it. Half an hour later he was hopelessly jammed,
with the trailer twisted aside and the cab wedged near
the sheer drop to the water. He gave it up and went
back to inspect his infected cargo.

She was asleep, but moaning faintly. He prodded her
awake with the jack-handle. "Can you crawl, kid? If you
can, come back to the door."

She nodded, and began dragging herself toward the
flashlight. She clenched her lip between her teeth to keep
from whimpering, but her breath came as a voiced murmur . . . *nnnng . . . nnnng . . .*

She sagged weakly when she reached the entrance, and
for a moment he thought she had fainted. Then she
looked up. "What next, skipper?" she panted.

"I . . . I don't know. Can you let yourself down to the
pavement.

She glanced over the edge and shook her head. "With
a rope, maybe. There's one back there someplace. If
you're scared of me, I'll try to crawl and get it."

"Hands to yourself?" he asked suspiciously; then he
thanked the darkness for hiding the heat of shame that
crawled to his face.

"I won't . . ."

He scrambled into the trailer quickly and brought back
the rope. "I'll climb up on top and let it down in front of
you. Grab hold and let yourself down."

A few minutes later she was sitting on the concrete
causeway looking at the wrecked draw. "Oh!" she muttered as he scrambled down from atop the trailer. "I
thought you just wanted to dump me here. We're stuck,
huh?"

"Yeah! We might swim it, but doubt if you could make
it."

"I'd try . . ." She paused, cocking her head slightly. "There's a boat moored under the bridge. Right over there."

"What makes you think so?"

"Water lapping against wood. Listen." Then she shook her head. "I forgot. You're not hyper."

"I'm not what?" Paul listened. The water sounds seemed homogeneous.

"Hyperacute. Sharp senses. You know, it's one of the symptoms."

He nodded, remembering vaguely that he'd heard something to that effect—but he'd chalked it up as hallucinatory phenomenon. He walked to the rail and shone his light toward the water. The boat was there—tugging its rope taut from the mooring as the tide swirled about it. The bottom was still fairly dry, indicating that a recent rower had crossed from the island to the mainland.

"Think you can hold onto the rope if I let you down?" he called.

She gave him a quick glance, then picked up the end she had previously touched and tied a loop about her waist. She began crawling toward the rail. Paul fought down a crazy urge to pick her up and carry her; plague be damned. But he had already left himself dangerously open to contagion. Still, he felt the drumming charges of conscience . . . *depart from me, ye accursed, for I was sick and you visited me not* . . .

He turned quickly away, and began knotting the end of the rope about the rail. He reminded himself that any sane person would desert her at once, and swim on to safety. Yet, he could not. In the oversized clothing she looked like a child, hurt and helpless. Paul knew the demanding arrogance that could possess the wounded—*help me, you've got to help me, you damn merciless bastard! . . . No, don't touch me there, damn you!* Too many times, he had heard the sick curse the physician, and the injured curse the rescuer. Blind aggression, trying to strike back at pain.

But the girl made no complaint except the involuntary hurt sounds. She asked nothing, and accepted his aid with a wide-eyed gratitude that left him weak. He thought that it would be easier to leave her if she would only beg or plead, or demand.

"Can you start me swinging a little?" she called as he lowered her toward the water.

Paul's eyes probed the darkness below, trying to sort the shadows, to make certain which was the boat. He used both hands to feed out the rope, and the light laid on the rail only seemed to blind him. She began swinging herself pendulum-wise somewhere beneath him.

"When I say 'ready,' let me go!" she shrilled.

"You're not going to drop!"

"Have to! Boat's out further. Got to swing for it. I can't swim, really."

"But you'll hurt your—"

"Ready!"

Paul still clung to the rope. "I'll let you down into the water and you can hang onto the rope. I'll dive, and then pull you into the boat."

"Uh-uh! You'd have to touch me. You don't want that, do you? Just a second now . . . one more swing . . . ready!"

He let the rope go. With a clatter and a thud, she hit the boat. Three sharp cries of pain clawed at him. Then —muffled sobbing.

"Are you all right?"

Sobs. She seemed not to hear him.

"Jeezis!" He sprinted for the brink of the draw-bridge and dived out over the deep channel. How far . . . down . . . down. . . . Icy water stung his body with sharp whips, then opened to embrace him. He fought to the surface and swam toward the dark shadow of the boat. The sobbing had subsided. He grasped the prow and hauled himself dripping from the channel. She was lying curled in the bottom of the boat.

"Kid . . . you all right, kid?"

"Sorry . . . I'm such a baby," she gasped, and dragged herself back to the stern.

Paul found a paddle, but no oars. He cast off and began digging water toward the other side, but the tide tugged them relentlessly away from the bridge. He gave it up and paddled toward the distant shore. "You know anything about Galveston?" he called—mostly to re-assure himself that she was not approaching him in the darkness with the death-gray hands.

"I used to come here for the summer, I know a little about it."

Paul urged her to talk while he plowed toward the island. Her name was Willie, and she insisted that it was for Willow, not for Wilhelmina. She came from Dallas, and claimed she was a salesman's daughter who was done in by a traveling farmer. The farmer, she explained, was just a wandering dermie who had caught her napping by the roadside. He had stroked her arms until she awoke, then had run away, howling with glee.

"That was three weeks ago," she said. "If I'd had a gun, I'd have dropped him. Of course, I know better now."

Paul shuddered and paddled on. "Why did you head south?"

"I was coming here."

"Here? To Galveston?"

"Uh-huh. I heard someone say that a lot of nuns were coming to the island. I thought maybe they'd take me in."

The moon was high over the lightless city, and the tide had swept the small boat far east from the bridge by the time Paul's paddle dug into the mud beneath the shallow water. He bounded out and dragged the boat through thin marsh grass onto the shore. Fifty yards away, a ramshackle fishing cottage lay sleeping in the moonlight.

"Stay here, Willie," he grunted. "I'll find a couple of boards or something for crutches."

He rummaged about through a shed behind the cottage and brought back a wheelbarrow. Moaning and laughing at once, she struggled into it, and he wheeled her to the house, humming a verse of *Rickshaw Boy*.

"You're a funny guy, Paul. I'm sorry . . ." She jiggled her tousled head in the moonlight, as if she disapproved of her own words.

Paul tried the cottage door, kicked it open, then walked the wheelbarrow up three steps and into a musty room. He struck a match, found an oil lamp with a little kerosene, and lit it. Willie caught her breath.

He looked around. "Company," he grunted.

The company sat in a fragile rocker with a shawl about her shoulders and a shotgun between her knees. She had been dead at least a month. The charge of buckshot had sieved the ceiling and spattered it with bits of gray hair and brown blood.

"Stay here," he told the girl tonelessly. "I'll try to get a dermie somewhere—one who knows how to sew a tendon. Got any ideas?"

She was staring with a sick face at the old woman. "Here? With—"

"She won't bother you," he said as he gently disentangled the gun from the corpse. He moved to a cupboard and found a box of shells behind an orange teapot. "I may not be back, but I'll send somebody."

She buried her face in her plague-stained hands, and he stood for a moment watching her shoulders shiver. "Don't worry . . . I will send somebody." He stepped to the porcelain sink and pocketed a wafer-thin sliver of dry soap.

"What's that for?" she muttered, looking up again.

He thought of a lie, then checked it. "To wash you off of me," he said truthfully. "I might have got too close. Soap won't do much good, but I'll feel better." He looked at the corpse coolly. "Didn't do her much good. Buckshot's the best antiseptic all right."

Willie moaned as he went out the door. He heard her crying as he walked down to the waterfront. She was still crying when he waded back to shore, after a thorough scrubbing. He was sorry he'd spoken cruelly, but it was such a damned relief to get rid of her . . .

With the shotgun cradled on his arm, he began putting distance between himself and the sobbing. But the sound worried his ears, even after he realized that he was no longer hearing her.

He strode a short distance inland past scattered fishing shanties, then took the highway toward the city whose outskirts he was entering. It would be at least an hour's trek to the end of the island where he would be most likely to encounter someone with medical training. The hospitals were down there, the medical school, the most likely place for any charitable nuns—if Willie's rumor were true. Paul meant to capture a dermie doctor or nurse and force the amorous-handed maniac at gunpoint to go to Willie's aid. Then he would be done with her. When she stopped hurting, she would start craving—and he had no doubt that he would be the object of her manual affections.

The bay was wind-chopped in the moonglow, no longer glittering from the lights along 61st Street. The oleanders along Broadway were choked up with weeds. Cats or rabbits rustled in the tousled growth that had been a carefully tended parkway.

Paul wondered why the plague had chosen Man, and not the lower animals. It was true that an occasional dog or cow was seen with the plague, but the focus was upon humanity. And the craving to spread the disease was Man-directed, even in animals. It was as if the neural entity deliberately sought out the species with the most complex nervous system. Was its onslaught really connected with the meteorite swarm? Paul believed that it was.

In the first place, the meteorites had not been predicted. They were not a part of the regular cosmic bombardment. And then there was the strange report that they were *manufactured* projectiles, teeming with frozen microorganisms which came alive upon thawing. In these days of tumult and confusion, however, it was hard. Nevertheless Paul believed it. Neuroderm had no first cousins among Earth diseases.

What manner of beings, then, had sent such a curse? Potential invaders? If so, they were slow in coming. One thing was generally agreed upon by the scientists: the missiles had not been "sent" from another solar planet. Their direction upon entering the atmosphere was wrong. They could conceivably have been fired from an interplanetary launching ship, but their velocity was about equal to the theoretical velocity which a body would obtain in falling sunward from the near-infinite distance. This seemed to hint the projectiles had come from another star.

Paul was startled suddenly by the flare of a match from the shadow of a building. He stopped dead still in the street. A man was leaning against the wall to light a cigarette. He flicked the match out, and Paul watched the cigarette-glow make an arc as the man waved at him.

"Nice night, isn't it?" said the voice from the darkness.

Paul stood exposed in the moonlight, carrying the shotgun at the ready. The voice sounded like that of an adolescent, not fullly changed to its adult timbre. If the youth wasn't a dermie, why wasn't he afraid that Paul might be one? And if he was a dermie, why wasn't he advancing in the hope that Paul might be as yet untouched?

"I said, 'Nice night, isn't it?' Whatcha carrying the gun for? Been shooting rabbits?"

Paul moved a little closer and fumbled for his flashlight. Then he threw its beam on the slouching figure in the shadows. He saw a young man, perhaps sixteen, reclining against the wall. He saw the pearl-gray face that characterized the final and permanent stage of neuroderm! He stood frozen to the spot a dozen feet away from the youth, who blinked perplexedly into the light. The kid was assuming automatically that he was another dermie! Paul tried to keep him blinded while he played along with the fallacy.

"Yeah, it's a nice night. You got any idea where I can find a doctor?"

The boy frowned. "Doctor? You mean you don't know?"

"Know what? I'm new here."

"New? Oh . . ." the boy's nostrils began twitching slightly, as if he were sniffing at the night air. "Well, most of the priests down at Saint Mary's were missionaries. They're all doctors. Why? You sick?"

"No, there's a girl . . . But never mind. How do I get there? And are any of them dermies?"

The boy's eyes wandered peculiarly, and his mouth fell open, as if he had been asked why a circle wasn't square. "You are new, aren't you? They're all dermies, if you want to call them that. Wh—" Again the nostrils were flaring. He flicked the cigarette away suddenly and inhaled a slow draught of the breeze. "I . . . I smell a non-hyper," he muttered.

Paul started to back away. His scalp bristled a warning. The boy advanced a step toward him. A slow beam of anticipation began to glow in his face. He bared his teeth in a wide grain of pleasure.

"You're not a hyper yet," he hissed, moving forward. "I've never had a chance to touch a nonhyper . . ."

"Stay back, or I'll kill you!"

The lad giggled and came on, talking to himself. "The padre says it's wrong, but . . . you smell so . . . so . . . ugh . . ." He flung himself forward with a low throaty cry.

Paul sidestepped the charge and brought the gun barrel down across the boy's head. The dermie sprawled howling in the street. Paul pushed the gun close to his face, but the youth started up again. Paul jabbed viciously with the barrel, and felt it strike and tear. "I don't want to have to blow your head off—"

The boy howled and fell back. He crouched panting on his hands and knees, head hung low, watching a dark puddle of blood gather on the pavement from a deep gash across his cheek. "Whatcha wanta do that for?" he whimpered. "I wasn't gonna hurt you." His tone was that of a wronged and rejected suitor.

"Now, where's Saint Mary's? Is that one of the hospitals? How do I get there?" Paul had backed to a safe distance and was covering the youth with the gun.

"Straight down Broadway . . . to the Boulevard . . . you'll see it down that neighborhood. About the fourth street, I think." The boy looked up, and Paul saw the extent of the gash. It was deep and ragged, and the kid was crying.

"Get up! You're going to lead me there."

Pain had blanketed the call of the craving. The boy struggled to his feet, pressed a handkercheif against the wound, and with an angry glance at Paul, he set out down the road. Paul followed ten yards behind.

"If you take me through any dermie traps, I'll kill you."

"There aren't any traps," the youth mumbled.

Paul snorted unbelief, but did not repeat the warning. "What made you think I was another dermie?" he snapped.

"Because there's no nonhypers in Galveston. This is a hyper colony. A nonhyper used to drift in occasionally, but the priests had the bridge dynamited. The nonhypers upset the colony. As long as there aren't any around to smell, nobody causes any trouble. During the day, there's a guard out on the causeway, and if any hypers come looking for a place to stay, the guard ferries them across. If nonhypers come, he tells them about the colony, and they go away."

Paul groaned. He had stumbled into a rat's nest. Was there no refuge from the gray curse? Now he would have to move on. It seemed a hopeless quest. Maybe the old man he met on his way to Houston had arrived at the only possible hope for peace: submission to the plague. But the thought sickened him somehow. He would have to find some barren island, find a healthy mate, and go to live a savage existence apart from all traces of civilization.

"Didn't the guard stop you at the bridge?" the boy asked. "He never came back today. He must be still out there."

Paul grunted "no" in a tone that warned against idle conversation. He guessed what had happened. The dermie guard had probably spotted some healthy wanderers; and instead of warning them away, he rowed across the drawbridge and set out to chase them. His body probably lay along the highway somewhere, if the hypothetical wanderers were armed.

When they reached 23rd Street, a few blocks from the heart of the city, Paul hissed at the boy to stop. He heard someone laugh. Footsteps were wandering along the sidewalk, overhung by trees. He whispered to the boy to take refuge behind a hedge. They crouched in the shadows several yards apart while the voices drew nearer.

"Brother James had a nice tenor," someone said softly. "But he sings his Latin with a western drawl. It sounds . . . well . . . peculiar, to say the least. Brother John is a stickler for pronunciation. He won't let Fra James solo. Says it gives a burlesque effect to the choir. Says it makes the sisters giggle."

The other man chuckled quietly and started to reply. But his voice broke off suddenly. The footsteps stopped a dozen feet from Paul's hiding place. Paul, peering through the hedge, saw a pair of brown-robed monks standing on the sidewalk. They were looking around suspiciously.

"Brother Thomas, do you smell—"

"Aye, I smell it."

Paul changed his position slightly, so as to keep the gun pointed toward the pair of plague-stricken monastics. They stood in embarrassed silence, peering into the darkness, and shuffling their feet uneasily. One of them suddenly pinched his nose between thumb and forefinger. His companion followed suit.

"Blessed be God," quavered one.

"Blessed be His Holy Name," answered the other.

"Blessed be Jesus Christ, true God and true Man."

"Blessed be . . ."

Gathering their robes high about their shins, the two monks turned and scurried away, muttering the Litany of the Divine Praises as they went. Paul stood up and stared after them in amazement. The sight of dermies running from a potential victim was almost beyond belief. He questioned his young guide. Still holding the handkerchief against his bleeding face, the boy hung his head.

"Bishop made a ruling against touching nonhypers," he explained miserably. "Says it's a sin, unless the nonhyper submits of his own free will. Says even then it's wrong, except in the ordinary ways that people come in contact with each other. Calls it fleshly desire, and all that."

"Then why did you try to do it?"

"I ain't so religious."

"Well, sonny, you better get religious until we come to the hospital. Now, let's go."

They marched on down Broadway encountering no other pedestrians. Twenty minutes later, they were standing in the shadows before a hulking brick building, some of whose windows were yellow with lamplight. Moonlight bathed the statue of a woman standing on a ledge over the entrance, indicating to Paul that this was the hospital.

"All right, boy. You go in and send out a dermie doctor. Tell him somebody wants to see him, but if you say I'm not a dermie, I'll come in and kill you. Now move. And don't come back. Stay to get your face fixed."

The youth stumbled toward the entrance. Paul sat in the shadow of a tree, where he could see twenty yards in all directions and guard himself against approach. Soon a black-clad priest came out of the emergency entrance, stopped on the sidewalk, and glanced around.

"Over here!" Paul hissed from across the street.

The priest advanced uncertainly. In the center of the road he stopped again, and held his nose. "Y-you're a nonhyper," he said, almost accusingly.

"That's right, and I've got a gun, so don't try anything."

"What's wrong? Are you sick? The lad said—"

"There's a dermie girl down the island. She's been shot. Tendon behind her heel is cut clean through. You're going to help her."

"Of course, but . . ." The priest paused. "You? A nonhyper? Helping a so-called dermie?" His voice went high with amazement.

"So I'm a sucker!" Paul barked. "Now get what you need, and come on."

"The Lord bless you," the priest mumbled in embarrassment as he hurried away.

"Don't sic any of your maniacs on me!" Paul called after him. "I'm armed."

"I'll have to bring a surgeon," the cleric said over his shoulder.

Five minutes later, Paul heard the muffled grunt of a starter. Then an engine coughed to life. Startled, he scurried away from the tree and sought safety in a clump of shrubs. An ambulance backed out of the driveway and into the street. It parked at the curb by the tree, engine running. A pallid face glanced out curiously toward the shadows. "Where are you?" it called, but it was not the priest's voice.

Paul stood up and advanced a few steps.

"We'll have to wait on Father Mendelhaus," the driver called. "He'll be a few minutes."

"You a dermie?"

"Of course. But don't worry. I've plugged my nose and I'm wearing rubber gloves. I can't smell you. The sight of a nonhyper arouses some craving, of course. But it can be overcome with a little will power. I won't infect you, although I don't understand why you nonhypers fight so hard. You're bound to catch it sooner or later. And the world can't get back to normal until everybody has it."

Paul avoided the startling thought. "You the surgeon?"

"Uh, yes. Father Williamson's the name. I'm not really a specialist, but I did some surgery in Korea. How's the girl's condition? Suffering shock?"

"I wouldn't know."

They fell silent until Father Mendelhaus returned. He came across the street carrying a bag in one hand and a brown bottle in the other. He held the bottle by the neck with a pair of tongs and Paul could see the exterior of the bottle steaming slightly as the priest passed through the beam of the ambulance's headlights. He placed the flask on the curb without touching it, then spoke to the man in the shadows.

"Would you step behind the hedge and disrobe, young man? Then rub yourself thoroughly with this oil."

"I doubt it," Paul snapped. "What is it?"

"Don't worry, it's been in the sterilizer. That's what took me so long. It may be a little hot for you, however. It's only an antiseptic and deodorant. It'll kill your odor, and it'll also give you some protection against picking up stray micro-organisms."

After a few moments of anxious hesitation, Paul decided to trust the priest. He carried the hot flask into the brush, undressed, and bathed himself with the warm aromatic oil. Then he slipped back into his clothes and reapproached the ambulance.

"Ride in back," Mendelhaus told him. "And you won't be infected. No one's been in there for several weeks, and as you probably know, the micro-organisms die after a few hours exposure. They have to be transmitted from skin to skin, or else an object has to be handled very soon after a hyper has touched it."

Paul warily climbed inside. Mendelhaus opened a slide and spoke through it from the front seat. "You'll have to show us the way."

"Straight out Broadway. Say, where did you get the gasoline for this wagon."

The priest paused. "That has been something of a secret. Oh well . . . I'll tell you. There's a tanker out in the harbor. The people left town too quickly to think of it. Automobiles are scarcer than fuel in Galveston. Up north, you find them stalled everywhere. But since Galveston didn't have any through-traffic, there were no cars running out of gas. The ones we have are the ones that were left in the repair shop. Something wrong with them. And we don't have any mechanics to fix them."

Paul neglected to mention that he was qualified for the job. The priest might get ideas. He fell into gloomy silence as the ambulance turned onto Broadway and headed down-island. He watched the back of the priests' heads, silhouetted against the headlighted pavement. They seemed not at all concerned about their disease. Mendelhaus was a slender man, with a blond crew cut and rather bushy eyebrows. He had a thin, aristocratic face—now plague-gray—but jovial enough. It might be the face of an ascetic, but for the quick blue eyes that seemed full of lively interest rather than inward-turning mysticism. Williamson, on the other hand, was a rather plain man, with a stolid tweedy look, despite his black cassock.

"What do you think of our plan here?" asked Father Mendelhaus.

"What plan?" Paul grunted.

"Oh, didn't the boy tell you? We're trying to make the

island a refuge for hypers who are willing to sublimate their craving and turn their attentions toward reconstruction. We're also trying to make an objective study of this neural condition. We have some good scientific minds, too —Doctor Relmone of Fordham, Father Seyes of Notre Dame, two biologists from Boston College. . . ."

"Dermies trying to cure the plague?" Paul gasped.

Mendelhaus laughed merrily. "I didn't say cure it, son. I said 'study it.'"

"Why?"

"To learn how to live with it, of course. It's been pointed out by our philosophers that things become evil only through human misuse. Morphine, for instance, is a product of the Creator; it is therefore good when properly used for relief of pain. When mistreated by an addict, it becomes a monster. We bear this in mind as we study neuroderm."

Paul snorted contemptuously. "Leprosy is evil, I suppose, because Man mistreated bacteria?"

The priest laughed again. "You've got me there. I'm no philosopher. But you can't compare neuroderm with leprosy."

Paul shuddered. "The hell I can't! It's worse."

"Ah? Suppose you tell me what makes it worse? List the symptoms for me."

Paul hesitated, listing them mentally. They were: discoloration of the skin, low fever, hallucinations, and the insane craving to infect others. They seemed bad enough, so he listed them orally. "Of course, people don't die of it," he added. "But which is worse, insanity or death?"

The priest turned to smile back at him through the porthole. "Would you call me insane? It's true that victims have frequently lost their minds. But that's not a direct result of neuroderm. Tell me, how would you feel if everyone screamed and ran when they saw you coming, or hunted you down like a criminal? How long would your sanity last?"

Paul said nothing. Perhaps the anathema was a contributing factor. . . .

"Unless you were of very sound mind to begin with, you probably couldn't endure it."

"But the craving . . . and the hallucinations . . ."

"True," murmured the priest thoughtfully. "The hallucinations. Tell me something else, if all the world was

blind save one man, wouldn't the world be inclined to
call that man's sight a hallucination? And the man with
eyes might even come to agree with the world."

Again Paul was silent. There was no arguing with
Mendelhaus, who probably suffered the strange delusions
and thought them real.

"And the craving," the priest went on. "It's true that
the craving can be a rather unpleasant symptom. It's the
condition's way of perpetuating itself. Although we're not
certain how it works, it seems able to stimulate erotic
sensations in the hands. We do know the micro-organisms
get to the brain, but we're not yet sure what they do
there."

"What facts have you discovered?" Paul asked cautiously.

Mendelhaus grinned at him. "Tut! I'm not going to tell
you, because I don't want to be called a 'crazy dermie.'
You wouldn't believe me, you see."

Paul glanced outside and saw that they were approaching the vicinity of the fishing cottage. He pointed out the
lamplit window to the driver, and the ambulance turned
onto a side road. Soon they were parked behind the
shanty. The priests scrambled out and carried the
stretcher toward the light, while Paul skulked to a safer
distance and sat down in the grass to watch. When Willie
was safe in the vehicle, he meant to walk back to the
bridge, swim across the gap, and return to the mainland.

Soon Mendelhaus came out and walked toward him
with a solemn stride, although Paul was sitting quietly in
the deepest shadow—invisible, he had thought. He arose
quickly as the priest approached. Anxiety tightened his
throat. "Is she . . . is Willie . . . ?"

"She's irrational," Mendelhaus murmured sadly. "Almost . . . less than sane. Some of it may be due to high
fever, but . . ."

"Yes?"

"She tried to kill herself. With a knife. Said something
about buckshot being the best way, or something . . ."

"Jeezis! Jeezis!" Paul sank weakly in the grass and covered his face with his hands.

"Blessed be His Holy Name," murmured the priest by
way of turning the oath aside. "She didn't hurt herself
badly, though. Wrist's cut a little. She was too weak to

do a real job of it. Father Will's giving her a hypo and a
tetanus shot and some sulfa. We're out of penicillin."

He stopped speaking and watched Paul's wretchedness
for a moment. "You love the girl, don't you?"

Paul stiffened. "Are you crazy? Love a little tramp
dermie? Jeezis . . ."

"Blessed be—"

"Listen! Will she be all right? I'm getting out of here!"
He climbed unsteadily to his feet.

"I don't know, son. Infection's the real threat, and
shock. If we'd got to her sooner, she'd have been safer.
And if she was in the ultimate stage of neuroderm, it
would help."

"Why?"

"Oh, various reasons. You'll learn, someday. But listen, you look exhausted. Why don't you come back to
the hospital with us? The third floor is entirely vacant.
There's no danger of infection up there, and we keep a
sterile room ready just in case we get a nonhyper case.
You can lock the door inside, if you want to, but it
wouldn't be necessary. Nuns are on the floor below. Our
male staff lives in the basement. There aren't any laymen
in the building. I'll guarantee that you won't be bothered."

"No, I've got to go," he growled, then softened his
voice: "I appreciate it though, Father."

"Whatever you wish. I'm sorry, though. You might be
able to provide yourself with some kind of transportation
if you waited."

"Uh-uh! I don't mind telling you, your island makes me
jumpy."

"Why?"

Paul glanced at the priest's gray hands. "Well . . . you
still feel the craving, don't you?"

Mendelhaus touched his nose. "Cotton plugs, with a little camphor. I can't smell you." He hesitated. "No, I
won't lie to you. The urge to touch is still there to some
extent."

"And in a moment of weakness, somebody might—"

The priest straightened his shoulders. His eyes went
chilly. "I have taken certain vows, young man. Sometimes
when I see a beautiful woman, I feel desire. When I see
a man eating a thick steak on a fast-day, I feel envy and
hunger. When I see a doctor earning large fees, I chafe
under the vow of poverty. But by denying desire's de-

mands, one learns to make desire useful in other ways. Sublimation, some call it. A priest can use it and do more useful work thereby. I am a priest."

He nodded curtly, turned on his heel and strode away. Halfway to the cottage, he paused. "She's calling for someone named Paul. Know who it might be? Family perhaps?"

Paul stood speechless. The priest shrugged and continued toward the lighted doorway.

"Father, wait . . ."

"Yes?"

"I—I am a little tired. The room . . . I mean, will you show me where to get transportation tomorrow?"

"Certainly."

Before midnight, the party had returned to the hospital. Paul lay on a comfortable mattress for the first time in weeks, sleepless, and staring at the moonlight on the sill. Somewhere downstairs, Willie was lying unconscious in an operating room, while the surgeon tried to repair the torn tendon. Paul had ridden back with them in the ambulance, sitting a few feet from the stretcher, avoiding her sometimes wandering arms, and listening to her delirious moaning.

Now he felt his skin crawling with belated hypochondria. What a fool he had been—touching the rope, the boat, the wheelbarrow, riding in the ambulance. There were a thousand ways he could have picked up a few stray micro-organisms lingering from a dermie's touch. And now, he lay here in this nest of disease. . . .

But strange—it was the most peaceful, the sanest place he'd seen in months. The religious orders simply accepted the plague—with masochistic complacency perhaps—but calmly. A cross, or a penance, or something. But no, they seemed to accept it almost gladly. Nothing peculiar about that. All dermies went wild-eyed with happiness about the "lovely desire" they possessed. The priests weren't wild-eyed.

Neither was normal man equipped with socially-shaped sexual desire. Sublimation?

"Peace," he muttered, and went to sleep.

A knocking at the door awoke him at dawn. He grunted at it disgustedly and sat up in bed. The door, which he had forgotten to lock, swung open. A chubby nun with a breakfast tray started into the room. She saw his face, then stopped. She closed her eyes, wrinkled her nose, and framed a silent prayer with her lips. Then she backed slowly out.

"I'm sorry, sir!" she quavered through the door. "I— I knew there was a patient in here, but I didn't know . . . you weren't a hyper. Forgive me."

He heard her scurrying away down the hall. Somehow, he began to feel safe. But wasn't that exactly what they wanted him to feel! He realized suddenly that he was trapped. He had left the shotgun in the emergency room. What was he—guest or captive? Months of fleeing from the gray terror had left him suspicious.

Soon he would find out. He arose and began dressing. Before he finished, Mendelhaus came. He did not enter, but stood in the hallway beyond the door. He smiled a faint greeting, and said, "So you're Paul?"

He felt heat rising in his face. "She's awake, then?" he asked gruffly.

The priest nodded. "Want to see her?"

"No, I've got to be going."

"It would do her good."

He coughed angrily. Why did the black-cassocked dermie have to put it that way? "Well it wouldn't do me any good!" he snarled. "I've been around too many gray-leather hides already!"

Mendelhaus shrugged, but his eyes bore a hint of contempt. "As you wish. You may leave by the outside stairway—to avoid disturbing the sisters."

"To avoid being touched, you mean!"

"No one will touch you."

Paul finished dressing in silence. The reversal of attitudes disturbed him. He resented the seeming "tolerance" that was being extended him. It was like asylum inmates being "tolerant" of the psychiatrist.

"I'm ready!" he growled.

Mendelhaus led him down the corridor and out onto a sunlit balcony. They descended a stone stairway while the priest talked over his shoulder.

"She's still not fully rational, and there's some fever. It wouldn't be anything to worry about two years ago, but now we're out of most of the latest drugs. If sulfa won't hold the infection, we'll have to amputate, of course. We should know in two or three days."

He paused and looked back at Paul, who had stopped on the stairway. "Coming?"

"Where is she?" Paul asked weakly. "I'll see her."

The priest frowned. "You don't have to, son. I'm sorry if I implied any obligation on your part. Really, you've done enough. I gather.that you saved her life. Very few nonhypers would do a thing like that. I—"

"Where is she?" he snapped angrily.

The priest nodded. "Downstairs. Come on."

As they re-entered the building on the ground floor, the priest cupped his hands to his mouth and called out, "Nonhyper coming! Plug your noses, or get out of the way! Avoid circumstances of temptation!"

When they moved along the corridor, it was Paul who felt like the leper. Mendelhaus led him into the third room.

Willie saw him enter and hid her gray hands beneath the sheet. She smiled faintly, tried to sit up, and failed. Williamson and a nun-nurse who had both been standing by the bedside turned to leave the room. Mendelhaus followed them out and closed the door.

There was a long, painful pause. Willie tried to grin. He shuffled his feet.

"They've got me in a cast," she said conversationally.

"You'll be all right," he said hastily. "It won't be long before you'll be up. Galveston's a good place for you. They're all dermies here."

She clenched her eyes tightly shut. "God! God! I hope I never hear that word again. After last night . . . that old woman in the rocking chair . . . I stayed there all alone . . . and the wind'd start the chair rocking. Ooh!" She looked at him with abnormally bright eyes. "I'd rather die than touch anybody now . . . after seeing that. Somebody touched her, didn't they, Paul? That's why she did it, wasn't it?"

He squirmed and backed toward the door. "Willie . . . I'm sorry for what I said. I mean—"

"Don't worry, Paul! I wouldn't touch you now." She clenched her hands and brought them up before her face, to stare at them with glittering hate. "I loathe myself!" she hissed.

What was it Mendelhaus had said, about the dermie

going insane because of being an outcast rather than because of the plague? But she wouldn't be an outcast here.
Only among nonhypers, like himself . . .

"Get well quick, Willie," he muttered, then hurriedly
slipped out into the corridor. She called his name twice,
then fell silent.

"That was quick," murmured Mendelhaus, glancing at
his pale face.

"Where can I get a car?"

The priest rubbed his chin. "I was just speaking to
Brother Matthew about that. Uh . . . how would you
like to have a small yacht instead?"

Paul caught his breath. A yacht would mean access to
the seas, and to an island. A yacht was the perfect solution. He stammered gratefully.

"Good," said Mendelhaus. "There's a small craft in dry
dock down at the basin. It was apparently left there because there weren't any dock crews around to get her
afloat again. I took the liberty of asking Brother Matthew
to find some men and get her in the water."

"Dermies?"

"Of course. The boat will be fumigated, but it isn't
really necessary. The infection dies out in a few hours.
It'll take a while, of course, to get the boat ready. Tomorrow . . . next day, maybe. Bottom's cracked; it'll need
some patching."

Paul's smile weakened. More delay. Two more days of
living in the gray shadow. Was the priest really to be
trusted? Why should he even provide the boat? The jaws
of an invisible trap, slowly closing.

Mendelhaus saw his doubt. "If you'd rather leave now,
you're free to do so. We're really not going to as much
trouble as it might seem. There are several yachts at the
dock; Brother Matthew's been preparing to clean one or
two up for our own use. And we might as well let you
have one. They've been deserted by their owners. And
. . . well . . . you helped the girl when nobody else
would have done so. Consider the boat as our way of
returning the favor, eh?"

A yacht. The open sea. A semitropical island, unin-
habited, on the brink of the Caribbean. And a woman,
of course—chosen from among the many who would be
willing to share such an escape. Peculiarly, he glanced at
Willie's door. It was too bad about her. But she'd get

along okay. The yacht . . . if he were only certain of Mendelhaus' intentions . . .

The priest began frowning at Paul's hesitation. "Well?"

"I don't want to put you to any trouble. . . ."

"Nonsense! You're still afraid of us! Very well, come with me. There's someone I want you to see." Mendelhaus turned and started down the corridor.

Paul lingered. "Who . . . what—"

"Come on!" the priest snapped impatiently.

Reluctantly, Paul followed him to the stairway. They descended to a gloomy basement and entered a smelly laboratory through a double-door. Electric illumination startled him; then he heard the sound of a gasoline engine and knew that the power was generated locally.

"Germicidal lamps," murmured the priest, following his ceilingward gaze. "Some of them are. Don't worry about touching things. It's sterile in here."

"But it's not sterile for your convenience," growled an invisible voice. "And it won't be sterile at all if you don't stay out! Beat it, preacher!"

Paul looked for the source of the voice, and saw a small, short-necked man bending his shaggy gray head over a microscope at the other end of the lab. He had spoken without glancing up at his visitors.

"This is Doctor Seevers, of Princeton, son," said the priest, unruffled by the scientist's ire. "Claims he's an atheist, but personally I think he's a puritan. Doctor, this is the young man I was telling you about. Will you tell him what you know about neuroderm?"

Seevers jotted something on a pad, but kept his eye to the instrument. "Why don't we just give it to him, and let him find out for himself?" the scientist grumbled sadistically.

"Don't frighten him, you heretic! I brought him here to be illuminated."

"Illuminate him yourself. I'm busy. And stop calling me names. I'm not an atheist; I'm a biochemist."

"Yesterday you were a biophysicist. Now, entertain my young man." Mendelhaus blocked the doorway with his body. Paul, with his jaw clenched angrily, had turned to leave.

"That's all I can do, preacher," Seevers grunted. "Entertain him. I know nothing. Absolutely nothing. I have some observed data. I have noticed some correlations. I

have seen things happen. I have traced the patterns of
the happenings and found some probable common de-
nominators. And that is all! I admit it. Why don't you
preachers admit it in your racket?"

"Seevers, as you can see, is inordinately proud of his
humility—if that's not a paradox," the priest said to Paul.

"Now, Doctor, this young man—"

Seevers heaved a resigned sigh. His voice went sour-
sweet. "All right, sit down, young man. I'll entertain you
as soon as I get through counting free nerve-endings in
this piece of skin."

Mendelhaus winked at his guest. "Seevers calls it
masochism when we observe a fast-day or do penance.
And there he sits, ripping off patches of his own hide to
look at through his peeping glass. Masochism—heh!"

"Get out, preacher!" the scientist bellowed.

Mendelhaus laughed mockingly, nodded Paul toward a
chair, and left the lab. Paul sat uneasily watching the back
of Seevers' lab jacket.

"Nice bunch of people really—these black-frocked ya-
hoos," Seevers murmured conversationally. "If they'd just
stop trying to convert me."

"Doctor Seevers, maybe I'd better—"

"Quiet! You bother me. And sit still, I can't stand to
have people running in and out of here. You're in; now
stay in."

Paul fell silent. He was uncertain whether or not
Seevers was a dermie. The small man's lab jacket
bunched up to hide the back of his neck, and the sleeves
covered his arms. His hands were rubber-gloved, and a
knot of white cord behind his head told Paul that he was
wearing a gauze mask. His ears were bright pink, but
their color was meaningless; it took several months for the
gray coloring to seep to all areas of the skin. But Paul
guessed he was a dermie—and wearing the gloves and
mask to keep his equipment sterile.

He glanced idly around the large room. There were
several glass cages of rats against the wall. They seemed
airtight, with ducts for forced ventilation. About half the
rats were afflicted with neuroderm in its various stages. A
few wore shaved patches of skin where the disease had
been freshly and forcibly inflicted. Paul caught the fleeting
impression that several of the animals were staring at him
fixedly. He shuddered and looked away.

He glanced casually at the usual maze of laboratory glassware, then turned his attention to a pair of hemispheres, suspended like a trophy on the wall. He recognized them as the twin halves of one of the meteorites, with the small jelly-pocket in the center. Beyond it hung a large picture frame containing several typewritten sheets. Another frame held four pictures of bearded scientists from another century, obviously clipped from magazine or textbook. There was nothing spectacular about the lab. It smelled of clean dust and sour things. Just a small respectable workshop.

Seevers' chair creaked suddenly. "It checks," he said to himself. "It checks again. Forty per cent increase." He threw down the stub pencil and whirled suddenly. Paul saw a pudgy round face with glittering eyes. A dark splotch of neuroderm had crept up from the chin to split his mouth and cover one cheek and an eye, giving him the appearance of a black and white bulldog with a mixed color muzzle.

"It checks," he barked at Paul, then smirked contentedly.

"What checks?"

The scientist rolled up a sleeve to display a patch of adhesive tape on a portion of his arm which had been discolored by the disease. "Here," he grunted. "Two weeks ago this area was normal. I took a centimeter of skin from right next to this one, and counted the nerve endings. Since that time, the derm's crept down over the area. I took another square centimeter today, and recounted. Forty per cent increase."

Paul frowned with disbelief. It was generally known that neuroderm had a sensitizing effect, but new nerve endings . . . No. He didn't believe it.

"Third time I've checked it," Seevers said happily. "One place ran up to sixty-five per cent. Heh! Smart little bugs, aren't they? Inventing new somesthetic receptors that way!"

Paul swallowed with difficulty. "What did you say?" he gasped.

Seevers inspected him serenely. "So you're a nonhyper, are you? Yes, indeed, I can smell that you are. Vile, really. Can't understand why sensible hypers would want to paw you. But then, I've insured myself against such foolishness."

He said it so casually that Paul blinked before he caught the full impact of it. "Y-y-you've done what?"

"What I said. When I first caught it, I simply sat down with a velvet-tipped stylus and located the spots on my hands that gave rise to pleasurable sensations. Then I burned them out with an electric needle. There aren't many of them, really—one or two points per square centimeter." He tugged off his gloves and exhibited pick-marked palms to prove it. "I didn't want to be bothered with such silly urges. Waste of time, chasing nonhypers—for me it is. I never learned what it's like, so I've never missed it." He turned his hands over and stared at them. "Stubborn little critters keep growing new ones, and I keep burning them out."

Paul leaped to his feet. "Are you trying to tell me that the plague causes new nerve cells to grow?"

Seevers looked up coldly. "Ah, yes. You came here to be illoooominated, as the padre put it. If you wish to be de-idiotized, please stop shouting. Otherwise, I'll ask you to leave."

Paul, who had felt like leaving a moment ago, now subsided quickly. "I'm sorry," he snapped, then softened his tone to repeat: "I'm sorry."

Seevers took a deep breath, stretched his short meaty arms in an unexpected yawn, then relaxed and grinned. "Sit down, sit down, m'boy. I'll tell you what you want to know, if you really want to know anything. Do you?"

"Of course!"

"You don't! You just want to know how you—whatever your name is—will be affected by events. You don't care about understanding for its own sake. Few people do. That's why we're in this mess. The padre now, he cares about understanding events—but not for their own sake. He cares, but for his flock's sake and for his God's sake—which is, I must admit, a better attitude than that of the common herd, whose only interest is in their own safety. But if people would just want to understand events for the understanding's sake, we wouldn't be in such a pickle."

Paul watched the professor's bright eyes and took the lecture quietly.

"And so, before I illuminate you, I want to make an impossible request."

"Yes, sir."

"I ask you to be completely objective," Seevers continued, rubbing the bridge of his nose and covering his eyes with his hand. "I want you to forget you ever heard of neuroderm while you listen to me. Rid yourself of all preconceptions, especially those connected with fear. Pretend these are purely hypothetical events that I'm going to discuss." He took his hands down from his eyes and grinned sheepishly. "It always embarrasses me to ask for that kind of cooperation when I know damn well I'll never get it."

"I'll try to be objective, sir."

"Bah!" Seevers slid down to sit on his spine, and hooked the base of his skull over the back of the chair. He blinked thoughtfully at the ceiling for a moment, then folded his hands across his small paunch and closed his eyes.

When he spoke again, he was speaking to himself: "Assume a planet, somewhat earthlike, but not quite. It has carboniferous life forms, but not human. Warm blooded, probably, and semi-intelligent. And the planet has something else—it has an overabundance of parasite forms. Actually, the various types of parasites are the dominant species. The warm blooded animals are the parasites' vegetables, so to speak. Now, during two billion years, say, of survival contests between parasite species, some parasites are quite likely to develop some curious methods of adaption. Methods of insuring the food supply —animals, who must have been taking a beating."

Seevers glanced down from the ceiling. "Tell me, youngster, what major activity did Man invent to secure his vegetable food supply?"

"Agriculture?"

"Certainly. Man is a parasite, as far as vegetables are concerned. But he learned to eat his cake and have it, too. He learned to perpetuate the species he was devouring. A very remarkable idea, if you stop to think about it. Very!"

"I don't see—"

"Hush! Now, let's suppose that one species of microparasites on our hypothetical planet learned, through long evolutionary processes, to stimulate regrowth in the animal tissue they devoured. Through exuding controlled amounts of growth hormone, I think. Quite an advancement, eh?"

Paul had begun leaning forward tensely.

"But it's only the first step. It let the host live longer, although not pleasantly, I imagine. The growth control would be clumsy at first. But soon, all parasite-species either learned to do it, or died out. Then came the contest for the best kind of control. The parasites who kept their hosts in the best physical condition naturally did a better job of survival—since the parasite-ascendancy had cut down on the food supply, just as Man wastes his own resources. And since animals were contending among themselves for a place in the sun, it was to the parasite's advantage to help insure the survival of his host-species—through growth control."

Seevers winked solemnly. "Now begins the downfall of the parasites—their decadence. They concentrated all their efforts along the lines of . . . uh . . . scientific farming, you might say. They began growing various sorts of defense and attack weapons for their hosts—weird biodevices, perhaps. Horns, swords, fangs, stingers, poisonthrowers—we can only guess. But eventually, one group of parasites hit upon—what?"

Paul, who was beginning to stir uneasily, could only stammer. Where was Seevers getting all this?

"Say it!" the scientist demanded.

"The . . . nervous system?"

"That's right. You don't need to whisper it. The nervous system. It was probably an unsuccessful parasite at first, because nerve tissue grows slowly. And it's a long stretch of evolution between a microspecies which could stimulate nerve growth and one which could direct and utilize that growth for the host's advantage—and for its own. But at last, after a long struggle, our little species gets there. It begins sharpening the host's senses, building up complex senses from aggregates of old style receptors, and increasing the host's intelligence within limits."

Seevers grinned mischievously. "Comes a planetary shake-up of the first magnitude. Such parasites would naturally pick the host species with the highest intelligence to begin with. With the extra boost, this brainy animal quickly beats down its own enemies, and consequently the enemies of its microbenefactor. It puts itself in much the same position that Man's in on Earth—lord it over the beasts, divine right to run the place, and all that. Now understand—it's the animal who's become intelligent, not the parasites. The parasites are operating on complex instinct patterns, like a hive of bees. They're wonderful neurological engineers—like bees are good structural engineers; blind instinct, accumulated through evolution."

He paused to light a cigarette. "If you feel ill, young man, there's drinking water in that bottle. You look ill."

"I'm all right!"

"Well, to continue: The intelligent animal became master of his planet. Threats to his existence were overcome—unless he was a threat to himself, like we are. But now, the parasites had found a safe home. No new threats to force readaption. They sat back and sighed and became stagnant—as unchanging as horseshoe crabs or amoeba or other Earth ancients. They kept right on working in their neurological beehives, and now they became cultivated by the animal, who recognized their benefactors. They didn't know it, but they were no longer the dominant species. They had insured their survival by leaning on their animal prop, who now took care of them with god-like charity—and selfishness. The parasites had achieved biological heaven. They kept on working, but they stopped fighting. The host was their welfare state, you might say. End of a sequence."

He blew a long breath of smoke and leaned forward to watch Paul, with casual amusement. Paul suddenly realized that he was sitting on the edge of his chair and gaping. He forced a relaxation.

"Wild guesswork," he breathed uncertainly.

"Some of it's guesswork," Seevers admitted. "But none of it's wild. There is supporting evidence. It's in the form of a message."

"Message?"

"Sure. Come, I'll show you." Seevers arose and moved toward the wall. He stopped before the two hemispheres. "On second thought, you better show yourself. Take down that sliced meteorite, will you? It's sterile."

Paul crossed the room, climbed unsteadily upon a bench, and brought down the globular meteorite. It was the first time he had examined one of the things, and he inspected it curiously. It was a near-perfect sphere, about eight inches in diameter, with a four-inch hollow in the center. The globe was made up of several concentric shells, tightly fitted, each apparently of a different metal. It was not seemingly heavier than aluminum, although the outer shell was obviously of tough steel.

"Set it face down," Seevers told him. "Both halves. Give it a quick little twist. The shells will come apart. Take out the center shell—the hard, thin one between the soft protecting shells."

"How do you know their purposes?" Paul growled as he followed instructions. The shells came apart easily.

"Envelopes are to protect messages," snorted Seevers.

Paul sorted out the hemispheres, and found two mirror-polished shells of paper-thin tough metal. They bore no inscription, either inside or out. He gave Seevers a puzzled frown.

"Handle them carefully while they're out of the protectors. They're already a little blurred . . ."

"I don't see any message."

"There's a small bottle of iron filings in that drawer by your knee. Sift them carefully over the outside of the shells. That powder isn't fine enough, really, but it's the best I could do. Felger had some better stuff up at Princeton, before we all got out. This business wasn't my discovery, incidentally."

Baffled, Paul found the iron filings and dusted the mirror-shells with the powder. Delicate patterns appeared —latitudinal circles, etched in iron dust and laced here and there with diagonal lines. He gasped. It looked like the map of a planet.

"I know what you're thinking," Seevers said. "That's what we thought too, at first. Then Felger came up with this very fine dust. Fine as they are, those lines are rows of pictograph symbols. You can make them out vaguely with a good reading glass, even with this coarse stuff. It's magnetic printing—like two-dimensional wire-recording. Evidently, the animals that printed it had either very powerful eyes, or a magnetic sense."

"Anyone understand it?"

"Princeton staff was working on it when the world went crazy. They figured out enough to guess at what I've just told you. They found five different shell-messages among a dozen or so spheres. One of them was a sort of a key. A symbol equated to a diagram of a carbon atom. Another symbol equated to a pi in binary numbers. Things like that—about five hundred symbols, in fact. Some we couldn't figure. Then they defined other symbols by what amounted to blank-filling quizzes. Things like—'A star is . . .' and there would be the unknown symbol. We would try to decide whether it meant 'hot,' 'white,' 'huge,' and so forth."

"And you managed it?"

"In part. The ruthless way in which the missiles were opened destroyed some of the clarity. The senders were guilty of their own brand of anthropomorphism. They projected their own psychology on us. They expected us to open the things shell by shell, cautiously, and figure out the text before we went further. Heh! What happens? Some machinist grabs one, shakes it, weighs it, sticks it on a lathe, and—brrrrrr! Our curiosity is still rather apelike. Stick our arm in a gopher hole to see if there's a rattlesnake inside."

There was a long silence while Paul stood peering over the patterns on the shell. "Why haven't people heard about this?" he asked quietly.

"Heard about it!" Seevers roared. "And how do you propose to tell them about it?"

Paul shook his head. It was easy to forget that Man had scurried away from his presses and his broadcasting stations and his railroads, leaving his mechanical creatures to sleep in their own rust while he fled like a bee-stung bear before the strange terror.

"What, exactly, do the patterns say, Doctor?"

"I've told you some of it—the evolutionary origin of the neuroderm parasites. We also pieced together their reasons for launching the missiles across space—several thousand years ago. Their sun was about to flare into a supernova. They worked out a theoretical space-drive, but they couldn't fuel it—needed some element that was scarce in their system. They could get to their outer planet, but that wouldn't help much. So they just cultured up a batch of their parasite-benefactors, rolled them into these balls, and fired them like charges of buckshot at various stars. Interception-course, naturally. They meant to miss just a little, so that the projectiles would swing into long elliptical orbits around the suns—close enough in to intersect the radiational 'life-belt' and eventually cross paths with planets whose orbits were near-circular. Looks like they hit us on the first pass."

"You mean they weren't aiming at Earth in particular?"

"Evidently not. They couldn't know we were here. Not at a range like that. Hundreds of light-years. They just took a chance on several stars. Shipping off their pets was sort of a last ditch stand against extinction—symbolic, to be sure—but a noble gesture, as far as they were concerned. A giving away of part of their souls. Like a man writing his will and leaving his last worldly possession to some unknown species beyond the stars. Imagine them standing there—watching the projectiles being fired out toward deep space. There goes their inheritance, to an unknown heir, or perhaps to no one. The little creatures that brought them up from beasthood."

Seevers paused, staring up at the sunlight beyond the high basement window. He was talking to himself again, quietly: "You can see them turn away and silently go back . . . to wait for their collapsing sun to reach the critical point, the detonating point. They've left their last mark—a dark and uncertain benediction to the cosmos."

"You're a fool, Seevers," Paul grunted suddenly.

Seevers whirled, whitening. His hand darted out forgetfully toward the young man's arm, but he drew it back as Paul sidestepped.

"You actually regard this thing as desirable, don't you?" Paul asked. "You can't see that you're under its effect. Why does it affect people that way? And you say I can't be objective."

The professor smiled coldly. "I didn't say it's desirable. I was simply pointing out that the beings who sent it saw it as desirable. They were making some unwarranted assumptions."

"Maybe they just didn't care."

"Of course they cared. Their fallacy was that we would open it as they would have done—cautiously. Perhaps they couldn't see how a creature could be both brash and intelligent. They meant for us to read the warning on the shells before we went further."

"Warning . . . ?"

Seevers smiled bitterly. "Yes, warning. There was one group of oversized symbols on all the spheres. See that pattern on the top ring? It says, in effect—'Finder-creatures, you who destroy your own people—if you do this thing, then destroy this container without penetrating deeper. If you are self-destroyers, then the contents will only help to destroy you.'"

There was a frigid silence.

"But somebody would have opened one anyway," Paul protested.

Seevers turned his bitter smile on the window. "You couldn't be more right. The senders just didn't foresee our monkey-minded species. If they saw Man digging out the nuggets, braying over them, chortling over them, cracking them like walnuts, then turning tail to run howling for the forests—well, they'd think twice before they fired another round of their celestial buckshot."

"Doctor Seevers, what do you think will happen now? To the world, I mean?"

Seevers shrugged. "I saw a baby born yesterday—to a woman down the island. It was fully covered with neuroderm at birth. It has some new sensory equipment—small pores in the fingertips, with taste buds and olfactory cells in them. Also a nodule above each eye sensitive to infrared."

Paul groaned.

"It's not the first case. Those things are happening to adults, too, but you have to have the condition for quite a while. Brother Thomas has the finger pores already. Hasn't learned to use them yet, of course. He gets sensations from them, but the receptors aren't connected to olfactory and taste centers of the brain. They're still linked with the somesthetic interpretive centers. He can touch various substances and get different perceptive combinations of heat, pain, cold, pressure, and so forth. He says vinegar feels ice-cold, quinine sharp-hot, cologne warm-velvet-prickly, and . . . he blushes when he touches a musky perfume."

Paul laughed, and the hollow sound startled him.

"It may be several generations before we know all that will happen," Seevers went on. "I've examined sections of rat brain and found the micro-organisms. They may be working at rerouting these new receptors to proper brain areas. Our grandchildren—if Man's still on Earth by then —can perhaps taste analyze substances by touch, qualitatively determine the contents of a test tube by sticking a finger in it. See a warm radiator in a dark room—by infrared. Perhaps they'll be some ultraviolet sensitization. My rats are sensitive to it."

Paul went to the rat cages and stared in at three gray-pelted animals that seemed larger than the others. They retreated against the back wall and watched him warily. They began squeaking and exchanging glances among themselves.

"Those are third-generation hypers," Seevers told him. "They've developed a simple language. Not intelligent by human standards, but crafty. They've learned to use their sensory equipment. They know when I mean to feed them, and when I mean to take one out to kill and dissect. A slight change in my emotional odor, I imagine. Learning's a big hurdle, youngster. A hyper with finger pores gets sensations from them, but it takes a long time to attach meaning to the various sensations—through learning. A baby gets visual sensations from his untrained eyes—but the sensation is utterly without significance until he associates milk with white, mother with a face shape, and so forth."

"What will happen to the brain?" Paul breathed.

"Not too much, I imagine. I haven't observed much happening. The rats show an increase in intelligence, but not in brain size. The intellectual boost apparently comes from an ability to perceive things in terms of more senses. Ideas, concepts, precepts—are made of memory collections of past sensory experiences. An apple is red, fruity-smelling, sweet-acid flavored—that's your sensory idea of an apple. A blind man without a tongue couldn't form such a complete idea. A hyper, on the other hand, could add some new adjectives that you couldn't understand. The fully-developed hyper—I'm not one yet—has more sensory tools with which to grasp ideas. When he learns to use them, he'll be mentally more efficient. But there's apparently a hitch.

"The parasite's instinctive goal is to insure the host's survival. That's the substance of the warning. If Man has the capacity to work together, then the parasites will help him shape his environment. If Man intends to keep fighting with his fellows, the parasite will help him do a better job of that, too. Help him destroy himself more efficiently."

"Men have worked together—"

"In small tribes," Seevers interrupted. "Yes, we have group spirit. Ape-tribe spirit, not race spirit."

Paul moved restlessly toward the door. Seevers had turned to watch him with a cool smirk.

"Well, you're illuminated, youngster. Now what do you intend to do?"

Paul shook his head to scatter the confusion of ideas.

"What can anyone do? Except run. To an island, perhaps."

Seevers hoisted a cynical eyebrow. "Intend taking the condition with you? Or will you try to stay nonhyper?"

"Take . . . are you crazy? I mean to stay healthy!"

"That's what I thought. If you were objective about this, you'd give yourself the condition and get it over with. I did. You remind me of a monkey running away from a hypodermic needle. The hypo has serum health-insurance in it, but the needle looks sharp. The monkey chatters with fright."

Paul stalked angrily to the door, then paused. "There's a girl upstairs, a dermie. Would you—"

"Tell her all this? I always brief new hypers. It's one of my duties around this ecclesiastical leper ranch. She's on the verge of insanity, I suppose. They all are, before they get rid of the idea that they're damned souls. What's she to you?"

Paul strode out into the corridor without answering. He felt physically ill. He hated Seevers' smug bulldog face with a violence that was unfamiliar to him. The man had given the plague to himself! So he said. But was it true? Was any of it true? To claim that the hallucinations were new sensory phenomena, to pose the plague as possibly desirable—Seevers had no patent on those ideas. Every dermie made such claims; it was a symptom. Seevers had simply invented clever rationalizations to support his delusions, and Paul had been nearly taken in. Seevers was clever. *Do you mean to take the condition with you when you go?* Wasn't that just another way of suggesting, "Why don't you allow me to touch you?" Paul was shivering as he returned to the third floor room to recoat himself with the pungent oil. Why not leave now? he thought.

But he spent the day wandering along the waterfront, stopping briefly at the docks to watch a crew of monks scrambling over the scaffolding that surrounded the hulls of two small sea-going vessels. The monks were caulking split seams and trotting along the platforms with buckets of tar and paint. Upon inquiry, Paul learned which of the vessels was intended for his own use. And he put aside all thoughts of immediate departure.

She was a fifty-footer, a slender craft with a weighted fin-keel that would cut too deep for bay navigation. Paul guessed that the colony wanted only a flat-bottomed vessel for hauling passengers and cargo across from the mainland. They would have little use for the trim seaster with the lines of a baby destroyer. Upon closer examination, he guessed that it had been a police boat, or Coast Guard craft. There was a gun-mounting on the forward deck, minus the gun. She was built for speed, and powered by diesels, and she could be provisioned for a nice long cruise.

Paul went to scrounge among the warehouses and locate a stock of supplies. He met an occasional monk or nun, but the gray-skinned monastics seemed only desirous of avoiding him. The dermie desire was keyed principally by smell, and the deodorant oil helped preserve him from their affections. Once he was approached by a wild-eyed layman who startled him amidst a heap of warehouse crates. The dermie was almost upon him before Paul heard, the footfall. Caught without an escape route, and assailed by startled terror, he shattered the man's arm with a shotgun blast, then fled from the warehouse to escape the dermie's screams.

Choking with shame, he found a dermie monk and sent him to care for the wounded creature. Paul had shot at other plague victims when there was no escape, but never with intent to kill. The man's life had been spared only by hasty aim.

"It was self-defense," he reminded himself.

But defense against what? Against the inevitable?

He hurried back to the hospital and found Mendelhaus outside the small chapel. "I better not wait for your boat," he told the priest. "I just shot one of your people. I better leave before it happens again."

Mendelhaus' thin lips tightened. "You shot—"

"Didn't kill him," Paul explained hastily. "Broke his arm. One of the brothers is bringing him over. I'm sorry, Father, but he jumped me."

The priest glanced aside silently, apparently wrestling against anger. "I'm glad you told me," he said quietly. "I suppose you couldn't help it. But why did you leave the hospital? You're safe here. The yacht will be provisioned for you. I suggest you remain in your room until it's ready. I won't vouch for your safety any farther than the building." There was a tone of command in his voice, and Paul nodded slowly. He started away.

"The young lady's been asking for you," the priest called after him.

Paul stopped. "How is she?"

"Over the crisis, I think. Infection's down. Nervous condition not so good. Deep depression. Sometimes she goes a little hysterical." He paused, then lowered his voice. "You're at the focus of it, young man. Sometimes she gets the idea that she touched you, and then sometimes she raves about how she wouldn't do it."

Paul whirled angrily, forming a protest, but the priest continued: "Seevers talked to her, and then a psychologist—one of our sisters. It seemed to help some. She's asleep now. I don't know how much of Seevers' talk she understood, however. She's dazed—combined effects of pain, shock, infection, guilt feelings, fright, hysteria—and some other things. Morphine doesn't make her mind any clearer. Neither does the fact that she thinks you're avoiding her."

"It's the plague I'm avoiding!" Paul snapped. "Not her."

Mendelhaus chuckled mirthlessly. "You're talking to me, aren't you?" He turned and entered the chapel through a swinging door. As the door fanned back and forth, Paul caught a glimpse of a candlelit altar and a stark wooden crucifix, and a sea of monk-robes flowing over the pews, waiting for the celebrant priest to enter the sanctuary and begin the Sacrifice of the Mass. He realized vaguely that it was Sunday.

Paul wandered back to the main corridor and found himself drifting toward Willie's room. The door was ajar, and he stopped short lest she see him. But after a moment he inched forward until he caught a glimpse of her dark mass of hair unfurled across the pillow. One of the sisters had combed it for her, and it spread in dark waves, gleaming in the candlelight. She was still asleep. The candle startled him for an instant—suggesting a deathbed and the sacrament of the dying. But a dog-eared magazine lay beneath it; someone had been reading to her.

He stood in the doorway, watching the slow rise of her breathing. Fresh, young, shapely—even in the crude cotton gown they had given her, even beneath the blue-white pallor of her skin—soon to become gray as a cloudy sky in a wintery twilight. Her lips moved slightly, and he backed a step away. They paused, parted moistly, showing thin white teeth. Her delicately carved face was thrown back slightly on the pillow. There was a sudden tightening of her jaw.

A weirdly pitched voice floated unexpectedly from down the hall, echoing the semisinging of Gregorian chant: *"Asperges me, Domine, hyssopo, et mundabor . . ."* The priest was beginning Mass.

As the sound came, the girl's hands clenched into rigid fists beneath the sheet. Her eyes flared open to stare wildly at the ceiling. Clutching the bedclothes, she pressed the fists up against her face and cried out: "No! Noooo! God, I won't!"

Paul backed out of sight and pressed himself against the wall. A knot of desolation tightened in his stomach. He looked around nervously. A nun, hearing the outcry, came scurrying down the hall, murmuring anxiously to herself. A plump mother hen in a dozen yards of starched white cloth. She gave him a quick challenging glance and waddled inside.

"Child, my child, what's wrong! Nightmares again?"

He heard Willie breathe a nervous moan of relief. Then her voice, weakly— "They . . . they made me . . . touch . . . Ooo, God! I want to cut off my hands!"

Paul fled, leaving the nun's sympathetic reassurance to fade into a murmur behind him.

He spent the rest of the day and the night in his room. On the following day, Mendelhaus came with word that the boat was not yet ready. They needed to finish caulking and stock it with provisions. But the priest assured him that it should be afloat within twenty-four hours. Paul could not bring himself to ask about the girl.

A monk brought his food—unopened cans, still steaming from the sterilizer, and on a covered tray. The monk wore gloves and mask, and he had oiled his own skin. There were moments when Paul felt as if he were the diseased and contagious patient from whom the others protected themselves. Like Omar, he thought, wondering —"which is the Potter, pray, and which the Pot?"

Was Man, as Seevers implied, a terrorized ape-tribe fleeing illogically from the gray hands that only wanted to offer a blessing? How narrow was the line dividing blessing from curse, god from demon! The parasites came in a devil's mask, the mask of disease. "Diseases have often killed me," said Man. "All disease is therefore evil." But was that necessarily true? Fire had often killed Man's club-bearing ancestors, but later came to serve him. Even diseases had been used to good advantage—artificially induced typhoid and malaria to fight venereal infections.

But the gray skin . . . taste buds in the fingertips . . . alien micro-organisms tampering with the nerves and the brain. Such concepts caused his scalp to bristle. Man— made over to suit the tastes of a bunch of supposedly beneficent parasites—was he still Man, or something else? Little bacteriological farmers imbedded in the skin, raising a crop of nerve cells—eat one, plant two, sow an olfactor in a new field, reshuffle the feeder-fibers to the brain.

Monday brought a cold rain and stiff wind from the Gulf. He watched the water swirling through littered gutters in the street. Sitting in the window, he watched the gloom and waited, praying that the storm would not delay his departure. Mendelhaus smiled politely, through his doorway once. "Willie's ankle seems healing nicely," he said. "Swelling's gone down so much we had to change casts. If only she would—"

"Thanks for the free report, Padre," Paul growled irritably.

The priest shrugged and went away.

It was still raining when the sky darkened with evening. The monastic dock-crew had certainly been unable to finish. Tomorrow . . . perhaps.

After nightfall, he lit a candle and lay awake watching its unflickering yellow tongue until drowsiness lolled his head aside. He snuffed it out and went to bed.

Dreams assailed him, tormented him, stroked him with dark hands while he lay back, submitting freely. Small hands, soft, cool, tender—touching his forehead and his cheeks, while a voice whispered caresses.

He awoke suddenly to blackness. The feel of the dream-hands was still on his face. What had aroused him? A sound in the hall, a creaking hinge? The darkness was impenetrable. The rain had stopped—perhaps its cessation had disturbed him. He felt curiously tense as he lay listening to the humid, musty corridors. A . . . faint . . . rustle . . . and . . .

Breathing! The sound of soft breathing was in the room with him!

He let out a hoarse shriek that shattered the unearthly silence. A high-pitched scream of fright answered him! From a few feet away in the room. He groped toward it and fumbled against a bare wall. He roared curses, and tried to find first matches, then the shotgun. At last he found the gun, aimed at nothing across the room, and jerked the trigger. The explosion deafened him. The window shattered, and a sift of plaster rustled to the floor.

The brief flash had illuminated the room. It was empty. He stood frozen. Had he imagined it all? But no, the visitor's startled scream had been real enough.

A cool draft fanned his face. The door was open. Had he forgotten to lock it again? A tumult of sound was beginning to arise from the lower floors. His shot had aroused the sleepers. But there was a closer sound—sobbing in the corridor, and an irregular creaking noise.

At last he found a match and rushed to the door. But the tiny flame revealed nothing within its limited aura. He heard a doorknob rattle in the distance; his visitor was escaping via the outside stairway. He thought of pursuit and vengeance. But instead, he rushed to the washbasin and began scrubbing himself thoroughly with harsh brown soap. Had his visitor touched him—or had the hands been only dream-stuff? He was frightened and sickened.

Voices were filling the corridor. The light of several candles was advancing toward his doorway. He turned to see monks' faces peering anxiously inside. Father Mendelhaus shouldered his way through the others, glanced at the window, the wall, then at Paul.

"What—"

"Safety, eh?" Paul hissed. "Well, I had a prowler! A woman! I think I've been touched."

The priest turned and spoke to a monk. "Go to the stairway and call for the Mother Superior. Ask her to make an immediate inspection of the sisters' quarters. If any nuns have been out of their rooms—"

A shrill voice called from down the hallway: "Father, Father! The girl with the injured ankle! She's not in her bed! She's gone!"

"Willie!" Paul gasped.

A small nun with a candle scurried up and panted to recover her breath for a moment. "She's gone, Father.

I was on night duty. I heard the shot, and I went to see if it disturbed her. She wasn't there!"

The priest grumbled incredulously. "How could she get out? She can't walk with that cast."

"Crutches, Father. We told her she could get up in a few days. While she was still irrational, she kept saying they were going to amputate her leg. We brought the crutches in to prove she'd be up soon. It's my fault, Father. I should have—"

"Never mind! Search the building for her."

Paul dried his wet skin and faced the priest angrily. "What can I do to disinfect myself?" he demanded.

Mendelhaus called out into the hallway where a crowd had gathered. "Someone please get Doctor Seevers."

"I'm here, preacher," grunted the scientist. The monastics parted ranks to make way for his short chubby body. He grinned amusedly at Paul. "So, you decided to make your home here after all, eh?"

Paul croaked an insult at him. "Have you got any effective—"

"Disinfectants? Afraid not. Nitric acid will do the trick on one or two local spots. Where were you touched?"

"I don't know. I was asleep."

Seevers' grin widened. "Well, you can't take a bath in nitric acid. We'll try something else, but I doubt if it'll work for a direct touch."

"That oil—"

"Uh-uh! That'll do for exposure-weakened parasites you might pick up by handling an object that's been touched. But with skin to skin contact, the bugs're pretty stout little rascals. Come on downstairs, though, we'll make a pass at it."

Paul followed him quickly down the corridor. Behind him, a soft voice was murmuring: "I just can't understand why nonhypers are so . . ." Mendelhaus said something to Seevers, blotting out the voice. Paul chafed at the thought that they might consider him cowardly.

But with the herds fleeing northward, cowardice was the social norm. And after a year's flight, Paul had accepted the norm as the only possible way to fight.

Seevers was emptying chemicals into a tub of water in the basement when a monk hurried in to tug at Mendelhaus' sleeve. "Father, the sisters report that the girl's not in the building."

"What? Well, she can't be far! Search the grounds. If she's not there, try the adjoining blocks."

Paul stopped unbuttoning his shirt. Willie had said some mournful things about what she would rather do than submit to the craving. And her startled scream when he had cried out in the darkness—the scream of someone suddenly awakening to reality—from a dazeworld.

The monk left the room. Seevers sloshed more chemicals into the tub. Paul could hear the wind whipping about the basement windows and the growl of an angry surf not so far away. Paul rebuttoned his shirt.

"Which way's the ocean?" he asked suddenly. He backed toward the door.

"No, you fool!" roared Seevers. "You're not going to —get him, preacher!"

Paul sidestepped as the priest grabbed for him. He darted outside and began running for the stairs. Mendelhaus bellowed for him to stop.

"Not me!" Paul called back angrily. "Willie!"

Moments later, he was racing across the sodden lawn and into the street. He stopped on the corner to get his bearings. The wind brought the sound of the surf with it. He began running east and calling her name into the night.

The rain had ceased, but the pavement was wet and water gurgled in the gutters. Occasionally the moon peered through the thinning veil of clouds, but its light failed to furnish a view of the street ahead. After a minute's running, he found himself standing on the seawall. The breakers thundered a stone's throw across the sand. For a moment they became visible under the coy moon, then vanished again in blackness. He had not seen her.

"Willie!"

Only the breakers' growl responded. And a glimmer of phosphorescence from the waves.

"Willie!" he slipped down from the seawall and began feeling along the jagged rocks that lay beneath it. She could not have gotten down without falling. Then he remembered a rickety flight of steps just to the north, and he trotted quickly toward it.

The moon came out suddenly. He saw her, and stopped. She was sitting motionless on the bottom step, holding her face in her hands. The crutches were stacked neatly against the handrail. Ten yards across the sand slope lay the hungry, devouring surf. Paul approached her slowly. The moon went out again. His feet sucked at the rainsoaked sand.

He stopped by the handrail, peering at her motionless shadow. "Willie?"

A low moan, then a long silence. "I did it, Paul," she muttered miserably. "It was like a dream at first, but then . . . you shouted . . . and . . ."

He crouched in front of her, sitting on his heels. Then he took her wrists firmly and tugged her hands from her face.

"Don't . . ."

He pulled her close and kissed her. Her mouth was frightened. Then he lifted her—being cautious of the now-sodden cast. He climbed the steps and started back to the hospital. Willie, dazed and weary and still uncomprehending, fell asleep in his arms. Her hair blew about his face in the wind. It smelled warm and alive. He wondered what sensation it would produce to the finger-pore receptors. "Wait and see," he said to himself.

The priest met him with a growing grin when he brought her into the candlelit corridor. "Shall we forget the boat, son?"

Paul paused. "No . . . I'd like to borrow it anyway."

Mendelhaus looked puzzled.

Seevers snorted at him: "Preacher, don't you know any reasons for traveling besides running away?"

Paul carried her back to her room. He meant to have a long talk when she awoke. About an island—until the world sobered up.

The Lineman

IT WAS AUGUST on Earth, and the newscast reported a
heat wave in the Midwest: the worst since 2065. A
letter from Mike Tremini's sister in Abilene said the
chickens were dying and there wasn't enough water for
the stock. It was the only letter that came for any of
Novotny's men during that fifty-shift hitch on the
Copernicus Trolley Project. Everybody read it and lux-
uriated in sympathy for Kansas and sick chickens.

It was August on Luna too. The Perseids rained down
with merciless impartiality; and, from his perch atop the
hundred-foot steel skeleton, the lineman stopped cranking the jack and leaned out against his safety belt to
watch two demolition men carrying a corpse out toward
Fissure Seven. The corpse wore a deflated pressure suit.
Torn fabric dragged the ground. The man in the rear
carried the corpse's feet like a pair of wheelbarrow
handles, and he continually tripped over the loose fabric; his head waggled inside his helmet as if he cursed
softly and continuously to himself. The corpse's helmet
was translucent with an interior coating of pink ice,
making it look like a comic figure in a strawberry ice
cream ad, a chocolate ragamuffin with a scoop for a
head.

The lineman stared after the funeral party for a time
until the team-pusher, who had been watching the slack
span of 800 MCM aluminum conductors that snaked half
a mile back toward the preceding tower, glanced up at
the hesitant worker and began bellowing into his micro-

388

phone. The lineman answered briefly, inspected the pressure gauge of his suit, and began cranking the jack again. With every dozen turns of the crank, the long snaking cable crept tighter across the lunar plain, straightening and lifting almost imperceptibly until at last the center-point cleared the ground and the cable swooped in a long graceful catenary between the towers. It trembled with fitful glistenings in the harsh sunglare. The lineman ignored the cable as he turned the crank. He squinted across the plains at the meteor display.

The display was not spectacular. It could be detected only as a slight turbulence in the layer of lunar dust that covered the ground, and an occasional dust geyser where a pea-sized bit of sky debris exploded into the crust at thirty miles per second. Sometimes the explosion was bright and lingering, but more often there was only a momentary incandescence quickly obscured by dust. The lineman watched it with nervous eyes. There was small chance of being hit by a stone of consequential size, but the eternal pelting by meteoric dust, though too fine to effect a puncture, could weaken the fabric of a suit and lead to leaks and blowouts.

The team-pusher keyed his mic switch again and called to the lineman on the tower. *"Keep your eyes on that damn jack, Relke! That clamp looks like she's slipping from here."*

The lineman paused to inspect the mechanism. *"Looks OK to me,"* he answered. *"How tight do I drag this one up?"*

The pusher glanced at the sagging span of steel-reinforced aluminum cable. *"It's a short stretch. Not too critical. What's the tension now?"*

The lineman consulted a dial on the jack. *"Going on forty-two hundred pounds, Joe."*

"Crank her up to five thousand and leave it," said the pusher. *"Let C-shift sag it in by the tables if they don't like it."*

"Yokay. Isn't it quitting time?"

"Damn near. My suit stinks like we're on overtime. Come on down when you reel that one in. I'm going back to the sleep wagon and get blown clear." The pusher shut off his oxygen while he transferred his hose connections from the main feeder supply to the walk-around bottles on his suit. He signaled "quitting time"

at the men on the far tower, then started moon-loping his
way across the shaggy terrain toward the train of rolling
barracks and machinery that moved with the construction crew as the 200 kilovolt transmission line inched
its way across the lunar landscape.

The lineman glanced up absently at the star-stung
emptiness of space. Motion caught his eye. He watched
with a puzzled frown, then hitched himself around to
call after the departing team-pusher.

"Hey, Joe!"

The pusher stopped on a low rise to look back.
"Relke?" he asked, uncertain of the source of the voice.

"Yeah. Is that a ship up there?" The lineman pointed
upward toward the east.

"I don't see it. Where?"

*"Between Arcturus and Serpens. I thought I saw it
move."*

The pusher stood on the low tongue of lava and
watched the heavens for a time. *"Maybe—maybe not.
So what if it is, Relke?"*

"Well . . ." The lineman paused, keying his mic nervously. *"Looks to me like it's headed the wrong direction
for Grater City. I mean—"*

The pusher barked a short curse. *"I'm just about fed
up with that superstitious drivel!"* he snapped. *"There*
aren't *any non-human ships, Relke. And there aren't any
non-humans."*

"I didn't say—"

"No, but you had it in mind." The pusher gave him a
scornful look and hiked on toward the caterpillar train.

"Yuh. If you say so, Joe," Relke muttered to himself.
He glanced again at the creeping point of light in the
blackness; he shrugged; he began cranking up the slack
span again. But the creeping point kept drawing his
gaze while he cranked. When he looked at the tension
indicator, it read 5,600 pounds. He grunted his an-
noyance, reversed the jack ratchet, and began letting out
the extra 600 pounds.

The shift-change signal was already beeping in his
headsets by the time he had eased it back down to
5,000, and the C-shift crewmen were standing around
the foot of the tower jeering at him from below.

"Get off it, boy. Give the men a chance."

"Come on down, Relke. You can let go. It ain't gonna drop."

He ignored the razzing and climbed down the trainward side of the tower. Larkin and Kunz walked briskly around to meet him. He jumped the last twenty-five feet, hoping to evade them, but they were waiting for him when his boots hit the ground.

"We want a little talk with you, Relke, my lad," came Larkin's rich, deceptively affable baritone.

"Sorry, Lark, it's late and I—" He tried to sidestep them, but they danced in and locked arms with him, one on each side.

"Like Lark told you, we want a little talk," grunted Kunz.

"Sure, Harv—but not right now. Drop by my bunk tank when you're off shift. I been in this strait jacket for seven hours. It doesn't smell exactly fresh in here."

"Then, Sonny, you should learn to control yourself in your suit," said Larkin, his voice all mellifluent with smiles and avuncular pedagoguery. *"Let's take him, Harv."*

They caught him in a double armlock, hoisted him off the ground, and started carrying him toward a low lava ridge that lay a hundred yards to the south of the tower. He could not kick effectively because of the stiffness of the suit. He wrenched one hand free and fumbled at the channel selector of his suit radio. Larkin jerked his stub antenna free from its mounting before Relke could put in a call for help.

"Tch, tch tch," said Larkin, waggling his head.

They carried him across the ridge and set him on his feet again, out of sight of the camp. *"Sit down, Sonny. We have seeeerious matters to discuss with you."*

Relke heard him faintly, even without the antenna, but he saw no reason to acknowledge. When he failed to answer, Kunz produced a set of jumper wires from his knee pocket and clipped their suit audio circuits into a three way intercom, disconnecting the plate lead from an r.f. stage to insure privacy.

"You guys give me a pain in the hump," growled the lineman. *"What do you want this time? You know damn well a dead radio is against safety rules."*

"It is? You ever hear of such a rule, Kunz?"

*"Naah. Or maybe I did, at that. It's to make things

easy for work spies, psych checkers, and time-and-motion men, ain't that it?"

"Yeah. You a psych checker or a time-and-motion man, Relke?"

"Hell, you guys know damn well I'm not—"

"Then what are you stalling about?" Larkin's baritone lost its mellowness and became an ominous growl. "You came nosing around, asking questions about the Party. So we let you in on it. We took you to a cell meeting. You said you wanted to join. So we let you in on two more meetings. Then you chickened out. We don't like that, Relke. It smells. It smells like a dirty informing rat!"

"I'm no damn informer!"

"Then why did you welsh?"

"I didn't welsh. I never said I'd join. You asked me if I was in favor of getting the Schneider-Volkov Act repealed. I said 'yes.' I still say 'yes.' That doesn't mean I want to join the Party."

"Why not, Relke?"

"Well, there's the fifty bucks, for one thing."

"Wh-a-a-at! One shift's wages? Hell, if that's all that's stopping you—Kunz, let's pay his fifty bucks for him, okay?"

"Sure. We'll pay your way in, Relke. I don't hold it against a man if he's a natural born tightwad."

"Yeah," said Larkin. "All you gotta do is sign up, Sonny. Fifty bucks, hell—that's less than union dues. If you can call that yellow-bellied obscenity a union. Now how about it, Relke?"

Behind the dark lenses of his glare goggles, Relke's eyes scanned the ground for a weapon. He spotted a jagged shard of volcanic glass and edged toward it.

"Well, Relke?"

"No deal."

"Why not?"

"That's easy. I plan on getting back to Earth someday. Conspiracy to commit mutiny rates the death penalty."

"Hear what he said, Lark? He calls it mutiny."

"Yeah. Teacher's little monitor."

"C'mere, informer."

They approached him slowly, wearing tight smiles. Relke dived for the shard of glass. The jumper wires jerked tight and broke loose, throwing them off balance for a moment. He came up with the glass shard in one fist and backed away. They stopped. The weapon was as good as a gun. A slit suit was the ultimate threat. Relke tore the dangling wires loose from his radio and backed toward the top of the ridge. They watched him somberly, not speaking. Larkin waved the lineman's stub antenna and looked at him questioningly. Relke held out a glove and waited for him to toss it. Larkin threw it over his shoulder in the opposite direction. They turned their backs on him. He loped on back toward the gravy train, knowing that the showdown had been no more than postponed. Next time would be worse. They meant to incriminate him, as a kind of insurance against his informing. He had no desire to be incriminated, nor to inform—but try to make them believe that.

Before entering the clean-up tank, he stopped to glance up at the heavens between Arcturus and Serpens. The creeping spot of light had vanished—or moved far from where he had seen it. He did not pause to search. He checked his urine bottle in the airlock, connected his hoses to the wall valves, and blew the barn-smell out of his suit. The blast of fresh air was like icy wine in his throat. He enjoyed it for a moment, then went inside the tank for a bath.

Novotny was waiting for him in the B-shift line crew's bunkroom. The small pusher looked sore. He stopped pacing when Relke entered.

"Hi, Joe."

Novotny didn't answer. He watched while Relke stowed his gear, got out an electric razor, and went to the wall mirror to grind off the blond bristles.

"Where you been?" Novotny grunted.

"On the line where you saw me. I jacked that last span up tighter than you told me. I had to let her back down a little. Made me late getting in."

The pusher's big hand hit him like a club between the shoulder blades, grabbed a handful of coverall, and jerked him roughly around. The razor fell to the end of the cord. Novotny let go in back and grabbed a handful in front. He shoved the lineman back against the wall.

Relke gaped at him blankly.

"Don't give *me* that wide blue-eyed dumb stare, you sonofabitch!" the pusher snapped. "I saw you go over the hill with Kunz and Larkin."

Relke's Adam's apple did a quick genuflection. "If you saw me go, you musta seen *how* I went."

Novotny shook him. "What'd they want with you?" he barked.

"Nothing."

Joe's eyes turned to dark slits. "Relke, I told you, I told the rest of my men. I told you what I'd do to any sonofabitch on my team that got mixed up with the Party. Pappy don't allow that crap. Now shall I do it to you here, or do you want to go down to the dayroom?"

"Honest, Joe, I'm not mixed up in it. I got interested in what Larkin had to say—back maybe six months ago. But I never signed up. I never even meant to."

"Six months? Was that about the time you got your Dear John letter from Fran?"

"Right after that, Joe."

"Well, that figures. So what's Larkin after you about now?"

"I guess he wonders why I asked questions but never joined."

"I don't want your guesses. What did he say out there, and what did you say to him?"

'He wanted to know why I didn't sign up, that's all."

"And you told him what?"

"No deal."

"So?"

"So, I came on back and took a shower."

Novotny stared at him for a few seconds. "You're lying," he grunted, but released him anyway. "OK, Relke, but you better listen to this. You're a good lineman. You've stayed out of trouble. You get along with the rest of the team. If you got out of line in some *other* way, I'd figure it was about time you let off some steam. I'd stick up for you. But get mixed up with the Party— and I'll stomp you. When I'm through stomping you, I'll report you off my team. Understand?"

"Sure, Joe."

Novotny grunted and stepped away from him. "No hard feelings, Relke."

"Naah." The lineman went back to the mirror and started shaving again. That his hand remained steady was a surprise to him. Novotny had never before laid a hand on him, and Relke hoped the first time would be the last. He had watched Joe mop up the dayroom with

Benet for playing fast and loose with safety rules while
working a hotstick job, and it put Benet in sick bay for
three days. Novotny was small, but he was built like a
bunker. He was a fair overseer, but he handled his men
in the only way he knew how to handle them on such a
job. He expected self-discipline and self-imposed obedience, and when he didn't get it, he took it as a personal
insult and a challenge to a duel. Out on the lava, men
were pressure-packed, hermetically sealed charges of
high explosive blood and bone; one man's folly could
mean the death of several others, and there was no recourse to higher authority or admonitions from the dean,
with a team on the lava.

"What's your grudge against the Party, Joe?" Relke
asked while he scraped under his neck.

"No grudge. Not as long as Benet, Braxton, Relke,
Henderson, Beasley, Tremini, and Novotny stay out of
it. No grudge at all. I'm for free love and nickel beer as
much as the next guy. But I'm not for getting my ass
shot off. I'm not for fouling up the whole Lunar project
just to get the Schneider-Volkov Act repealed, when you
can't get it repealed that way anyhow. I'm not for facing
a General Space Court and getting sentenced to blowout.
That's all. No grudge."

"What makes you think a general strike couldn't force
repeal, Joe?"

The pusher spat contemptuously at the disposal chute
and missed. "A general strike on the Lunar Project?
Hell, Relke, use your head. It'd never work. A strike
against the government is rough to pull off, even on
Earth. Up here, it'd be suicide. The Party's so busy yelling about who's right and who's wrong and who's getting
a raw deal—and what they ought to do about it—that
they forget the important point: who's in the driver's seat.
So what if we shut down Copernicus and all the projects
like this one? Copernicus has a closed ecology, its own
plant-animal cycle, sure. We don't need much from
Earth to keep it running—but there's the hitch: don't
need *much*. The ecology slips out of balance now and
then. Every month or two it has to get a transfusion from
Earth. Compost bacteria, or a new strain of algae because
our strain starts mutating—it's always something like
that. If a general strike cut us off from Earth, the World
Parliament could just sit passing solemn gas through their

waffle-bottom chairs and wait. They could debate us to death in two months."

"But world opinion—"

"Hell, *they* make world opinion, not *us*."

Relke stopped shaving and looked around. "Joe?"

"Yah."

"Kunz and Larkin'd kill me for telling you. Promise not to say anything?"

The pusher glowered at him for a moment. "Look, Relke, nobody brutalizes Joe Novotny's men, I'll handle Kunz and Larkin. You'd better spill. You think it's informing if you tell *me?*"

Relke shook his head. "Guess not. OK, Joe. It's this: I've been to three cell meetings. I heard some stuff. I think the strike's supposed to start come sundown."

"I heard that too. If it does, we'll all be—" He broke off. The cabin's intercom was suddenly blaring.

Attention, all personnel, attention. Unidentified bird at thirty degrees over horizon, south-southwest, braking fire for landing in our vicinity. All men on the line take cover. Safety team to the ready room on the double. Rescue team scramble, rescue team scramble.

Relke rolled the cord neatly around the razor and stared at it. "I'll be damned," he muttered. "It *was* a ship I saw. What ship would be landing way the hell out here?" He glanced around at Novotny.

The pusher was already at the periscope viewer, his face buried in the sponge rubber eyepieces. He cranked it around in a search pattern toward the south-southwest.

"See anything?"

"Not yet . . . *yeah,* there she is. Braking in fast—now what the hell!"

"Give me a look."

They traded turns at the viewer.

"She's a fusion furnace job. Cold fusion. Look at that blue tail."

"Why land way out here?"

The hatch burst open and the rest of the men spilled in from the dayroom. A confused babble filled the cabin. "I tole ya and I tole ya!" said Bama Braxton. "That theah mine shaff at Tycho is the play-yun evvy-dance. Gennlemen, weah about to have stranjuhs in ouah midst."

"Cut that superstitious bullspit, Brax," Novotny

grunted. "There *aren't* any aliens. We got enough bogeys around here without you scaring the whoop out of yourself with that line of crap."

"Theah ahn't no aliens!" Braxton howled. "Theah ahn't no *aliens?* Joe, youah bline to the play-yun evvy-dance!"

"He right, Joe," said Lije Henderson, the team's only Negro and Bama's chief crony. "That mine shaff speak fo' itself."

"That mine's a million years old," Joe snorted, "and they're not even sure it's a mine. I said drop it."

"That *ship* speak fo' itself!"

"Drop it! This isn't the first time a ship overshot Crater City and had to set down someplace else. Ten to one it's full of Parliament waffle-bottoms, all complaining their heads off. Maybe they've got a meteor puncture and need help quick."

The closed-circuit intercom suddenly buzzed, and Novotny turned to see the project engineer's face on the small viewer.

"Are all your men up and dressed, Joe?" he asked when Novotny had answered the call.

"EVERYBODY PIPE DOWN! Sorry, Suds. No—well, except for Beasley, they're up. Beasley's logging sack time."

"The hell Beasley is!" complained Beasley from his bunk. "With you verbing nouns of a noun all yapping like—"

"Shut up, Beez. Go on, Suds."

"We got contact with that ship. They've got reactor troubles. I tried to get Crater City on the line, but there's an outage on the circuit somewhere. I need some men to take a tractor and backtrack toward Copernicus. Look for a break in the circuit."

"Why call me?"

"The communication team is tied up, Joe."

"Yeah, but I'm not a communic—"

"Hell!" Brodanovitch exploded. "It doesn't take an electronics engineer to splice a broken wire, does it?"

"OK, Suds, we'll go. Take it easy. What about that ship?"

The engineer paused to mop his face. He looked rather bleak suddenly. "I don't know if it's safe to tell you. But you'll find out anyhow. Watch out for a riot."

"Not a runaway reactor—"

"Worse, Joe. Women."

"WOMEN!" It was a high piping scream from Beasley. "Did he say *women?*" Beasley was out of bed and into his boots.

"WOMEN!" They came crowding around the intercom screen.

"Back off!" Novotny barked. "Go on, Suds."

"It's a troupe of entertainers, Joe. Clearance out of Algiers. They say they're scheduled for a performance in Crater City, come nightfall. That's all I know, except they're mostly women."

"Algiers! Jeez! Belly dancers . . . !"

The room was a confused babble.

"Wait a minute," said Suds. His face slid off the screen as he talked to somebody in the boss tank. Moments later he was back. "Their ship just put down, Joe. Looks like a safe landing. The rescue team is out there. You'll pass the ship on the way up the line. Get moving."

"Sure, Suds." Novotny switched off and looked around at the sudden scramble. "I'll be damned if you do!" he yelled. "You can't all go. Beasley, Henderson—"

"No, bigod you don't, Joe!" somebody howled. "Draw straws!"

"OK. I can take three of you, no more."

They drew. Chance favored Relke, Braxton, and Henderson. Minutes later they crowded into the electric runabout and headed southeast along the line of stately steel towers that filed back toward Copernicus. The ship was in sight. Taller than the towers, the nacelles of the downed bird rose into view beyond the broken crest of a distant lava butte. She was a freight shuttle, space-constructed and not built for landing on Earth. Relke eyed the emblem on the hull of her crew nacelle while the runabout nosed onto the strip of graded roadbed that paralleled the transmission line back to Crater City. The emblem was unfamiliar.

"That looks like the old *RS Voltaire,*" said the lineman. "Somebody must have bought her, Joe. Converted her to passenger service."

"Maybe. Now keep an eye on the telephone line."

The pusher edged the runabout toward the trolley rods. The overhead power transmission line had been energized by sections during the construction of it, and the line was hot as far as the road had been extended. Transformer stations fed energy from the 200 kilovolt circuit into the 1,500 volt trolley bars that ran down the center of the roadbed. Novotny stopped the vehicle at the end of the finished construction and sidled it over until the feeler arms crackled against the electrified bus rods and locked in place. He switched the batteries to "charge" and drove on again.

"Relke, you're supposed to be watching that talk circuit, not the ship."

"OK, Joe, in a minute."

"You horny bastard, you can't see their bloomers through that titanium hull. Put the glasses down and watch the line."

"OK, just a minute. I'm trying to find out who owns her. The emblem's—"

"Now, dammit!"

"No marking on her except her serial number and a picture of a rooster—and something else that's been painted over."

"RELKE!"

"Sure, Joe, OK."

"Girls!" marveled Lije Henderson. "Whenna lass time you touch a real girl, Brax?"

"Don' ass me, Lije, don' evum ass me. I sweah, if I evum touch a lady's li'l pink fingah right now, I could—"

"Hell, I could jus' sittin' heah lookin' at that ship. Girls. God! Lemme have those glasses, Relke."

Novotny braked the runabout to a halt. "All right, get your helmets on," he snapped. "Pressure your suits. I'm going to pump air out."

"Whatthehell! *Why*, Joe?"

"So you can get out of this heap. You're walking back. I'll go on and find the break myself."

Braxton squealed like a stuck pig; a moment later all three of them were on him. "Please, Joe. . . . Fuh the love a heaven, Joe, have a haht. . . . Gawd, *women!*"

"Get off my lap, you sonofabitch!" he barked at Braxton, who sat on top of him, grabbing at the controls. "Wait—I'll tell you what. Put the damn binoculars down and watch the line. Don't say another damn word about dames until we find the break and splice it. Swear to that, you bastards, and you can stay. I'll stop at their

ship on our way back, and then you can stare all you
want to. OK?"

"Joe, I sweah on a stack of—"

"All right, then watch the line."

They drove on in silence. The ship had fired down on
a flat stretch of ground about four miles from the construction train, a few hundred yards from the trolley
road. They stared at it as the runabout crawled past,
and Novotny let the vehicle glide to a halt.

"The ramp's out and the ladder's down," said Relke.
"Somebody must have come out."

"Unglue your eyes from that bird and look around,"
Novotny grunted. "You'll see why the ladder's down."
He jerked his thumb toward a row of vehicles parked
near the massive ship.

"The rescue team's wagons. But wheah's the rescue
team?"

No crewmen were visible in the vicinity of the ship
or the parked runabouts. Novotny switched on the radio,
punched the channel selector, and tried a call, reading
the call code off the side of the safety runabout.

*"Double Able Niner, this is One Four William. Talk
back, please."*

They sat in silence. There was nothing but a hiss of
solar interference from the radio and the sound of heavy
breathing from the men.

"Those lucky ole bastahds!" Braxton moaned. "You
know wheah they gone, gennlemen? I taya weah they
gone. They clambered right up the ladies' ladduh, thass
wheah. You know wheah they gone? I taya, alright—"

"Knock it off. Let's get moving. Tell us on the way
back."

"Those lucky ole—"

The runabout moved ahead across the glaring land.
Relke: "Joe?"

"Yeah?"

"Joe, on our way back, can we go over and see if
they'll let us climb aboard?"

Novotny chuckled. "I thought you were off dames,
Relke. I thought when Fran sent you the Dear John,
you said dames were all a bunch of—"

"Damn, Joe! You could have talked all day without
saying 'Fran.'" The lineman's throat worked a brief

spasm, and he stared out across the broken moonscape with dismal eyes.

"Sorry I mentioned it," Novotny grunted. "But sure, I guess one of us could walk over and ask if they mind a little more company on board."

Lije: *"One* of us! Who frinstance—*you?"*

Joe: "No, you can draw for it—not now, you creep! Watch the line."

They watched in silence. The communication circuit was loosely strong on temporary supports beside the roadbed. The circuit was the camp's only link with Crater City, for the horizon interposed a barrier to radio reception, such reception being possible only during the occasional overhead transits of the lunar satellite station which carried message-relaying equipment. The satellite's orbit had been shifted to cover a Russian survey crew near Clavius, however, and its passages over the Trolley Project were rare.

"I jus' *thought,"* Lije muttered suddenly, smacking his fist in his palm.

Relke: "Isn't that getting a little drastic, Lije?"

"I jus' thought. If we fine that outage, less don' fix it!"

Joe: "What kind of crazy talk is that?"

"Lissen, you know what ole Suds want to call Crater City *fo'? He* want to call 'em so's they'll senn a bunch of tank wagons down heah and tote those gals back to town. Thass what he want to call 'em fo'!"

Braxton slapped his forehead. "Luvva God! He's right. Y'all heah that? Is he right, Joe, or is he right?"

"I guess that's about the size of it."

"We mi'not evum get a look at 'em!" Braxton wailed. "Less don' fix it, Joe!"

"I sweah, if I evum touch one of theah precious li'l fingahs, I'd—"

"Shut up and watch the line."

Relke: "Why didn't he use a bridge on the circuit and find out where the break was, Joe?"

"A bridge won't work too well on that line."

"How fah we gonna keep on drivin', Joe?"

"Until we find the break. Relke, turn up that blower a little. It's beginning to stink in here."

"Fresh ayah!" sighed Braxton as the breeze hit them from the fan.

Relke: "I wonder if it's fresh. I keep wondering if it doesn't come out foul from the purifier, but we've been living in it too long to be able to tell. I even dream about it. I dream about going back to Earth and everybody runs away from me. Coughing and holding their noses. I can't get close to a girl even in a dream anymore."

"Ah reckon a head-shrinker could kill hisself a-laughin' over that one."

"Don't talk to me about head shrinkers."

"Watch the damn line."

Braxton: "Talk about *dreams!* Listen, I had one lass sleep shift that I oughta tell y'all about. Gennlemen, if she wasn't the ohnriest li'l—"

Novotny cursed softly under his breath and tried to keep his eyes on both the road and the communications circuit.

Relke: "Let 'em jabber, Joe. I'll watch it."

Joe: "It's bad enough listening to a bunch of jerks in a locker room bragging about the dames they've made. But Braxton! Braxton's got to brag about his dreams. Christ! Send me back to Earth. I'm fed up."

"Aww, Joe, we got nothin' else to talk about up heah."

They drove for nearly an hour and a half without locating the out-age. Novotny pulled the runabout off the hot trolleys and coasted to a stop. "I'm deflating the cab," he told them. "Helmets on, pressure up your suits."

"Joe, weah not walkin' back from heah!" Bama said flatly.

"Oh, blow yourself out, Brax!" the pusher said irritably. "I'm getting out for a minute. C'mon, get ready for vacuum."

"Why?"

"Don't say *why* to me outside the sleep-tank, corn pone! Just do it."

"Damn! Novotny's in a humah! Les say 'yassah' to him, Bama."

"You too, Lije!"

"Yassah."

"Can it." Novotny got the pressure pumped down to two pounds, and then let the rest of the air spew out slowly into vacuum. He climbed out of the runabout and loped over to the low-hanging spans of the communication circuit. He tapped into it with the suit audio and listened for a moment. Relke saw his lips moving as he tried a call, but nothing came through the lineman's suit radio. After about five minutes, he quit talking and beckoned the rest of them back to the runabout.

"That was Brodanovitch," he said after they were inside and the pressure came up again. "So the circuit break must be on up ahead."

"Oh, hell, we'll *navah* get a look at those ladies!"

"Calm down. We're going back—" He paused a moment until the elated whooping died down. "Suds says let them send a crew out of Copernicus to fix it. I guess there's no hurry about moving those people out of there."

"The less hurry, the bettuh . . . *hot dawg!* C'mon, Joe, roll it!" Bama and Lije sat rubbing their hands. Only Relke seemed detached, his enthusiasm apparently cooled. He sat staring out at the meteor display on the dust-flats. He kept rubbing absently at the ring finger of his left hand. There was no ring there, nor even a mark on the skin. The pusher's eye fell on the slow nervous movement.

"Fran again?" Joe grunted.

The lineman nodded.

"I got my Dear John note three years ago, Relke."

Relke looked around at him in surprise. "I didn't know you were married, Joe."

"I guess I wasn't as married as I thought I was."

Relke stared outside again for awhile. "How do you get over it?"

"You don't. Not up here on Luna. The necessary and sometimes sufficient condition for getting over a dame is the availability of other dames. So, you don't."

"Hell, Joe!"

"Yeah."

"The movement's not such a bad idea."

"Can it!" the pusher snapped.

"It's true. Let women come to Crater City, or send us home. It makes sense."

"You're only looking at the free love and nickel beer end of it, Relke. You can't raise kids in low gravity. There are five graves back in Crater City to prove it. Kids' graves. Six feet long. They grow themselves to death."

"I know but . . ." He shrugged uncomfortably and watched the meteor display again.

"When do we draw?" said Lije. "Come on Joe, less draw for who goes talk ouah way onto the ship."

Relke: "Say, Joe, how come they let dames in an entertainment troupe come to the moon, but they won't let our wives come? I thought the Schneider-Volkov Act was supposed to keep all women out of space, period."

"No, they couldn't get away with putting it like that. Against the WP constitution. The law just says that all personnel on any member country's lunar project must be of a single sex. Theoretically some country—Russia, maybe—could start an all-girl lunar mine project, say. Theoretically. But how many lady muckers do you know? Even in Russia."

Lije: "When do we draw? Come on, Joe, less draw."

"Go ahead and draw. Deal me out."

Chance favored Henderson. "Fast-uh, Joe. Hell, less go fastuh, befo' the whole camp move over theah."

Novotny upped the current to the redline and left it there. The long spans of transmission line, some of them a mile or more from tower to tower, swooped past in stately cadence.

"There she is! Man!"

"You guys are building up for a big kick in the rump. They'll never let us aboard."

"Theah's two more cahs pahked over theah."

"Yeah, and still nobody in sight on the ground."

Novotny pulled the feelers off the trolleys again. "OK, Lije, go play John Alden. Tell 'em we just want to look, not touch."

Henderson was bounding off across the flats moments after the cabin had been depressurized to let him climb out. They watched him enviously while the pressure came up again. His black face flashed with sweat in the sunlight as he looked back to wave at them from the foot of the ladder.

Relke glanced down the road toward the rolling construction camp. "You going to call in, Joe? Ought to be able to reach their antenna from here."

"If I do, Brodanovitch is sure to say 'haul-ass on back to camp.' "

"Never mind, then! Forget I said it!"

The pusher chuckled. "Getting interested, Relke?"

"I don't know. I guess I am." He looked quickly toward the towering rocket.

"Mostly you want to know how close you are to being rid of her, maybe?"

"I guess—Hey, they're letting him in."

"That lucky ole bastuhd!" Bama moaned.

The airlock opened as Lije scaled the ladder. A helmet containing a head of unidentifiable gender looked out and down, watching the man climb. Lije paused to wave. After a moment's hesitancy, the space-suited figure waved back.

"Hey, up theah, y'all mind a little company?"

The party who watched him made no answer. Lije shook his head and climbed on. When he reached the lock, he held out a glove for an assist, but the figure stepped back quickly. Lije stared inside. The figure was holding a gun. Lije stepped down a rung. The gun beckoned impatiently for him to get inside. Reluctantly Lije obeyed.

The hatch closed. A valve spat a jet of frost, and they watched the pressure dial slowly creep to ten psi. Lije watched the stranger unfasten his helmet, then undid his own. The stranger was male, and the white goggle marks about his eyes betrayed him as a spacer. His thin dark features suggested Semitic or Arabic origins.

"Parlez-vous français?"

"Naw," said Lije. "Sho' don't. Sorry."

The man tossed his head and gave a knowing snort. "Ah! Afrique-Américain. Yais. I had forgotten. I misthought you African. Apologeez?"

"Needn' bothuh," said Lije. "Coss, if you feelin' apologetic, you might put that pistola back in yo' boot."

"Ho?" The man looked down at the gun in his hand as if he had forgotten it. "Ho! It is first necessaire that we find out who you are," he explained, and brandished the weapon under Lije's nose. He grinned a flash of white teeth. "Who send you here?"

"Nobody send me. I come unduh my own steam. Some fellas in my moonjeep pulled cahds, and I—"

"Whup! You are—ah *tin Unteroffizier? Mais non,* wrong sprach—you *l'officiale?* Officer? Company man?"

"Who, me? Lahd, no. I'm juss a hot-stick man on B-shif'. You muss be lookin' fo' Suds Brodanovitch."

"Why you come to this ship?"

"Well, the fellas and I heard tell theah was some gals, and we—"

The man waved the gun impatiently and pressed a button near the inner hatch. A red indicator light went on.

"Yes?" A woman's voice, rather hoarse. Lije's chest heaved with sudden emotion, and his sigh came out a bleat.

The man spoke in a flood of French. The woman did not reply at once. Lije noticed the movement of a viewing lens beside the hatch; it was scanning him from head to toe.

The woman's voice shifted to an intimate contralto. "OK, dearie, you come right in here where it's nice and warm."

The inner hatch slid open. It took Lije a few seconds to realize that she had been talking to him. She stood there smiling at him like a middle-aged schoolmarm.

"Why don't you come on in and meet the girls?"

Eyes popping, Lije Henderson stumbled inside.

He was gone a long time.

When he finally came out, the men in Novotny's runabout took turns cursing at him over the suit frequency. *"Fa chrissake, Henderson, we've been sitting here using up oxy for over an hour while you been horsing around . . ."* They waited for him with the runabout, cabin depressurized.

Lije was panting wildly as he ran toward them. *"Lissen to the bahstud giggle,"* Bama said disgustedly.

"Y'all juss don' know, y'all juss don' KNOW!" Lije was chanting between pants.

"Get in heré, you damn traitor!"

"Hones', I couldn' help myself. I juss couldn'."

"Well, do the rest of us get aboard her, or not?" Joe snapped.

"Hell, go ahead, man! It's wide open. Evahthing's wide open."

"Girls?" Relke grunted.

"Girls. God yes! Girls."

"You coming with us?" Joe asked. Lije shook his head and fell back on the seat, still panting. *"Lahd, no! I couldn't stand it. I juss want to lie heah and look up at*

ole Mamma Earth and feel like a human again." He grinned beatifically. *"Y'all go on."*

Braxton was staring at his crony with curious suspicion. *"Man, those must be some entuhtainuhs! Whass the mattah with you, Lije?"*

Henderson whooped and pounded his leg. *"Hoo hoo! Hooeee! Entuhtainuhs, he says. Hoo-hooeee! You mean y'all still don' know what that ship is?"*

They had already climbed out of the tractor. Novotny glared back in at Lije. *"We've been waiting to hear it from you, Henderson,"* he snapped.

Lije sat up grinning. *"That's no stage show troupe! That ship, so help me Hannah, is a—hoo hoo hooee—is a goddam flyin' HO-house."* He rolled over on the seat and surrendered to laughter.

Novotny looked around for his men and found himself standing alone. Braxton was already on the ladder, and Relke was just starting up behind.

"Hey, you guys come back here!"

"Drop dead, Joe."

Novotny stared after them until they disappeared through the lock. He glanced back at Lije. Henderson was in a grinning beatific trance. The pusher shrugged and left him lying there, still wearing his pressure suit in the open cabin. The pusher trotted after his men toward the ship.

Before he was halfway there, a voice broke into his headsets. *"Where the devil are you going, Novotny? I want a talk with you!"*

He stopped to glance back. The voice belonged to Brodanovitch, and it sounded sore. The engineer's runabout had nosed in beside Novotny's; Suds sat in the cab and beckoned at him angrily. Joe trudged on back and climbed in through the vehicle's coffin-sized airlock. Brodanovitch glared at him while the pusher removed his helmet.

"What the devil's going on over there?"

"At the ship?" Joe paused. Suds was livid. "I don't know exactly."

"I've been calling Safety and Rescue for an hour and a half. Where are they?"

"In the ship, I guess."

"You *guess!*"

"Hell, chief, take it easy. We just got here. I don't know what's going on."

"Where are your men?"

Novotny jerked his thumb at the other runabout. "Henderson's in there. Relke and Brax went to the ship."

"And that's where you were going just now, I take it," Suds snarled.

"Take that tone of voice and shove it, Suds! You know where you told me to go. I went. Now I'm off. We're on our own time unless you tell us different."

The engineer spent a few seconds swallowing his fury. "All right," he grunted. "But every man on that rescue squad is going to face a Space Court, and if I have any say about it, they'll get decomped."

Novotny's jaw dropped. "Slow down, Suds. Explosive decompression is for mutiny or murder. What're you talking about?"

"Murder."

"Wha-a-at?"

"That's what I call it. A demolition man—Hardin, it was—had a blowout. With only one man standing by on the rescue gear."

"Meteor dust?"

"Yeah."

"Would it have made any difference if Saftey and Rescue had been on the job?"

Suds glowered. "Maybe, maybe not. An inspector might have spotted the bulge in his suit before it blew." He shook an angry finger toward the abandoned Safety & Rescue vehicles. "Those men are going to stand trial for negligent homicide. It's the principle, damn it!"

"Sure, Suds. I guess you're right. I'll be right back."

Henderson was sleeping in his pressure suit when Novotny climbed back into his own runabout. The cab was still a vacuum. He got the hatch closed, turned on the air pumps, then woke Henderson.

"Lije, you been with a woman?"

"Nnnnnngg-nnnng! I hope to tell!" He shot a quick glance toward the rocket as if to reassure himself as to its reality. "And man, was she a little—"

Joe shook him again. "Listen. Brodanovitch is in the next car. Bull mad. I'll ask you again. You been with a woman?"

"Woman? You muss of lost yoah mine, Joe. Lass

time I saw a woman was up at Atlanta." He rolled his
eyes up toward the Earth crescent in the heavens. "Sure
been a long ole time. Atlanta . . . *man!*"

"That's better."

Lije jerked his head toward Brodanovitch's jeep.
"What's ole wet blanket gonna do? Chase those gals out
of here, I 'spect?"

"I don't know. That's not what he's frothing about,
Lije. Hardin got killed while the S&R boys were shacking
up over there. Suds doesn't even *know* what's in that
ship. He acts like he's got about a dozen troubles running
loose at once, and he doesn't know which way to grab."

"He don't even *know?* How we evah gonna keep him
from findin' out?" Lije shot another glance at the ship
and jumped. "Uh-oh! Looka theah! Yonder they come.
Clamberin' down the ladies' ladduh. Theah's Joyce and
Lander and Petzel—other one looks like Crump. Half
the Safety team, Joe. Hoo-eee! They got that freshly
bred look. You can evum tell it from heah. Uh-oh!"

Brodanovitch had climbed out of his runabout. Bellowing at his mic, he charged toward the ship. The S&R men
took a few lopes toward their vehicles, saw Brodanovitch,
and stopped. One man turned tail and bolted for the
ladder again. Gesturing furiously, the engineer bore
down on them.

"Leave the radio off, Joe. Sure glad we don' have to
listen to that bull bellow."

They sat watching the safety men, who managed
somehow to look stark naked despite their bulgey pressure suits. Suds stalked toward them like an amok run-
ner, beating a gloved fist into his palm and working his
jaw at them.

"Suds don' know how to get along with men when he
want to get along with 'em, and he don't know how to fuss
at 'em when he don't want to get along. Man, look how
he rave!"

"Yeah. Suds is a smart engineer, but he's a rotten
overseer."

The ship's airlock opened again and another man
started out. He stopped with one foot on the top rung of
the ladder. He looked down at Brodanovitch and the
S&R men. He pulled his leg back inside and closed the
hatch. Novotny chuckled.

"That was Relke, the damn fool."

Lije smote his forehead. "Look at Suds! They tole him! They went an *tole* him, Joe. We'll nevah get back in that ship now."

The pusher watched the four figures on the plain. They were just standing there. Brodanovitch had stopped gesticulating. For a few seconds he seemed frozen. His head turned slowly as he looked up at the rocket. He took three steps toward it, then stopped.

"He gonna have apoplexy, thass what he gonna have."

Brodanovitch turned slowly. He gave the S&R men a blank look, then broke into a run toward his tractor.

"I'd better climb out," Joe said.

He met the engineer beside the command runabout. Sud's face was a livid mask behind the faceplate. *"Get in,"* he snapped at the pusher.

As soon as they were inside, he barked, "Drive us to Crater City."

"Slow down, Suds."

"Joe. That ship. Damn brothel. Out to fleece the camp."

"So what're you going to do in Crater City?"

"Tell Parkeson, what else?"

"And what's the camp going to be doing while you're gone?"

That one made him pause. Finally he shook his head. "Drive, Joe."

Novotny flipped the switch and glanced at the gauges. "You haven't got enough oxygen in this bug to last out the trip."

"Then we'll get another one."

"Better take a minute to think it over, Suds. You're all revved up. What the hell can Parkeson do?"

"What can he *do?* What can—migawd, Joe!" Suds choked.

"Well?"

"He can get that ship out of here, he can have those women interned."

"How? Suppose they refuse to budge. Who appointed Parkeson king of creation? Hell, he's only *our* boss, Suds. The moon's open to any nation that wants to send a ship, or to any corporation that can get a clearance. The W.P. decided that a long time ago."

"But it's illegal—those women, I mean!"

"How do you know? Maybe their racket's legal in

Algiers. That's where you told me they had clearance from, didn't you? And if you're thinking about the Schneider-Volkov Act, it just applies to the Integrated Projects, not wildcat teams."

Brodanovitch sat silent for a few moments, his throat working. He passed a shaky hand over his eyes. "Joe, we've got to keep discipline. Why can't I ever make the men understand that? On a moon project, it's discipline or die. You know that, Joe."

"Sure I know it. You know it. Parkeson knows it. The First Minister of the Space Ministry knows it. But the men don't know it, and they never will. They don't know what the word 'discipline' means, and it's no good trying to tell them. It's an overseer's word. It means your outfit's working for you like your own arms and legs. One brain and one body. When it cracks, you've just got a loose handful of stray men. No coordination. You can see it, but they can't see it. 'Discipline' is just a dirty word in the ranks, Suds."

"Joe, what'll I do?"

"It's your baby, not mine. Give it first aid. Then talk to Parkeson later, if you want to."

Suds sat silent for half a minute, then: "Drive back to the main wagon."

Novotny started the motors. "What are you going to do?"

"Announce Code Red, place the ship off limits, put an armed guard on it, and hope the Crater City crew gets that telephone circuit patched up quick. That's all I can do."

"Then let me get a safe distance away from you before you do it."

"You think it'll cause trouble?"

"Good Lord, Suds, use your head. You've got a campful of men who haven't been close to a dame in months and years, even to talk to. They're sick, they're scared, they're fed-up, they want to go home. The Party's got them bitter, agitated. I'd hate to be the guy who puts those women off limits."

"What would you do?"

"I'd put the screws on the shift that's on duty. I'd work hell out of the crews that are supposed to be on the job. I'd make a horrible example out of the first man to goof off. But first I'd tell the off-duty team pushers they can take their crews over to that ship, one crew at a time, and in an orderly manner."

"*What?* And be an accomplice? Hell, no!"

"Then do it your own way. Don't ask me."

Novotny parked the runabout next to the boss-wagon. "Mind if I use your buggy for awhile, Suds?" he asked. "I left mine back there, and I've got to pick up my men."

"Go ahead, but get them back here—fast."

"Sure, Suds."

He backed the runabout out again and drove down to B-shift's sleep-wagon. He parked again and used the airlock phone. "Beasley, Benet, the rest of you—come on outside."

Five minutes later they trooped out through the lock. "What's the score, Joe?"

"The red belts are ahead, that's all I know."

"Come on. you'll find out."

"Sleep! I haven't had no sleep since—*Say!* You takin' us over to that ship, Joe?"

"That's the idea."

"YAYHOO!" Beasley danced up and down. "Joe, we love ya!"

"Cut it. This is once-and-once-only. You're going once, and you're not going again."

"Who says?"

"Novotny says."

"But *why?*" Benet wailed.

"What did you say?"

"I said 'why!' "

"OK. I'll tell you why. Brodanovitch is going to put the ship off limits. If I get you guys in under the wire, you've got no gripe later on—when Suds hangs out the big No."

"Joe, that's chicken."

Novotny put on the brakes. "Get out and walk back, Benet."

"Joe—!"

"Benet."

"Look, I didn't mean anything."

Novotny paused. If Brodanovitch was going to try to do things the hard way, he'd lose control of his own men unless he gave them loose rein for a while first— keeping them reminded that he still *had* the reins. But

Benet was getting out of hand lately. He had to decide.
Now.

"Look at me, Benet."

Benet looked up. Joe smacked him. Benet sat back,
looking surprised. He wiped his nose on the back of a
glove and looked at the red smear. He wiped it again.
The smear was bigger.

"You can stay, Benet, but if you do, I'll bust your
hump after we get back. You want it that way?"

Benet looked at the rocket; he looked at Joe; he
looked at the rocket. "Yeah. We'll see who does the
busting. Let's go."

"All right, but do you see any other guys taking their
teams over?"

"No."

"But you think you're getting a chicken deal."

"Yeah."

The pusher drove on, humming to himself. As long as
he could keep them alternately loving him and hating
him, everything was secure. Then he was Mother. Then
they didn't stop to think or rationalize. They just reacted to Mother. It was easy to handle men reacting,
but it wasn't so easy to handle men thinking. Novotny
liked it the easy way, especially during a heavy meteor
fall.

"It is of no importance to me," said Madame d'Annecy,
"if you are the commandant of the whole of space,
M'sieur. You wish entrance, I must ask you to contribute
thees small fee. It is not in my nature to become unpleasant like thees, but you have bawl in my face,
M'sieur."

"Look," said Brodanovitch, "I didn't come over here
for . . . for what you think I came over here for." His
ears reddened. "I don't want a girl, that is."

The madame's prim mouth made a small pink O of
sudden understanding. "Ah, M'sieur, I begin to see.
You are one of those. But in that I cannot help you. I
have only girls."

The engineer choked. He started toward the hatch. A
man with a gun slid into his path.

"Permit yourself to be restrained, M'sieur."

"There are four men in there that are supposed to
be on the job, and I intend to get them. And the others
too, while I'm at it."

"Is it that you have lost your boy friend, perhaps?"

Brodanovitch croaked incomprehensibly for a moment, then collapsed onto a seat beside the radar table that Madame d'Annecy was using for an accounting desk. "I'm no fairy," he said.

"I am pleased to hear it, M'sieur. I was beginning to pity you. Now if you will please sign the sight draft. so that we may telecast it—"

"I am *not* paying twelve hundred dollars just to get my men out of there!"

"I do not haggle, M'sieur. The price is fixed."

"Call them down here!"

"It cannot be done. They pay for two hours, for two hours they stay. Undisturbed."

"All right, let's see the draft."

Madame d'Annecy produced a set of forms from the map case and a small gold fountain pen from her ample bosom. "Your next of kin, M'sieur?" She handed him a blank draft.

"Wait a minute! How did you know where my account—"

"Is it not the correct firm?"

'Yes, but how did yo know?" He looked at the serial number on the form, then looked up accusingly. "This is a telecopy form. You have a teletransmitter on board?"

"But of course! We could not risk having payment stopped after services rendered. The funds will be transferred to our account before you leave this ship. I assure you, we are well protected."

"I assure you, you are all going to jail."

Madame d'Annecy threw back her head and laughed heartily. She said something in French to the man at the door, then smiled at the unhappy engineer. "What law prevails here, M'sieur?"

"UCOJE does. Uniform Code of Justice, Extraterrestrial. It's a semi-military—"

"U.N.-based, I believe?"

"Certainly."

"Now I know little of thees matters, but my attorneys would be delighted, I am certain, if you can tell me: which articles of thees UCOJE is to be used for inducing us to be incarcerated?"

"Why . . . Uh . . ." Suds scratched nervously at one

corner of his moustache. He glanced at the man with the gun. He gazed forlornly at the sight draft.

"Exactly!" Mme d'Annecy said brightly. "There have been no women to speak of on the moon since the unfortunate predicament of *les enfants perdus.* The moonborn grotesque ones. How could they think to pass laws against thees—thees *ancien* establishment, thees *maison intime*—when there are no women, eh M'sieur?"

"But you falsified your papers to get clearance. You must have."

"But no. Our clearance is 'free nation,' not 'world federal.' We are an entertainment troupe, and my government's officials are most lenient in defining 'entertainment.' *Chacun à son gout,* eh?"

Suds sat breathing heavily. "I can place this ship off limits."

"If you can do that, if the men do not come"—she shrugged eloquently and spread her hands—"then we will simply move on to another project. There are plenty of others. But do you think thees putting us off limits will make you very popular with your men?"

"I'm not trying to win a popularity contest," Suds wheezed. "I'm trying to finish the last twelve miles of this line before sundown. You've got to get out of here before there's a complete work stoppage."

"Thees project. It is important? Of an urgent nature?"

"There's a new uranium mine in the crater we're building toward. There's a colony there without an independent ecology. It has to be supplied from Copernicus. Right now, they're shooting supplies to them by rocket missile. It's too far to run surface freight without trolley service— or reactor-powered vehicles the size of battleships and expensive. We don't have the facilities to run a fleet of self-powered wagons that far."

"Can they not run on diesel, perhaps?"

"If they carry the oxygen to burn the diesel with, and if everybody in Copernicus agrees to stop breathing the stuff."

"*Embarras de choix.* I see."

"It's essential that the line be finished before nightfall. If it isn't, that mine colony will have to be shipped back to Copernicus. They can't keep on supplying it by bird. And they can't move out any ore until the trolley is ready to run."

Mme d'Annecy nodded thoughtfully. "We wish to make the cordial entente with the lunar workers," she murmured. "We do not wish to cause the *bouleversement* —the disruption. Let us then negotiate, M'sieur."

"I'm not making any deals with you, lady."

"Ah, but such a hard position you take! I was but intending to suggest that you furnish us a copy of your camp's duty roster. If you will do that, Henri will not permit anyone to visit us if he is—how you say?—goofing off. Is it not that simple?"

"I will not be a party to robbery!"

"How is it robbery?"

"Twelve hundred dollars! Pay for two day-hitches. Lunar days. Nearly two months. And you're probably planning to fleece them more than once."

"*A bon marché!* Our expenses are terrific. Believe me, we expect no profit from this first trip."

"First trip and last trip," Suds grumbled.

"And who has complained about the price? No one so far excepting M'sieur. Look at it *thus* it is an investment." She slid one of the forms across the table. "Please to read it, M'sieur."

Suds studied the paper for a moment and began to frown. "*Les Folies Lunaires*, Incorporated . . . a North African corporation . . . in consideration of the sum of one hundred dollars in hand paid by—who?—Howard Beasley!—aforesaid corporation sells and grants to Howard Beasley . . . *one share of common stock!*"

"M'sieur! Compose yourself! It is no fraud. Everybody gets a share of stock. It comes out of the twelve hundred. Who knows? Perhaps after a few trips, there will even be dividends. M'sieur? But you look positively ill! Henri, bring brandy for the gentleman."

"So!" he grated. "That's the way it goes, is it? Implicate everybody—nobody squawks."

"But certainly. It is for our own protection, to be sure, but it is really stock."

"Blackmail."

"But no, M'sieur. All is legal."

Henri brought a plastic cup and handed it to him; Suds shook his head.

"Take it, M'sieur. It is real brandy. We could bring only a few bottles, but there is sufficient pure alcohol for the mixing of cocktails."

The small compartment was filled with the delicate perfume of the liquor; Brodanovitch glanced longingly at the plastic cup.

"It is seventy-year-old Courvoisier, M'sieur. Very pleasant."

Suds took it reluctantly, dipped it toward Mme d'Annecy in self-conscious toast, and drained it. He acquired a startled expression; he clucked his tongue experimentally and breathed slowly through his nose.

"Good Lord!" he murmured absently.

Mme d'Annecy chuckled. "M'sieur has forgotten the little pleasures. It was a shame to gulp it so. *Encore, Henri.* And one for myself, I think. Take time to enjoy this one, M'sieur." She studied him for a time while Henri was absent. She shook her head and began putting the forms away, leaving out the sight draft and stock agreement which she pushed toward him, raising one inquisitive brow. He gazed expressionlessly at them. Henri returned with the brandy; Madame questioned him in French. He seemed insistently negative for a time, but then seemed to give grudging assent. *"Bien!"* she said, and turned to Brodanovitch: "M'sieur, it will be necessary only for you to purchase the share of stock. Forget the fee."

"What?" Suds blinked in confusion.

"I said—" The opening of the hatch interrupted her thought. A dazzling brunette in a filmy yellow dress bounced into the compartment, bringing with her a breath of perfume. Suds looked at her and emitted a loud guttural cluck. A kind of glazed incredulity kneaded his face into a mask of shocked granite wearing a supercilious moustache. The girl ignored his presence and bent over the table to chat excitedly in French with Mme. d'Annecy. Suds's eyes seemed to find a mind and will of their own; involuntarily they contemplated the details of her architecture, and found manifest fascination in the way she relieved an itch at the back of one trim calf by rubbing it vigorously with the instep of her other foot while she leaned over the desk and bounced lightly on tiptoe as she spoke.

"M'sieur Brodanovitch, the young lady wishes to know —M'sieur Brodanovitch?—*M'sieur!*"

"What—? Oh." Suds straightened and rubbed his eyes. "Yes?"

"One of your young men has asked Giselle out for a walk. We have pressure suits, of course. But is it safe to promenade about this area?" She paused. "M'sieur, *please!*"

"What?" Suds shook his head. He tore his eyes away from the yellow dress and glanced at a head suddenly thrust in through the hatch. The head belonged to Kelke. It saw Brodanovitch and withdrew in haste, but Suds made no sign of recognition. He blinked at Madame again.

"M'sieur, is it safe?"

"What? Oh. I suppose it is." He gulped his brandy and poured another.

Mme. d'Annecy spoke briefly to the girl, who, after a hasty *merci* and a nod at Suds went off to join Relke outside. When they were gone, Madame smilingly offered her pen to the engineer. Suds stared at it briefly, shook his head, and helped himself to another brandy. He gulped it and reached for his helmet. La d'Annecy snapped her fingers suddenly and went to a locker near the bulkhead. She came back with a quart bottle.

"M'sieur will surely accept a small token?" She offered the bottle for his inspection. "It is Mumms 2064, a fine year. Take it, M'sieur. Or do you not care for champagne? It is our only bottle, and what is one bottle of wine for such a crowd? Take it—or would you prefer the brandy?"

Suds blinked at the gift while he fastened his helmet and clamped it. He seemed dazed. She held the bottle out to him and smiled hopefully. Suds accepted it absentmindedly, nodded at her, and stepped into the airlock. The hatch slid closed.

Mme. d'Annecy started back toward her counting table. The alarm bell burst into a sudden brazen clamor. She looked back. A red warning signal flashed balefully. Henri burst in from the corridor, eyed the bell and the light, then charged toward the airlock. The gauge by the hatch showed zero pressure. He pressed a starter button, and a meter hummed to life. The pressure needle crept upward. The bell and the light continued a frenetic complaint. The motor stopped. Henri glanced at the gauge, then swung open the hatch. *"Allons! Ma foi, quelle merde!"*

Mme. d'Annecy came to peer around him into the small cubicle. Her subsequent shriek penetrated to the farthest corridors. Suds Brodanovitch had missed his last chance to become a stockholder.

"It wasn't yo' fault, Ma'am," said Lije Henderson a few minutes later as they half-led half-carried her to her compartment. "He knew beetuh than to step outside with that bottle of booze. You didn't know. You couldn' be 'spected to know. But he been heah long enough to know—a man make one mistake, thass all. BLOOIE."

Blooie was too graphic to suit Madame; she sagged and began retching.

"C'mon, Ma'am, less get you in yo hammock." They carried her into her quarters, eased her into bed, and stepped back out on the catwalk.

Lije mopped his face, leaned against a tension member, and glanced at Joe. "Now how come you s'pose he had that bottle of fizzling giggle water up close to his helmet that way, Joe?"

"I don't know. Reading the label, maybe."

"He sho' muss have had something on his mine."

"Well, it's gone now."

"Yeah. BLOOIE. Man!"

Relke had led the girl out through the lock in the reactor nacelle in order to evade Brodanovitch and a possible command to return to camp. They sat in Novotny's runabout and giggled cozily together at the fuzzy map of Earth that floated in the darkness above them. On the ship's fuselage, the warning light over the airlock hatch began winking, indicating that the lock was in use. The girl noticed it and nudged him. She pointed at the light.

"Somebody coming out," Relke muttered. "Maybe Suds. We'd better get out of here." He flipped the main switch and started the motor. He was backing onto the road when Giselle caught his arm.

"Beel! Look at the light!"

He glanced around. It was flashing red.

"Malfunction signal. Compressor trouble, probably. It's nothing. Let's take a ride. Joe won't care." He started backing again.

"Poof!" she said suddenly.

"What?"

"Poof. It opened, and *poof*—" She puckered her lips and blew a little puff of steam in the cold air to show him. "So. Like smoke."

He turned the car around in the road and looked back again. The hatch had closed. There was no one on the ladder. "Nobody came out."

"*Non.* Just poof."

He edged the car against the trolley rails, switched to autosteering, and let it gather speed.

"Beel?"

"Yeah, kid?"

"Where you taking me?"

He caught the note of alarm in her voice and slowed down again. She had come on a dare after several drinks, and the drinks were wearing off. The landscape was frightening alien, and the sense of falling into bottomlessness was ever-present.

"You want to go back?" he asked gloomily.

"I don't know. I don't like it out here."

"You said you wanted some ground under your feet."

"But it doesn't feel like ground when you walk on it."

"Rather be inside a building?"

She nodded eagerly.

"That's where we're going."

"To your camp?"

"God, no! I'm planning to keep you to myself."

She laughed and snuggled closer to him. "You can't. Madame d'Annecy will not permit—"

"Let's talk about something else," he grunted quickly.

"OK. Let's talk about Monday."

"Which Monday?"

"Next Monday. It's my birthday. When is it going to be Monday, Bill?"

"You said *Bill.*"

"Beel? That's your name, isn't eet? Weeliam Q. Relke, who weel not tell me what ees the *Q?*"

"But you said *Bill.*"

She was silent for a moment. "OK, I'm a phony," she muttered. "Does the inquisition start now?"

He could feel her tighten up, and he said nothing. She waited stiffly for a time. Gradually she relaxed against him again. "When's it going to be Monday?" she murmured.

"When's it going to be Monday where?"

"Here, anywhere, silly!"

He laughed. "When will it be Monday all over the universe?"

She thought for a moment. "Oh. Like time zones. OK, when will it be Monday here?"

"It won't. We just have periods, hitches, and shifts. Fifty shifts make a hitch, two hitches make a period. A period's from sunrise to sunrise. Twenty-nine and a half days. But we don't count days. So I don't know when it'll be Monday."

It seemed to alarm her. She sat up. "Don't you even have *hours?*" She looked at her watch and jiggled it, listened to it.

"Sure. Seven hours in a shift. *We* call them hours, anyhow. Forty-five seconds longer than an Earth hour."

She looked up through the canopy at the orb of Earth. "When it's Monday on Earth, it'll be Monday here too," she announced flatly.

Relke laughed. "OK, we'll call it that."

"So when will it start being Monday on Earth?"

"Well, it'll start at twenty-four different times, depending on where you are. Maybe more than twenty-four. It's August. Some places, they set the clocks ahead an hour in Summer."

She looked really worried.

"You take birthdays pretty seriously?" he asked.

"Only this one. I'll be—" She broke off and closed her mouth.

"Pick a time zone," Relke offered, "and I'll try to figure out how long until Monday starts. Which zone? Where you'd be now, maybe?"

She shook her head.

"Where you were born?"

"That would be—" She stopped again. "Never mind. Forget it." She sat brooding and watching the moonscape.

Relke turned off the road at the transformer station. He pulled up beside a flat-roofed cubicle the size of a sentry-box. Giselle looked at it in astonishment.

"*That's* a building?" she asked.

"That's an entrance. The 'building's' underground. Come on, let's seal up."

"What's down there?"

"Just a transformer vault and living quarters for a substation man."

"Somebody *lives* down there?"

"Not yet. The line's still being built. They'll move somebody in when the trolley traffic starts moving."

"What do we want to go down there for?"

He looked at her forlornly. "You'd rather go back to the ship?"

She seemed to pull herself together professionally. She laughed and put her arms around him and whispered something in French against his ear. She kissed him hard, pressed her forehead against his, and grinned. "C'mon, babee! Let's go downstairs."

Relke felt suddenly cold inside. He had wanted to see what it felt like to be alone with a woman again in a quiet place, away from the shouting howling revelry that had been going on aboard the ship. Now he knew what it was going to feel like. It was going to feel counterfeit. "Christ!" he grunted angrily. "Let's go back!" He reached roughly around her and cut on the switch again. She recoiled suddenly and gaped at him as he started the motor and turned the bug around.

"Hey!" She was staring at him oddly, as if seeing him for the first time.

Relke kept his face averted and his knuckles were white on the steering bar. She got up on her knees on the seat and put her hands on his shoulders. "Bill. Good Lord, you're *crying!*"

He choked out a curse as the bug hit the side of the cut and careened around on the approach to the road. He lost control, and the runabout went off the approach and slid slowly sideways down a gentle slope of crushed-lava fill. A sharp clanking sound came from the floor plates.

"Get you suit sealed!" he yelled. "Get it sealed!"

The runabout lurched to a sudden stop. The cabin pressure stayed up. He sat panting for a moment, then started the motor. He let it inch ahead and tugged at the steering bar. It was locked. The bug crept in an arc, and the clanking resumed. He cut off the motor and sat cursing softly.

"What's wrong?"

"Broke a link and the tread's fouled. We'll have to get out."

She glanced at him out of the corner of her eye. He was glowering. She looked back toward the sentrybox entrance to the substation and smiled thoughtfully.

It was chilly in the vault, and the only light came from the indicator lamps on the control board. The pressure gauge inside the airlock indicated only eight pounds of air. The construction crew had pumped it up to keep some convection currents going around the big transformers, but they hadn't planned on anyone breathing it soon. He changed the mixture controls, turned the barostat up to twelve pounds, and listened to the compressors start up. When he turned around, Giselle was taking off her suit and beginning to pant.

"*Hey,* stay in that thing!" he shouted.

His helmet muffled his voice, and she looked at him blankly. "*What?*" she called. She was gasping and looking around in alarm.

Relke sprinted a few steps to the emergency rack and grabbed a low pressure walk-around bottle. When he got back, she was getting blue and shaking her head drunkenly. He cracked the valve on the bottle and got the hose connection against her mouth. She nodded quickly and sucked on it. He went back to watch the gauges. He found the overhead lighting controls and turned them on. Giselle held her nose and anxiously sipped air from the bottle. He nodded reassuringly at her. The construction crews had left the substation filled with nitrogen-helium mixture, seeing no reason to add rust-producing moisture and oxygen until someone moved into the place; she had been breathing inert gases, nothing more.

When the partial oxygen pressure was up to normal, he left the control panel and went to look for the communicator. He found the equipment, but it was not yet tied into the line. He went back to tell the girl. Still sipping at the bottle, she watched him with attentive brown eyes. It was the gaze of a child, and he wondered about her age. Aboard ship, she and the others had seemed impersonal automata of Eros; painted ornaments and sleekly functional decoys designed to perform stereotyped rituals of enticement and excarnation of desire, swiftly, lest a customer be kept waiting. But here in stronger light, against a neutral background, he noticed suddenly that she was a distinct individual. Her lipstick had smeared. Her dark hair kept spilling out in tangled wisps from beneath a leather cap with fleece ear flaps. She wore a pair of coveralls, several sizes too large and rolled up about the ankles. With too much rouge on her solemnly mischievous face, she looked ready for a role in a girls' school version of *Chanticler*.

"You can stop breathing out of the can," he told her. "The oxygen pressure's okay now."

She took the hose from her mouth and sniffed warily. "What was the matter? I was seeing spots."

"It's all right now."

"It's cold in this place. Are we stuck here?"

"I tried to call Joe, but the set's not hooked up. He'll come looking for us."

"Isn't there any heat in here? Can't you start a fire?"

He glanced down at the big 5,000 kva transformers in the pit beyond the safety rail. The noise of corona discharge was very faint, and the purr of thirty-two cycle hum was scarcely audible. With no trucks drawing power from the trolley, the big pots were cold. Normally, eddy current and hysteresis losses in the transformers would keep the station toast-warm. He glanced at a thermometer. It read slightly under freezing: the ambient temperature of the subsurface rock in that region.

"Let's try the stationman's living quarters," he grunted. "They usually furnish them fancy, as bunk tanks go. Man has to stay by himself out here, they want to keep him sane."

A door marked PRIVATE flipped open as they approached it. A cheery voice called out: *"Hi, Bo. Rugged deal, ain't it?"*

Giselle started back in alarm. "Who's there?"

Relke chuckled. "Just a recorded voice. Back up, I'll show you."

They moved a few paces away. The door fell closed. They approached it again. This time a raucous female squawked at them: *"Whaddaya mean coming home at this hour? Lemme smell your breath."*

Giselle caught on and grinned. "So he won't get lonesome?"

"Partly, and partly to keep him a little sore. The stationmen hate it, but that's part of the idea. It gives them something to talk back to and throw things at."

They entered the apartment. The door closed itself, the lights went on. Someone belched, then announced: *"I get just as sick of looking at you as you do looking at me, button head. Go take a bath."*

Relke flushed. "It can get pretty rough sometimes. The tapes weren't edited for mixed company. Better plug your ears if you go in the bathroom."

Giselle giggled. "I think it's cute."

He went into the kitchenette and turned on all the
burners of the electric range to help warm the place.
"Come stand next to the oven," he called, "until I see if
the heat pumps are working." He opened the oven door.
A libidinous purr came from within.

*"Dah-ling, now why bother with breakfast when you
can have meee?"*

He glanced up at Giselle.

"I didn't say it," she giggled, but posed invitingly.

Relke grinned and accepted the invitation.

"You're not crying now," she purred as he released her.

He felt a surge of unaccountable fury, grunted, "Excuse
me," and stalked out to the transformer vault. He looked
around for the heat pumps, failed to find them, and went to
lean on the handrail over-looking the pit. He stood there
with his fists in his pockets, vaguely anguished and enraged, for no reason he understood. For a moment he had
been too close to feeling at home, and that brought up the
wrath somehow. After a couple of minutes he shook it off
and went back inside.

"Hey, I wasn't teasing you," Giselle told him.

"What?"

"About crying."

"Listen," he said irritably, "did you ever see a looney
or a spacer without leaky eyes? It's the glare, that's all."

"Is that it? Huh—want to know something? I can't
cry. That's funny. You're a man and you can cry, but I
can't."

Relke watched her grumpily while she warmed her behind at the oven. *She's not more than fifteen*, he decided
suddenly. It made him a little queasy. *Come on, Joe,
hurry.*

"You know," she went on absently, "when I was a little
girl, I got mad at . . . at somebody, and I decided I was
never going to cry anymore. I never did, either. And you
know what?—now I can't. Sometimes I try and I try, but
I just *can't.*" She spread her hands to the oven, tilted them
back and forth, and watched the way the tendons worked
as she stiffened her fingers. She seemed to be talking to
her hands. "Once I used an onion. To cry, I mean. I cut
an onion and rubbed some of it on a handkerchief and
laid the hankerchief over my eyes. I cried that time, all
right. That time I couldn't stop crying, and nobody could

make me stop. They were petting me and scolding me and shaking me and trying to give me smelling salts, but I just couldn't quit. I blubbered for two days. Finally Mother Bernarde had to call the doctor to give me a sedative. Some of the sisters were taking cold towels and—"

"Sisters?" Relke grunted.

Giselle clapped a hand to her mouth and shook her head five or six times, very rapidly. She looked around at him. He shrugged.

"So you were in a convent."

She shook her head again.

"So what if you were?" He sat down with his back to her and pretended to ignore her. She was dangerously close to that state of mind which preceeds the telling of a life history. He didn't want to hear it; he already knew it. So she was in a nunnery; Relke was not surprised. Some people had to polarize themselves. If they broke free from one pole, they had to seek its opposite. People with no middle ground. Black, or if not black, then white, never gray. Law, or criminality. God, or Satan. The cloister, or a whorehouse. Eternally a choice of all or nothing-at-all, and they couldn't see that they made things that way for themselves. They set fire to every bridge they ever crossed —so that even a cow creek became a Rubicon, and every crossing was on a tightrope.

You understand that too well, don't you, Relke? he asked himself bitterly. There was Fran and the baby, and there wasn't enough money, and so you had to go and burn a bridge—a 240,000-mile bridge, with Fran on the other side. And so, after six years on Luna, there would be enough money; but there wouldn't be Fran and the baby. And so, he had signed another extended contract, and the moon was going to be home for a long long time. *Yeh, you know about burned bridges, all right, Relke.*

He glanced at Giselle. She was glaring at him.

"If you're waiting for me to say something," she snapped, "you can stop waiting. I don't have to tell you anything."

"I didn't ask you anything."

"I was just a novice. I didn't take permanent vows."

"All *right.*"

"They wouldn't let me. They said I was—unstable. They didn't think I had a calling."

"Well, you've got one now. Stop crawling all over me like I said anything. I didn't ask you any questions."

"You gave me that pious look."

"Oh, garbage!" He rolled out of the chair and loped off to the room. The stationman's quarters boasted its own music system and television (permanently tuned to the single channel that broadcast a fairly narrow beam aimed at the lunar stations). He tried the television first, but solar interference was heavy.

"Maybe it'll tell us when it's going to be Monday," she said, coming to watch him from the doorway.

He gave her a sharp look, then softened it. The stove had warmed the kitchen, and she had stepped out of the baggy coveralls. She was still wearing the yellow dress, and she had taken a moment to comb her hair. She leaned against the side of the doorway, looking very young but excessively female. She had that lost pixie look and a tropical climate tan too.

"Why are you looking at me that way?" she asked. "Is this all we're going to do? I mean, just wait around until somebody comes? Can't we dance or something?" She did a couple of skippity steps away from the door jamb and rolled her hips experimentally. One hip was made of India rubber. "Say! Dancing ought to be fun in this crazy gravity." She smirked at him and posed alluringly.

Relke swallowed, reddened, and turned to open the selector cabinet. *She's only a kid, Relke.* He paused, then dialed three selections suitable for dancing. *She's only a kid, damn it!* He paused again, then dialed a violin concerto. *A kid—back home they'd call her "jail bait."* He dialed ten minutes' worth of torrid Spanish guitar. *You'll hate yourself for it, Relke.* He shuddered involuntarily, dialed one called *The Satyricon of Lily Brown, an orgy in New African Jazz (for adults only).*

He glanced up guiltily. She was already whirling around the room with an imaginary partner, dancing to the first selection.

Relke dialed a tape of Palestrina and some plainchant, but left it for last. Maybe it would neutralize the rest.

She snuggled close and they tried to keep time to the music—not an easy task, with the slow motion imposed by low gravity mismatched to the livelier rhythms of dancing on Earth. Two attempts were enough. Giselle flopped down on the bunk.

"What's that playing now, Bill?"

"Sibelius. Concerto for Something and Violin. I dunno."

"Bill?"

"Yeah."

"Did I make you mad or something?"

"No, but I don't think—" He turned to look at her and stopped talking. She was lying on her back with her hands behind her head and her legs cocked up, balancing her calf on her other knee and watching her foot wiggle. She was lithe and brown and . . . ripe.

"Damn," he muttered.

"Bill?"

"Uh?"

She wrinkled her nose at him and smiled. "Don't you even know what you wanted to come over here for?"

Relke got up slowly and walked to the light switch. He snapped it.

Oh, dahling!" said a new voice in the darkness. *"What if my husband comes home!"*

After Sibelius came the Spanish guitar. The African jazz was wasted.

Relke sat erect with a start. Giselle still slept, but noises came from the other room. There were voices, and a door slammed closed. Shuffling footsteps, a muffled curse. "Who's there?" he yelled "Joe?"

The noises stopped, but he heard the hiss of someone whispering. He nudged the girl awake with one elbow. The record changer clicked, and the soft chant of an *Agnus Dei* came from the music system.

"Oh, God! It's Monday!" Giselle muttered sleepily.

"A dame," grunted a voice in the next room.

"Who's there?" Relke called again.

"We brought you some company." The voice sounded familiar. A light went on in the other room. "Set him down over here, Harv."

Relke heard rattling sounds and a chair scraped back. They dumped something into the chair. Then the bulky silhouette of a man filled the doorway. "Who's in here, anyhow?" He switched on the lights. The man was Larkin. Giselle pulled a blanket around herself and blinked sleepily.

"Is it Monday?" she asked.

A slow grin spread across Larkin's face. "Hey Harv!" he called over his shoulder. "Look what we pulled out of the grab bag! Come look at lover boy. . . . Now, Harv— is that sweet? Is that romantic?"

Kunz looked over Larkin's shoulder. "Yuh. Real homey, ain't it. Hiyah, Rat. Lookit that cheese he's got with him. Some cheese. Round like a provolone, huh? Hiyah, cheesecake, know you're in bed with a rat?"

Giselle glanced questioningly at Relke. Relke was surveying the tactical situation. It looked unpromising. Larkin laughed.

"Look at him, Harv—wondering where he left his shiv. What's the matter, Relke? We make you nervous?" He stepped inside, Kunz followed.

Relke stood up in bed and backed against the wall. "Get out of the way," he grunted at Giselle.

"Look at him!" Larkin gloated. "Getting ready to kick. You planning to kick somebody, sonny?"

"Stay back!" he snapped. "Get out of here, Giselle!"

"A l'abri? Oui—" She slid off the bed and darted for the door. Kunz grabbed at her, but she slipped past. She stopped in the doorway and backed up a step. She stared into the next room. She put her hand to her mouth. "Oh! Oh!" she yelped. Larkin and Kunz glanced back at her. Relke lunged off the bed. He smashed against Larkin, sent him sprawling into Kunz. He dodged Giselle and sprinted for the kitchen and the cutlery rack. He made it a few steps past the door before he saw what Giselle had seen. Something was sitting at the table, facing the door. Relke stopped in his tracks and began backing away. The something at the table was a blistered caricature of a man, an icy frost-figure in a deflated pressure suit. Its mouth was open, and the stomach had been forced up through . . . He closed his eyes. Relke had seen men blown out, but it hadn't gotten any pleasanter to look at since the last time.

"Get him, Harv!"

They pinned his arms from behind. "Heading for a butcher knife, Relke?" He heard a dull crack and felt his head explode. The room went pink and hazy.

"That's for grabbing glass on us the other day, Sonny."

"Don't mess him up too much, Lark. The dame's here."

"I won't mess him up. I'll be real clean about it."

The crack came again, and the pink haze quivered with black flashes.

"That's for ratting on the Party, Relke."

Dimly he heard Giselle screaming at them to stop it.

"Take that little bitch in the other room and play house with her, Harv. I'll work on Sonny awhile, and then we'll trade around. Don't wear her out."

"Let go," she yelled. "Take your hands off—listen, I'll go in there with you if you'll quite beating him. Now stop—"

Another crack. The pink haze flew apart, and blackness engulfed him. Time moved ahead in jerks for awhile. First he was sitting at the table across from the corpse. Larkin was there too, dealing himself a hand of solitaire. Loud popular music blared from the music system, but he could hear Kunz laughing in the next room. Once Giselle's voice cried out in protest. Relke moved and groaned. Larkin looked his way.

"Hey, Harv—he's awake. It's your turn."

"I'm busy," Kunz yelled.

"Well, hurry up. Brodanovitch is beginning to thaw."

Relke blinked at the dead man. "Who? Him? Brodan—" His lips were swollen, and it was painful to talk.

"Yeah, that's Suds. Pretty, isn't he? You're going to look like that one of these days, kid."

"You—killed—Suds?"

Larkin threw back his head and laughed. "Hey, Harv, hear that? He thinks we killed Suds."

"What happened to him, then?"

Larkin shrugged. "He walked into an airlock with a bottle of champagne. The pressure went down quick, the booze blew up in his face, and there sits Suds. A victim of imprudence, like you. Sad looking schlemazel, isn't he?"

"Wha'd you bring him here for?"

"You know the rules, Sonny. A man gets blown out, they got to look him over inch by inch, make sure it wasn't murder."

Giselle cried out again in protest. Relke started to his feet, staggering dizzily. Larkin grabbed him and pushed him down.

"Hey, Harv! He's getting frisky. Come take over. The gang'll be rolling in pretty quick."

Kunz came out of the bunkroom. Larkin sprinted for

the door as Giselle tried to make a run for it. He caught her and dragged her back. He pushed her into the bunkroom, went in after her, and closed the door. Relke lunged at Kunz, but a judo cut knocked numbness into the side of his neck and sent him crashing against the wall.

"Relke, get wise," Harv growled. "This'll happen every now and then if you don't join up."

The lineman started to his feet. Kunz kicked him disinterestedly. Relke groaned and grabbed his side.

"We got no hard feelings, Relke. . . ." He chopped his boot down against the back of Relke's neck. "You can join the Party any time."

Time moved ahead in jerks again.

Once he woke up. Brodanovitch was beginning to melt, and the smell of brandy filled the room. There were voices and chair scrapings and after a while somebody carried Brodanovitch out. Relke lay with his head against the wall and kept his eyes closed. He assumed that if the apartment contained a friend, he would not still be lying here on the floor; so he remained motionless and waited to gather strength.

"So that's about the size of it," Larkin was telling someone. "Those dames are apt to be dynamite if they let them into Crater City. We've got enough steam whipped up to pull off the strike, but what if that canful of cat meat walks in on Copernicus about sundown? Who's going to have their mind on politics?"

"Hell, Lark," grunted a strange voice. "Parkeson'll never let them get in town."

"No? Don't be too damn sure. Parkeson's no idiot. He knows trouble's coming. Hell, he could *invite* them to Crater City, pretend he's innocent as a lamb, just didn't know what they are, but take credit for them being there."

"Well, what can we do about it?"

"Cripple that ship."

"Wha-a-at?"

"Cripple the ship. Look, there's nothing else we can do on our own. We've got no orders from the Party. Right before we break camp, at sundown, we cripple the ship. Something they can't fix without help from the base."

"Leave them *stuck* out here?"

"Only for a day or two. Till the Party takes over the base. Then *we* send a few wagons out here after dark and pick up the wenches. Who gets credit for dames showing up? The Party. Besides, it's the only thing we dare do without orders. We can't be sure what'd happen if Parkeson walked in with a bunch of Algerian whores about the time the show's supposed to start. And says, 'Here, boys, look what Daddy brought.' "

"Parkeson hasn't got the guts."

"The hell he hasn't. He'd say *that* out of one side of his mouth. Out of the other side, he'd be dictating a vigorous protest to the WP for allowing such things to get clearance for blasting off, making it sound like they're at fault. That's just a guess. We've got to keep those women out of Crater City until we're sure, though. And there's only one way; cripple the ship."

There were five or six voices in the discussion, and Relke recognized enough of them to understand dimly that a cell meeting was in progress. His mind refused to function clearly, and at times the voices seemed to be speaking in senseless jargon, although the words were plain enough. His head throbbed and he had bitten a piece out of the end of his tongue. He felt as if he were lying stretched out on a bed of jagged rocks, although there was only the smooth floor under his battered person.

Giselle cried out from the next room and beat angrily on the door.

Quite mindlessly, and as if his body were being directed by some whimsical puppet master, Relke's corpse suddenly clambered to its feet and addressed itself to the startled conspirators.

"Goddam it, gentlemen, can't you let the lady out to use the crapper?"

They hit him over the head with a jack handle.

He woke up again. This time he was in the bunkroom. A faint choking sound made him look up. Giselle sat on the foot of the bed, legs tightly crossed, face screwed up. She was trying to cry.

"Use an onion," he told her thickly, and sat up. "What's the matter?"

"It's Monday now."

"Where are they?"

"They left. We're locked in."

He fell back with a groan. A stitch in his side felt like a broken rib. He turned his face to the wall. "What's so great about Monday?" he muttered.

"Today the others are taking their vows."

When he woke up again, Novotny was watching him from the foot of the bed. The girl was gone. He sat up and fell back with a groan.

"Fran," he said.

"It wasn't Fran, it was a hustler," said Joe. "I had Beasley take her back. Who busted you?"

"Larkin and Kunz."

"It's a good thing."

"What?"

"They saved me the trouble. You ran off with the jeep."

"Sorry."

"You don't have to be sorry. Just watch yourself, that's all."

"I wanted to see what it was like, Joe."

"What? Playing house with a wench?"

He nodded.

"What was it like?"

"I don't know."

"You woke up calling her Fran."

"I did?"

"Yah. Before you start feeling that way, you better ask Beasley what they did together on the rug while you were asleep, Romeo."

"What?"

"She really knows some tricks. Mme. d'Annecy really educates her girls. You been kissing and cooing with her, Relke?"

"I'm sick, Joe. Don't."

"By the way, you better not go back. The Madame's pretty sore at you."

"Why?"

"For keeping the wench gone so long. There was going to be a show. You know, a circus. Giselle was supposed to be in it. You might say she had the lead role."

"Who?"

"Giselle. Still feel like calling her Fran?—Hey! if you're going to vomit, get out of bed."

Relke staggered into the latrine. He was gone a long time.

"Better hurry up," Novotny called. "Our shift goes on in half an hour."

"I can't go on, Joe."

"The hell you can't. Unless you want to be sent up N.L.D. You know what they do to N.L.D. cases."

"You wouldn't report me N.L.D."

"The hell I wouldn't, but I don't have to."

"What do you mean?"

"Parkeson's coming, with a team of inspectors. They're probably already here, and plenty sore."

"About the ship? The women?"

"I don't know. If the Commission hear about those bats, there'll be hell to pay. But who'll pay it is something else."

Relke buried his face in his hands and tried to think. "Joe, listen. I only half remember, but . . . there was a cell meeting here."

"When?"

"After Larkin and Kunz worked me over. Some guys came in, and . . ."

"Well?"

"It's foggy. Something about Parkeson taking the women back to Crater City."

"Hell, that's a screwy idea. Who thinks that?"

Relke shook his head and tried to think. He came out of the latrine mopping his face on a towel. "I'm trying to remember."

Joe got up. "All right. Better get your suit. Let's go pull cable."

The lineman breathed deeply a few times and winced at the effect. He went to get his suit out of the hangar, started the routine safety check, and stopped halfway through. "Joe, my suit's been cut."

Novotny came to look. He pinched the thick corded plastic until the incision opened like a mouth. "Knife," he grunted.

"Those sons of—"

"Yah." He fingered the cut. "They meant for you to find it, though. It's too conspicious. It's a threat."

"Well, I'm fed up with their threats. I'm going to—"

"You're not going to do anything, Relke. *I'm* going to do it. Larkin and Kunz have messed around with my men one time too often."

"What have you got in mind, Joe?"

"Henderson and I will handle it. We'll go over and have a little conference with them, that's all."

"Why Henderson? Look, Joe, if you're going to stomp them, it's *my* grudge, not Lije's."

"That's just it. If I take you, it's a grudge. If Lije and I do it, it's just politics. I've told you guys before—leave the politics to me. Come on, we'll get you a suit from the emergency locker."

They went out into the transformer vault. Two men wearing blue armbands were bending over Brodanovitch's corpse. One of them was fluently cursing unknown parties who had brought the body to a warm place and allowed it to thaw.

"Investigating team," Novotny muttered. "Means Parkeson is already here." He hiked off toward the emergency lockers.

"Hey, are you the guy that left this stiff near a stove?" one of the investigators called out to Relke.

"No, but I'll be glad to rat on the guys that did, if it'll get them in trouble," the lineman told him.

"Never mind. You can't hang them for being stupid."

"What are you going to do with *him?*" Relke asked, nodding at the corpse.

"Promote him to supervisory engineer and give him a raise."

"Christ but they hire smart boys for the snooper team, don't they? What's your I.Q., friend? I bet they had to breed you to get you smart."

The checker grinned. "You looking for an argument, Slim?"

Relke shook his head. "No, I just asked a question."

"We're going to take him back to Copernicus and bury him, friend. It takes a lot of imagination to figure that out, doesn't it?"

"If he was a class three laborer, you wouldn't take him back to Copernicus. You wouldn't even bury him. You'd just chuck him in a fissure and dynamite the lip."

The man smiled. Patient cynicism was in his tone. "But he's *not* a class three laborer, Slim. He's Mister S. K. Brodanovitch. Does that make everything nice and clear?"

"Sure. Is Parkeson around?"

The checker glanced up and snickered. "You're a chum of his, I guess? Hear that, Clyde? We're talking to a wheel."

Relke reddened. "Shove it, chum. I just wondered if he's here."

"Sure, he's out here. He went over to see that flying bordello you guys have been hiding out here."

"What's he going to do about it?"

"Couldn't say, friend."

Novotny came back with an extra suit.

"Joe, I just remembered something."

"Tell me about it on the way back."

They suited up and went out to the runabout. Relke told what he could remember about the cell meeting.

"It sounds crazy in a way," Novotny said thoughtfully. "Or maybe it doesn't. It *could* mess up the Party's strike plans if Parkeson brought those women back before sundown. The men want women back on the moon project. If they can get women bottlegged in, they won't be quite so ready to start a riot on the No Work Without a Wife theme."

"But Parkeson'd get fired in a flash if—"

"If Parliament got wind of it, sure. Unless he raised the squawk later himself. UCOJE doesn't mention prostitution. Parkeson could point out that some national codes on Earth tolerate it. Nations with delegates in the Parliament, and with work teams on the moon. Take the African team at Tycho. And the Japanese team. Parkeson himself is an Aussie. Whose law is he supposed to enforce?"

"You mean maybe they can't keep ships like that from visiting us?"

"Don't kid yourself. It won't last long. But maybe long enough. If it goes on long enough, and builds up, the general public will find out. You think that wouldn't cause some screaming back home?"

"Yeah. That'll be the end."

"I'm wondering. If there turns out to be a profit in it for whoever's backing d'Annecy, well—anything that brings a profit is pretty hard to put a stop to. There's only one sure way to stop it. Kill the demand."

"For women? Are you crazy, Joe?"

"They could bring in decent women. Women to marry. That'll stop it."

"But the kids. They can't have kids."

"Yeah, I know. That's the problem, and they've got to start solving it sometime. Hell, up to now, they haven't been trying to solve it. When the problem came up, and the kids were dying, everybody got hysterical and jerked the women back to Earth. That wasn't a solution, it was an evasion. The problem is growth-control—in low gravity. It ought to have a medical answer. If this d'Annecy dame gets a chance to keep peddling her wares under the counter, well—she'll force them to start looking for a solution."

"I don't know, Joe. Everybody said homosexuality would force them to start looking for it—after Doc Reiber made his survey. The statistics looked pretty black, but they didn't do anything about it except send us a shipful of ministers. The fairies just tried to make the ministers."

"Yeah, but this is different."

"I don't see how."

"Half the voters are women."

"So? They didn't do anything about homosex—"

"Relke, wise up. Listen, did you ever see a couple of Lesbians necking in a bar?"

Relke snickered. "Sure, once or twice."

"How did you feel about it?"

"Well, this once was kind of funny. You see, this one babe had on—"

"Never mind. You thought it was funny. Do you think it's funny the way MacMillian and Wickers bill and coo?"

"That gets pretty damn nauseating, Joe."

"Uh-huh, but the Lesbians just gave you a giggle. Why?"

"Well, I don't know, Joe it's—"

"I'll tell you why. You like dames. You can understand other guys liking dames. You like dames so much that you can even understand two dames liking each other. You can see what they see in each other. But it's incongruous, so it's funny. But you *can't* see what two fairies see in each other, so that just gives you a bellyache. Isn't that it?"

"Maybe, but what's that got to do with the voters?"

"Ever think that maybe a woman would feel the same way in reverse? A dame could see what MacMillian and Wickers see in each other. The dame might morally disapprove, but at the same time she could sympathize. What's more, she'd be plenty sure that she could handle that kind of competition if she ever needed to. She's a woman, and wotthehell, Wickers is only a substitute woman. It wouldn't worry her too much. Worry her morally, but not as a personal threat. Relke, Mme d'Annecy's racket is a personal threat to the home girl and the womenfolk."

"I see what you mean."

"Half the voters are women."

Relke chuckled. "Migod, Joe, if Ellen heard about that ship . . ."

"Ellen?"

"My older sister. Old maid. Grim."

"You've got the idea. If Parkeson thinks of all this . . ." His voice trailed off. "When is Larkin talking about crippling that ship?"

"About sundown, why?"

"Somebody better warn the d'Annecy dame."

The cosmic gunfire had diminished. The Perseid shrapnel still pelted the dusty face of the plain, but the gram-impact-per-acre-second had dropped by a significant fraction, and with it fell the statisticians's estimate of dead men per square mile. There was an ion storm during the first half of B-shift, and the energized spans of high voltage cable danced with fluttering demon light as the trace-pressure of the lunar "atmosphere" increased enough to start a glow discharge between conductors. High current surges sucked at the line, causing the breakers to hiccup. The breakers tried the line three times, then left the circuit dead and waited for the storm to pass. The storm meant nothing to the construction crews except an increase in headset noise.

Parkeson's voice came drawling on the general call frequency, wading waist-deep through the interference caused by the storm. Relke leaned back against his safety strap atop the trusswork of the last tower and tried to listen. Parkeson was reading the Articles of Discipline, and listening was compulsory. All teams on the job had stopped work to hear him. Relke gazed across the plain toward the slender nacelles of the bird from Algiers in the distance. He had gotten used to the ache in his side where Kunz had kicked him, but it was good to rest for a time and watch the rocket and remember brown legs and a yellow dress. Properties of Earth. Properties belonging to the communion of humanity, from which fellowship a Looney was somehow cut off by 238,000 miles of physical separation.

"We've got a job to finish here," Parkeson was telling the men.

Why? What was in space that was worth the wanting? What followed from its conquest? What came of finishing the job?

Nothing.

Nothing.

Nothing. Nothing anybody ever dreamed of or hoped for.

Parkeson scolded on. *"I know the question that's foremost in your minds,"* his voice continued, *"but you'd better forget it. Let me tell you what happens if this line isn't finished by sundown.* (But by God, it *will* be finished!) *Listen, you wanted women. All right, now you've all been over to visit the uh—'affectionate institution'—and you got what you wanted; and now the work is behind schedule. Who gives a damn about the project, eh! I know what you're thinking. 'That's Parkeson's worry.' OK, so let's talk about what you're going to breathe for the next couple of periods. Let's talk about how many men will wind up in the psycho-respiratory ward, about the overload on the algae tanks. That's not your responsibility either, is it? You don't* have *to breathe and eat. Hell, let Nature take care of air and water, eh? Sure. Now look around. Take a good look. All that's between you and that hungry vacuum out there is ten pounds of man-made air and a little reinforced plastic. All that keeps you eating and drinking and breathing is that precarious life-cycle of ours at Copernicus. That plant-animal feedback loop is so delicately balanced that the biology team gets the cold shakes every time somebody sneezes or passes gas. It has to be constantly nursed. It has to be planned and kept on schedule. On Earth, Nature's a plenum. You can chop down her forests, kill off her deer and buffalo and fill her air with smog and hot isotopes; the worst you can do is cause a few new deserts and dust bowls, and make things a little unpleasant for a while.*

"Up here, we've got a little bit of Nature cooped up in a bottle, and we're in the bottle too. We're cultured like mold on agar. The biology team has to chart the ecology for months in advance. It has to know the construction and survey teams are going to deliver exactly what they promise to deliver, and do it on schedule. If you don't deliver, the ecology gets sick. If the ecology gets sick, you get sick.

"Do you want another epidemic of the chokers like we had three years back? That's what'll happen if there's a work slowdown while everybody goes off on a sex binge at that ship. If the line isn't finished before sundown, the

*ecology gets bled for another two weeks to keep that mine
colony going, and the colony can't return wastes to our
cycle. Think it over, but think fast. There's not much time.
'We all breathe the same air'—on Earth, that's just a political slogan. Here, we all breathe it or we all choke in it.
How do you want it, men?"*

Relke shifted restlessly on the tower. He glanced down
at Novotny and the others who lounged around the foot
of the steel skeleton listening to Parkeson. Lije caught his
eye. He waved at Relke to haul up the hoist-bucket. Relke
shook his head and gave him a thumbs-down. Henderson
gestured insistently for him to haul it up. Relke reeled the
bucket in. It was empty, but chalked on the sides and bottom was a note from Lije: "They tell me what L and K
did to you and yr girl. I and Joe will take care of it, right
after this sermon. You can spit on my fist first if you
want. Lije."

Relke gave him a half-hearted screw-twist signal and
let the bucket go. Revenge was no good, and vicarious revenge was worse than no good; it was hollow. He thought
of asking Joe to forget it, but he knew Joe wouldn't listen.
The pusher felt his own integrity was involved, and a matter of jurisdictional ethics: nobody can push my men
around but me. It was gang ethics, but it seemed inevitable somehow. Where there was fear, men huddled in
small groups and counted their friends on their fingers, and
all else was Foe. In the absence of the family, there
had to be the gang, and fear made it quarrelsome, jealous,
and proud.

Relke leaned back against his strap and glanced up toward Earth. The planet was between quarter and half
phase, for the sun was lower in the west. He watched it
and tried to feel something more than a vague envy. Sometimes the heartsick nostalgia reached the proportions of
idolatrous adoration of Gaea's orb overhead, only to sub-
side into a grudging resentment of the gulf between worlds.
Earth—it was a place where you could stop being afraid,
a place where fear of suffocation was not, where fear of
blowout was not, where nobody went berserk with the
chokers or dreamed of poisoned air or worried about
shorthorn cancer or burn blindness or meteoric dust or
low-gravity muscular atrophy. A place where there was
wind to blow your sweat away.

Watching her crescent, he felt again that vague anger

of separation, that resentment against those who stayed at
home, who had no cause for constant fear, who could live
without the tense expectancy of sudden death haunting
every moment. One of them was Fran, and another was
the one who had taken her from him. He looked away
quickly and tried to listen to the coordinator.

"*This is no threat*," Parkeson was saying. "*If the line
isn't finished on time, then the consequences will just happen, that's all. Nobody's going to punish you, but there are
a few thousand men back at the Crater who have to
breathe air with you. If they have to breathe stink next
period—because you guys were out having one helluva
party with Madame d'Annecy's girls—you can figure how
popular you'll be. That's all I've got to say. There's still
time to get the work back on schedule. Let's use it.*"

Parkeson signed off. The new engineer who was replacing Brodanovitch gave them a brief pep-talk, im-
plying that Parkeson was a skunk and would be forced to
eat his own words before sundown. It was the old hard-
guy-soft-guy routine: first a bawling-out and then a
buttering-up. The new boss offered half of his salary to
the first team to forge ahead of its own work schedule. It
was not stated nor even implied that Parkeson was paying
him back.

The work was resumed. After half an hour, the safety
beeper sounded on all frequencies, and men switched back
to general call. Parkeson and his party were already heading back toward Copernicus.

"*Blasting operation at the next tower site will occur in
ten minutes*," came the announcement. "*Demol team
requests safety clearance over all of zones two and three,
from four forty to five hundred hours. There will be
scatter-glass in both zones. Zone two is to be evacuated
immediately, and all personnel in zone three take line-of-
sight cover from the red marker. I repeat: there will be
scatter-glass . . .*"

"That's us," said Novotny when it was over. "Everybody come on. Brax, Relke, climb down."

Braxton swore softly in a honey-suckle drawl. It never
sounded like cursing, which it wasn't, but like a man
marveling at the variety of vicissitudes invented by an
ingenious universe for the bedevilment of men. "I sweah,
when the angels ahn't shootin' at us from up in Perseus,
it's the demol boys. Demol says froggie, and ev'body

jumps. It gives 'em that suhtain feelin' of impohtance. Y'all know what I think? I got a thee-orry. I think weah all really dead, and they don't tell us it's hell weah in, because not tellin' us is paht of the tohture."

"Get off the damn frequency, Brax, and stay off!" Novotny snapped when the Alabaman released his mic button. "I've told you and Henderson before—either learn to talk fast, or don't talk on the job. If somebody had a slow leak, he'd be boiling blood before he could scream— with you using the frequency for five minutes to say 'yeah.' "

"Mistuh Novotny! My mothuh always taught me to speak slowly and de-stinct-ly. If you think that yo' Yankee upbringin' . . ."

Joe rapped on his helmet until he shut up, then beckoned to Henderson. "Lije, we got twenty minutes."

"Yeah, Joe, want to go see a couple of guys now?" He flashed white teeth and stared back toward the barrack train.

"Think we can handle it in twenty minutes?"

"I don't know. It seem like a short time to do a real good job of it, but maybe if we don't waste any on preliminary fisticuffin' . . ."

"Hell, they didn't waste any ceremony on Relke."

"Less go, then!" He grinned at Relke and held out his fist. "Spit on it?"

Relke shook his head. Henderson laughed. "Wanted to see if you'd go ptooey in your helmet."

"Come on, Lije. The rest of you guys find cover."

Relke watched the two of them lope off toward the rolling barracks. "Hey, Joe," he called after a few seconds.

The lopers stopped to look back. "Relke?"

"Yeah. Don't lose."

"What?"

"They'll say I sicced you. Don't lose."

"Don't worry." They loped again. The longer Relke watched them, the less he liked the idea. If they didn't do a pretty thorough job on Kunz and Larkin, things would be worse for Relke than if they did nothing at all. Then there was the movement to think about; he didn't know to what extent *they* looked out for their own.

Relke walked out of the danger zone and hiked across the hill where he could get a clear view of the rocket. He stopped for a while on the slope and watched four distant figures moving around on the ground beneath the towering ship. For a moment, he thought they were women, but then he saw that one of them was coiling mooring cable, and he knew they were ship's crew. What sort of men had the d'Annecy women been able to hire for such a job? he wondered.

He saw that they were getting ready to lift ship. *Lift ship!*

Relke was suddenly running toward them without knowing why. Whenever he topped a rise of ground and could see them, he tried calling them, but they were not using the project's suit frequency. Finally he found their voices on the seldom used private charter band, but they were speaking French.

One of the men looped a coil of cable over his shoulder and started up the ladder toward the lock. Relke stopped atop an outcropping. He was still two or three miles from the ship. The "isobar" valve system for the left knee of his suit had jammed, and it refused to take up the increased pressure caused by flexure. It was like trying to bend a fully inflated rubber tire, and he hobbled about for a moment with one leg stiff as a crutch.

"Listen!" he called on the p.c. frequency. "You guys at the ship. Can you hear me?" He was panting, and he felt a little panicky. The man on the ladder stopped climbing and looked around.

There was a staccato exchange in French.

"No, no! Over here. On the rock." He waved at them and jumped a few times. "Look toward the camp. On the rock."

They conversed heatedly among themselves for a time.

"Don't any of you speak English?" he begged.

They were silent for a moment. "Whoevair ees?" one of them ventured. "You conversation with wrong radio, M'sieur. Switch a button."

"No, no. I'm trying to call you . . ."

A carrier drowned him out.

"We close for business," the man said. "We go now." He started climbing again.

"Listen!" Relke yelled. "Ten thousand dollars. Everything."

"You crazy man."

"Look, it won't get you in any trouble. I've got plenty in the bank. I'll pay—"

The carrier cut him off again.

"You crazy. Get off the air. We do not go to Earth now."

"Wait! Listen! Tell Giselle . . . No, let me talk to her. Get her to use the radio. It's important."

"I tell you, we close for business now." The man climbed in the airlock. The others climbed up behind. They were jeering at him. This time it sounded like Arabic. He watched until they were all inside.

White fury lanced the gound and spread in a white sheet beneath the ship and roiled up in a tumult of dust and expanding gasses. It climbed on a white fan, gathering velocity. Relke could still make it out as a ship when its course began arcing away from the vertical. It was beginning a trajectory in the direction of Copernicus. When it was out of sight, he began trudging back toward the work site. He was nearly an hour overdue.

"Where you been?" Novotny asked him quietly after watching him hobble the last quarter of a mile in stony silence. He was squinting at the lineman with that faintly puzzled look that Relke recognized as a most ominous omen. The squint was lopsided because of a cut under one eye, and it looked like a chip was missing from a tooth.

Relke showed his stiff leg and bounced the heel against the ground a couple of times. "I walked too far, and the c.p. valves got jammed. Sorry, Joe."

"You don't have to be sorry. Let's see."

The pusher satisfied himself that the suit was malfunctioning. He waved the lineman toward the barrack train. "Go to supply and get it fixed. Get back on the double. You've slowed us down."

Relke paused. "You sore, Joe?"

"We're on duty. I don't get sore on duty. I save it up. Now—haul ass!"

Relke hobbled off. "What about . . . what you went for Joe?" he called back. "What happened?"

"I told you to keep your nose out of politics!" the pusher snapped. "Never mind what happened."

Joe, Relke decided, was plenty sore. About something. Maybe about a beating that backfired. Maybe about Relke taking an hour awol. Either way, he was in trouble. He thought it over and decided that paying a bootleg ship ten thousand to take him back to Earth with them hadn't been such a hysterical whim after all.

But then he met Larkin in the supply wagon. Larkin

was stretched out flat on his back, and a medic kept saying, "Who did it to you? Who did it to you?" and Larkin kept telling him to go to hell out of a mouth that looked like a piece of singed stew meat. Kunz was curled up on a blanket and looked even worse. He spat in his sleep and a bit of tooth rattled across the deck.

"Meanest bunch of bastards I ever saw," the clerk told Relke while he checked in the suit. "They don't even give you a chance. Here were these two guys sleeping in their bunks and not bothering anybody, and what do you think?"

"I quit thinking. What?"

"Somebody starts working them over. Wham. Don't even wake them up first. Just wham. You ever see anything like it? Mean, John, just mean. You can't even get a shift's sleep anymore. You better go to bed with a knife in your boot, John."

"It's Bill."

"Oh. What do you suppose makes a guy that mean anyway?"

"I don't know. Everybody's jumpy, I guess."

The clerk looked at him wisely. "There you have put your finger on it, John. Looney nerves. The jitters. Everybody's suit-happy." He leaned closer and lowered his voice. "You know how I tell when the camp's getting jittery?"

"Listen, check me out a suit. I've got to get back to the line."

"Now wait, this'll surprise you. I can tell better than the psych checkers when everybody's going on a slow panic. It's the sleeping bag liners."

"What?"

"The bed wetters, John. You'd be surprised how many grown men turn bed wetters about the middle of a hitch. At first, nobody. Then somebody gets killed on the line. The bag liners start coming in for cleaning. By the end of the hitch, the wash tank smells like a public lavatory, John. Not just the men, either. Some of the engineers. You know what I'm doing?"

"Look, Mack, the suit . . ."

"Not Mack. Frank. Look, I'll show you the chart." He got out a sheet of paper with a crudely drawn graph on it. "See how it goes? The peak? I've done ten of them."

"Why?"

The clerk looked at him blankly. "For the idea box, John. Didn't you know about the prizes? Doctor Esterhall ought to be glad to get information like this."

"Christ, they'll give you a medal, Charley. Now give me my damn suit before I get it myself. I'm due on the line."

"OK, OK. You got the jitters yourself, haven't you?" He went to get the suit. "I just happened to think," he called back. "If you've been turning in liners yourself, don't worry about me. I don't keep names, and I don't remember faces."

"You blab plenty, though," Relke grumbled to himself.

The clerk heard him. "No call to get sore, John."

"I'm not sore, I'm just in a hurry. If you want to beg for a stomping, it's nothing to me."

The clerk came back bristling. "Who's going to stomp?"

"The bed wetters, I guess." He started getting into the suit.

"Why? It's for science, isn't it?"

"Nobody likes to be watched."

"There you put your finger on it, John. It's the watching part that's worst. If they'd only quit watching us, or come out where we could see them! You know what I think? I think there's some of them among us. In disguise." The clerk smirked mysteriously at what-he-knew-but-wouldn't-tell.

Relke paused with a zipper half-way up. "Who do you mean—watching? Checkers?"

The clerk snorted and resumed what he had been doing when Relke entered: he was carefully taping his share of stock in Mme. d'Annecy's venture up on the wall among a display of pin-ups. "You know who I mean," he muttered.

"No, I don't."

"The ones that dug that mine, that's who."

"Aliens? Oh, bullspit."

"Yeah? You'll see. They're keeping an eye on us, all right. There's a guy on the African team that even talked to some of them."

"Nuts. He's not the first guy that ever talked to spooks.

Or demons. Or saucer pilots. You don't have to be a Looney to be a lunatic."

That made the clerk sore, and he stomped off to his sanctum to brood. Relke finished getting into the suit and stepped into the airlock. Some guys had to personify their fear. If there was no danger, somebody must be responsible. They had to have an Enemy. Maybe it helped, believing in gremlins from beyond Pluto. It gave you something to hate when your luck was bad.

He met Joe just outside the lock. The pusher was waiting to get it.

"Hey, Pappy, I own up. I was goofing off awhile ago. If you want to be sore—" Relke stopped. Something was wrong. Joe was breathing hard, and he looked sick.

"Christ, I'm not sore! *Not now!*"

"What's wrong, Joe?"

The pusher paused in the hatchway. "Run on back to the line. Keep an eye on Braxton. I'm getting a jeep. Back in a minute." He went on inside and closed the hatch.

Relke trotted toward the last tower. After a while he could hear Braxton talking in spasms on the frequency. It sounded like sobbing. He decided it *was* sobbing.

"Theah just isn't any God," Bama was moaning. "Thea just couldn't be a God and be so mean. He was the bes' friend a man evah had, and he nevah did nothin' to deserve it. Oh, God, oh, God, why did it have to be *him?* I've done penance fo' what my gran'pa did to his, an' I been as color blind as any Yankee evah bohn, an' I love him like my own brother. Theah jus' can't be any God in Heaven, to treat a man that way, when he been so . . ." Braxton's voice broke down into incoherent sobbing.

There was a man lying on the ground beside the tower. Relke could see Benet bending over him. Benet was clutching a fistful of the man's suit. He crossed himself slowly and stood up. A safety team run-about skidded to a halt beside the tower, and three men piled out. Bennet spread his hands at them in a wide shrug and turned his back.

"What happened?" Relke asked as he loped up to Beasley.

"Bama was welding. Lije walked over to ask him for a wrench or something. Bama turned around to get it, and Lije sat down on the strut with the hot weld."

"Blow out?"

"He wasn't that lucky. Call it a fast slowout."

Novotny drove up, saw the safety jeep, and started bellowing furiously at them.

"Take it easy, chum. We got here as quick as we could."

"Theah jus' can't be any God in Heaven . . ."

They got Henderson in the safety runabout. Novotny manufactured a hasty excuse to send Braxton off with them, for grief had obviously finished his usefulness for awhile. Everybody stood around in sickly silence and stared after the jeep.

"Benet, you know how to pray," Novotny muttered. "Say something, altar boy."

"Aw, Joe, that was fifteen years ago. I haven't lived right."

"Hell, who has? Go ahead."

Benet muttered for a moment and turned his back. *"In nomine Patris et Filii et Spiritus Sancti . . ."* He paused.

"Can't you pray in English?" Joe asked.

"We always said it in Latin. I only served at a few masses."

"Go ahead."

Benet prayed solemnly while they stood around with bowed heads and shuffled their boots in the dust. Nobody understood the words, not even Benet, but somehow it seemed important to listen.

'Requiem aeternam dona ei, Domine. Et lux perpetua luceat . . .'

Relke looked up slowly and let his eyes wander slowly across the horizon. There were still some meteorites coming in, making bright little winks of fire where they bit into the plain. Deadly stingers out of nowhere, heading nowhere, impartially orbiting, random as rain, random as death. The debris of creation. Relke decided Braxton was wrong. There was a God, all right, maybe personal, maybe not, but there was a God, and He wasn't mean. His universe was a deadly contraption, but maybe there wasn't any way to build a universe that wasn't a deadly contraption—like a square circle. He made the contraption and He put Man in it, and Man was a fairly deadly contraption himself. But the funny part of it was, there wasn't a damn thing the universe could do to a man that a man wasn't built to endure. He could even endure it when it killed him. And gradually he could get the better of it. It was the consistency of matched qualities—random mercilessness and human endurance—and it wasn't mean, it was a fair match.

"Poor Lije. God help him."

"All right," Novotny called. "Let's pull cable, men."

"Yeah, you know what?" said Beasley. "Those dames went to Crater City. The quicker we get the line finished, the quicker we get back. Damn Parkeson anyhow!"

"Hell, why do you think he let them go there, Beeze?" Tremini jeered. "So we'd work our butts off to finish quick, that's why. Parkeson's no idiot. If he'd sent them packing for somewhere else, maybe we'd finish, maybe we wouldn't."

"Cut the jawing. Somebody run down and get the twist out of that span before she kinks. Relke, start taking up slack."

Atop the steel truss that supported the pendulous insulators, the lineman began jacking up the slack line. He glanced toward the landing site where the ship had been, and it was hard to believe it had ever been there at all. A sudden improbable dream that had come and gone and left nothing behind. Nothing? Well, there was a share of stock . . .

"Hey, we're all capitalists!" Relke called.

Benet hooted. "Take your dividends out in trade."

"Listen, someday they'll let dames come here again and get married. That's one piece of community property you better burn first."

"That d'Annecy dame thought of everything."

"Listen, that d'Annecy dame is going to force an issue. She'll clean up, and a lot of guys will throw away small fortunes, but before it's over, they'll let women in space again. Now quit jawing, and let's get to work."

Relke glanced at the transformer station where he had taken the girl. He tried to remember what she looked like, but he got Fran's face instead. He tried to transmute the image into Giselle's, but it stayed Fran. Maybe he hadn't really seen Giselle at all. Maybe he had looked at her and seen Fran all along, but it had been a poor substitution. It had accomplished one thing, though. He felt sorry for Fran now. He no longer hated her. She had stuck it out a long time before there had been another guy. And it was harder for a wife on Earth than it was for a husband on Luna. She had to starve in the midst of plenty. He had only to deny himself what he couldn't get anyhow, or even see. She was the little girl with her nose against the bakery window. He was only fasting in the desert. It was easy; it put one beyond temptation. To fast in a banquet hall, one had to be holy. Fran wasn't holy. Relke doubted he'd want a wife who was holy. It could get damnably dull.

A quick glance at Earth told him it was still in the skyless vault. Maybe she'll come, if they ever let them come, he thought wistfully. Maybe the guy'll be a poor substitute, and she'll figure out who she's really married to, legal instruments not-withstanding. Maybe . . . O God, let her come! . . . women had no business on Luna, but if they didn't then neither did men, nor Man, who had to be a twosome in order to be recognizably human.

"Damn it, Relke, work that jack!" Joe yelled. "We got to build that line!"

Relke started cranking again, rocking his body to the rhythm of the jack, to the rhythm of echoes of thought. Got to build the line. Damn it, build the line. Got to build the line. Build the damn it line. The line was part of a living thing that had to grow. The line was yet another creeping of life across a barrier, a lungfish flopping from pool to pool, an ape trying to walk erect across still another treeless space. Got to build the line. Even when it kills you, got to build the line, the bloody endless line. The lineman labored on in silence. The men were rather quiet that shift.

Vengeance for Nikolai

THE DISTANT THUNDER of the artillery was only faintly audible in the dugout. The girl sat quietly picking at her hands while the colonel spoke. She was only a slip of a girl, all breast and eyes, but there was an intensity about her that made her unmistakably beautiful, and the colonel kept glancing at her sidelong as if his eyes refused to share the impersonal manner of his speech. The light of a single bare bulb glistened in her dark hair and made dark shadows under deep jade eyes already shadowed by weeping. She was listening intently or not at all. She had just lost her child.

"They will not kill you, *grazhdanka,* if you can get safely past the lines," said the colonel. He paced slowly in the dugout, his boot heels clicking pleasantly on the concrete while he sucked at a long cigaret holder and milked his thumbs behind his back in solemn thought. "These Americans, you have heard about their women? No, they will not kill you, unless by accident in passing the lines. They may do other things to you—forgive me!— it is war." He stopped pacing, straddled her shadow, and looked down at her with paternal pity. "Come, you have said nothing, nothing at all. I feel like a swine for asking it of you, but there is no other hope of beating back this attack. And I am ordered to ask you. Do you understand?"

She looked up. Light filled her eyes and danced in them with the moist glittering of a fresh grief already an ancient grief old as Man. "They killed my Nikolai,"

451

she said softly. "Why do you speak to me so? What can it mean? The bombardment—I know nothing—I cannot think of it. Why do you torment me?"

The colonel betrayed no impatience with her, although he had gone over it twice before. "This morning you tried to leap off the bridge. It is such a shame to die without purpose, *dushka*. I offer you a purpose. Do you love the Fatherland?"

"I am not a Party member, *Tovarish Polkovnik*."

"I did not ask if you love the Party, my dear. However, you should say *'parties,'* now that we are tolerating those accursed Menshevist deviationists again. Bah! *They* even name members of the *Gorodskoi* Soviets these days. We are becoming a two party republic. How sickening! Where are the old warrior Bolsheviks? It makes one weep. . . . But that is not the question I asked if you love the Fatherland."

She gave a hesitant nod.

"Then think of the Fatherland, think of vengeance for Nikolai. Would you trade your life for that? I know you would. You were ready to fling it away."

She stirred a little; her mind seemed to re-enter the room. "This Ami *Gyenyeral*. Why do you wish him dead?"

"He is the genius behind this assault, my child. Who would have thought the Americans would have chosen such an unlikely place for an invasion? And the manner of it! They parachuted an army ninety miles inland, instead of assaulting the fortified coastline: He committed half a million troops to deliberate encirclement. Do you understand what this means? If they had been unable to drive to the coast, they would have been cut off, and the war would very likely be over. With *our* victory. As it was, the coast defenders panicked. The airborne army swept to the sea to capture their beachhead without need of a landing by sea, and now there are two million enemy troops on our soil, and we are in full retreat. *Flight* is a better word. General Rufus MacAmsward gambled his country's entire future on one operation, and he won. If he had lost, they would likely have shot him. Such a man is necessarily mad. A megalomaniac, an evil genius.

Oh, I admire him very much! He reminds me of one of their earlier generals, thirty years ago. But that was before their Fascism, before their Blue Shirts.

"And if he is killed?"

The colonel sighed. He seemed to listen for a time to the distant shellfire. "We are all a little superstitious in wartime," he said at last. "Perhaps we attach too much significance to this one man. But they have no other generals like *him*. He will be replaced by a competent man. We would rather fight competent men than fight an unpredictable devil. He keeps his own counsels, that is so. We know he does not rely heavily upon his staff. His will rules the operation. He accepts intelligence but not advice. If he is struck dead—well, we shall see."

"And I am to kill him. It seems unthinkable. How do you know I can?"

The colonel waved a sheaf of papers. "Only a woman can get to him. We have his character clearly defined. Here is his psychoanalytic biography. We have photostats of medical records taken from Washington. We have interviews with his ex-wife and his mother. Our psychologists have studied every inch of him. Here, I'll read you—but no, it is very dry, full of psychiatric jargon. I'll boil it down.

"MacAmsward is a champion of the purity of womanhood, and yet he is a vile old lecher. He is at once a baby and an old man. He will kneel and kiss your hand—yes, really. He is a worshipper of womanhood. He will court you, convert you, pay you homage, and then expect you to—forgive me—to take him to bed. He could not possibly make advances on you uninvited, but he expects you—as a goddess rewarding a worshipper—to make advances on *him*. He will be your abject servant, but with courtly dignity. His life is full of breast symbols. He clucks in his sleep. He has visited every volcano in the world. He collects anatomical photographs; his women have all been bosomy brunettes. He is still in what the Freudians call the oral stage of emotional development—emotionally a two-year-old. I know Freud is bad politics, but for the Ami, it is sometimes so."

The colonel stopped. There was a sudden tremor in the earth. The colonel lurched, lost his balance. The floor heaved him against the wall. The girl sat still, hands in her lap, face very white. The air shock followed the earth shock, but the thunder clap was muted by six feet of concrete and steel. The ceiling leaked dust.

"Tactical A-missile," the colonel hissed. "Another of them! If they keep it up, they'll drive us to use Lucifer. This is a mad dog war. Neither side uses the H-bomb, but in the end one side or the other will have to use it. If the Kremlin sees certain defeat, we'll use it. So would Washington. If you're being murdered, you might as well take your killer with you if you can. Bah! It is a madness. I, Porphiry Grigoryevich, am as mad as the rest. Listen to me, Marya Dmitriyevna, I met you an hour ago, and now I am madly in love with you, do you hear? Look at you! Only a day after a bomb fragment dashed the life out of your baby, your bosom still swelled with unclaimed milk and dumb grief, and yet I dare stand here and say I am in love with you, and in another breath ask you to go and kill yourself by killing an Ami general! Ah, ah! What insane apes we are! Forget the Ami general. Let us both desert, let us run away to Africa together, to Africa where apes are simpler. There! I've made you cry. What a brute is Phorphiry, what a brute!"

The girl breathed in gasps. "Please, *Tovarish Polkovnik!* Please say nothing more! I will go and do what you ask, if it is possible."

"I only ask it, *dushka*, I cannot command it. I advise you to refuse."

"I will go and kill him. Tell me how! There is a plan? There must be a plan. How shall I pass the lines? How shall I get to him? What is the weapon? How can I kill him?"

"The weapon, you mean? The medical officer will explain that. Of course, you'll be too thoroughly searched to get even a stickpin past the lines. They often use fluoroscopy, so you couldn't even swallow a weapon and get it past them. But there's a way, there's a way—I'll let the *vrach* explain it. I can only tell you how to get captured, and how to get taken to MacAmsward after your capture. As for the rest of it, you will be directed by posthypnotic suggestion. Tell me, you were an officer in the Woman's Defense Corps, the home guard, were you not?"

"Yes, but when Nikki was born, they asked for my resignation."

"Yes, of course, but the enemy needn't find out you're

inactive. You have your uniform still? . . . Good! Wear it. Your former company is in action right now. You will join them briefly."

"And be captured?"

"Yes. Bring nothing but your ID tags. We shall supply the rest. You will carry in your pocket a certain memorandum addressed to all home guard unit commanders. It is in a code the Ami have already broken. It contains the phrase: 'Tactical bacteriological weapons immediately in use.' Nothing else of any importance. It is enough. It will drive them frantic. They will question you. Since you know nothing, they can torture nothing out of you.

"In another pocket, you will be carrying a book of love poetry. Tucked in the book will be a photograph of General Rufus MacAmsward, plus two or three religious ikons. Their Intelligence will *certainly* send the memorandum to MacAmsward; both sides are that nervous about germ weapons. It is most probably that they will send him the book and the picture—for reasons both humorous and practical. The rest will take care of itself. MacAmsward is all ego. Do you understand?"

She nodded. Porphiry Grigoryevich reached for the phone.

"Now I am going to call the surgeon," he said. "He will give you several injections. Eventually, the injections will be fatal, but for some weeks, you will feel nothing from them. Post-hypnotic urges will direct you. If your plan works, you will not kill MacAmsward in the literal sense. Literally, he will kill himself. If the plan fails, you'll kill him another way if you can. You were an actress, I believe?"

"For a time. I never got to the Bolshoi."

"But excellent! His mother was an actress. You speak English. You are beautiful, and full of grief. It is enough. You are the one. But do you really love the Fatherland enough to carry it out?"

Her eyes burned. "I hate the killers of my son!" she whispered.

The colonel cleared his throat. "Yes, of course. Very well, Marya Dmitriyevna, it is death I am giving you. But you will be sung in our legends for a thousand years. And by the way—" He cocked his head and looked at her oddly. "I believe I really do love you, *dushka.*"

With that, he picked up the phone.

Strange exhilaration surged within her as she crawled through the brush along the crest of the flood embankment, crawled hastily, panting and perspiring under a smoky sun in a dusty sky while Ami fighters strafed the opposite bank of the river where her company was retreating. The last of the Russ troops had crossed, or were killed in crossing. The terrain along the bank where she crawled was now the enemy's. There was no lull in the din of battle, and the ugly belching of artillery mingled with the sound of the planes to batter the senses with a merciless avalanche of noise; but the Ami infantry and mechanized divisions had paused for regrouping at the river. It would be a smart business for the Americans to plunge on across the river at once before the Russians could reorganize and prepare to defend it, but perhaps they could not. The assault had carried the Ami forces four hundred miles inland, and it had to stop somewhere and wait for the supply lines to catch up. Marya's guess—and it was the educated guess of a former officer—was that the Ami would bridge the river immediately under air cover and send mechanized killer-strikes across to harass the retreating Russ without involving infantry in an attempt to occupy territory beyond the river.

She fell flat and hugged the earth as machine gun fire traversed the ridge. A tracer hit rock a yard from her head, spraying her with dust, and sang like a snapped wire as it shot off to the south. The spray of bullets travelled on along the ridge. She moved ahead again.

The danger was unreal. It was all part of an explosive symphony. She had the manna. She could not be harmed. Nothing but vengeance lay ahead. She had only to crawl on.

Was it the drug that made her think like that? Was there an euphoric mixed in the injections? She had felt nothing like this during the raids. During the raids there was only fear, and the struggle to remember whether she had left the teapot boiling while the bombs blew off.

Macbeth. Once she had played Lady Macbeth upon the Moscow stage. How did it go? *The raven himself is hoarse that croaks the fatal entrance of Duncan under my battlements. Come, you spirits that tend on mortal thoughts, unsex me here, and fill me, from crown to toe, top-full of direst cruelty!*

But that wasn't quite it. That wasn't quite what she felt. It was a new power that dwelt in her bosom. It was something else.

Her guard uniform was caked with mud, and the insignia was torn loose from her collar. The earth scuffed her knees and the brush scratched her arms. She kept falling flat to avoid the raking fire of her own machine guns. And yet it was necessary that she stay on the ridge and appear to be seeking a way across the river.

She was too intent upon watching the other side to notice the sergeant. She crawled over a corpse and nearly fell in the foxhole with him. She had been crawling along with her pistol in hand, and the first she saw of the sergeant was his boot. It stamped down on her gun hand. He jammed the muzzle of a tommy-gun against the side of her throat.

"Drop it, sister! *Voyennoplyennvi!*"

She gasped in pain—her hand—and stared up at him with wide eyes. A lank young Ami with curly hair and a quid of tobacco in one cheek.

"Moya rooka—my hand!"

He kept his boot heel on the gun, but let her get her hand free. "Get down in here!"

She rolled into the hole. He kicked the gun toward the river.

"Hey, Cap!" he yelled over his shoulder. "I got a guest. One of the commissar's ladies." Then to the girl: "Before I kill you, what are you doing on this side of the river, spy?"

"Most chyeryez ryekoo . . ."

"I don't speak it. No savvy. *Ya nye govoryu . . ."*

Marya was suddenly terrified. He was lean and young and pale with an unwelcome fear that would easily allow him to fire a burst into her body at close range. The Ami forces had been taking no prisoners during the running battle. The papers called them sub-human beasts because of it, but Marya was sufficiently a soldier to know that prisoners of war were a luxury for an army with stretchy logistic problems, and often the luxury could not be afforded. One Russian lieutenant had brought his men to the Ami under a while flag, and the Ami captain had shot him in the face and ordered his platoon to pick off the others with rifle fire as they tried to flee. In a sense, it was retaliatory. The Russians had taken no prisoners during the Ami airborne landings, and she had seen some Ami airmen herded together and machine-gunned. She hated it. But as an officer, she knew there were times of necessity.

"Please don't shoot," she said in English. "I give up. I can't get across the river anyway."

"What are you doing on this side?" he demanded.

"My company was retreating across the bridge. I was the last to start across. Your artillery hit the bridge. The jets finished it off with their rockets." She had to shout to be heard above the roar of battle. She pointed down the river. "I was trying to make it down to the ford. Down there you can wade across."

It was all true. The sergeant thought it over.

"Hey, Cap!" he yelled again. "Didn't you hear me? What'll I do with her?"

If there was an answer, it was drowned by shellfire.

"Undress!" the sergeant barked.

"What?"

"I said to take off your clothes. And no tricks. Strip to the skin."

She went sick inside. So now it started, did it? Well, let it come! For the Fatherland! For Nikolai. She began unbuttoning her blouse. She did not look at the Ami sergeant. Once he whistled softly. When she had finished undressing, she looked up defiantly. His face had changed. He moistened his lips and swore softly under his breath. He crossed himself and edged away. Deep within her, something smiled. He was only a boy.

"Well, what are you cursing about?" she asked tonelessly.

"If I didn't think you would I mean I wish this gun if I had time I'd but you'd stab me in the back but when I think about what they'll do to you back there . . .

"Jeezis!" he said fervently, wagging his head and rolling his quid into the other cheek. "Put the underwear and the blouse back on, roll up the rest of it, and start crawling down the slope. Aim for that slit trench down there. I'll be right behind you."

"She's quite a little dish, incidentally," the Ami captain was saying on the field telephone. "Are we shooting

prisoners now, or are we sending them back . . . Yeah?"
He listened for awhile. A mortar shell came screaming
down nearby and they all sat down in the trench and
opened their mouths to save eardrums. "To who?" he
said when it was over. "Slim? Oh, to you . . . Yeah, that's
right, a photograph of Old Brass Butt in person. I can't
read the other stuff. It's in Russky. . . . Just a minute."
He covered the mouthpiece and looked up at the sergeant. "Where's the rest of your squad, Sarge?"

The sergeant swallowed solemnly. "I lost all my men
except Price and Vittorio, sir. They were wounded and
went to the rear."

"Damn! Well, they're sending up replacements tonight,
and we're all going back for a breather, as soon as they
get here. So you might as well march her on back yourself." He glanced thoughtfully at the girl. "Good God!"
he murmured.

Marya was surrounded by several officers. They were
all looking at her hungrily. She thought quickly.

"You have searched me," she said cooly. "Would you
gentlemen allow me to put on my skirt? I have submitted
to capture. As an officer, I expect . . ."

"Look, lady, what you expect doesn't matter a damn!"
snapped a lieutenant. "You're a prisoner of war, and
you're lucky to be alive. Besides. you are now about to
have the high privilege of lying down with six . . ."

"Quiet, Sam!" grunted the captain. "We can't do it.
Lady, put on the rest of your clothes and get going."

"Why?" the lieutenant yelled. "That damned sergeant
is going to . . ."

"Shut up! Can't you see she's no peasant? Christ, man,
this war doesn't make you *all* swine, does it? Sergeant,
trade that Chicago typewriter for a forty-five, and take
her back to Major Kline for interrogation. Don't touch
her, you hear?"

"Yes, sir."

The captain scribbled an order in his notebook, tore
out the page, and handed it to the sergeant. "You can
probably hitch a ride on the chow wagon part of the way.
It's going to get dark pretty soon, so keep a leash on her.
If anybody starts a gang rape, blow his guts out." He
grinned ruefully. "If we are going to pass it up ourselves,
by damn, I want to make sure nobody else does it." He
glanced at the Russian girl and reddened. "My apologies,

lieutenant. We're not really bastards. We're just a long way from home. After we wipe ot this Red Disease (he spat out the words like bites of tainted meat) you'll see we're not so bad. I hope you'll be treated like an officer and a gentlewoman, even if you are a commie." He bowed slightly and offered the first salute.

"But I'm not—well, thank you, Captain," she said, and returned the salute. . . .

They sat spraddle-legged in the back of the truck as it bounced along the shell-pocked road. The guns had fallen silent, but the sky was full of Ami squadrons jetting toward the sunset. Pilotless planes and rocket missiles painted swift vapor trails across the heavens, and the sun colored them with blood. She breathed easier now, and she was very tired. The Ami sergeant sat across from her and kept his gun trained on her and appeared very ill-at-ease. He blushed several times for no apparent cause. She tried to shut him out of her consciousness and think of nothing. He was a doggy sort of a pup, and she disliked him. The Ami were all doggy pups. She had met them before. There was something of the spaniel in them.

Nikolai, Nikolai, my breasts ache for you, and they burst with your milk, and I must drain them before I die of it. My baby, my bodykins, my flesh torn from my flesh, my baby, my pain, my Nikki Andreyevich, come milk me—but no, now it is death, and we can be one again. How wretched it is to ache with milk and mourn you . . .

"Why are you crying?" the sergeant grunted after awhile.

"You killed my baby."

"I what?"

"Your bombers. They killed my baby. Only yesterday."

"Damnation! So that's why you're—" He looked at her blouse and reddened again.

She glanced down at herself. She was leaking a little, and the pressure was maddening. So that's what he was blushing about!

There was a crushed paper cup in the back of the truck. She picked it up and unfolded it, then glanced doubtfully at the sergeant. He was looking at her in a kind of mournful anguish.

"Do you mind if I turn my back?" she asked.

'Hell's bells!" he said softly, and put away his gun.

"Give me your word you won't jump out, and I won't even look. This war gives me a sick knot in the gut." He stood up and leaned over the back of the cab, watching the road a head and not looking at her, although he kept one hand on his holster and one boot heel on the hem of her skirt.

Marya tried to dislike him a little less than before. When she was finished, she threw out the cup and buttoned her blouse again. "Thank you, sergeant, you can turn around now."

He sat down and began talking about his family and how much he hated the war. Marya sat with her eyes closed and her head tilted back in the wind and tried not to listen.

"Say, how can you have a baby and be in the army?" he asked after a time.

"Not the army. The home guard. Everybody's in the home guard. Please, won't you just be quiet awhile?"

"Oh. Well. Sure, I guess."

Once they bailed out of the truck and lay flat in the ditch while two Russian jets screamed over at low altitude, but the jets were headed elsewhere and did not strafe the road. They climbed back in the truck and rolled on. They stopped at two road blocks for MP shakedowns before the truck pulled up at a supply dump. It was pitch dark.

The sergeant vaulted out of the truck. "This is as far as we ride," he told her. "We'll have to walk the rest of the way. It's dark as the devil, and we're only allowed a penlight." He flashed it in her face. "It would be a good chance for you to try to break for it. I hate to do this to you, sis, but put your hands together behind your back."

She submitted to having her wrists bound with telephone wire. She walked ahead of him down the ditch while he pointed the way with the feeble light and held one end of the wire.

"I'd sure hate to shoot you, so please don't try anything."

She stumbled once and felt the wire jerk taut.

"You've cut off the circulation; do you want to cut off the hands?" she snapped. "How much farther do we have to go?"

The sergeant seemed very remorseful. "Stop a minute.

I want to think. It's about four miles." He fell silent. They stood in the ditch while a column of tanks thundered past toward the front. There was no traffic going the other way.

"Well?" she asked after awhile.

"I was just thinking about the three Russky women they captured on a night patrol awhile back. And what they did to them at interrogation."

"Go on."

"Well, it's the Blue Shirt boys that make it ugly, not so much the army officers. It's the political heel snappers you've got to watch out for. They see red and hate Russky. Listen, it would be a lot safer for you if I took you in after daylight, instead of at night. During the day there's sometimes a Red Cross fellow hanging around, and everybody's mostly sober. If you tell everything you know, then they won't be so rough on you."

"Well?"

"There's some deserted gun emplacements just up the hill here, and an old command post. I guess I could stay awake until dawn."

She paused, wondered whether to trust him. No, she shouldn't. But even so, he would be easier to handle than half a dozen drunken officers.

"All right, Ami, but if you don't take wires off, your medics will have to amputate my hands."

They climbed the hill, crawled through splintered logs and burned timbers, and found the command post underground. Half the roof was caved in, and the place smelled of death and cartridge casings, but there was a canvas cot and a gasoline lantern that still had some fuel in it. After he had freed her wrists, she sat on the cot and rubbed the numbness out of her hands while he opened a K-ration and shared it with her. He watched her rather wistfully while she ate.

"It's too bad you're on the wrong side of this war," he said. "You're okay, as Russkies go. How come you're fighting for the commies?"

She paused, then reached down and picked up a handful of dirt from the floor, kneaded it, and showed it to him, while she nibbled cheese.

"Ami, this had the blood of my ancestors in it. This ground is mine. Now it has the blood of my baby in it; don't speak to me of sides, or leaders, or politics." She held the soil out to him. "Here, look at it. But don't touch. It's mine. No, when I think about it, go ahead and *touch*. Feel it, smell it, taste a little of it the way a peasant would to see if it's ripe for planting. I'll even give you a handful of it to take home and mix with your own. It's mine to give. It's also mine to fight for." She spoke clamly and watched him with deep jade eyes. She kept working the dirt in her hand and offering it to him. "Here! This is Russia. See how it crumbles? It's what they'll bury you in. Here, take it." She tossed it at him. He grunted angrily and leaped to his feet to brush himself off.

Marya went on eating cheese. "Do you want an argument, Ami?" she asked, chewing hungrily while she talked. "You will get awfully dirty, if you do. I have a simple mind. I can only keep tossing handfuls of Russia at you to answer your ponderous questions."

He did an unprecedented thing. He sat down on the floor and began—well, almost sobbing. His shoulders heaved convulsively for a moment. Marya stopped eating cheese and stared at him in amazement. He put his arms across his knees and rolled his forehead on them. When he looked up, his face was blank as a frightened child's.

"God, I want to go home!" he croaked.

Marya put down the K-ration and went to bend over him. She pulled his head back with a handful of his hair and kissed him. Then she went to lie down on the cot and turned her face to the wall.

"Thanks, Sergeant," she said. "I hope they don't bury you in it after all."

When she awoke, the lantern was out. She could see him bending over her, silhouetted against the stars through the torn roof. She stifled a shriek.

"Take your hands away!"

He took them away at once and made a choking sound. His silhouette vanished. She heard him stumbling among the broken timbers, making his way outside. She lay there thinking for awhile, thoughts without words. After a few minutes, she called out.

"Sergeant? Sergeant!"

There was no answer. She started up and kicked something that clattered. She went down on her knees an felt for it in the dark. Finally she found it. It was his gun.

"*Sergeant!*"

After awhile he came stumbling back. "Yes?" he asked softly.

"Come here."

His silhouette blotted the patch of stars again. She felt for his holster and shoved the gun back in it.

"Thanks, Ami, but they would shoot you for that."

"I could say you grabbed it and ran."

"Sit down, Ami."

Obediently he sat.

"Now give me your hands again," she said, then, whispering: "No, please! Not there! Not there."

The last thing would be vengeance and death, but the next to the last thing was something else. And it was clearly in violation of the captain's orders.

It was the beating of the old man that aroused her fury. They dragged him out of the bunker being used by Major Kline for questionings, and they beat him about the head with a piece of hydraulic hose. "They" were immaculately tailored Blue Shirts of the Americanist Party, and "he" was an elderly Russian major of near retirement age. Two of them held his arms while the third kicked him to his knees and whipped him with the hose.

"Just a little spanking, commie, to learn you how to recite for teacher, see?"

"Whip the bejeezis out of him."

"Fill him with gasoline and stick a wick in his mouth."

"Give it to him!"

They were very methodical about it, like men handling an unruly circus animal. Marya stood in line with a dozen other prisoners, waiting her turn to be interrogated. It was nine in the morning, and the sun was evaporating the last of the dew on the tents in the camp. The sergeant had gone into the bunker to report to Major Kline and present the articles her captors had taken from her person. He had been gone ten minutes. When he came out, the Blue Shirts were still whipping the prisoner. The old man had fainted.

"He's faking."

"Wake him up with it, Mac. Teach him."

The sergeant walked straight toward her but gave no sign of recognition. He did not look toward the whistle and slap of the hose, although his face seemed slightly pale. He drew his gun in approaching the prisoners and a guard stepped into his path.

"Halt! You can't . . ."

"Major Kline's orders, Corporal. He'll see Marya Dmitriyevna Lisitsa next. Right now. I'm to show her in."

The guard turned blankly to look at the prisoners.

"*That* one," said the sergeant.

"The girl? Okay, you! *Shagom marsh!*"

She stepped out of line and went with the sergeant, who took her arm and hissed, "Make it easy on yourself," out of the corner of his mouth. Neither looked at the other.

It was dark in the bunker, but she could make out a fat little major behind the desk. He had a poker expression and a small moustache. He kept drumming his fingers on the desk and spoke in comic grunts.

"So this is the wench," he muttered at the sergeant. He stared at Marya for a moment, then thundered: "Attention! Hit a brace! Has nobody taught you how to salute?"

Her fury congealed into a cold knot. She ignored the command and refused to answer in his own language. "*Ya nye govoryu po Angliiski!*" she snapped.

"I thought you said she spoke English," he grunted at the sergeant. "I thought you said you'd talked to her."

She felt the sergeant's fingers tighten on her arm. He hesitated. She heard him swallow. Then he said, "Yes sir, I did. Through an interpreter."

Bless you, little sergeant! she thought, not daring to look her thanks at him.

"*Hoy, McCoy!*" the major bellowed toward the door.

The man who came in was not McCoy, but one of the Americanist Blue Shirts. He gave the major a cross-breasted Americanist salute and barked the slogan: "*Ameh'ca Fust!*"

"America First," echoed the major without vigor and without returning the political salute. "What is it now?"

"I regrets to repoaht, suh, that the cuhnel is dead of a heaht condition, and can't answeh moa questions."

"I told you to loosen him up, not kill him. Damn! Well, no help for it. Get him out. That's all, Purvis, that's all."

"Ameh'ca Fust!"

"Yeah."

The Blue Shirt smacked his heels, whirled, and hiked out. The interpreter came in.

"McCoy, I hate this job. Well, there she is. Take a gander. She's the one with the bacteriological memo and the snap of MacAmsward. I'm scared to touch it. They'll want this one higher up. Look at her. A fine piece, eh?"

"Distinctly, sir," said McCoy, who looked legal and regal and private-school-polished.

"Yes, well, let's begin. Sergeant, wait outside till we're through."

She was suddenly standing alone with them, eyes bright with fury.

"Why did you begin using bacteriological weapons?" Kline barked.

The interpreter repeated the question in Russian. The question was a silly beginning. No one had yet made official accusations of germ warfare. She answered with a crisp sentence, causing the interpreter to make a long face.

"She says they are using such weapons because they dislike us, sir."

The major coughed behind his hand. "Tell her what will happen to her if she does that again. Let's start over." He squinted at her. "Name?"

"Imya?" echoed McCoy.

"Marya Dmitriyevna."

"Familiya?"

"Lisitsa."

"It means 'fox', sir. Possibly a lie."

"Well, Marya Dmitriyevna Fox, what's your rank?"

"V kakom vy chinye?" snapped McCoy.

"Starshii Lyeityenant," said the girl.

"Senior lieutenant, sir."

"You see, girl? It's all straight from Geneva. Name, rank, serial number, that's all. You can trust us. . . . Ask her if she's with Intelligence."

"Razvye'dyvatyel naya sluzhba?"

"Nyet!"

"Nyet, eh? How many divisions are ready at the front?"

"Skol'ko na frontye divizii?"

"Ya nye pomnyu!"

"She says she doesn't remember."

"Who is your battalion commander, Lisitsa?"

"Kto komandir va'shyevo batalyona?"

"Ya nye pomnyu!"

"She says she doesn't remember."

"Doesn't, eh? Tell her I know she's a spy, and we'll shoot her at once."

The interpreter repeated the threat in Russian. The girl folded her arms and stared contempt at the major.

"You're to stand at attention!"

"Smirno!"

She kept her arms folded and stood as she had been standing. The major drew his forty-five and worked the slide.

"Tell her that I am the sixteenth bastard grandson of Mickey Spillane and blowing holes in ladies' bellies is my heritage and my hobby."

The interpreter repeated it. Marya snorted three words she had learned from a fisherman.

"I think she called you a castrate, sir."

The major lifted the automatic and took casual aim. Something in his manner caused the girl to go white. She closed her eyes and murmured something reverent in favor of the Fatherland.

The gun jumped in Kline's hand. The crash brought a yell from the sergeant outside the bunker. The bullet hit concrete out the doorway and screamed off on a skyward ricochet. The girl bent over and grabbed at the front of her skirt. There was a bullet hole in front and in back where the slug had passed between her thighs. She cursed softly and fanned the skirt.

"Tell her I am a terrible marksman, but will do better next time," chuckled Kline. "Good thing the light shows through that skirt, eh, McCoy—or I might have burned the 'tender demesnes.' There! Is she still cursing me?"

"Fluently, sir."

"I must have burned her little white hide. Give her a second to cool off, then ask what division she's from."

"Kakovo vy polka?"

"Ya nye pomnyu!"

"She has a very poor memory, sir."

The major sighed and inspected his nails. They were grubby. "Tell her," he muttered, "that I think I'll have her assigned to C company as its official prostitute after our psychosurgeons make her a nymphomaniac."

McCoy translated. Marya spat. The major wrote.

"Have you been in any battles, woman?" he grunted. *"V kakikh srazhyeniyakh vy oochast'vovali?"*

"Ya nye pomnyu!"

"She says—"

"Yeah, I know. It was a silly question." He handed the interpreter her file. "Give these to the sergeant and have him take her up to Purvis. I haven't the heart to whip information out of a woman. Slim's queer; he loves it." He paused, looking her over. "I don't know whether to feel sorry for her, or for Purvis. That's all, McCoy."

The sergeant led her to the Blue Shirts' tent. "Listen," he whispered. "I'll sneak a call to the Red Cross." He appeared very worried in her behalf.

The pain lasted for several hours. She lay on a cot somewhere while a nurse and a Red Cross girl took blood samples and smears. They kept giving each other grim little glances across the cot while they ministered to her.

"We'll see that the ones who did it to you are tried," the Red Cross worker told her in bad Russian.

"I speak English," Marya muttered, although she had never admitted it to her interrogators, not even to Purvis.

"You'll be all right. But why don't you cry?"

But she could only cry for Nikolai now, and even that would be over soon. She lay there for two days and waited.

After that, there was General MacAmsward, and a politer form of questioning. The answers, though, were still the same.

"Ya nye pomnyu!"

What quality or quantity can it be, laughably godlike, transubstantially apelike, that abides in the flesh of brutes and makes them men? For General MacAmsward was indeed a man, although he wished to be only a soldier.

There are militarists who love the Fatherland, and militarists who love the Motherland, and the difference between them is as distinct as the difference between the drinkers of bourbon and the drinkers of rye. There are the neo-Prussian zombies in jackboots who stifle their souls to make themselves machines of the Fatherland, but MacAmsward was not one of them. MacAmsward was a Motherland man, and Mother was never much interested in machines. Mother raised babies into champions, and a champion is mightier than the State; never is he a tool of the State. So it was with Rufus MacAmsward, evil genius by sworn word of Porphiry Grigoryevich.

Consider a towering vision of Michael the Archangel carrying a swagger stick. Fresh from the holy wars of Heaven he comes, striding past the rows of white gloved orderlies standing at saber salute, their haloes (M-1, official nimbus) studded with brass spikes. The archangel's headgear is a trifle rakish, crusted with gold laurel and dented by a dervish devil's bullet. He ignores the thrones and dominations, but smiles democratically at a lowly cherub and pauses to inquire after the health of his grandmother.

Grandmother is greatly improved.

Immensely reassured, General MacAmsward strides into his quarters and hangs up his hat. The room is in darkness except for the light from a metal wall lamp that casts its glare around the great chair and upon the girl who sits in the great chair at the far end of the room. The girl is toying with a goblet of wine, and her dark hair coils in thick masses about her silk-clad shoulders. The silk came by virtue of the negligence of the general's ex-wife in forgetting to pack. The great chair came as a prize of war, having been taken from a Soviet People's Court where it is no longer needed. It is massive as an episcopal throne—a fitting seat for an archangel—and it is placed on a low dais at the head of a long table flanked by lesser chairs. The room is used for staff conference, and none would dare to sit in the great chair except the general—or, of course, a lovely grief-stung maiden.

The girl stares at him from out of two pools of shadow. Her head is slightly inclined and the downlight catches only the tip of her nose. The general pauses with his hand on his hat. He turns slowly away from the hat rack, brings himself slowly to attention, and gives her a solemn salute. It is a tribute to beauty. She acknowledges it with a nod. The general advances and sits in the simple chair at the far end of the long table. The general sighs with fervor, as if he had not breathed since entering the door. His eyes have not left her face. The girl puts down the glass.

"I have come to kill you," she said. "I have come to nurse you to death with the milk of a murdered child."

The general winced. She had said it three times before,

once for each day she had resided in his house. And for
the third time, the general ignored it.

"I have seen to it, my child," he told her gravely.
"Captain Purvis faces court martial in the morning. I have
directed it. I have directed too that you be repatriated
forthwith, if it is your wish, for this is only common justice after what that monster has done to you. Now however let me implore you to remain with us and quit the
forces of godlessness until the war is won and you can
return to your home in peace."

Marya watched his shadowy figure at the far end of
the table. He was like Raleigh at the court of Beth, at
once mighty and humble. Again she felt the surge of
exhilaration, as when she had crawled along the ridge at
the river, ducking machine gun fire. It was the voice of
Macbeth's wife whispering within her: *Come to my
woman's breasts, and take my milk for gall, you murder-
ing ministers, wherever in your sightless substances you
wait on nature's mischief!* It was the power of death
in her bosom, where once had been the power of life.

She arose slowly and leaned on the table to stare at
him fiercely. "Murderer of my child!" she hissed.

"May God in His mercy—"

"Murderer of my child!"

"Marya Dmitriyevna, it is my deepest sorrow." He
sat watching her gravely and seemed to lose none of his
lofty composure. "I can say nothing to comfort you. It
is impossible. It is my deepest sorrow."

"There is something you can do."

"Then it is done. Tell me quickly."

"Come here." She stepped from the table to the edge
of the dais and beckoned. "Come to me here. I have
secrets to whisper to the killer of my son. Come."

He came and stood down from her so that their faces
were at the same level. She could see now that there was
real pain in his eyes. Good! Let it be. She must make
him understand. He must know perfectly well that she
was going to kill him. And he must know how. The necessity of knowing was not by any command of Porphiry's;
it was a must that she had created within herself. She was
smiling now, and there was a new quickness in her ges-
tures.

"Look at me, high killer. I cannot show you the broken
body of my son. I can show you no token or relic. It is

all buried in a mass grave." Swiftly she opened the silk
robe. "Look at me instead. See? How swollen I am again.
Yes, here! A token after all. A single drop. Look, it is his,
it is Nikolai's."

MacAmsward went white. He stood like a man hypno-
tized.

"See? To nourish life, but now to nourish death. Your
death, high killer. But more! My son was conceived in
love, and you have killed him, and now I come to you.
You will give me another, you see. Now we shall conceive him in hate, you and I, and you'll die of the death
in my bosom. Come, make hate to me, killer."

His jaw trembled. He took her shoulders and ran his
hands down her arms and closed them over hers.

"Your hands are ice," he whispered, and leaned forward to kiss a bare spot just below her throat, and
somehow she was certain that he understood. It was a
preconscious understanding, but it was there. And still he
bent over her.

*Come, thick night, and pall thee in the dunnest smoke
of hell, that my keen knife see not the wound it makes* . . .

Of course the general had been intellectually convinced that it was entirely a figure of speech.

The toxin's work was quickly done. A bacterial toxin,
swiftly lethal to the non-immunized, slowly lethal to
Marya who could pass it out in her milk as it formed.
The general slept for half an hour and woke up with a
raging fever. She sat by the window and watched him
die. He tried to shout, but his throat was constricted. He
got out of bed, took two steps, and fell. He tried to crawl
toward the door. He fell flat again. His face was crimson.

The telephone rang.

Someone knocked at the door.

The ringing stopped and the knocking went away.
She watched him breathe. He tried to speak, but she
turned her back to him and looked out the window at
the shell-pocked countryside. Russia, Nikolai, and even
the Ami sergeant who had wanted to go home, it was for
them that she listened to his gasping. She lit one of his
American cigarets and found it very enjoyable. The phone
was ringing furiously again. It kept on ringing.

The gasping stopped. Someone was hammering on
the door and shouting. She stood enjoying the cigaret and
watching the crows flocking in a newly planted field. The

earth was rich and black here, the same soil she had tossed at the Ami sergeant. It belonged to her, this soil. Soon she would belong to it. With Nikolai, and maybe the Ami sergeant.

The door crashed loose from its hinges. Three Blue Shirts burst in and stopped. They looked at the body on the floor. They looked at Marya.

"What has happened here?"

The Russian girl laughed. Their expressions were quite comical. One of them raised his gun. He pulled the trigger six times.

"Come . . . Nikki Andreyevich . . . come . . ."

One of them went over and nudged her with his boot, but she was already dead. She had beaten them. She had beaten them all.

The American newspapers printed the truth. They said that General MacAmsward had died of poisoned milk. But that was all they said. The *whole* truth was only sung in Russian legend for the next one thousand years.